PROMISES

Reviewer's Praise for the Writing of E. G. Lewis

Witness is a love story, and a good one.
—Christy Award Winner, Jill Williamson

Mr. Lewis weaves the lore seamlessly into the adventure, blending meticulous research and practiced storytelling into a delightfully satisfying tale you won't soon forget. —It Is To Write

Promises is one of those unique books that keeps getting better and better. After letting his readers settle into life in Appalachian Kentucky, Mr. Lewis catapults them, and his strong female protagonist, off to New York, London, Paris, and beyond.
— Northwest Book Review

Witness will keep you glued to your seat turning pages long into the night. And the characters are just wonderful! I love Rivkah and feel like she's family now! I highly, highly recommend his books. You will be moved by God and E.G. Lewis' writing as much as I was..I am sure of it! —Michelle Vasquez

Author E. G. Lewis has a wonderful skill with his writing, hiding deep and serious research under simple, honest story-telling. There's no feel of being overwhelmed with teaching in *Disciple,* neither religious nor historical. To research so deeply and tread so lightly is a wonderful talent . —Sheila Deeth

Witness is worthy of so much more than a 5 star rating. It's an emotional story full of fiction but also full of actual events...
—Molly Edwards

Promises is provocative, descriptive and in tune with the human psyche...He draws us in with such craft and precision that before you know it you just have to keep reading. —Tracy Krauss

God, as depicted in *Apostle* is ever-present in the characters' lives, but never intrusive in the tale or the history.
—Gregory Thomas

Reviewer's Praise for the Writing of E. G. Lewis

The true delight of "The Seeds of Christianity" is not just the great storyline, but the historical setting the author so brilliantly depicts. You feel the heat of the potter's kiln on your face and the cool of the wine grapes on your bare feet as everyday life in the ancient Middle East comes alive on each page. —Bruce Judisch

It was a gripping story, not in a who-dun-it manner but rather in a way that made me want to learn what happened next, to be part of their story. —Wyndy Callahan

A great adventure, some intriguingly imaginative concepts, wonderful characters, and a beautiful sense of Southern Oregon scenery and community (with touches of India, London, and more besides), *Lost* is a very enjoyable novel which really does satisfy. —Summit Book Reviews

You will rejoice and cry at various times. These are novels that will transport you to a different world. —Isabelle Lusier

This book delves into the humanity and depravity of both the Jewish and Roman peoples, medicine, the military and economics...and all with a bit of humor. —Tammy Litke

There are a lot of really interesting elements that co-exist quite naturally with the breathtaking descriptions of the Oregon scenery, while touching glimpses into the emotional make up of the characters flow seamlessly into scenes of high intensity action. *Lost* is a mystery, romance, action, thriller rolled into one. —Tracy Krauss

An unlikely team of committed adventurers have to solve the problems or risk the loss of several hundred people already assumed dead. In *Lost*, E.G. Lewis mixes facts with fiction to provide an entertaining and exciting novel. — Anne Baxter

Books by E. G. Lewis

<u>The Seeds of Christianity™ Series</u>

WITNESS — Book One

DISCIPLE — Book Two

APOSTLE — Book Three

MARTYR — Book Four

<u>The Mountain Memories Trilogy</u>

PROMISES — Book One

LOST — Book Two

<u>Christian Non-Fiction</u>

At Table with the Lord - Foods of the First Century

All Things Christmas - The History & Traditions of Advent and Christmas

In Three Days - The History & Traditions of Lent and Easter

PROMISES

~ Book One ~
of the
Mountain Memories Trilogy

A Novel

By

E. G. Lewis

Cape Arago Press
PO Box 771
North Bend, OR 97459
www.capearagopress.com

Published by Cape Arago Press, P.O. Box 771 North Bend, OR 97459

ISBN 13: 978-0-9825949-1-9
ISBN 10: 09825949-1-7

1. Fiction: Romantic Suspense 2.Fiction: Women's Fiction

Promises

I stood at the window of my condominium watching snow blanket Central Park. Despite the apartment's warmth, I tugged my mother's shawl tighter and crossed my arms protectively. I wasn't working today. I never do on this, my least favorite day of the year.

It hasn't always been like this. I loved winters as a little girl. Every fall I'd check out the wooly bears' coats and spy on the squirrels to see how many nuts they'd gathered, searching for clues about the coming winter.

In Eastern Kentucky where I grew up, the weather turned frigid after Christmas. In January we had frost on the inside of the windows, extra quilts on the bed, and the *Warm Morning* heat stove in the living room set to high. January also brought snow, deep snow that filled the hollows and drifted over the back porch steps.

Those deep snows meant no school and going sledding with my younger brothers. Even today, I smile when I recall coming inside cold, wet and invigorated. We'd hang our gloves, coats and knit hats on a rack in front of the stove to dry and hurry to our rooms to change. When we returned Momma always had mugs of hot cocoa waiting on the kitchen table. She warned us to take baby sips so we wouldn't burn our tongues.

We, of course, never listened.

Sometimes, if the snow was just right, she'd send me outdoors with a big spoon and a bowl. After carefully scraping away the crusty top layer so I didn't get soot from the chimney, I'd fill the bowl and Momma would turn it into snow ice cream. I'll never forget how soothing it felt on my sore tongue.

Those were happy times for us all, me, my two brothers, and Momma and Daddy. Life seemed simple then and the future looked as perfect as perfect can be. Everything changed the year I turned fifteen and Momma took sick. She died the following January.

Folks back home say I look just like her, that we could be twins. It's true; more and more when I look in the mirror it's her I see. Those same people think I rely upon her good looks to earn my living. In a way, I suppose I do. But it takes more than good bones and a nice figure to make it to the top as a model.

On melancholy days like today I remind myself that Momma was not so much taken from me, as she was given to me...even if only for a short while. She guided me in life and continues to guide me in death. A few days before she passed over, I sat at her bedside and made certain promises. Promises I've done my level best to keep.

The thought that I might have fallen short, that I somehow let her down, never ceases to haunt me.

BOOK ONE
KENTUCKY WOMAN

~ 1 ~

Witch's Fingers.

That's what Mary Jane called them as a little girl. On stormy nights when witches tried to claw their way into her bedroom, she'd scream for Momma.

Her mother would be there in an instant, the stairway light glowing behind her like the Madonna's halo. She'd slide into the bed, kiss away her fears and rock her back to sleep.

Sleet pinged against her bedroom window like buckshot off a steel drum the night before her mother's funeral. The wind grabbed the gnarled oak beside the house, shaking its bare branches and sending dead twigs clattering across their tin roof. She'd woken several times to the sound of its branches scraping her bedroom wall.

"Mary Jane, the boys are nearly ready," her father called from the bottom of the stairway. "How about you?"

"All but my dress."

She sat the newspaper aside. The worn linoleum felt cold and brittle under her feet. Tightening the blue chenille bathrobe she'd pulled on over her slip, she jammed her toes into the matted fleece of her slippers. She'd slept in this attic bedroom shoehorned into the eaves of their modest, story-and-a-half clapboard house all her life. Its knee walls and sloping ceiling always seemed warm and protective.

But today they felt cold and foreboding.

Mary Jane went to her desk and returned with a pair of scissors. At fifteen, she was tall—5' 11"—and stooped to avoid banging her head. The mattress quivered beside her. She felt a nudge and glanced down. Her orange tabby, Marmalade, stared up at her from the patchwork quilt. When she didn't immediately pet him, he marched forward and butted her again.

She scooped him up, pressing him to her cheek. "Good old Marmuls." She listened to the comforting rumble of his little motor. "You always know when I need a pick-me-up."

She reached for her newspaper, making practice snips in the air with the scissors. Then, frowning in concentration, she started the first tentative cut. Seconds later her mother's obituary separated from the page and drifted into her lap.

Mary Jane opened her white Bible, tucked in the small rectangle of newsprint and watched it disappear as the pages fanned shut.

From now on, her life would be divided into two parts, before Momma died and after Momma died.

The family returned from the cemetery to find their small house overflowing with well wishers. Ladies from the church set up a makeshift buffet in the kitchen and people milled around plate-in-hand. The women claimed the living room, relegating the men and their tobacco to the porch.

Mary Jane took Estil's hand. "Let's go for a walk." She glanced around the room. "All these people make me nervous."

He helped her on with her coat and escorted her through the men clustered on both sides of the porch. One side argued mining, the other farming. They threaded between them and walked hand-in-hand down the path to the garden. A gust of wind shook the apple trees as they passed, showering them with ice. She folded her collar up and leaned into his shoulder.

Estil put his arm around her. "Let's go inside the barn. It'll get you out of the wind."

He opened the door of the attached shed and led Mary Jane inside. Muted sunlight streamed in through dusty cobwebs on the windows. The distinctive smell of burley tobacco lingered where they'd sorted and graded their tobacco crop two months earlier. Discarded bits of dry leaves and stems lay scattered on the dirt floor, crunching underfoot.

Mary Jane and Estil clung to each other in the privacy of the grading room. She wept into the scratchy wool of his overcoat, soaking it with her tears. He lifted her chin and kissed her. She pressed against him, savoring the strength of his embrace. She let him hold her for a long time before reluctantly pushing away.

"I don't know how I'm going to make it without Momma." She gave him an upward glance. "For the first time, I think I truly understand the old spiritual *Sometimes I Feel Like a Motherless Child."*

Estil's expression darkened for an instant.

She noticed and touched his cheek. "I shouldn't have said that. I didn't mean it to be hurtful."

He wrapped her in his arms and kissed the top of her head. "In different ways, we're both motherless children now."

"Do you ever miss your Mom?"

"Not often. I learned a long time ago to avoid expectations. She does her thing; I do mine."

She tried to read Estil's eyes, wondering how much of what he said was true and how much was macho posturing.

"It would be alright to miss her just a little now and then."

"And it's just as alright *not* to miss her. We're talking about a woman who moved to California with her boyfriend leaving a 16 -month-old son behind."

He stepped away, rolling his shoulders as he paced. “Look. I know you mean well, MJ, but this is nothing like you and your Mom.” He raised two fingers, one entwined around the other. “You two were this close. Your mother left because she had to. Mine ran off to be someone else’s whore.”

Estil frowned at the rough oak post beside him.

Mary Jane watched his right hand tighten into a fist and moved to stop him.

He relaxed the fist at her touch.

She kissed him long and hard to heal the hurt she’d caused. They were both flushed and breathless when they separated.

He glanced around the dusty room. “You know, I’m not deaf, dumb and blind. I understand how people in this county feel about my father. Say what you want, Pop was there for me when she wasn’t. Some days I can almost convince myself he cares.”

~ 2 ~

Mary Jane and Estil stood facing each other beside his pickup, holding hands as they said good-bye.

He reached for her.

Out of the corner of her eye she noticed the curtain in the living room window jerk aside. Feeling her father's watchful eye, she rested a hand on the front of Estil's shoulder, keeping him at arm's length. "Call me tonight?"

"Always do."

She gave him a chaste kiss.

Mary Jane rested her elbow on the gatepost and smiled as she watched his pickup disappear from view. The smile slipped from her face when she turned.

Her father waited on the porch, white shirtsleeves folded back over his muscular forearms. His breath making smoky puffs in the January air.

"Where have you been?" he asked as her foot touched the steps.

"Walking. Talking."

"Didn't I see you coming out of the barn?"

Mary Jane nodded. "Uh huh. I got cold. We went inside to get out of the wind."

"It was plenty warm in the house."

"We wanted to be alone."

"You don't need to be alone with the likes of Estil Estep. It doesn't look good."

Her father stood between her and the door. Those few feet felt like miles.

"What do you mean?"

"You know what I mean."

"I hope I don't." She tossed her hair back and stepped around him to go inside.

After hanging up her coat, Mary Jane gathered the plates and napkins left on living room tables. She carried a handful into the kitchen and stacked them on the drainboard. Her best friend, Stephanie Brown, followed with cups clinking in her hands.

"Where's the golden boy off to?"

"Estil wanted to throw his rock."

"He wanted to what?"

Mary Jane squirted detergent into the sink and ran hot water over it. She swished her hand to make bubbles, enjoying its familiar lemony scent.

"He went home to throw his rock."

"You have to explain that one."

"Estil has this football-shaped rock, that's all."

"And he throws it?"

"He thinks it'll strengthen his passing arm. He says it's like those heavy bats baseball players swing." Mary Jane smiled. "He spent a whole afternoon poking around the quarry until he found just the right one. He throws it back and forth across his front yard almost every night."

Stephanie pulled the faucet to her side of the sink. "So, are you two lovebirds making any, you know, plans?"

In a part of the state where many girls married right out of high school and more than a few dropped out to get married, it was not an inappropriate question.

"Sometimes we talk about going to the University of Kentucky together, if that's what you mean." Mary Jane passed her a sudsy plate.

"No. I meant like engagement rings, wedding bells, the pitter-patter of little feet."

"What would make you say that?"

"Gosh, I don't know. You and Estil have been an item ever since you started sharing peanut butter sandwiches at Vacation Bible School. He's really cute, Captain of the football team, and his family owns most of Blackstone County. If that isn't a catch, what is?"

"You know there are things more important than good looks and money."

"I'm not sure I do. Tell me."

Mary Jane's eyes sparkled. "Having someone nice who cares about you and loves you. Someone I could love right back and have kids with and make a family." She grinned and reached for another plate. "See. It's not complicated."

"And you've never thought about what it might be like making kids with Estil?"

"We're still in high school."

"You've absolutely, never, ever thought about it?"

Mary Jane skimmed off some foam and tossed it in Stephanie's direction. "What if I have? Is that so terrible?"

"Of course not. You're the prettiest girl in school; you deserve him."

"Beauty is in the eye of the beholder."

"Stow the modesty. I've seen the way people, boys, look at you."

"They do that to all the girls."

"Let's trade. I get to be the long-legged, blue-eyed blond and you're short with mousy-brown hair. See how things feel from this side."

Mary Jane's Aunt Louise popped her head around the corner. "Yoo Hoo, it's me. Do you girls need any help?"

"You could clean up leftovers," Mary Jane said. "There's room in the fridge."

Weezie began spooning leftovers into storage containers and passed the empties over to the sink. She looked from one girl to the other. "It sure quieted down in here since I came in. Did I interrupt your secrets?"

"We'd pretty much exhausted the subject."

"Oh, really?"

Stephanie cupped her hand around her mouth and whispered, "We were talking about boyfriends, the golden boy, Estil Estep."

"What else do teenage girls talk about?" She pulled out a chair and turned it to face the sink. "Don't stop on my account. I don't hear many juicy tidbits at my age." She fluttered her hands at them. "Go on...go on. What about him?"

"I told her I'm surprised she's not making plans. If it were me, I'd do more than wear his class ring. At the very least, I'd spend my study halls practicing writing Stephanie Estep in my theme book."

Weezie's brow knotted. "Like your father, I have reservations about the Estep family. Randall Estep's messy divorces and public affairs have been, to say the least, scandalous."

Mary Jane whirled around ready to declare the son innocent of his father's sins.

Weezie's raised hand, stopped her. "Still, Estil seems like a nice young man. He sent flowers to the funeral home. We'll give him some points there. He's good looking and, of course, he's got those muscles. I recall some young girls liking muscles."

Mary Jane concentrated on the dishes.

"Still, his father hardly qualifies as the ideal role model, though far be it from me to judge. The bottom line, girls, is that matrimony is a sacred union." She tapped her knee for emphasis. "It must be approached cautiously and only after prayerful consideration."

"Will you two stop it? I'm not ready to marry anyone."

"Miss Aw Shucks here also claims not to be the prettiest girl in school."

"Steph, enough already."

"I'm sure there are many attractive young women at your school," Weezie said, "but there's a difference between polite modesty and plain foolishness. The Bible says pride is sinful, however, it also enjoins us not to hide our light under a bushel."

"See." Stephanie licked her finger and marked a point in the air. "I win."

Weezie glanced at the kitchen clock. Felix the Cat's round, bobbing eyes snapped back and forth in time with his twitching tail, ticking away the seconds. "Look at that time. Stephanie, would you be a dear and carry these casserole dishes out to my car?"

She waited until Stephanie left the room then slipped an arm around Mary Jane's shoulder. A retired librarian, Weezie contributed to her niece and nephews' education by giving them daily watchwords.

"Our watchword for tomorrow will be *Pertinacious*: to hold on firmly, to be persistent."

Rechecking the doorway, she looked Mary Jane in the eye.

"You know, it's not my job to tell you you're beautiful, nor yours to tell yourself you're not. Christian humility doesn't require a lovely woman to pretend she's ugly. Rather, she must acknowledge that every person is equally beautiful in God's eyes. You inherited your mother's good looks. It's a gift. And like anything the Lord gives it can be a blessing...or a curse."

Her aunt's words sent a chill up Mary Jane's spine.

~ 3 ~

Temperatures dropped all afternoon as a winter storm swept through the Appalachians. Snow fell, bringing its peculiar hush. Mary Jane put away the supper dishes, went upstairs and changed for bed. The evening's stillness seeped into her room as she retreated into a book.

John Combs tapped on the stairway door leading up to his daughter's bedroom. "MJ, are you still awake?"

She closed her book over a finger. "Present and accounted for."

"Can I come up and talk?"

"Sure."

She put the book aside as her father ascended the steep stairway. He sat a small paper sack on her desk without comment then spun the straight-backed wooden chair at her desk around and straddled the seat. Folding his big hands across the chair's back, her father leaned forward and rested his chin on them.

Mary Jane sat on the bed in her nightgown with the quilt bunched around her waist. Her cat, Marmalade, lay sprawled across her lap.

After quietly studying his daughter for several moments, her father sighed and murmured, "Sad, sad day."

She nodded.

He continued staring.

Mary Jane wiggled her legs, dislodging the cat, and lifted the covers chest high.

"What is it, Daddy?"

"You're so lovely. In this light you bear an amazing resemblance to your mother." His voice sounded weary, defeated. By the time his words reached her, they seemed worn-out from the journey. "She was your age when we met. I can't look at you without seeing her."

She swallowed hard and, in a tiny voice, said, "You've told

me that before,"

"Yes, I suppose I have."

Her father's eyes drifted around the small room cataloging minute details as if the answer he sought lay hidden in the knotted strings of a tennis shoe, the lines of discolored paint on the ceiling where the roof leaked three winters ago, or blond hairs tangled in the bristles of her hairbrush.

"We tried for years before she got pregnant. We'd almost given up. Then one day, there you were. And now you're all I have to remember her by."

It seemed a struggle for him to maintain a consistent train of thought. She wondered if he'd forgot what he came for, or was merely reflecting the emptiness hanging over their household.

"I'm sorry for the episode on the porch. I've had a lot on my mind these last few weeks."

"I know you were never thrilled about me dating Estil, but don't blame him. He didn't kill Momma; cancer did."

"You're my daughter. A father's entitled to worry." He opened his hands like a preacher at Sunday service. "Honey, you're young. Estil's your first real boyfriend. These feelings can be overwhelming. I don't want to see you hurt."

"A minute ago you said Momma was my age when you two began dating."

He straightened in the chair. "But I wasn't Estil Estep. I respected your mother."

"He respects me. What is it you think we do?"

Her father's strong hands clenched and unclenched the back of the chair. "If I even suspected he tried anything, he and I would have a man-to-man talk he'd never forget."

"We've been good. I swear it. Estil's my friend. I need him right now."

"Even though she was sick, your mother convinced me to allow you to keep company with him. I don't think she'd want me to forbid you to see him now."

He rubbed his sandpapery palms together.

"You don't know the Estep's like I do. All my life, I've watched them cheat everyone in Blackstone County. First it was Estil's grandfather, now it's his father. Someday it will be him. The Estep's think they own everything they touch, land... livestock...coal. Women aren't any different. Sooner or later, Estil's going to try to claim what he thinks is rightfully his."

Seeing his daughter wiping her eyes on the bed sheet, he stopped. He ran his fingers through his hair and shook his head. "I didn't come here to argue about Estil. I don't know how I ended up doing it."

She sniffed. "Why did you come?"

"I know life feels confused right now, but I wanted you to know I'll take care of you and your brothers. I'll always be here for you, no matter what."

Although her father came offering reassurance, the conviction in his voice frightened her. Her mother's death had driven home the futility of counting on the future. She no longer believed there was such a thing as certainty this side of eternity.

"Hear me?" he asked, when she didn't respond.

"Yes, I hear you," she replied. Her soft voice was barely audible in the quiet room.

"And one more thing." He touched the lunch sack, rustling its stiff brown paper. "Your mother left this for you. She wanted you to have it after she passed." He looked around and shrugged. "I guess that's all I came to say."

Her father unfolded himself from the chair, returned it to the kneehole of her desk, and headed for the stairs.

"Daddy?"

He paused on the first step, glancing back.

"Thanks. I love you."

"I love you, too. Goodnight, Baby."

Mary Jane listened to her father descend the stairs. She heard the familiar squeak as he put his foot on the next to last step and the metallic click of the latch sliding into its mortise when the door closed.

She'd started to retrieve the sack when the phone rang.

It was Estil. "MJ?"

"Hi."

"Are you alone?"

She giggled. "No. Actually, I've got another fella here in bed with me."

"His name better be Marmalade, or I'm gonna be sore."

"We'd better not stay on too long. I turned the ringer off downstairs like always, but Daddy may have heard my phone."

"What's the problem?"

"It's just my father's concern for his little girl. He wasn't pleased when we went off to the barn today."

"At least your father's interested in you, which is more than I can say."

"Your dad wouldn't like hearing you say that."

"He's not here. He left for Frankfort, there's a coal convention at the State Capitol. Probably busy greasing palms."

"Aren't you being a little hard on him? Don't forget, Estep Mining Company is your family's business."

"And I want no part of it. It's not like I blame Pop, or anything. He didn't choose to be an Estep anymore than I did."

"You make it sound like you're being held captive."

"I am. Nobody asked if coal mining was what I wanted. I'm supposed to want it and, if I don't, pretend I do. That's the difference between us, MJ. Your world's wide open; you have options, choices. My future was decided before I was born. Fortunately, fate dealt me a wild card. Football's my ticket out."

Marmalade adjusted positions on her bed, meowing several times as he made a nest in the covers.

"Hey. I heard your boyfriend meow." Estil chuckled. "Now I can sleep tonight."

~ 4 ~

Mary Jane cradled the phone and retrieved the sack her father left. Feeling like a small child on Christmas morning, she removed the package and turned it in her hands.

Momma wrapped this herself, she thought. The thin red ribbon with its cluster of long curlicues proved it. She hugged the package and closed her eyes, remembering.

"Make them curly, Momma."

With the exuberance only five-year-olds have, she spooled off yards of ribbon, offering them to her mother by the handful. Mary Jane hopped from one foot to the other, bubbling-over with excitement as she watched her mother wrap presents.

"Make it curly, Momma. Make it curly."

"Keep your pants on." Her mother gave the package a final once over. Then, opening the scissors, she trapped a piece of ribbon between her thumb and the blade. She zipped it along, curling the ribbon into tight spirals as Mary Jane squealed with delight.

Beneath the ribbon and wrapping paper lay a department store glove box. Inside she found a single envelope with her name written across it in expansive script. She slowly lifted it out of the box and turned it in her hand. It was sealed with a gold medallion embossed with a heart.

Mary Jane shifted in the bed. Sliding closer to the light, she ran a fingernail under the flap. The stiff paper crinkled as she removed the letter from its envelope. Unfolding it, she began to read.

My dear, dear Mary Jane—

You are my beautiful daughter whom I cherish more than life itself. Flesh of my flesh, you are the embodiment of the love your father and I shared. You lived within me for nine months and you'll stay in my heart forever.

I suppose, deep down all mothers are pretty much the same. I've watched you mature in wisdom and grace with boundless pride. Ever since you were a little girl, I've dreamed of seeing you grown-up with babies of your own.

But it wasn't to be. The specialists in Lexington tell me there's nothing more they can do. So, rather than remain far from my family, I've come home to die.

Even though I believe with all my heart that greater things await us on the other side, I'm not ready to go. But I've come to accept that it's His will, not mine, which must be done. You see, we're all part of an eternal plan far beyond our understanding. You, your brothers, your father...everyone, always was and always will be in God's hands. That is my comfort as I prepare to leave you.

Throughout my illness, my thoughts have centered on you. On the way back from Lexington I decided to write this letter. And, though very tired, I insisted your father stop at Cumberland Falls. We honeymooned there, you know. We stayed at the DuPont Lodge and even managed to see a moonbow one night. As a new bride I considered it an omen; especially since there are only a half-dozen places in the world where it can be seen.

I just heard Weezie's "Yoo Hoo" at the door. I must put this aside.

We ended up talking several hours. I find myself doing this a lot these days. Time is short and I have to say all that is in my heart while I still have the chance.

Thanksgiving's come and gone and Christmas is hard upon us. Not a very merry one this year, I'm afraid. Sorry. Though the doctors tell me it can't happen, I'm determined to last into January. I don't want to cloud all future Christmases with memories of my death.

My thoughts are running in as many directions as a flock of frightened sheep. I'm very tired, which makes it doubly difficult. But I swore I'd finish this letter before I rest, and I will.

A wonderfully strange thing has happened, Mary Jane. I've begun having moments of clarity, visions. I won't waste time on explanations; the process isn't important. Though I will confess

I've discussed this with the visiting nurse. She insists it's a side effect of the pain medication. I can't and won't accept that.

It's been like flipping pages in a photo album. I see you doing things, going places, meeting people. The images aren't always easy to interpret as they flash by, but I've done my best. And, oh the things I've seen.

Perhaps it's Weezie having just left, but I want to end this letter with a watchword. This is my watchword, not for just a day or a week, but for the rest of your life. TRUST: an assured reliance on the character, strength or truth of someone or something. Trust God. Trust your values, trust those who love you and, most important of all, trust yourself.

You're destined for great things, my darling daughter. I felt it the moment they placed you in my arms. You were only a few seconds old and complaining mightily about being thrust into this cruel world. Suddenly our eyes met. You calmed. We looked at each other and I felt it. I really did. And now I've seen it.

Don't roll your eyes like that. This is your mother talking. I see that little smirk of yours. I'm serious; I was there.

Stay true to yourself and what you know to be right. Remember the promises you made at my bedside. Get up each morning, look in the mirror, and tell yourself you're special, because you are.

They say a bride should wear something old and something new, something borrowed and something blue. I'm giving you something old to wear on your wedding day. Your great grandmother wore this necklace on her wedding day. My mother wore it on hers, and I wore it on mine. I'm giving it to you now so you can wear it on yours.

Hugs and kisses and love forever,

Momma

Mary Jane opened the small package of folded tissue. A silver necklace with a delicate filigreed cross tumbled into her palm.

~ 5 ~

John Combs returned to work at Estep Mining Company's Blossom Gulch Mine No. 3 the morning after his wife's funeral.

Mary Jane rose early, threw on a robe and padded down to the kitchen to fix his breakfast. Despite her resolve to fill the gap left by her mother's death, she knew even this simple task could intimidate her if she let it.

You can do this, she told herself. Didn't you watch Momma often enough to know the routine?

Walking by memory, she crossed the dark living room and clicked on the kitchen light. Circles of frost clung to the inside of the cold windowpanes. She filled the coffeemaker and turned it on. While it hissed and belched she put bacon in a skillet and started it frying. Mary Jane glanced up from pouring coffee and gave her father a proud smile. "Morning, Daddy, breakfast's ready."

John Combs paused in the doorway. The welcoming smell of coffee, bacon and fresh bread filled the little kitchen. His eyes moved from his smiling daughter to the table. He kissed her on the forehead and pulled out a chair.

"You shouldn't have gone to all this trouble. I could do with a bowl of cereal."

"If that's all you needed, Momma wouldn't have fixed you eggs and meat every morning. How many times did she say, 'If you work hard you have to eat."

She stood beside the table trying not to fidget.

He took a bite and chewed for a moment. "Umm!" He nodded and smiled as he washed it down with a sip of coffee. "Tastes every bit as good as what your Momma made."

By the time he finished she had his lunchbox packed and waiting.

It was dark when her father returned from the mine. Mary

Jane heard the crunch of tires on the gravel drive and pushed aside the curtain. His eyes had the sunken, empty look of a concentration camp survivor. He shuffled to the porch bent with fatigue.

She heard the clump of his work boots on the steps and opened the door to greet him. Unlacing his steel-toed boots, he pulled them off without a word. He came through the back door and dropped them beside a cardboard box of kindling.

Mary Jane felt both pride and anger watching him limp through the kitchen like a beaten fighter. Pride for the sacrifices he made to provide for them, and anger at what the mine did to him. Estep Mining Company wasn't just grinding coal they were grinding down the men who mined it.

While he sifted through the evening paper, Mary Jane tied on an apron and began setting the supper table. She heated a casserole left from the day before. An apple cobbler from the refrigerator became dessert. She made a fresh pot of coffee and put out bread and butter.

The short rest improved her father's appearance, but did nothing for his mood. He frowned at his plate while the children said Grace.

"Did you have a bad day at work?" Mary Jane asked.

He buttered his bread with angry slaps of his knife. "You'd do well not to concern yourself with things in the mine."

Halfway through the meal, her father slammed his fist on the table. All three children jumped. Brent's fork slipped from his fingers, clattering onto his plate. Brian's mouth dropped. Mary Jane bolted upright and folded her hands in her lap.

"A man was almost killed today."

"What happened?" they asked in unison.

"A section of belt ripped apart without warning. The last 40 feet of it whipsawed out like a bullwhip." He looked at their stunned faces. "Ever have someone snap you with a towel in gym class?"

They all had.

He spread his hands wide apart. “Imagine that tiny piece of terrycloth is an industrial belt this wide.”

“What about the man?”

“He must’ve had an angel beside him. The end of the belt slammed into his mantrip tearing the seat to pieces. If he hadn’t leaped out of the car, it would’ve been him along with it.”

Her father dropped his head into his hands. “I could tell something wasn’t right, but I couldn’t get to the shutoff in time. I’ve told Estep over and over the belt needed to be replaced.” He curled his big hands into fists. “He keeps saying patch it. I’ve patched it so many times there’s no belt left. It’s nothing but a bunch of patches chasing each other around the sprockets.”

“Did they replace the belt today?” Brent asked.

His father didn’t look up. “What do you think?”

Mary Jane smiled when the phone rang. “Hi.”

“Missed you at school today,” Estil said.

“Maybe in another day or so.”

“How are you doing?”

“I was okay until Daddy got home from work. He was upset about an accident at the mine.”

“I heard about it. A belt snapped down in No. 3. That’s all Pop talked about.”

“Oh yeah, what’d he say?”

“They had to shut down to fix the belt. The down time cost him a bunch of lost production and the belt destroyed the seats on one of those little cars they use to come and go. It’ll cost over five hundred bucks to fix it.”

“What about the man in the car?”

“No big deal; he wasn’t hurt. Pop said it’s a good thing. Otherwise, they would’ve had to shut down for a safety inspection. That’s the last thing he wants.”

“I can imagine.”

~ 6 ~

By March the weather had cleared and the wind whispered promises of spring. It became possible to work out-of-doors again. In January, the Bly Granite and Marble Company agreed to place Olivia Comb's grave marker as soon as weather permitted. True to their word, they poured the footing on the second Friday in March and set the marker the following Monday. Mary Jane stopped on her way home from school to inspect their handiwork.

She knew the spots where wild jonquils bloomed and kept a lookout for them. She noticed several clumps of bright yellow heads swaying in the breeze and grinned through the school bus window. The next morning she poked a Mason jar into her bookbag and picked a handful of jonquils on her way to the cemetery.

The afternoon sun warmed her back as she climbed the slope to her mother's grave. She laid the flowers on the grass and dug out the jar. Wiping beads of perspiration from her forehead with the back of her hand, she filled the jar at the hydrant and returned.

She circled the new marker several times inspecting it for flaws. Not finding any, she sat down. The corner of its black granite base provided a convenient seat. She curled her legs back and placed her left arm across the monument's top, almost hugging it. Her fingers caressed the rough, grainy surface along the stone's upper edge.

"Hi, Momma. It's me, Mary Jane." She centered the jar on the base, rotating it to the flower's best advantage.

"Your new stone looks nice, and right on time like they promised."

She reached out and fluffed the blooms in the jar. "I brought some jonquils like we used to pick when I was little. They're the first of the season. I remember how you always said, 'You know springtime's coming when the jonquils pop up.'"

Her finger traced the freshly cut letters. She reached the last line, *Beloved Wife and Mother*, and whispered, "Oh God...I miss you so much, Momma. Why did you have to go and get sick?"

She rested her cheek against the cold stone and sobbed. After a minute or two, she dug in her pocket for a tissue, wiped her eyes and blew her nose.

"Aunt Weezie and Uncle Cash came by last weekend." She sniffed and hiccupped like a child who'd been spanked. She took a deep breath and cleared her throat. "Weezie keeps telling me we're going to get through this. I wish I believed that. Her watchword for me that day was *Saturine*: having a melancholy or morose disposition. I couldn't argue. I don't smile much anymore."

She shifted her hip on the hard granite. "In case you're wondering, the boys have been little snots. They always pestered me, but it's worse now. Weezie said it's their way of grieving. 'This too will pass', she says. It sure doesn't feel like it to me. They don't do anything around the house and Daddy's so wrapped up with problems at the mine that he ignores them. I complain and complain, but nobody listens."

Her eyes narrowed and she lowered her voice to a conspiratorial whisper.

"Maybe I shouldn't tell you this, but I'm going to anyway. You know Mrs. Jackson, the widow lady at church? She's been giving us cakes and pies. She stalks Daddy after Sunday service. She waits in the parking lot with an armload of goodies and a face full of smiles. It's downright unseemly. I don't like it, not one darned bit. The boys gobble the stuff right up. I won't eat anything she makes."

Mary Jane shaded her eyes with a hand and squinted into the sun streaming through the locust trees that gave Locust Grove Cemetery its name. The sun's angle told her she needed to finish up, get home and start supper.

"I'm still dating Estil, of course. He's been real sweet lately. He even sent flowers to the funeral home and sat beside me at church. I gave him a big kiss for being so nice. Actually, I give him lots of kisses," she said, blushing. "It's not Estil's fault Daddy works in the Estep's coal mine."

She checked her watch. "I'd better be going. I have to walk home. I browned some hamburger for chili last night. All I need to do is warm it up with a couple of jars of tomatoes and add some beans. While it's heating, I'll make corn bread. That'll give the boys something else to complain about."

Mary Jane stood up and stretched. The sun sat low on the horizon. It'd be dusk by the time she got home. She picked up her bookbag and tossed it over a shoulder.

"Bye, Momma." She patted a kiss onto the marker. "I haven't forgotten the promises I made."

~ 7 ~

The first weeks of summer vacation passed pleasantly. Mary Jane awoke to the coos of mourning doves and, after getting her father off to work, set her own schedule. Housework became less of a problem. She had time to read, hangout with Stephanie, or putter in the garden.

She'd looked forward to summer vacation expecting to have more time with Estil, but her father had other ideas. He imposed strict limits on where, and how often, she could see him. Despite her howls of protest, he dug in his heels and made the rules stick. Although she still talked to Estil on the phone most evenings, they were allotted only a single date each weekend.

Just when she'd decided things couldn't get worse, they did. Estil's mother called suggesting he spend July with her in California.

"It's crazy," Estil said. "I hardly hear from her and now she wants me to fly across the country to spend time with her."

"Is that what you told her?"

"I said I'd think about it."

"Did she give any reason for wanting to see you?"

"She talked about me growing up and this being our last chance to connect. You know, sentimental stuff."

"Have you ever talked to her about your feelings?"

"Don't go getting all feminine on me. You know I'm not into touchy-feely."

Estil's ambivalence toward his mother bothered Mary Jane. She and Momma had been so close. Hardly a day went by that she didn't think of her. Estil insisted his situation was different. She still found it difficult to imagine anyone not having warm feelings for their mother.

"She's right," Mary Jane said. "You should go. This summer is the quiet before the storm. You've got another year of high school and then you're off to UK. If you don't see her now, you'll always wish you had."

Before he left, he invited Mary Jane to go on an all-day horseback ride. And, to her surprise, her father didn't object.

Morning dew wet their boots as they piled tack into the bed of Estil's pickup. They loaded two horses into a trailer, hitched onto it and headed off.

"You're gonna love this spot," Estil said. "It has lots of trails winding through the trees."

They left the truck behind and plunged into the shadowy world of a mature forest. Despite the warm day, the air felt cool against her skin.

Estil knew the way and took the lead whenever the trail narrowed. Mary Jane had pulled her hair into a ponytail and threaded out the back of a baseball cap. It bobbed and swayed in time to the horse's movements.

Estil wore a white Stetson and rode tall in the saddle. She enjoyed watching the muscles in his back and shoulders ripple under his tee shirt. The primordial surroundings, the feel of the horse beneath her, and Estil's physique were powerful stimulants.

Around noon, Estil turned onto a sloping trail leading to a wide meadow. They watered their horses in a small, stream-fed lake then turned them loose to graze. After washing up, they retired to a limestone outcropping to eat the picnic lunch Mary Jane packed.

Afterwards Estil leaned against an oak tree and motioned her to sit in front of him. Without consciously planning it, she closed her eyes and began timing her breaths to his. It united them in an indescribable way. She wondered if Estil felt it as well.

He nuzzled her neck. "Sure will miss you."

"I'm going to miss you, too." She tilted her head letting his lips follow the curve of her neck. "Are you looking forward to your trip?"

He rocked his hand in the air. “The mountains are all dry and brown.”

“I meant the time with your mom.”

“We’ll see.”

“Think you’ll meet any girls?”

He looked surprised. “They have girls in California?”

She gave him a poke.

He squeezed her. “None like you, at least.”

He was lying through his teeth and she loved him for it. Twisting in his arms, she turned and kissed him. He tightened his arms around her and traced the curve of her hip through her jeans. She relaxed and let him touch her, enjoying the feel of his hand.

Estil rolled his shoulders, stretched and yawned. It was a lazy summer afternoon, ideal for cloud watching and daydreaming. She took his hands in hers and tugged his arms tight around her. She felt their time together slipping away and wanted to make the most of what remained.

Estil leaned forward and kissed her cheek. “You’re sure quiet. What sort of thoughts are running around inside your head?”

“Oh, I was just caught up in the beauty of this place. I guess I sort of drifted away.” She swept her hand in a wide arc. “So all of this belongs to your dad, huh?”

“My grandfather bought it years ago, about 200 acres. It backs up to the Daniel Boone National Forest.” He pointed at the mountain behind them. “The line’s somewhere over the ridge.”

“Just think, when you take over the company it’ll be yours.”

“Not if I can help it.”

“How can you not like this place? It’s paradise.”

“This place is fine. I meant the company. I’m just about as interested in what Pop does as he is in what I do.”

She patted his hand. “I bet he cares more about you than

you realize."

"Keep making bets like that and you'll go broke."

"Still, it's nice he keeps it as a place to ride, and maybe hunt or fish."

"You don't know my Pop. He's craftier than that. He doesn't do anything for the fun of it. Look around. There's tons of hardwood timber out there."

Mary Jane did look around. At the tall trees, at the pond with a family of ducks trailing V's behind them, at a red-tailed hawk circling in the distance.

"He'd cut this all down and haul it away?"

"In a heartbeat."

"So why hasn't he?"

"Like you said, it's a nice place to ride. Meanwhile, the longer he waits, the more the trees are worth."

"If he selectively logged, it could remain a pristine wilderness."

Estil picked up a twig, peeled it and stuck it between his teeth. "Nah, he'll clear-cut it."

The defiant undertone in Estil's voice stunned her. "Why?"

"It's underlain with coal. He'll strip mine the whole place."

Mary Jane looked around with new eyes. She'd knew what strip mines did to the landscape. She'd felt their house shake when strip miners blew the tops off mountains to get at the coal. Watched bulldozers shove the overburden into the surrounding valleys, burying lakes and streams.

She stared over at the hillside opposite them imagining it gone, flat as a pancake. Beside it would be waste heaps a hundred feet high oozing runoff as acidic as vinegar, with coal sludge pooled in every depression and tire track.

They'd probably grade a road right through the spot where she and Estil were sitting. She could almost hear the gears grinding as overloaded coal trucks clattered past belching diesel smoke.

"Don't you need permits to do that?"

Estil twisted the stick in his teeth. "That's no problem."

"What about all those new mining regulations?"

"The mining lobby's got most of the politicians in their hip pocket. Oh, they bluster and fume for the TV cameras, but things never really change. This is coal country, Sweetheart. Get with the program."

"But...but if he comes in and decimates this place, won't he have to put it back together again?"

Estil shook his head and chuckled. He stared at the ground for a moment, developing an explanation simple enough for her to understand. "Okay, here's the way it works. They have rules; you contest them. They require bonds; you get them lowered. You hire experts who'll say whatever you want them to."

"Once they find out how much it's really going to cost, they'll come looking for your dad and make him pay up."

Estil laughed again. "Estep Mining Company would never develop this site. Pop will set up a dummy corporation and sell the mining rights to them on a per-ton royalty. They strip out the coal and he pockets the money. Then, surprise! The new company runs out of cash and files bankruptcy."

"Is that how your family operates, Estil?"

"I'm simply saying such things have been known to happen."

"But there's magic here. This place is beautiful."

"So's a pile of cash." He flicked the stick away. "And you can't have 'em both."

"It sounds like you admire him."

"Deep down, I guess we're a lot alike; we get what we go after."

For the first time she saw the side of the Esteps her father talked about. The sound of the wind rushed through the trees like an approaching freight train. She looked at the meadow again. A bit of its magic had already slipped away.

~ 8 ~

Mary Jane leaned on the wrought iron gate gulping in deep breaths. She'd been home alone when the phone rang and was bursting to tell someone her good news. Deciding to share the news with her mother, she closed up the house and headed for the cemetery. It came into view when she rounded the curve and, seeing it so close at hand, she broke into a giddy run.

She brushed aside stray wisps of hair and berated herself for not taking time to cut some flowers. She's rushed away without giving them a thought.

The gate's rusty hinges creaked in protest when she pushed it back. Grinning, Mary Jane jogged up the low hill to her mother's grave and dropped onto the base of the marker. Her left arm found its familiar spot half-resting, half-hugging her mother's black granite stone.

"Hi, Momma, it's me again. I've got news, big news."

Mary Jane heard a strange noise beside her and jerked around. A curious cow from a nearby herd had wandered over to the fence separating her pasture from the cemetery. The buckskin colored Jersey slowly chewed her cud and stared at Mary Jane with big cow eyes, politely waiting to hear the news.

She pointed to the grazing herd. "Did your friends there send you over to spy?" She gave a happy chuckle. "Go ahead and eavesdrop. See if I care."

Turning her back to the cow, in her most controlled and mature voice she said, "Guess what, Momma? I've got a job."

Then she lost it.

"That's right, I said job. Yeah, a job...like in work and paydays and savings accounts and money for college tuition. Mr. Pence from the Piggly Wiggly Market called me not half-an-hour ago. He's going to hire me." She slapped her knee. "Can you believe it? I'm going to be a grocery checker at The Pig."

Eyes gleaming, Mary Jane sighed with satisfaction. The locust trees bordering the cemetery filtered the hot July sun, throwing a checkerboard of bright and dark splotches around her. From here on out, she'd be a working girl, she thought, smoothing her tee shirt.

"I filled out the application about a million years ago. When I didn't hear anything, I figured it must've gone into the round file. I gave up hope and then... Bang! Out of the blue, Mr. Pence called me for an interview.

"I brushed my hair back and let it fall over my shoulders and wore my blue dress and good shoes, and a brand new pair of hose. I sat there nice and straight, all prim and proper 'n' ladylike. I made eye contact, smiled and nodded just like they tell you to. And it worked; I got the job."

A sudden look of alarm crossed her face.

"Don't worry. I'm not thinking of quitting school. It's only part-time, Friday nights and all day Saturday. I'll be in church every Sunday morning just like always."

Her face clouded as the implications of what she'd just said sank in. She bit her lip, mulling it over.

"Boy, oh, Boy, Estil's not going to like this. Not even a little bit." She rested her forehead on her fist. "I won't be able to go to any football games this fall and he's counting on me being there like always."

She'd been so excited about the job she never gave him a thought. Well, he would just have to understand. This job was as important to her as football was to him.

"I better get back home before someone misses me. She pushed herself up, touched her lips and tapped the top of her mother's marker. "Love you, Momma."

The cow remained next to the fence, staring. Mary Jane looked over and grinned. "You can go back and make your report now."

She skipped back down the little hill laughing with each step she took.

~ 9 ~

Estil didn't find out about her job until he returned from California. Mary Jane had figured it right, he *was* upset. They argued. He threatened. She returned his class ring. She knew she'd won when she saw his face.

He guessed maybe, just maybe, he could live with her working on game nights. Mary Jane promised to try to get some Fridays off. She took the ring back and they kissed and made up.

"Run! Lift those knees. C'mon ladies, let's get a move on."

Grunting in the sun, Estil and the rest of the team ran laps until Coach Carson decided they'd paid for their poor performance in the scrimmage. They grumbled that Carson had no favorites. He treated them all like dirt.

The sweat-drenched players were limping toward the showers when Carson's gravelly voice bellowed, "Estep!"

Inwardly groaning, Estil dropped back from the pack and walked to where the coach stood.

"When are you going to learn to follow my plays? If I tell you wide right, I want to see that ball go to the right, not down the middle."

He sighed. "I had an open receiver. We scored."

"How many times must I tell you? Follow orders. Your arm won't always get you out of trouble."

"Yessir," Estil mumbled. These daily harangues were taking their toll. He'd begun to question his commitment to football. If the alternative hadn't been Estep Coal Company, he would've told Carson where to go.

"Walk you to the shower." Carson patted him on the back. "Buck up. I'm going to make you a champion whether you like it or not."

Estil grinned.

The coach gave him a sidelong glance. He couldn't afford to alienate his petulant star. Estil's raw power would make the Marauders unbeatable. One way or another, Carson needed to covert this wild stallion into a saddle horse.

The Bly Marauders started the season strong, winning three conference games in a row. Sportswriters around the state took a hard look at the Southeast Conference. Searching for a catchy story angle, a local sportswriter dubbed him Estil "The Arm" Estep. It stuck and Estil "The Arm's" name popped up in newspapers as far away as Lexington and Louisville.

"Hey, Dude, your fan club's waiting outside," a player said as Estil rounded the corner.

"Fan club? What are you talking about?"

"MJ. She's out there pantin' for ya, man. You better take the edge off before she decides to leave with me."

Estil took a few steps, stopped and turned halfway round to glance back. "You know, Ron, you gotta get yourself a steady girl. You and MJ?" He shook his head. "Not in this lifetime. These fantasies of yours are getting downright bizarre."

Estil walked away chuckling. Passing the laundry cart, he tossed in his soiled jersey and hung his pads over the side.

He found Mary Jane waiting under the security light, leaning against the wall with one knee bent. She wore tight jeans with western boots. Her suede jacket had fringe running across the back and down the arms. Under it she had a soft pink blouse with the collar folded up and two buttons undone. His class ring dangled from a chain around her neck.

Hearing his cleats on the concrete, she turned. "Good game, Mr. Quarterback."

"Did you see it?"

"Every play."

"What are you doing here?"

"I'm waiting for you to change so we can go out."

"Why didn't you tell me you were coming?"

"I wanted to surprise you."

"Well, you did."

Her eyes narrowed. "Did you have plans?"

"No. I just didn't expect you."

She reached up and touched the black grease paint under his eyes. "Just because you've still got your war paint on, doesn't mean you have to be so feisty."

Her hand traced his cheek, dropped onto his muscular shoulder then slipped around his neck. "Missed you," she whispered, putting her other arm around him and lifting her face for a kiss.

He held her around the waist, kissing her several times.

His hair was a mass of sweaty ringlets and she ran her fingers through the damp tendrils along the back of his neck. "Glad I came?"

He answered with a muffled grunt. She turned her head aside, giggling softly as he nuzzled her neck. She took a deep breath, inhaling his strong, masculine scent. It rekindled the excitement she'd felt watching him on the field.

"Let me get a look at you."

His pants were smudged with dirt and grass-stained. He had dribbles of dried blood from multiple scrapes and scratches on his shins and a large purple bruise was forming on his left arm. She touched it lightly. "You need to tell those mean boys not to play so rough. I don't like it when they beat on you."

He reached for her. "How about seconds?"

She kept him at arm's length. "Put some clothes on and we'll get a burger. I'll be waiting in your truck. There's plenty more where that came from."

Estil maneuvered his pickup up the steep incline leading to the overlook and parked. The October night was crisp and clear with countless stars twinkling above them. Lights from the houses below lay scattered across the valley like confetti after a party. He put his arm over the back of the seat and Mary Jane slid close.

"Everything all right?" she asked.

"Sure."

"When you came out of the locker room it felt like you didn't want to see me."

"Lately I've been thinking you haven't wanted to see me."

"Whatever gave you an idea like that?"

Estil relaxed his grip on her shoulder. Turning to the window, he drummed his fingers on the steering wheel, silently counting the stars.

"Well, you didn't come to any pre-season practices and this is the first regular game you've been to. I'm the starting quarterback. How does it look for me to not even have a date? It feels like something's changed."

"Something has changed. I've taken on lots more responsibility since Momma died. I couldn't come watch your pre-season practice, I had to can peaches."

Since her mother's death, she craved the comfort of their relationship. The prospect of going to the football game, the anticipation of being with him, buoyed her spirits all week. But they no longer connected the way they once had. The more she sought depth and understanding, the more superficial Estil seemed.

Still fuming, he reached behind the seat and extracted a bottle of beer from a cooler he kept there.

"How do you manage to always have a stock of beer in a dry county?"

"We're right on the state line." His teeth gleamed in the moonlight when he grinned. He twisted the cap off of the long-necked bottle and flicked it away.

"Must you drink that?"

"It helps me unwind." He took a long pull on the bottle.

She hated it when he drank. Not only did she dislike kissing him when his breath smelled of alcohol, but drinking also lowered his inhibitions.

He belched loudly. "You oughta take a drink now and then. It might loosen you up."

"Which do you want, me or that beer?"

Estil ran his eyes up and down her then dangled the bottle by its neck, rocking it back and forth. Waves of foam, yellow through the brown bottle, sloshed up the side. He stuck his arm out the window and up-ended it. When it was empty, he tossed it over the edge of the parking area where it clanked among the other dead soldiers hiding in the bushes.

"Happy?"

She answered by leaning into him.

"You know how important football is."

"Important to you."

"Spit it out, what's eating you?"

"I just wish you could understand that right now I have important priorities like two younger brothers to take care of, housework and my job."

"How could I have forgotten your job?" He voice was thick with sarcasm.

"I've got to get some money together if I'm going to go to college. Friday's our busiest night at the store. I begged and begged Mr. Pence to let me off."

"In other words, you don't have time for me?"

"I didn't say that."

"That's what I heard."

"Look, I've got the night off. You won your game. We're together. Stop fussing and enjoy it."

She snuggled against him. He wrapped his arms around her and they necked for several minutes, melting away the strain of being apart. She pressed herself against him as he kissed her, sensing a need in Estil's touch that excited her. She closed her eyes and whispered his name as he kissed along her throat.

Snapping her eyes open, Mary Jane grabbed his hands and pushed them away.

The darkness couldn't hide Estil's displeasure.

Overheated and breathing hard, they glared at each other like prizefighters at the end of a round.

"What is it you want from me?"

He smacked the steering wheel. "I just want things to be settled and secure like they used to be."

"Believe me, I wish I could turn back the clock more than you do. Things have changed, there's no going back."

She rested her head on his shoulder. Her hair had a faint, fruity smell, from the apricot shampoo she bought at the Dollar General Store. He toyed with her ponytail then kissed her cheek before encircling her in his arms once again. Mary Jane sighed with contentment.

After a few minutes, his fondling yanked her back to reality. "Don't touch me like that, Estil."

"Jeez, MJ, I thought we had something."

"No, you had something. I could do without the help-yourself-hands."

She'd been an unwitting accomplice, she thought, adjusting her blouse. After several weeks apart, Estil wasn't the only one feeling needy. Yet admitting to having needs and desires that were, on the whole, not unlike his own, would only reinforce his determination to break down her resistance.

Meanwhile, he scowled out the window.

She tried placating him by rubbing his shoulder.

He shrugged her hand away and continued sulking.

When he reached for another beer, she said, "Why don't you take me home."

~ 10 ~

Her spat with Estil left Mary Jane too upset to sleep. She tossed and turned, reminding herself that her father worked the next day and she had a full shift at the Piggly Wiggly Market. She was reading when the phone rang.

"MJ?"

"Yes."

"Reading?"

"Uh-huh."

"Listen, Babe, I'm really sorry. I don't know what got into me tonight. I must have taken a hit to the head during the game or something. I know how tough it's been for you. I shouldn't have acted the way I did. It's just that we haven't been together much and I really missed you. Can you forgive me?"

She sat in the bed nodding. Same old Estil, act first and think later, especially when under pressure.

"You're not saying anything."

"Yes." She forced the word out over the lump in her throat. "Yes, I forgive you."

Estil seemed at a loss as to what to do next. After a pause he said, "Love you, sleep tight."

"You're looking glum." Stephanie took a seat at the lunch table. "Let me guess, man trouble?"

Mary Jane gave a little start. "Am I that transparent?"

"Let's just say I've seen that look before." Stephanie's brown eyes twinkled. "What's the golden boy done now?"

"I made a special effort to go to the game last Friday. Not only did I lose the pay, but now I owe my soul to Mr. Pence. My sacrifices meant nothing to Estil. The only thing he wanted to do was head to Hennick's Hill and fool around."

"And you two aren't speaking."

“He called up and apologized, but I’m still mad about it.”

“So the big guy needed his horns clipped. Are you saying you don’t enjoy a little affection now and then?”

“I’m normal. Being in Estil’s arms and making-out is...nice. But this isn’t about affection; it’s about me wanting him to be supportive, understanding, and empathetic.”

“Not asking for much, are we?” Stephanie unwrapped her sandwich and studied it for a minute, frowning.

The two girls ate in silence.

“In case you haven’t noticed, Estil’s turned into quite the strapping young lad. Men have certain built-in biological urges, physical needs.”

Mary Jane frowned. “You’re as bad as he is. To hear him tell it, I’m causing him horrendous physiological pain.”

“You’re keeping him on an awfully long leash. Maybe you ought to offer a little sample.”

“Let the deli counter give away the samples. Besides, his fingers find their way to places where they shouldn’t be without my assistance. I refuse to become a sex object.”

Stephanie chuckled. “Take a look in the mirror the next time you step out of the shower. You already are a sex object.”

~ 11 ~

"Mr. Pence, I need to talk to you."

Mary Jane moved with athletic grace as she chased her boss down the cracker aisle, dodging grocery carts and weaving between customers.

"Can't you see I'm busy right now, MJ?" he said over his shoulder and headed for the back room.

Pence shouldered his way through the double doors, ignoring a sign that warned: *Beware of Outgoing Traffic.*

Mary Jane started to follow, but came to an abrupt stop. The swinging doors snapped open in front of her, crashing against the sides of the milk coolers as a grocery stocker wheeled out a cart of canned goods. Sidestepping the cart, she straightened a teetering case of canned corn as he passed. Then, she made a beeline across the back aisle and dashed into the stockroom in time to see her boss disappear into his office.

Mary Jane hurried past rolling racks filled with trays of fresh bread and rolls, pallets of soda and around mountains of canned goods. When she reached his open office door, she drew to a halt and paused to catch her breath. She tidied her hair and smoothed her uniform, silently rehearsing her plea.

She tapped on the doorframe. "Mr. Pence, may I speak with you?"

He waved her in. "I'll be through in a minute."

Mary Jane sat on the folding chair in front of Pence's desk, tucked her skirt around her legs and folded her hands in her lap. "I didn't mean to interrupt your work," she whispered, knowing full well she had.

When he finished, Mary Jane gave him a nervous smile. "How are you today, Mr. Pence?"

"Busy," he shoved aside an inventory report. "This is about taking Friday night off, isn't it?"

She lowered her eyes and nodded.

"Look, I'm not trying to be hard-nosed, but you know Friday's our busiest day of the week. It's going to be crazier than usual with the playoffs .

"Please, Mr. Pence, just this one time. I'll never ask for another thing ever again."

"You've already taken a Friday off for a football game. You promised you'd never ask again, yet here you are."

She berated herself for not anticipating his response and preparing a rebuttal. "I didn't expect the Marauders to make it into the playoffs."

"The work doesn't go away. If you're not here someone else has to do your job."

"I'll make the hours up, I swear I will. What if I find somebody to swap shifts with?"

"You won't find anyone; it just doesn't want to work."

"I know Friday's going to be busy. I, I could come in Thursday night right after school and help roll cold cuts for deli trays, or make Cole slaw and potato salad. The stockers work all night on Fridays, what if I came in after the game and swept floors?"

Pence knew he'd be a goner if he looked her in the eye. Though she seemed naively unaware of her ability to do it, she could wrap him around her little finger in a heartbeat. She affected most men that way. On Friday nights when the checkout lines snaked halfway down the grocery aisles, he'd watched burly men in sweat-stained work clothes bag their own groceries and thank her for the privilege just for one of her smiles.

"I'll do anything, Mr. Pence. I've only been to one game all season and this is the final playoff." She fingered the class ring dangling around her neck. "Please let me go."

"What if the Marauders win and go to the State Finals?"

"That won't be any problem. The State Finals are at Cardinal Stadium in Louisville on a Sunday afternoon. I work Fridays and Saturdays, remember?"

"But you'll surely want to go over on Saturday. There'll be parties you wouldn't want to miss."

"I already talked to Daddy. He thinks motels are full of riff-raff and I'm too young to be staying there. I told him Stephanie would be with me, but that didn't change his mind. If the Marauders get into the State Finals, we'll drive up Sunday morning and come back after the game."

"It's a long trip back and forth in a single day."

"It's mostly interstate, a bunch of us girls will ride together. It'll be fun."

He sighed and supposed he could spare her this one time.

Eyes sparkling, she gave him a disarming smile and then, realizing she'd run long on her break, jumped out the chair and jogged back to her checkout stand.

Competing on their home turf and relying on Estil's strong passing, Bly defeated Russellville 42-13, clinching a spot in the state finals

Mary Jane waited for Estil after the game at their usual rendezvous point. He slipped out for a few victory kisses and then, suggesting she wait inside, went back to shower. He came out later and found her shivering.

"I told you to come inside." Estil wrapped his arms around her. "Why are you out here in the cold?"

"I don't like standing outside the locker room knowing everyone in there's running around naked. I planned to wait in your truck, but it isn't here."

"Whaddaya think happened?"

"It must've been stolen."

Estil grinned and removed a key from his pocket. "Let's see if this fits anything."

He led her to a brand new 4-wheel-drive pickup, unlocked the door and motioned her in. "See. You worry too much." He steadied her as she stretched her leg to climb into the high cab.

"Wow, some truck. Whose is it?"

"Mine."

"What happened to the old one?"

"I traded it in." He gunned the engine. "Went down to the Ford garage yesterday and got this baby."

"You didn't say anything about getting a new truck."

"Do I have to report everything I do?" He saw the look on her face and reached for her hand. "I didn't mean that to come out the way it did. Jeez, you're still cold." He slid his hand along her thigh. "We'll have to get you warmed-up."

"I see the button right here." Grinning, she moved the temperature control to warm and clicked on the blower.

She ran her eyes around the cab. Even though it still had a new car smell, the truck felt familiar. Estil's gun rack stretched across the back window just as always. The tiny football cleats hung from the mirror in his old truck dangled in front of her. She laughed and pointed to a bronze-toned statue on the dash. "Even St. Christopher moved with you."

Estil rubbed St. Christopher's head. "I couldn't leave ol' Chris behind."

Mary Jane leaned back, inspecting the truck's interior a second time. "How did you ever afford it?"

"I used the money I had in savings."

"You told me your grandfather left that money to pay your college tuition. There wasn't anything wrong with the old truck."

"Are you kidding? It was an old Estep Mining Company truck. Pop's Superintendent beat the life out of the springs in the year and a half he drove it. I'm going to win the championship. I deserved something better."

"But now you don't have money for college."

"Don't need it. Those scouts keep knocking at my door. I'm going to be a star, MJ. I'm headed for the big time."

After shutting the engine off, Estil extended his arm along the seat back. She slid beside him and they kissed. His arm curled around her and they spent time warming each other.

"I've missed you," she whispered, resting her head on his shoulder. Her hand moved along the side of his face, tracing the rocky outcropping of his cheekbone. She interlaced her fingers with his. "What's the big time, Estil?"

"I'm thinking I could play for one of the top schools, Michigan, Perdue, Nebraska, USC...the ones you see on TV.

"What happened to us going to UK together?" Her voice sounded small and timid.

He pushed a button, lowering the window beside him. He looked out for a second, spit and then raised it. Groping behind the seat, Estil extracted a bottle of beer.

"I see everything important moved to your new truck."

"I'm too big for the University of Kentucky. The Marauders cleaned everybody's clock this year and we'll win the state championship. I told the coach to send tonight's game films to Notre Dame."

"Notre Dame? You're not even Catholic."

Estil shook his head and laughed until he choked. He patted her knee. "Please tell me you didn't actually think all of those guys running around in gold helmets were former altar boys."

She crossed her arms. "I never thought about it one way or the other."

"Well, maybe you should." He used the beer bottle as a pointer while he lectured. "Let me put this in terms you can understand. When they call a huddle, they're not gathered in a circle rattling their rosary beads 'n' praying for a touchdown. The only thing Notre Dame's coach wants to know is how far I can pitch the football. I could be the freakin' Dalai Lama trotting around in a red robe and sandals for all they care."

Mary Jane sighed as Estil droned on. She hadn't begged a night off from work so he could lecture her on the preferences of college football coaches.

~ 12 ~

Estil completed an undefeated season with a playoff sweep. As a high school All-American his picture appeared on the sports pages of *USA Today* and in national magazines. The first Sunday in December, on the strength of his passing, the Bly Marauders won the Kentucky Class A Football State Championship. They awarded Estil the most valuable player trophy and Carson's peers elected him Coach of the Year.

The week before Christmas break the school dedicated a section in their trophy case to him. They retired his number and displayed the jersey he'd worn in his last game. Beside it sat the State Championship trophy with a miniature quarterback on top.

Some mornings Estil came in early, pausing in front of the case to read his name on the trophy. Afternoons, when he finished in the weight room and the office doors were locked, the halls dark and everyone gone home, he'd stand and quietly stare.

Throughout the season and into the playoffs, recruiters beat a path to Estil's door. It was a courtship with Estil the belle of the ball. He reveled in their attention, finding the validation he'd never gotten from his father.

Unimaginably, it ended as quickly as it began.

After succumbing to the lure of fame, he found himself high and dry in the middle of an NCAA-imposed recruiting Quiet Period. The rules said no recruiters could contact him until after New Year's. A long three week wait.

Estil didn't discuss his anxieties with anyone, not Coach Carson, not Mary Jane and certainly not his father. Bottled-up inside, his concerns drove him to absurd imaginings. He worried the recruiters might never return, that they'd find someone else to take his place. He reread the rules and found he couldn't sign until February. This further upset him.

The days remained short, the weather cold. All through the Christmas break he worked out in the school's weight room and jogged untold miles around the track to keep his legs in shape. In the evenings when he couldn't sit still enough to watch TV, he'd throw his rock across the yard or call Mary Jane.

After what seemed like an interminable wait, February rolled around and Estil agreed to sign a National Letter of Intent with the University of Michigan.

Randall Estep developed a sudden interest in football now that his son had a national reputation and arranged an elaborate dinner in his honor at the Blackstone Country Club.

Estil invited Mary Jane and, like everything about their relationship, it created complications. They not only scheduled the signing on her father's birthday, but she didn't have a dress suitable for a Country Club dinner. She negotiated a compromise. They'd go to Weezie's in the afternoon, leaving her free to go to the Country Club. She still had the problem of the clothes and solved it by bowing out.

"This is your day, not mine, Estil. You don't need me."

"For cryin' out loud, how can you say that? You have to be there. Otherwise I'll come off like some dateless geek."

She hemmed and hawed, then confessed, "I don't have anything to wear."

"Wear clothes."

"That's easy for you to say. I bet you're getting a new suit."

With prodding, he admitted he was.

"I can't afford a fancy party dress. I'm sorry."

"What if I gave you a dress as an early Valentine's Day present?"

"You don't know anything about women's clothes."

"Dad's wife, Adelle, does. She knows every dress store from here to Timbuktu."

So, with Stephanie along for moral support, Mary Jane and Adelle went shopping in Lexington. Not quite thirty, Adelle got along well with the girls. She treated them to manicures and took them out to lunch at her favorite restaurant. Afterwards, they hit the dress shops. Over Mary Jane's objections, Adelle settled on a slinky, three-piece Persian red outfit.

She tiptoed out of the dressing room, head swiveling and arms folded across her chest. "I can't wear this. I feel half-naked."

The neckline on the sleeveless top plunged. Mary Jane fingered the sparkly beads running down the front of the matching jacket. She loved the jacket, but it didn't even meet in the middle. It seemed designed to direct a viewer's eyes straight to her bust.

Stephanie gave a wolfish growl. "Man, you look hot. The golden boy's eyes will pop out when he sees you in that."

Adelle lifted Mary Jane's hands, pulling her arms away from her chest. "Put your arms at your sides so I can see how it fits." She circled, tugging and adjusting. "There now, take a look in the three-way mirror. You'll like what you see."

It wasn't a dress Mary Jane would have chosen, but since it was a gift she felt uncomfortable saying so.

"You look like a statue," Adelle said. "Relax. Move around naturally."

Mary Jane watched the longish skirt swirl around her legs when she walked, flashing tantalizing glimpses of thigh. Stephanie was right, it was one sexy dress. "What happens when I sit down?" Mary Jane asked, flipping the side split aside to demonstrate.

Adelle slipped her arm around Mary Jane's shoulder and caught her eye in the mirror. "Every man in the place is going to know you've got great legs."

"The top's cut too low, my bra shows."

"We'll get you a pushup bra with half cups."

"That'll show even more."

Adelle motioned her aside. "It's high time you started thinking about what you want out of life. Most of the girls I went to school with clerk in dime stores, or wait tables. They're married to truck drivers and miners and live in crappy, rundown trailers. They've got a couple of bratty kids and bellies stuck out t' here with another."

She glanced around and lowered her voice. "Listen. You and I are better than that. You're too good looking to waste time on some mechanic. You need to offer a preview of coming attractions."

"What if I don't want to?"

Adelle winked. "You marry some loser and he's gonna want to go for a ride every night of the week." She tossed her bleached-blond hair over her shoulder. "I don't know about you, but it'll be a cold day in Hell when I sign-on to be some grease monkey's circus pony."

They found a pair of matching high heels and Adelle insisted she get a lacy bra and panty set. Mary Jane, who usually bought white cotton, protested the extravagance. "No one's even going to see them."

Adelle gave her a coy wink. "Don't count on it."

When Adelle dropped her off, Mary Jane tucked her packages under her arm, hurried up to her room and hung the dress in the back of her closet. Neither her father nor the boys asked about it, which suited her just fine.

Mary Jane was alone at home getting ready. She pulled her hair into a French twist and was finishing her makeup when Estil honked.

She stepped out and looked up at the door on Estil's pickup. How would she ever stretch her leg up into the truck with those side splits? Why hadn't she thought of that in the store? She sighed and offered Estil her arm.

Too late now. He'd see whatever he saw.

Under the dome light, Mary Jane noticed a telltale glow in Estil's cheeks when he slid in. He'd already begun celebrating.

~ 13 ~

"We're sitting with Pop and Adelle and Coach Carson and his wife." Estil said. He studied the table for a moment then assigned places. "That's the head of the table, so Pop will sit there. Adelle will be on his left, putting you here."

Sitting next to Randall Estep made Mary Jane uncomfortable. "Suppose we sat over there?"

Estil shook his head. "This is the only way. See, boy-girl, boy-girl, boy-girl."

After dessert, Adelle and Mrs. Carson slipped away. Estil and his coach fell into a discussion of Big Ten football leaving Mary Jane alone with Randall Estep.

"You look lovely tonight, MJ."

She smiled politely, thanking him for the compliment.

"I especially like the way you fixed your hair."

She thanked him again.

He winked. "Putting it up means you'll let your hair down later tonight, hmmm?"

"Yes, I suppose that's true."

"What do you do when you let your hair down?"

"Just what you'd imagine; remove the pins and brush it out."

Estil had a pen out diagramming a play for Coach Carson. Mary Jane decided to join Adelle and Mrs. Carson and started to rise.

Estep rested a hand on her arm. "Don't rush away. We seldom have a chance to talk." He stared into her cleavage. "And I do enjoy seeing you."

She reluctantly settled back into the chair.

"I love the color of your dress. It gives your cheeks a warm glow."

"Adelle picked it out."

"So she said. Did you two have time for girl talk?"

"She had some interesting things to share."

He leaned back in his chair. "Quite a gal, isn't she?"

"Where did you ever find her?"

"On a business trip to Nashville, actually." His face softened when he smiled. "I walked into this little, hole-in-the-wall lounge one night and there she was."

"Like a diamond in the rough."

He nodded. "We hit it off right away."

"I can imagine."

He glanced at the thigh-high split in her dress and smiled. "Estil's done all right for himself, too."

"Yes, a football scholarship to the University of Michigan is quite an achievement."

"Well, an acorn doesn't fall far from the tree."

"You played football?"

"I referred to my achievements at Estep Mining Company."

"Yes, Estil's mentioned his feelings for Estep Mining."

He leaned forward. "I've worried he hasn't given the company serious consideration."

She took a sip of water. "He talks about it all the time."

Estep winked over the rim of his coffee cup. "That dress looks like it'd be easy to slip out of."

"I wouldn't know. This is the first time I've worn it."

"Well, I'm sure you'll find out before the night's over."

"Yep, just before I hop into my jammies."

Estep's hand brushed her knee beneath the tablecloth. Mary Jane told herself it was accidental until he began caressing her thigh.

"I love this dress," he whispered.

"Your wife said older men would." Mary Jane looked up and smiled. "Speaking of Adelle, here she comes now."

Mary Jane grabbed Estil's hand. "Let's dance." When they got to the dance floor, she made it clear she wanted to leave.

"Wait here. I'll go tell Pop."

She watched him lean down to speak into his father's ear. When he tried to straighten, his father grabbed his lapel and held fast.

"Tonight's your night. Use the guest house. Adelle and I won't bother you."

"You don't understand, Pop. Her father would never allow it."

"You're the one who doesn't understand. Her old man works for me, remember?"

"I'd rather do things my way."

His father wouldn't let him leave. Faced with having the lapel ripped off his new suit, Estil stayed to hear the rest.

"You're an Estep. It's time to act like it. If you want something, take it!"

His father glanced across the room. Seeing Mary Jane watching, he flashed a smile and held up a finger indicating *just one more minute.*

"When the fruit's ripe, you pick it."

Estil tried to reply, but his father cut him off.

"You'll toss her aside when you leave for Michigan anyway. Or is the football field the only place you can score?"

Estil pried his father's fingers loose and left without a word.

On the way to Hennick's Hill, Estil stopped at a rural market and purchased a couple of bottles of Coca-Cola. As he walked around the back of the truck, he poured out half of his, replacing it with whiskey.

After they parked, Mary Jane reached for her Coke, and in the dark, grabbed his by mistake. She took a sip and began choking and coughing.

Estil chuckled.

“Why didn’t you stop me?” she sputtered.

“You need to loosen up.”

She pointed at the offending bottle “Any more and I’ll be throwing-up.”

Estil pensively stared off at the dark silhouette of the mountains. Scraps of a faraway train whistle drifted up to them, sounding as lonely and forlorn as his mood.

She slid closer and entwined her fingers in his. “Feeling let down?”

“What makes you say that?”

“Call it intuition. You spend months anticipating something and then it’s here and gone in a flash.”

Estil shook his head. “I was thinking about something Pop said at the Country Club.”

“What’d he say?”

“It’s not important.”

After several fruitless stabs at conversation she gave up. They lapsed into an uncomfortable silence spent listening to the engine click and tap as it cooled.

Estil rested his hand on Mary Jane’s knee. It remained there briefly then slipped inside her skirt and up her leg. She pushed him away, wondering again why she’d let Adelle talk her into this outfit. Estil’s hand kept returning like a pesky fly that refused to leave the picnic.

Exasperated, she wrapped her hands around his. Her slim fingers barely contained his brawny fists. She looked him in the eye. “Settle down, Big Guy,” she whispered. “I know you’re excited about signing the letter of intent. You ought to be, but this isn’t the time or the place.”

He easily forced her hand apart. “How would you know?”

Estil drummed his fingers on the steering wheel and resumed staring out the window. Their breath formed moist fog on the inside of the windows. Here they were again, she thought, eyeing each other across a line drawn in the sand.

Straightening in the seat, Estil shoved his hand into his coat pocket. He smiled for the first time since he'd parked the truck. "You know, we've never talked about what's going to happen to us when I go away to Michigan."

"What do you want to happen?"

"I'd like you to wait for me."

"I'm not sure it would be the best thing for either of us."

The words were out of her mouth before she could stop them. For months events had been building to this moment. The excitement she'd felt when Estil asked her to go steady had gradually dribbled away, yet driven by habit, fear, or insecurity they both continued pretending otherwise.

"Don't be so sure." He placed a small box in her hand.

Her eyes widened when she glanced down at the velvet-covered box.

"Surprised?"

Unable to speak, she swallowed hard and nodded.

"Open it."

A diamond solitaire ring sparkled in the moonlight. She knew she should be giddy with excitement, but she felt only apprehension.

"Don't be bashful. Try it on."

Robot-like, she did as he instructed. She wished with all her heart Estil hadn't done what he just did. There'd be no more pretending now.

~ 14 ~

The ring on her finger felt strange, unnatural. "It's...it's beautiful, Estil. This is so unexpected. You shouldn't have."

He put a finger to her lips. "Don't talk, just feel." He kissed her and whispered, "Say you want me as much as I want you."

"This is happening too fast. I'm not ready."

"But you've got the ring. It's what you're always saying you want."

"I said I wanted an engagement ring?"

"Yes, over and over. Now there's nothing to stop us."

At first Estil's words didn't make sense. And then they did.

"I've talked about commitment and saving myself for marriage. A ring doesn't change anything." She slipped the ring off and fit it back into the box. "I'm sorry, Estil. I can't take this."

Estil jammed the box back into his pocket. "Oh, I forgot. You're the precious virgin Mary. You just don't get it, do you?"

"I get it. I get it all too well."

"Then act like it. I'm tired of being your lapdog. You're not as special as you think you are. There are plenty of girls who'd put out for me if they had the chance."

"Poor dear, whatever will you do? All those girls crazy in heat and only one Estil to satisfy them, maybe you should have them take numbers."

She suddenly stopped. Something was wrong with this picture. He'd said it. Stephanie had said it. And she just said it herself. If there were girls who'd give in to his advances, and there surely were, why not cast your line where the fish were biting? All at once, everything snapped into place.

Resting an arm along the back of the seat, she turned to face him. "Why are we still going steady?"

"You're not making sense."

"I never attended one of your practices. I missed most of

the games. I didn't even make it to all the playoffs. You're obviously unhappy, yet we haven't broken-up. Why?"

He glared at her.

"It's because you can't face the possibility that someone somewhere had the chance to sleep with you and turned it down."

"That's crazy talk, psycho-babble."

"Not for the great Estil 'The Arm' Estep it isn't."

Estil reached for his soda bottle. "The University of Michigan is only the beginning. After college, I'm going to play in the pros. Do you know how much a pro team pays its starting quarterback?"

She refused to take his bait.

"I'll make millions. I don't need my father's coal mines, I don't need you, I don't need anybody." His voice softened. "When I retire from the game, I'll do play-by-play commentary for the networks."

He gestured at the lights in the valley floor. "Do you want to spend your life in one of those little cracker boxes down there, working your fingers to the bone, scrimping and saving, shopping at the Dollar General Store?"

"Is that really how you feel?"

"You betcha." He emptied his bottle and swiped the back of his hand across his mouth. "This dumpy town can't hold me back. By the time I'm finished, Bly will be known for something other than the busted heads of striking coal miners. He faced her and smiled. "I'm going to be famous and you could be part of it."

"Sure I could. Fame and fortune all mine if I put out for you tonight. Let some other girl enjoy Estil 'The Penis' Estep."

"Read the handwriting on the wall, sister. This train's leaving the station whether you're on it, or not."

"Let it go." She smoothed her skirt. "Take me home, Estil."

He studied her for several moments then shook his head. "No. Not this time."

~ 15 ~

Estil placed his hands on Mary Jane's shoulders and pressed her onto the seat.

She tried to resist, but he easily overpowered her.

His fingers caught the neckline of her dress, tearing the sheer fabric.

"You're ripping my clothes!"

"You can't get to the candy if you don't open the wrapper."

Mary Jane twisted and squirmed, batting his hands away. She tried not to sound as terrified as she was. "This isn't the way it's supposed to be. Let's talk this out."

"Don't make thing any worse than they are. I'll get what I want one way or another."

"You've had too much to drink. Let me drive us home."

"Don't start raggin' on me about my drinking." He tossed her legs onto the seat, jamming her head against the door.

Magazine articles said to protect yourself by scratching and gouging an assailant's eyes. Mary Jane freed an arm and lashed at him.

Estil whipped out his hand and caught her wrist. He squeezed so tightly her fingers went numb. A slim girl couldn't battle an athlete who easily bench-pressed 240 pounds. Estil threw a football-sized rock across his yard. On a good day, Mary Jane might lob a softball to first base.

Having made his point, Estil tossed her hand aside and bunched her skirt around her waist. She covered her face, whimpering when he forced a knee between her legs.

Mary Jane strained beneath him, struggling to breathe. She stroked his cheek and tried to make her voice tender. "Think about what you're doing."

"Shut up, MJ. I'm not buyin' what you're sellin'. It's self-serve tonight."

"This is my first time," she sobbed. "Please Estil, not like this."

He grunted and fumbled with his zipper. Cursing when he couldn't get it unzipped, he leaned his head on the passenger's armrest and arched his back to get more room.

While he concentrated on the zipper, Mary Jane groped for the door handle. She found it and pulled with all her might.

The door popped open, the dome light came on, and Estil lurched forward.

With one hard shove she sent him tumbling face-first onto the gravel parking lot. Mary Jane righted herself. Slamming the door shut, she punched the automatic lock. Both doors locked with a satisfying thunk.

Adrenaline surged through her. She jumped behind the wheel and turned the key.

The engine came to life with a throaty roar.

Disoriented and confused, Estil staggered to his feet.

She rested her hands on the steering wheel, feeling the reassuring throb of the truck's engine. Heart hammering, Mary Jane dropped it into reverse and tromped on the accelerator.

The big pickup leaped back.

Braking, she cut the wheel hard left, shifted and gunned the engine.

The truck fishtailed, etching a circle in the loose gravel.

Rocks spewed back at Estil, forcing him to his knees. He bent down and covered his head.

The truck's tires grabbed hold and she shot forward.

Estil raised his head in time to watch Mary Jane and his new truck disappear down the park's entrance road.

Shaking and praying, she navigated the twisting drive with quick flicks of her wrist.

Estil ran to the edge of parking area.

The brake lights flashed briefly when she made a rolling stop. Then she turned onto the highway and sped away into the night.

Mary Jane tugged her clothing back together as she drove. She parked the truck in front of the house and gave a sigh of relief. The lights were out, everyone asleep. Tossing the keys into the ashtray, she hung Estil's class ring around St. Christopher and tiptoed to her room.

The following morning the truck was gone.

After her father left for work, Mary Jane gathered the torn remnants of her new outfit and threw them into the fire barrel along with a bag of trash and several old newspapers. She tossed in a lighted match and went back inside.

~ 16 ~

Estil had been out of Mary Jane's life for six months by time the new school year began. For reasons she never understood people assumed she wanted to hear the latest gossip concerning him.

She didn't.

He'd been right. There were plenty of girls ready for a roll in the hay with the golden boy. And, freed from her stabilizing influence, he cut a wide swath through Bly's female population leaving behind a string of broken-hearted victims. This series of hasty affairs and one-night stands established a pattern he would continue throughout his college career.

Mary Jane hadn't dated since they broke-up. Not because of any feelings she harbored for Estil, she enjoyed life more without him. But most of the young men around town, intimidated by her good looks and history as Estil's ex-steady, were afraid to ask her out.

All that changed the first day of the new school year when she met the young man she'd marry.

"Let's take Inorganic Chemistry together," Mary Jane suggested. "We could be lab partners."

Stephanie shook her head. "I don't need the science credit like some people I know.

"But it'd be fun."

"It'd be work."

School was less important since Del Crandall gave her an engagement ring. Unlike Mary Jane, whose future remained a blank page, Stephanie had her life mapped out. Graduate, get married, study cosmetology and live happily ever after.

So Mary Jane took Chemistry alone. Her only previous experience consisted of passing the room and noticing the noxious odors seeping under the door. The other worldliness of the lab created a sense of anticipation. Anticipation mingled with the fear she'd mix the wrong stuff and blow herself to bits.

The bell rang, starting the class. As the teacher closed the door, a new boy, tall and lanky with a shock of sandy-brown hair, rushed into the classroom with an armful of books.

He stood at the front of the room rocking from foot to foot looking for a place to sit. His face brightened when he saw the empty spot across from Mary Jane. He scampered into it and dumped his books onto the countertop. They toppled over and slid across the slick counter.

Mary Jane saw them careening at her and launched herself onto the counter to stop them. Shaken, but unhurt, she returned to her stool as he re-stacked the books.

The teacher invited the students to take a few minutes and wander around the room to familiarize themselves with the lab.

The young man, all arms and legs, rose and extended his hand. "Hi. My name's Jeremy Tilden. We moved into town over the summer. Sorry about the books. I didn't realize the tabletop was so slick." He slid a book back and forth, demonstrating.

"I'm Mary Jane Combs." She shook his hand. "Don't worry about it."

The teacher tapped the lectern. "One thing before we begin. I want everyone to look across the sink. See the person sitting over there? He or she is your lab partner. If they're you're best friend, fine. If they're a perfect stranger, that's okay too. Both of your names will be on all lab reports. So your grade depends upon your partner's performance almost as much as your own. This is your chance to change seats."

Mary Jane glanced over at Jeremy. He gave her a nervous smile then looked away. In that split-second Mary Jane detected the fear of rejection in his eyes.

The legs of her stool scraped the floor when she slid it back. Hearing the noise, Jeremy turned. Mary Jane leaned across the counter with a reassuring smile and extended her hand. "Hi,

Partner."

He gave a huge sigh of relief and grinned back.

"You won't regret this. I'm good in science and I study a lot. I'll tutor you if you need help. I'll do all our labs." Jeremy knew he was talking too fast, but couldn't stop himself.

"All you'll have to do is take notes and write reports." Thinking it over, he added, "I'll even write the reports if you want me to. You'll be glad we're partners."

And she was. Without Jeremy the class material would have been immensely boring. Somehow, he made it interesting. His genuine enthusiasm for chemistry astounded her.

When exam time drew near, they began meeting in the evenings and on weekends so Jeremy could prep her for the coming test. It benefited them both. His nervousness faded as they became better acquainted and she passed the exam with flying colors.

Mary Jane worked Friday nights and every Saturday, so Sunday afternoons became their time together. Their dates were casual, friendly, and devoid of the sexual tension she'd endured with Estil. They went to museums, saw performances by the local drama club, or took in exhibits at the community college.

Jeremy had a quiet confidence and seemed without ego. Content to share her company, he viewed her as a person, not a sex object, and his treatment of her bordered on chivalrous. By Christmas, they'd developed a deep and affectionate friendship.

~ 17 ~

The start of the second half of their senior year carried a sense of curious anticipation for the students in Mrs. Warnoski's Family Living Skills class. At their last meeting before the holidays, she'd predicted exciting changes. When questioned, she gave them a cagey smile and refused to elaborate.

A plump, matronly lady, she sat at her desk wearing her standard white blouse and navy blue suit. She nodded to the students as they came in, checking off their names in her attendance book.

When the bell rang, she placed her hand atop a stack of workbooks on the corner of her desk. "I promised exciting times this semester and so they will be. You'll be participating in an experimental program."

A rising chorus of groans filled the classroom.

"You're all getting married today."

Warnoski stood in front of the chalkboard looking at her student's shocked expressions with a self-satisfied grin. "The curriculum council thought that instead of making you carry around pretend babies you should experience the give and take of married life."

That elicited more groans.

"Here's how it works. First you'll be paired-up. Then each week you and your mate will get an event card to deal with. Some are good, some bad and some in-between. It may be a job re-location, or buying a house, the car breaking down, getting laid-off at work, a baby on the way...all sorts of things. And I expect you to address them maturely.

"You'll sit and discuss the problem with your partner and come up with a resolution. You'll write down your response and hand it in at the end of the week. Do you have questions?"

"Can we get a divorce?" a boy in the back hollered.

"Each deck of life events is different. So yes, divorce is one of the events you may encounter. But no, you cannot get a divorce just because you decide you don't like your partner."

A girl raised her hand. "How were the partners matched?"

"To make this a meaningful exercise I matched you randomly." Mrs. Warnoski smiled. "I sorted the class into two groups, boys and girls. Then I alphabetized the lists and paired them in reverse order, the first girl with the last boy and so on."

Everyone's head swiveled as the students tried to guess who their partner would be.

"As I call your names, one member of each team will come up and get your workbook. Your first event card is inside the front cover. Responses are due Friday. I'll pass out new cards each Monday." She cleared her throat. "Karen Adams and Thomas Young, Sally Breatherd and Zack Yancey, Mary Jane Combs and–"

The room erupted in a chorus of male catcalls, all asking to picked as Mary Jane's partner.

Head down, Mary Jane stared at her desktop.

"Picking up where we left off, Mary Jane Combs and Jeremy Tilden."

The fellow behind Jeremy leaned forward and whispered, "Hey Germy, I still have notes from Sex Ed if you need them."

Head down, Jeremy walked to the front of the room to get their workbook amid continued heckling.

The next day during study hall, they met in the school library to begin work. Mary Jane flipped through the workbook, looking more and more depressed as she turned the pages. She looked across the table and at an equally glum Jeremy.

"Why did I ever sign up for a course called Family Living Skills?"

"For the same reason I did. It seemed like an easy grade without much homework."

"Did you hear everyone yelling when she announced my

name? I kept wishing the floor would open up and swallow me. I swear, all boys are sex-starved morons."

Jeremy reached for the workbook. "That's not a fair statement."

"It seems accurate to me."

"You can't just write off half the human race." He opened the workbook and began scanning the instructions. "We're not all alike, you know."

Mary Jane shot him a surprised look.

"Well, I'm not a moron anyway."

She laughed. "I'm sorry, Jeremy. I meant them, not you. You're sweet as can be."

Jeremy beamed at her compliment.

"Look at all those exercises," Mary Jane said. "Don't I have enough on my plate already?"

"I don't know anything about this Family Living stuff," Jeremy said. "My parents never even told me the facts of life."

She patted his hand. "Don't worry. We'll find a quiet spot and I'll explain exactly how it works."

Jeremy's glare quieted her chuckles.

She fanned the workbook's pages and gave a low whistle. "I can't afford to fail this class."

"You're not the Lone Ranger, MJ. Somehow, someway I've got to squeeze out an A."

"Why must you get an A?"

"Anything less will torpedo my GPA." Jeremy tugged at his lip. "I've worked hard to get accepted into a Pre-Med Program and there are scholarships I'm hoping to get. I can't let four years of work go down the drain."

The low afternoon sun shone through the library windows highlighting every nick and scratch on the varnished oak tabletop between them. Mary Jane leaned back in her chair and studied him. Crossing her arms, she watched the sunlight filter through

Jeremy's hair and asked herself, *Jeremy, a doctor*?

She tried to imagine him in...oh say, ten or fifteen years. Mature, but still boyishly handsome, coming down a hospital corridor wearing a white coat. Tall, confident, clipboard in hand, moving briskly and nodding to the nurses he passed. It fit.

"So you want to be a doctor?"

Afraid of disapproval, or worse yet, ridicule, he seemed reluctant to take full ownership of his dream.

"Why?"

"Well, it's no secret people call me Germy. When I was nine or ten, I got an encyclopedia and studied germs. I came across researchers like Louis Pasteur and Jonas Salk. The more I found out, the more interested I became." He shrugged. "Maybe that's why it doesn't bother me anymore when people call me Germy."

Mary Jane leaned forward, resting her forearm on the table. "I'll make you a deal. You're doing the hard work in Chemistry; I'll pick up the slack in Family Living Skills. One way or another, my new husband will get the A he needs."

~ 18 ~

The screen door slammed behind Brent as he came into the house. He thumped his schoolbooks down and scanned the brochures his sister had spread across the coffee table.

"Whatcha doin'?"

"I'm getting ready for college. I stopped at the Counselor's Office today and got everything I need. Here's a University of Kentucky catalog." She waved it for him to see. "And application forms, transcript requests, the Federal Student Financial Aid forms, dorm information sheet, and an application for a campus job."

Brent gave them a cursory glance, and shrugged. "Is there anything to eat?"

"Have an apple. I'll start supper in a little while."

He tossed his jacket on the back of a chair and headed into the kitchen.

"Aren't you interested in any of this?"

"Why should I be?"

"It's exciting. Just think, we'll be the first generation in our family to get a college education. I'll blaze the trail. Brian's next, and then you."

Brent slouched against the kitchen doorway and took a bite of apple. "There's plenty of work right here in Bly. I can always get a job in one of the mines."

"If you ever set foot in a mine, you'd better plan on spending your day looking back over your shoulder, Mister. I'll be right behind you, ready to grab you by the ear and haul your sorry butt right out of there. Do you hear me?"

When he didn't answer she shouted, "I said, 'Do you hear me?'"

"I heard you already. Now leave me alone."

"Whether you know it or not, you are going to college." She smiled. "Now enjoy your apple."

She and Jeremy submitted their applications in mid-January. He wanted to get a semester at Bly onto his transcript before he sent it in. Mary Jane could have sent hers earlier, but thought mailing them together would bring good luck. After checking and double-checking her paperwork, she whispered a prayer and sealed the envelope.

She watched their envelopes disappear into the Out of Town slot at the Post Office with a nervous smile.

They stopped for coffee afterwards and Jeremy studied her face across the small table. He took her hand. "You'll be accepted. Don't worry"

But she did. Things got bleaker when Jeremy received his acceptance six weeks later and she heard nothing. He insisted her application needed time to work its way to the top of the stack. The power of Jeremy's reassurances waned with each passing day. The end of March drew near and still no word.

The UK basketball team played in the NCAA National Semifinals on the 31st and her father invited Jeremy to watch with them. The day before the game the mailman brought Mary Jane's acceptance. Without a word to anyone, she bought a squeeze tube of icing and drew a map of Kentucky on top of a cake. Alongside an arrow from Bly to Lexington she wrote, *MJ's headed to UK.*

At halftime her father walked into the kitchen and read the icing. "It's true, you've been accepted?"

She blinked and nodded.

He wrapped her in his arms, hugging her tightly. After kissing her forehead, he hollered, "Brian, bring the camera."

Attracted by the commotion, Brent wandered in. Seeing a cake, he reached for the knife. His father pulled him back. "Nobody touches the cake until we take pictures."

He kept his arm around Mary Jane's shoulder as Brian aimed and snapped. When the photos were over, John Combs cut a slice of cake and extended the plate to her. "The first piece goes to my daughter, the college student."

~ 19 ~

Mary Jane worked full time after graduation, earmarking most of each paycheck for her college savings account. In September they had a going away party for her in the break room at the Piggly Wiggly market. She grew misty-eyed thinking how much she'd miss her co-workers. She was especially grateful to Mr. Pence who'd hired her without any experience.

On her last morning at home she walked to the Locust Grove Cemetery.

"Hi Momma, it's me." She took her familiar seat on the marker's base. "I'm leaving for UK today and I wanted to tell you good-bye.

"I won't be around for a while, probably not until Thanksgiving break. We're going in Jeremy's car so I won't have a way back unless he's coming home. You'd like him; he's real polite. Shoot. Even Daddy likes him. We go out on dates now and I've kissed him a few times."

Mary Jane recalled early Saturday mornings and footsteps on the porch. One of her brothers matter-of-factly saying, "Germy," and her father's face brightening when he glanced up to see Jeremy crossing the room.

"Jeremy," he'd say, waving an arm. "Welcome. Come in and have some coffee."

Before she knew it, the four of them, Jeremy, Brian, Brent and her father, would be deep into discussions of valve lifters, camshafts and clutch bearings. Smiling, she'd slip away to work.

"You know how Daddy always said nobody's good enough for his little girl, right? I think he's decided Jeremy just about is. I still haven't declared a major. It'll be business, most likely marketing."

Mary Jane closed her eyes and imagined herself in a business suit walking along a busy downtown street. A rhythmic tapping intruded on her daydream. She blinked and looked around. Her eyes followed the sound to a woodpecker in one of the locust trees behind the cemetery. So much for her dreams about the world of big business.

She rose. “Bye, Momma. I’ll make you proud of me. I promise.” She tugged her sweater a little tighter, patted a kiss onto the top of the marker and left.

Jeremy passed her walking home from the cemetery, honked and stopped to pick her up.

Her father shook Jeremy’s hand and clapped him on the back as they prepared to leave. After asking how the car was running, he warned him to watch the traffic. Jeremy packed her bags in the car. Brian and Brent each gave her a quick hug and wished her well. Her father squeezed her tightly, whispered he loved her and admonished her to mind her morals.

“Will you and the boys be okay?”

“We’ll do fine. It’s time those two buzzards learned to fend for themselves. They’ve had it too easy with you around here.”

She stretched up to kiss him on the cheek. “I love you, Daddy.”

“I love you too, Sweetheart. You go do your thing and don’t worry about us. We’ll be here when you come back.”

She started to turn away, but he pulled her back. “There’ll be big changes around here by the time you get back.”

“What do you mean?”

“I mean Randall Estep’s about to get his comeuppance.”

“How do you know?”

“Cause I’m the one’s going to do it. I’ve decided to let certain people know what’s been going on down at Blossom Gulch No.3.” His expression hardened. “Things won’t change unless I do.”

“Won’t you get in trouble?”

“Make you a deal. I’ll worry about Estep; you worry about your schoolwork. Hear me?”

She grinned. "Yes. I hear you, Daddy."

Mary Jane waved back as they pulled away. Wanting a parting glimpse of the little white house where she'd spent her life, Mary Jane glanced into the side mirror. She watched her father step off the porch and walk into the road. He stood there with his hands on his hips, staring at their car as they drove away.

Estep Mining was loading a coal train when they went through town. Mary Jane raised her window, shutting out the locomotive's throb. They passed familiar stores and shops, and then they were on the highway weaving their way toward the interstate.

The closer they got to Lexington, the happier Mary Jane became. She cracked the window, leaned back and let the wind whip through her hair. She threw her head back and laughed for the sheer joy of it.

Going away to college had seemed an unattainable dream. Yet here she was on her way to UK as free as a bird on the wing. No more cleaning house, fixing lunches, cooking supper and doing dishes. No more Friday night checkout lines at Piggly Wiggly.

I've escaped, she thought. I'm free...I'm free.

Lexington was everything Bly was not. She'd grown up surrounded by forested hills and mountains. The lack of them lent the area a refreshing openness. People in Bly tended to clannishness and were suspicious of strangers. Folks at the college were welcoming and friendly. Lexington also had shopping malls and 24-hour restaurants.

She loved being on campus. It was a happening place pulsing with energy. People, some famous, others merely notorious, appeared for lectures, plays and concerts. For the first time since her mother died, Mary Jane placed herself first, vowing to live each day trying to be the person Momma wanted her to be.

She enjoyed being with Jeremy more and more. They had a satisfying, if low-key, relationship. They could take a walk, snuggle on a bench and kiss and hug without the expectation of more. It was a mutual thing with no pressure on either side. He wasn't ready for a serious relationship and neither was she.

The college assigned her a job in the cafeteria working the breakfast shift. Always an early-riser, the smell of sausage and bacon frying and bread toasting reminded her of mornings back home. Food Services remitted Mary Jane's pay to the business office to offset her housing cost. She paid her tuition with Federal loans and used her savings account for books and pocket money. She lived happily, but frugally, taking meals in the cafeteria and walking, rather than using the bus.

Life was good.

~ 20 ~

John Combs arrived at the Blossom Gulch Mine No. 3 in early morning shadows. Damp fog lingered in the air, blurring the outlines of conveyors rising high into the sky. Ignoring the familiar background clatter of belts and pulleys, he walked underneath machinery transferring fresh coal into the washing and sorting towers. Workers coming off the graveyard shift waved as he passed.

Combs walked into the metal building containing the mine offices. He turned down a hall and snatched a clipboard off a nail. As he walked toward the locker room he leafed through the smudged and crumpled yellow sheets jammed helter-skelter under the clip. Seeing nothing urgent among the repair requests, he sat the clipboard aside and donned his hard hat.

He stuck his head around the wall and nodded to the men sitting on a bench. "Earl. Tom. Charlie."

Discarded towels lay in a pile beside them. The damp locker room floors and walls emitted a subtle, but persistent mustiness. Returning his greeting, the men continued dressing.

"How was your shift? Is everything running smoothly, any shutdowns or equipment problems?"

Earl side-armed his hard hat onto the rack, stood up and stretched. "You worry too much, John. It'll give you ulcers." He slapped him on the back and left.

"I have to," he called after him. "Men's lives are on the line."

Charlie Johnson rose from the bench. Tall and lean, he dug a cigarette pack out of his jacket pocket. He removed one and tapped it against the pack as he spoke. "Let Estep do the worryin', Johnnie Boy." He struck a match on the wall and cupped a hand around the end of his cigarette as he lit it. He took a deep drag. "He owns this stinkin' hole in the ground, not you."

"What about you, Tom?"

He never glanced up from tying his boot. "I say this place was screwed-up the day they hired me, and it'll be just as screwed up the day I leave."

John Combs crossed the yard to the mineshaft. Ahead in the metal shed surrounding the entrance to Blossom Gulch No. 3 he noticed the unexpected flash of headlights.

Something didn't feel right.

They were gone by the time he reached the shed. Mantrips, the electric vehicles used to move about the mine, were parked against one wall. He walked along, resting his hand on the housing of each motor. He eventually found a warm one and checked its number. It was a foreman's car.

Folding his tall frame into the low-slung seat of his mantrip, John Combs headed down into the mine. Squat, no-frills vehicles designed for low clearance, the mantrips had an overall height of less than 30 inches. Ordinarily, they ferried four men in and out of the mine. But, since he did maintenance and repair work, his had been modified to accommodate the toolboxes, equipment and spare parts he needed to keep things running.

The mantrip's motor sounded like the buzz of a far-off bee, growing steadily louder as the car descended. Two, four, six...eight hundred feet, down and down he went. At somewhere over a thousand feet, the grade leveled out. The hum of Combs' mantrip reverberated along the narrow passageways and into adjoining rooms carved out of the coal.

The first residents of what became Blackstone County scratched their coal out of exposed seams. These primitive mines were nothing more than crude caves sunk into the face of a hillside. As the nation's appetite for coal grew, they began going deeper and deeper into the earth. For years they used a method of mining called *room and pillar*.

They removed the coal either by blasting, or in later years, with continuous cutters. As they progressed along the seam removing the coal, the miners left large empty areas behind — the rooms. A grid of timber-reinforced coal pillars interspersed throughout the rooms supported the ceiling.

This method left significant amounts of coal untouched

and, to boost yields, mine owners sometimes ordered the men to rob the pillars. That is, after depleting the seam, they removed the coal pillars as they retreated, betting that timber alone could keep the ceiling from crashing down on them.

Longwall mining eventually replaced rooms and pillars. First, they exposed the face of the seam using the traditional method. Then a cutter moved back and forth along this face removing coal. Portable hydraulic roof supports, called shields, supported the ceiling while the men worked. When the cutter reached the limit of its extension, everything moved forward. Without shields for support, the roof behind the active area gradually collapsed, filling the mined-out area.

Combs turned into the active area and coasted to a stop. Hopping out, he glanced around. Blossom Gulch No. 3 operated around the clock. He had fifteen minutes before the start of the next shift to conduct his inspection. He moved quickly, following a routine honed by daily repetition. He checked the air quality sensors first. Methane levels safe. Allowable limits of carbon monoxide and carbon dioxide.

He hummed to himself as he worked. The night before he'd received a call at home from an official at the Mine Safety office. Change was coming.

After checking the drive track and cutter head, he walked the length of the 900-foot seam face. His gloved hand regularly tested the conveyor belt as he passed. He shone his light onto the ceiling each time he stopped, inspecting the roof bolts securing the rock above him.

Satisfied, he headed back the way he'd come by crossing over to the shields that ran the length of the dig. Pairs of heavy-duty hydraulic cylinders on each shield forced a thick metal pan against the mine's roof. He checked them carefully. These shields prevented the roof from collapsing on the men as they worked.

At the next to last set he noticed a dark puddle of hydraulic fluid soaking into the dirt. Running his light around, he found identical breaks in several pairs of adjoining lines.

His foot struck something hard. He looked down at a pile of

roof bolts. Aiming his light at the roof he saw empty bolt holes and an ominous bulge in the overlying rock. Without hydraulic support, the shields were buckling under the strain.

He'd have to shut the mine down to stabilize the roof and repair those shields. Combs checked his watch. In a few minutes the entire crew would be clocked-in and on their way down. Estep hated having men standing around when they were on the clock.

He ran to his mantrip and returned with an impact wrench. Picking up one of the roof bolts, he began driving it back in. Bits of gravel-sized rock rained down on him as he worked.

All at once, the earth above him groaned. The sound made the hair on the back of his neck prickle. The ceiling seemed to liquefy. Everything above him was in motion. For a split-second he stood frozen, mesmerized.

An inner voice screamed, "Get out!"

He turned to run.

A fissure opened. Rocks began to fall.

The last thing John Combs heard was the piercing shriek of tearing metal as the shields ripped apart and the roof crashed down upon him.

~ 21 ~

Mary Jane's life at UK fell into a comfortable routine. Rise early, tiptoe around the room so as not to wake her roommate, grab a quick shower, dress, do her hair and makeup, hurry across campus in the pre-dawn darkness and clock-in for work at the dining hall.

As she walked to work, her thoughts returned to the previous evening. She and Jeremy had attended a pep rally. She wore her UK sweatshirt and a stand sold hot spiced cider. They watched a flurry of sparks from a bonfire rush into the night sky and cheerleaders, silhouetted by the flames, formed pyramids on each other's shoulders.

Despite the cold, she would always remember the fire being hot on her face. She tugged Jeremy's arm around her and snuggled into the reassurance of his embrace. Leaning her head back to kiss him, she detected traces of Old Spice on his cheek

At that moment, life seemed as perfect as perfect could be. She would seal that stolen kiss in her memory for the rest of her life, along with every detail of the following day.

Mary Jane yawned from lack of sleep as she worked her station. A couple of hours into her shift, Jeremy wandered in for breakfast looking as tired as she felt. She checked the clock and smiled; he was as predictable as the sunrise. She liked that about him.

He ordered the usual, a cinnamon roll and two strips of bacon. She studied the pan of rolls, found the biggest one and cut it out for him. After choosing the longest pieces of bacon, she poured his coffee and rang up the sale.

The morning continued to drag. Mary Jane was wiping down tables when she glanced up and saw Ernie Mellman coming in.

A member of the Campus Security Force, Ernie was middle-aged and gregarious with a ready smile. On one of her first days, Ernie asked her about home. When she confessed to being a Blackstone County escapee, he gave a knowing chuckle and said they still had a missing person file on him in Pike County.

Knowing they'd grown up less than a hundred miles apart gave them the basis for friendship. Ernie took his break about the same time each day and they often talked about the way things were back home.

But it was too early for his break.

She looked up and read the somber expression on his face. A quiver of fear swirled in her stomach. Something's happened, she thought, something bad.

A second earlier she had nothing on her mind. Now a million possibilities crowded her thoughts as her dreams collapsed into a heap of what might have been.

Jeremy saw her face and moved beside her before Ernie said a word. He slipped his arm around her, though she hardly noticed.

"I have some bad news, MJ. Why don't we sit down over here?" Ernie directed her to a table. "I'm sorry to be the one to tell you, but we received a call from Bly a few minutes ago. There's been an accident back home."

"Was it Brian or Brent?" she asked, her voice shaky.

Jeremy's hand tightened on her shoulder.

Ernie shook his head. "Neither. It's your father. The accident occurred at the Blossom Gulch mine."

"How many men were hurt?"

His expression turned grim. "Only your father."

"What happened?"

"We don't have any information about the accident. Mercy Hospital in Bly called us."

Mary Jane felt as though she might collapse. She leaned against Jeremy for support.

She started making plans. “The boys will need me.” She looked up at Jeremy. “I’ve got to get home. Can you drive me back?”

He nodded. Pulling out his handkerchief, he dabbed away the tears rolling down her cheeks. “We’ll leave right away.”

Ernie cleared his throat. “That won’t be necessary.”

She buried her face in her hands. “Oh, God, he’s already gone. Daddy’s dead.”

“No he’s not. Your father was alive when they called. He’s seriously injured, but alive and on his way to Chandler Medical Center here at the University.”

Jeremy took charge. “Splash some cold water on your face. We’ll ditch these books and walk over to the hospital. I’ll wait there with you.”

Her father went directly into surgery. Given his head injuries, they told her there were few, if any, guarantees. She and Jeremy moved to the surgical waiting room. Weezie, Cash and her brothers arrived about one o’clock. The surgeons were still working. With family there, Jeremy slipped away.

The surgeon came to see them late that night. Her father was in recovery. From there he’d go to intensive care. They’d done the best they could.

The metal shield cut deep into her father’s skull, damaging critical brain function. Emphasizing again the uncertainty of his situation, the surgeon told them he expected him to survive. What his condition would be, no one could predict.

The following days became a blur. An endless parade of surgeons, neurologists and other specialists, nurses, therapists, residents and interns passed in and out of Mary Jane’s life. She slept in waiting room chairs, or beside her father’s bed holding his hand. Night blended into day. Days came and went. She prayed by herself and with the family when Weezie formed them into a circle around his bed.

Finally she faced the decision she’d known was coming ever since Ernie Mellman walked into the cafeteria. She went to the

Registrar's office and withdrew from the University.

Someone had to pay the bills and keep house for Brent and Brian. Someone would have to care for her father when he came home. By default, the task fell to her. Steeling herself, she called her former boss, Mr. Pence, and asked for her old job back.

Mary Jane slumped in the backseat of the car wrapped in a blanket. Even though Cash had the heater on full blast, she couldn't stop shaking. She stared out the window, watching trees whiz by.

As happy as she'd been going, she was equally unhappy returning. She'd tried to escape and failed. The evil arm of fate found her even in Lexington. And now circumstances were dragging her back to where she didn't want to be.

Her father remained behind at a rehabilitation facility. He continued making slow, but steady, progress and his doctors predicted he would come home in a few weeks.

Mary Jane looked around as they entered Bly. It surprised her how shabby the little town had become in the short time she'd been away. She noted each scrap of litter, every dusty store window and each curl of peeling paint. She frowned at the black, sooty streaks on the tin roofs beside each chimney. She watched old men shuffling along in threadbare overalls and shuddered. She noticed a switch engine assembling a unit train of coal and decided then and there that she hated every particle of coal in every hopper car on every railroad track in the world.

She cried herself to sleep for weeks; cried until she ran out of tears. Her college career ended almost before it began. Her life, her dreams and her ambitions were all swept away like dry leaves before a winter wind.

~ 22 ~

"Whew! It's chilly today."

Mary Jane dug a pair of woolen gloves out of her jacket and slipped them on. She shifted on the cold granite base of her mother's tombstone. Folding her collar up against the wind, she chose her words carefully.

"Good thing I brought gloves; it's getting cold." Snow blanketed the winter-browned grass around her.

She looked up at the dark clouds dumping snow on the Cumberland Mountains. "No sense in beating around the bush, I need to talk to you about Daddy. I've waited until I got everything sorted out before I came over. It is now and, well, I've brought good news and I've brought bad news."

Stray snowflakes landed in Mary Jane's blond hair, glistened like diamonds for an instant, then melted. She took a deep breath and began.

"The good news is that the hospital called to say Daddy can come home. It'll be a few more days, but he'll be back for Christmas. The boys and I are going to buy a tree and decorate it with lights and tinsel just like the old days. Brent climbed up into the attic and pulled down the box with all our ornaments. We'll run garlands around the doorways and put a wreath above the fireplace. His nurses say it might help him remember things."

She tugged her sleeve down over her hand and brushed away the accumulated snow on top of the marker. "Oh, I've got some more good news. Mr. Pence down at the Piggly Wiggly says I can stay on full-time for as long as I want. I've penciled out our finances. Daddy's disability payments will cover his care, and I'll be able to keep the household running with my paychecks."

She paused and ran her finger around the granite's deeply-etched letters, cleaning out the snow. Tiring of that, she brushed back her bangs and exhaled. Her breath turned to smoke in the frigid air.

"Okay, now for the bad stuff. The doctor said Daddy's

probably never going to get much better than he is right now. It's as if he's had a stroke, or...or something. One side of him doesn't work very well. They're pretty sure he can see out of both eyes. At least his pupils contract if the doctor shines a light in them. Sometimes he follows people around with his eyes. Other times he doesn't seem to notice anything that's going on."

The air around her danced with tiny flakes, the kind that brought heavy accumulations and deep drifts. The snow turned the locust trees bordering the cemetery into shadowy sentinels.

She paused to brush snow off her cheeks before continuing. "Daddy doesn't talk any more. Mostly, he sits and occasionally babbles. I don't know if he recognizes me or not."

Verbalizing her father's condition made it all the more real. Her shoulders visibly sank under the weight of what she knew lay ahead.

The dam holding back her frustrations broke apart. Overcome with rage, Mary Jane pounded her fists on the top of the monument. The more she flailed the unresponsive granite, the harder she sobbed. The tears and cold air caused her nose to run. Her lips trembled when she tried to speak.

"Aw hell, Momma! Why don't you march right up to God and ask him why he can't find somebody else to beat-up on. I've always tried to do what's right. This isn't fair! Why'd he have to go picking on Daddy? Did he run out of bad people to curse? The poor man can't walk. He can't talk. He can't dress or feed himself. He can't even stand up like a man to pee. He's a child, Momma, a 55-year-old infant."

Her hands stung and ached, but she continued smacking the stone. Her words poured out in anguished sobs. Fueled by her frustration, Mary Jane's voice grew louder and louder, reverberating across the deserted cemetery.

"I can't handle this. Do you hear? I can't handle this. I dreamed of going to college. What kind of future do I have now? What am...I...going...to do?"

As fast as it came, her anger drained away. Exhausted, she

folded her arms on the top of the granite monument, laid her head down and wept. Her shoulders quivered as tears soaked her coat sleeves. She was covered with snow when she lifted her head. Shaking it off, she dug tissues out of her pockets and wiped her face, drying her cheeks before they chapped.

"It's time for me to go. I've said all I can say. I need to get out of here."

She started to rise, but stopped halfway up. A look of fright and pain distorted her normally beautiful features. "Oh, Lord. I'm sorry, Momma. I don't know what I was thinking. None of this is your fault."

She remained locked in a half crouch, one hand resting on the stone for support, her body twisted in anticipation of turning away to leave, her face reflecting her inner anguish. "I never meant for this to happen. I didn't mean to say those awful things. I'm sorry."

Tiny snowflakes spun and swirled around her. Mary Jane heaved herself the rest of the way up, turned and ran. She staggered along the snow-covered gravel path never stopping for a backward glance. As she stumbled down the hill, over and over she repeated, "I'm sorry...I'm sorry."

When she reached the parking area, she jogged to her car and brushed the windshield clean with a gloved hand. Reaching to open the car door, she paused to catch her breath. As she stood there alone in the cold, with snow falling all around and wind whipping at her hair, a great stillness descended upon her and a unexpected warmth wrapped itself around her.

Her mother took her to a Christmas Eve candlelight service when Mary Jane was five. She'd sat speechless, awed by the splendor of the twinkling lights and dancing shadows, basking in the grandeur of something larger than herself.

She had that same feeling. Bowing her head, she accepted the message of peace and forgiveness carried on each snowflake. When she looked up again, for the first time since leaving UK, she was no longer afraid.

~ 23 ~

It was the Christmas season and they decorated the house as she'd told her mother they would. Friends and neighbors began dropping by once John Combs came home. The piney smell of the tree and garlands helped mask the sickroom smell that lingered no matter how hard Mary Jane scrubbed.

She came to anticipate their shocked looks when they saw what he'd become. Some averted their eyes and talked about the weather. Others headed for the door suddenly remembering forgotten appointments.

As the details of his condition spread, the visits slowed and finally stopped.

"Thanks for coming over, Steph. I'm really starved for company." Mary Jane held the storm door open. She watched Stephanie's nose wrinkle as she entered the house.

"I know how hurtful this sounds," Stephanie said, "but every time I come over I leave begging God never to let me end up like your Dad."

"It's not hurtful; it's the truth. You think the same thought doesn't go through my mind? We all get on the same train never knowing what station it's going to stop at."

She rubbed her hands together, smiled. "So, how are you doing? How's Del? How's married life?"

Stephanie's face glowed. "I'm doin' great. Beauty school's great, Del's great, everything's great." She looked at Mary Jane. "And you...you're not so great. Are you feeling well?"

"I'm tired, that's all. I'm always burning the candle at both ends."

Stephanie glanced across the room at Mary Jane's father. "I'd better go say hello."

His hair had grown back and covered the place where surgeons repaired his skull. He still had several irregular patches of puckered scar tissue on the back of his head where skin grafts covered spots the shields gouged and ripped.

John Combs sat rigid as a statue, staring straight ahead. A green tank mounted behind his wheelchair fed oxygen into a plastic hose snaking up to clip in his nose. He seemed oblivious to the game show playing on the television set. Combs' right hand, the good one, tapped his leg incessantly to the beat of a song only he heard.

Stephanie stepped into his line of sight and dropped to one knee. "Hello, Mr. Combs, how are you feeling today?" she asked in a loud voice. She took his hand. "I'm MJ's friend, Stephanie. Remember me?"

He didn't acknowledge her.

She pulled a tissue from the dispenser on his wheelchair and blotted away saliva oozing out the side of his mouth. Stephanie tried several more times to elicit a response, never succeeding.

"I'm going to visit with Mary Jane now." She patted his hand as she rose. "You take care."

In the kitchen, Mary Jane rested her forehead in her hands while Stephanie made tea.

"It seems so unfair." Stephanie leaned around the corner and glanced into the living room. "What purpose does this serve? Why's he here?"

"He's here to be loved."

"Is it always this bad?"

"He has his good days and his bad days." Mary Jane frowned. "Truth is, even his best days are barely mediocre."

"Where are the boys?"

"It's hard for them to see him like this. They usually find something to do that takes them out of the house after supper. They're not around much until Daddy's gone to bed."

"So you're doing everything by yourself? What about baths and dressing and, well, you know?"

“He has a catheter. I have to empty the bag and keep everything clean.”

“You mean you have to...”

Mary Jane looked away and nodded. Color crept up her neck and spread across her face. “I concentrate on the task at hand and tell him about my day at work.”

“What happens when you’re not here?”

“We have a home health nurse who comes every morning. I wake Daddy up and feed him breakfast. After I leave for work, she bathes and dresses him and takes care of the toilet stuff. The nurse stays until an aide arrives. When I get home, the aide leaves.”

Mary Jane rubbed her eyes and yawned. Reliving her day tired her out almost as much as living it.

Stephanie reached and patted her hand. “You didn’t deserve this.”

“Who does?”

“You're a good daughter.”

Mary Jane’s lower lip quivered. She bit it, trying to hold back her tears. “I know I have no right to complain. He’s the one suffering, not me. But I don't want to be a good daughter anymore.”

Stephanie rubbed Mary Jane’s neck as she sobbed.

“I’ve taken care of the house ever since Momma died. I washed and cleaned and cooked. I planted a garden and put up fruits and vegetables. I had six weeks of freedom at UK and now this. When, for God’s sake, is it going to be my turn?”

In the living room, her father began making noises.

She wiped her face with the sleeve of her blouse and hollered, “Coming, Daddy.”

Mary Jane disappeared for a minute and returned muttering. Throwing open a cupboard door, she rummaged among the pill bottles lining the bottom shelf. When she found the one she wanted, she snatched it up and jerked the cap off, sending it rolling across the counter.

"I have to give him a pain pill. The fluid in his catheter is tinged pink. He's getting another bladder infection, which means another round of antibiotics. I just got the last one cleared up."

She threw the medicine bottle back in the cupboard and slammed the door. "Be right back.

She returned moments later. "We'll give the pill time to take hold then he'll be ready for bed."

Stephanie refilled their cups while she was gone. Mary Jane drank in silence. After a minute, she put the cup down and gave Stephanie a wry look. "After that little outburst, you have to be wondering just how good of a daughter I really am, huh?"

Her father went to bed with no trouble. Mary Jane turned off the television and returned to the kitchen. The only sound in the house was the steady ticking of the kitchen clock. She studied the clock face imbedded in Felix's abdomen.

"We've got about a half-an-hour before the boys come back." She turned to face Stephanie straight on. "There's something I want to talk to you about."

Mary Jane's voice grew whisper soft. "I'm going to tell you something and if you ever breathe a word of it to another living soul, I'll swear I never said it. Then I'll come back late at night and kill you in your sleep. Understand?"

"Yeah, cross my heart and all that stuff. What is it?"

"It's Daddy."

"I know he has to weigh on your mind."

"It's not that. It's..." Mary Jane gritted her teeth and looked around the kitchen.

"You can tell me anything, what is it?'

"Most of the time he's in a world of his own. That's most of the time, but every once in a while he sort of comes out of it. Don't get me wrong. It's not like he hops out of his wheelchair and skips across the room snapping his fingers and whistling *Blue Suede Shoes*, or anything. But he almost seems to know where he is. He speaks well enough that I can understand him."

"Wow! That's great. Maybe he's getting better and–." Stephanie's words trailed away when she saw the look on Mary Jane's face. "Or...maybe it isn't so great after all."

"He watches me as I walk past and calls me by my Mother's name."

"Oh, Lordy."

"You can say that again. He reaches for me and gets mad when I won't sit in his lap."

Stephanie reached over and patted Mary Jane's knee. "I know this has to hurt, but sometimes people like your Dad get confused."

"There's more. A couple of weeks ago, when I put him to bed he tried to pull me in. I know he seems weak. Since the accident, he's gotten so thin he looks like he'll blow away in the next windstorm. Don't let that fool you. In spite of his injuries, he's still surprisingly strong."

Mary Jane glanced up at the clock and listened for footsteps. Not hearing any, she took a deep breath and continued. "Daddy says things, things a man might say to his wife. It's getting so I'm afraid to be alone with him."

"You've got to tell someone about this."

Mary Jane pounded her fists on the table. "I am, you idiot. I'm telling you!"

"No. I mean someone who can do something, his doctor or the day nurse."

"I can't. Daddy's out of his head. If I say anything they might come and take him away. What if they locked him up, charged him with a crime? He had a reputation in this community. I can't ruin his good name."

"You mean he..."

"No, no, no. He's never done anything like what you're

thinking. I'll swear to it on a stack of Bibles ten feet tall. He's groped me a few times, that's all."

Jaw clenched and brows lowered, she stared at Stephanie waiting for her acknowledgement.

Stephanie nodded.

"Groped. Understand? It's nothing worse than what I put up with from Estil."

"Do your brothers know about this?"

"Of course not. I'd die if they found out. Imagine how it would look if he somehow managed to pull me into bed and they walked in?"

"What are you going to do?"

"Same as I have been, I suppose. I'll keep pushing his hand away and saying, 'Not tonight, Sweetie' or 'We'll have fun later.'"

"Well, at least you're getting good practice for married life."

"Boy, aren't I lucky to have someone who's so sympathetic."

Both of their heads spun around when they heard a key in the living room lock. Putting her finger to her lips, Mary Jane caught Stephanie's eyes and shook her head as Brian and Brent entered the house.

~ 24 ~

Mary Jane slogged through each day in a fog of exhaustion. She attributed the fatigue to her heavy workload, but as much as anything it resulted from pent-up frustration. It'd been a year since her father's accident and no one had come forward with details. The corrosiveness of the anger she kept bottled up ate away at her.

She decided early on that her father's accident wasn't an accident. Somehow, Randall Estep had a hand in it. But he hadn't acted alone. She knew Estep wouldn't go crawling around in the coal. Someone else did his dirty work. Who?

Mary Jane felt surrounded by a conspiracy of silence. Bly was a small town, a closed circle where everyone knew everyone else's business. Yet there'd been not a word. Almost as if the accident never happened. Someone had to know. They had to.

Some days it took all the willpower she had not to blurt out to one of her customers, "Don't you care? What if it'd been your husband?"

Oh, she still smiled and chatted with the ladies as she checked their groceries. She inquired about their husbands and children and mentioned the coupon sale on *Hungry Man* TV dinners while inside her spirit withered.

Someone somewhere knew the truth. Mary Jane studied the customer's faces as they shopped, wondering. She began to distrust everyone, even strangers on the street. What was left, suspecting the people at church?

One night, after settling their father into bed, Mary Jane gathered her brothers around the kitchen table. She'd poured glasses of milk and put a platter of cookies on the table.

She glanced from one boy to the other. "We have to deal with the fact Daddy will probably be like he is now for the rest of his life."

Both of the boys shifted in their chairs.

"Did the doctors tell you something?" Brian asked. As the oldest functioning male in the household, he felt it his responsibility to take the lead.

"They don't have to. You can find out all you need to know by spending a few hours with him."

"Is he going to die?" Brent asked.

"Someday, none of us gets out of here alive. His doctors have said more than once there's always the risk of a cerebral hemorrhage or a stroke. If it happens, well, it happens. We needn't worry about it this evening."

Marmalade wove between their legs rubbing and purring. When no one reached down to pet him, he retreated to a corner and groomed himself.

Her answer didn't satisfy Brent. "What's going to happen to us, MJ?"

"That's what I want to talk about. It's just the three of us now. Since I'm the only one who's over 18, I'm the only one who can legally act on Daddy's behalf, or ours. I think whatever decisions are made, we should make together."

Her brothers nodded in agreement.

"We need to know we can count on each other no matter what. I think we should put our hands together and promise we'll always stick together."

Taking the initiative, Brian stretched out his arm. Brent quickly dropped his hand over his brother's. Mary Jane wrapped her hands around theirs and closed her eyes. The only sound in the quiet kitchen was the clock's steady ticking. Felix's big eyes snapped back and forth, taking in all they said and did.

"We pledge ourselves to each other forever," Mary Jane said. "Though miles and years may come between us, we promise to remain true to each other and ready to help whenever and however we can."

"So help me God," Brian added. Brent and Mary Jane

repeated their bother's oath.

They released each other's hands and opened their eyes, blinking in the light. The power of their pact hung in the air and none of them wanted to break the spell by being the first to speak.

Mary Jane looked at her brothers and smiled. They were good boys. Barely three years had passed since their mother's death and they'd changed so much, especially after their father's accident.

Brian worked after school at the Burger Barn. Each payday he kept a few dollars back and gave the rest to Mary Jane. She could see him trying on the role of man of the house to see how it fit.

Brent, too, had matured. He did things around the house without being asked, helping wherever he could. He still looked to Brian for direction, but became more independent each day.

Mary Jane's eyes misted up. She swallowed the lump in her throat and whispered, "I love you guys."

Both boys looked at the floor and mumbled I love you.

~ 25 ~

Several months later Mary Jane rose early, showered, dressed in her work uniform and went downstairs. The living room lay in familiar early morning shadows. She opened the curtains and peeked in at her father. He lay on his side with his back to her.

She tiptoed in, unhooked his drainage bag and dumped the stale urine. After attaching a new bag, she said, "Morning, Daddy." She lifted the blind. "It's chilly outside; the grass is white with frost." She tugged the blanket over his shoulder. "I'll turn the heat up so the room can warm while I fix breakfast."

She spun the dial on the *Warm Morning* heater in the living room. Her parent's bedroom and the kitchen relied upon it for warmth. A second later she heard a reassuring thump as the pilot light ignited the burner.

Mary Jane smiled when she heard one of her brothers snoring as she passed their door. She snapped on the kitchen light, poured dry cat food into Marmalade's dish and filled the coffee maker.

The sun crept over the eastern horizon and poured through the windows, projecting shadows of oak leaves on the wall. Mary Jane removed a cup and bowl from the cupboard, sat them on her father's tray and added a spoon. Since his accident, his breakfasts of meat, eggs, pan bread and coffee had dwindled to hot cereal, buttered toast and Ovaltine.

She put two slices of wheat bread in the toaster and pushed it down. Opening a bin in the Hoosier cabinet, she scooped out some oatmeal. She waited until bubbles danced around the bottom of the pan, tossed in a pinch of salt and dumped the oats, stirring them for a few seconds until they dispersed.

Mary Jane had the refrigerator door half-open when she jerked to a stop. Felix the Cat's unmoving eyes peered down at her. His pendulum tail hung limp. Sometime during the night, he'd run down.

"Rise 'n' shine, Daddy. Breakfast is here."

She relied on the nightlight to see her way. Her father preferred not having the overhead on right away. When he didn't respond, Mary Jane sat his tray on the nightstand.

"Daddy, it's time to get up. You have to eat."

Getting no response, she stepped closer. "I'm going to be late for work."

He still didn't respond.

Her chest tightened as she stared down at her father in the dark room.

"Daddy?"

Mary Jane put a hand on his shoulder to shake him then jerked it back. He was dead.

Returning his breakfast to the kitchen, she went back to his room and fell into a flurry of activity. She aligned his slippers with the edge of the bed and took the crumpled *TV Guide* out of the pocket of his wheelchair. She smoothed his blanket, re-tucked the corners, and folded his coverlet across the foot of the bed. Then she tidied his nightstand and put the sickroom supplies on a closet shelf. Scooping up yesterday's pajamas, she crammed them into his hamper.

Mary Jane looked at him lying in the bed. She brushed a lock of hair off his forehead, smoothing it back with her hand.

Her mind raced. Who to call? It was clearly too late for paramedics. The police...his doctor? Remembering the home health nurse, she breathed a sigh of relief. She'd know what to do.

What about his funeral and the church? She needed to call the man at Locust Grove Cemetery, and Reverend Martin, and the monument company, and Aunt Weezie. She had to let Mr. Pence know she wouldn't be in for work. Brian and Brent were still asleep; she had to tell them.

The next few days passed in fog of guilt and thoughts of what might have been. She handled the funeral preparations mechanically. The day itself passed in a blur of activity. The table filled with casseroles and the house with people as it had four years earlier following her mother's death.

And then it was over.

That evening in her room Mary Jane knelt in the dark and prayed for the strength to do what it took to hold the family together.

"What now?" Stephanie asked.

They were alone in the house with their feet on the coffee table, drinking bottles of Coke from the refrigerator. Mary Jane tilted a can of salted peanuts to Stephanie. She scooped out a handful, ate some and fed the remainder into her bottle.

"Who knows?" Mary Jane replied, with a shrug. She studied the sweat forming on the outside of the hourglass-shaped bottle and rocked it in her hand, watching peanuts swirl.

"Well, you must have some plans."

"Try to go back to college, I suppose."

"Back to UK?"

"It's too late for that. I couldn't afford it anyway." Mary Jane's expression turned somber. "I wouldn't know anyone. Jeremy left the term after I did."

"I'd forgotten about him transferring to Johns Hopkins. Ever hear from him?"

Mary Jane shook her head. "He dropped by before he left for Baltimore. The house stank to high heaven and I looked a fright. Probably just as well. He doesn't need me dragging him down. If I go back at all, it'll have to be night classes at the community college. Brian and Brent are both still in high school. No matter what, I have to keep working at The Pig."

"So you go to community college, then what?"

"You know, Steph, I woke up this morning remembering the time Daddy took us to the State Fair. They had this bumper car ride."

Mary Jane gripped an imaginary steering wheel. "I decided

to drive from one end of the enclosure to the other." Her hand sliced through the air, pointing at the far wall. "I planned to go straight across, which is impossible. Every whipstitch someone ran into me, spinning me around and knocking me off course. I'd get back on track and somebody else would plow into me."

Mary Jane thumped her empty bottle down on the table. "That is exactly the way life's been ever since Momma got sick. I've gotten knocked off course so many times I'm not sure I know where I'm headed anymore."

"Jeez, I didn't mean to get you all down in the dumps."

Mary Jane lifted her arms, stretched and yawned. She spun on the couch to face Stephanie, folding her right leg onto the cushion and hooking her left one over it.

"Don't worry about it. It's probably too soon to be talking about this stuff, but I've given it a little thought. Brian graduates in a few months and Brent will be a junior in the fall. I've got my job at Piggly Wiggly as long as I want it and a place to live." She glanced around the room.

"I'm just going to tread water until..." her sentence faded into a shrug.

~ 26 ~

Mary Jane continued working at the Piggly Wiggly grocery and enrolled in evening classes at the local community college just as she'd said. Brian graduated from high school that spring and worked full-time during the summer. He continued giving her the bulk of his earnings. Rather than add it to the household account, she put the money away for his college expenses.

In the fall before Brian left for the University of Kentucky, Mary Jane divided the family savings giving him a third. Brent entered his junior year of high school and she started another term of night classes. The expense of books and tuition overwhelmed her.

Mary Jane sank onto the sofa beside Stephanie. "It's hopeless. Whatever made me think I could afford college?"

Stephanie lowered her newspaper. "Things look bleak right now, but they can change."

"I wish I had your optimism." Mary Jane nudged out a wrinkle in the throw rug with her toe and picked a tuft of cat hair off the sofa arm. "Face it, Steph, I always end up with too much month at the end of my money. I can't keep this house up and still have enough for tuition. And these night classes are killing me. By the end of the day, I'm as exhausted as my checking account. Unless my fairy godmother knocks on the door with a sack of gold, I'm finished."

Stephanie turned the page of her newspaper, read for a minute then grinned. "Knock, knock."

"I'm not in the mood for jokes."

Stephanie persisted.

"Okay. I'll bite. Who's there?"

"Your fairy godmother."

"My fairy godmother who?"

"Your fairy godmother, Stephanie, and she's found the solution to your problem."

Spinning the paper around for Mary Jane to see, Stephanie pointed to an advertisement for the Miss Cumberland Valley competition, a preliminary step to the Miss Kentucky Pageant.

"A beauty pageant? Things may be bleak, but I'm not desperate enough to parade around in my skivvies."

"It's a scholarship competition, see?"

Mary Jane smirked. "And strippers are *exotic dancers*. It's a peep show." She flipped her hair aside. "Besides, don't you have to be Apple Butter Queen, or Miss Dill Pickle, or something to get in?"

"Nope. Says right here, *Open to all.*"

"Forget it." Mary Jane lifted her chin. "I have my dignity."

"You have too much dignity for your own good," Stephanie yelled and rattled the paper in her face.

"I'm not going to prance around without any clothes on."

Stephanie dropped the newspaper into her lap and leaned her arm across the back of the sofa. "Ever gone swimming?"

"Sure."

"Did you have any clothes on?"

"A bathing suit."

Stephanie gave her a smug smile. "I rest my case, your honor."

"Case? You've got no case. Everyone else wore a bathing suit. It's not the same." Mary Jane shook her head. "Not the same at all."

"O-o-o-okay. What's your alternative?"

"I don't have one."

"Look-it. Here's the deal. The swimsuit competition takes barely a minute, one lousy, stinking minute. You walk out there, let them admire your ass-ets and walk off. You act like no one's ever given you the once over."

"Of course they have, but I never put myself on display and invited them to do it."

Stephanie pounded her fist on the arm of the sofa. "You're beautiful. You can win this thing." She pointed to the ad. "They're offering thousands of dollars in scholarships. How many cans of string beans do you have to run over the scanner to make that kinda dough?"

Mary Jane was in a panic the night of the competition.

She and Weezie had searched the pattern catalogs at the fabric store and made a dress for the evening gown competition. Stephanie, who'd completed Beauty College, did her hair and makeup.

They finished the interviews and were halfway through the evening gown competition. Mary Jane came off the stage and walked toward Stephanie, biting her lip. The swimsuit competition came next.

"I can't do this, Steph. I'm telling you, I can't do this."

"You can and you will."

"No, I can't do this."

Stephanie jammed a swimsuit into her hand and pointed to their left. "You will get behind that curtain and put this thing on now."

Mary Jane took the suit and moped away.

"Wait," Stephanie hollered. She ran over and handed her two pieces of what looked like moleskin cut into the shape of flowers. "I almost forgot these."

"Corn plasters?"

"They're nipple covers. It's chilly out there on stage. Stick 'em on and be quick. I still have to fix your suit."

After some last minute fussing with her hair, Stephanie had Mary Jane bend forward and rest her elbows on a nearby table. When she did, Stephanie slipped her hand under the bottom edge of her suit and jerked it up, exposing a round cheek.

Mary Jane shrieked. "What are you doing back there?"

"Making sure your suit doesn't ride up. Hold still. This'll only take a minute." Stephanie rested an arm on Mary Jane's back and exposed the other buttock. Whipping out an aerosol can, she sprayed something cold and sticky on both sides.

"That feels awful. What is it?"

"Butt glue."

"What if I didn't want my butt glued?"

"Quit your bellyachin'."

Mary Jane fumed while Stephanie rolled the suit down, carefully smoothing it into place. "There." She gave her a reassuring pat on the bottom. "Now everything will stay covered-up."

Mary Jane rose and wiggled her rear end around, scowling at the feel of the adhesive. "Was that necessary?" She reached around and ran her fingers along the bottom edge. "What if I can't get it off?"

"It'll come off." Stephanie waved the can at her. "It's *Cramer's Firm Grip*. They use it to stick Ace Bandages on the football players at the high school. I borrowed it from one of the trainers."

"Who said I wanted to play football?"

She grinned. "You should be grateful. My fallback option was the industrial adhesive section at the Western Auto store."

"Well, it feels yucky."

"Deal with it. They deduct points for wedgies." Stephanie put her hands on Mary Jane's shoulders, spun her around and gave her a push. "Now get out there and strut your stuff."

Mary Jane joined the parade of young woman preparing to go onstage. A medley of up-tempo music throbbed in the air. With each beat of the music, Mary Jane thought, *I can't do this.*

The line inched forward. One at a time, the contestants disappeared through the curtain into the spotlight. After a few moments and a round of polite applause, they returned at the opposite end. Safely behind the curtain, they milled around killing time until the swimsuit finale.

I can't do this.

Mary Jane's anxiety increased with each step she took. Three girls ahead of her.

I can't do this.

Two girls.

I can't do this.

One girl.

I can't do this.

No girls in front of her.

The introduction to the next song began. The stage manager gave her a little nudge. Mary Jane drew in a deep breath and stepped into the lights.

An unexpected surge of confidence swept through her as she stepped out to wild applause. I can do this, she thought, moving across the stage with practiced steps. The next Miss Cumberland Valley stood tall, threw her shoulders back and gave each of the judges a winning smile as she passed.

~ 27 ~

"This dumpy town can't hold me back. I'm going to be famous. By the time I'm finished, Bly will be known for something other than the busted heads of striking coal miners."– Estil Estep

New Year's Day 1985 dawned clear and cold in Bly. Estil Estep and the Michigan Wolverines were playing the Arizona Sun Devils in the Rose Bowl and Bly was in a frenzy.

Like most families around town, Mary Jane planned a Rose Bowl buffet. She began her preparations early and clicked on the TV to listen to the Rose Parade as she worked. She was sliding a ham into the oven when Brian came through the front door.

"I guess you heard, Estil didn't win the Heisman Trophy." He couldn't conceal his satisfaction.

"Oh yeah, according to the sports section he came in second."

"I wonder how he felt."

Mary Jane chuckled. "You don't know? How are you and Jennifer enjoying UK?"

"It's great. Different from what you imagine, but still great."

Beaming with pride, Mary Jane grabbed him and pulled him into her arms. "I'm so happy for you. Keep living your dream."

Hearing footfalls outside, Mary Jane pushed the curtain aside in time to watch Stephanie struggle up the steps. Del hovered next to her extending a helping hand.

"How's it feel watching Estil again," Stephanie asked when they were alone, "any second thoughts, regrets, do-overs?"

Mary Jane stared at her plate, tracing swirls in the ranch dip with a stalk of celery. "Estil Estep, Estil the Arm, born rich to a mother who abandoned him and a father who ignored him, desperate for recognition, hungry for love and unable to find either." Mary Jane drew a deep breath and shook her head. "Nope, no regrets."

Mary Jane began cutting the cake and putting the slices on plates. Stephanie arranged forks on the table.

"In answer to your original question," Mary Jane said. "I hope Estil throws a bunch of touchdown passes and gets the big fat pro football contract he's always wanted. Few of us have our dreams come true. Maybe he'll be one of the lucky ones."

Despite pre-game hype, the game was boring. The teams spent the first half trading the ball back and forth. Arizona restricted Estil to short throws, making him one frustrated quarterback.

Throughout the second half Estil paced the sidelines restlessly. He'd counted on winning the Heisman and didn't. His performance today was, at best, mediocre. His dreams were this close to becoming reality and he felt them slipping away. All of his old fears and insecurities returned.

With barely a minute left and the score tied 15 all, Michigan got the ball. As he went onto the field, the coach said, "Position the ball for the kicker. A field goal will win it."

Cursing his luck, Estil jammed on his helmet. He'd broken curfew the night before and his head throbbed. For weeks he'd dreamed of a blowout game with lots of passes, lots of touchdowns, lots of razzle-dazzle. He wanted to show the scouts what he could do. Instead the kicker would be the game's hero.

No he wouldn't, Estil thought. They expected long bombs, and, by God, that's what they'd get. He called a pass play in the huddle.

As he took his place behind the center, Estil thought of Mary Jane. He wondered if she was watching...even pictured her in front of the TV.

He glanced up and down the line. What did she think of him now? How would she feel when he got his pro contract? After checking his receivers a final time, Estil Estep began the last cadence he'd ever call.

The smell of fresh-popped corn filled the house. "Who wants popcorn?" Mary Jane called from the kitchen.

"Forget your popcorn and get in here. The game's ending."

"Okay, okay. Here I come." Mary Jane clambered between chairs and wiggled her way onto the sofa. "What's happening?"

"Minute t' go, score tied. He's going to set them up for a field goal."

The camera closed in tight on Estil. He took the snap and pulled away from the center. Defenders poured across the line.

Mary Jane watched Estil scamper back and forth, bobbing and weaving to avoid tackles. A stampede of opposing players bore down on him.

Mary Jane tensed in anticipation of the impending collision.

In desperation, Estil tried to handoff the ball to his last remaining blocker.

She had a frightening premonition and shouted, "Don't do it!"

Time seemed to move in slow motion. Defenders descended on Estil from all sides. A player read the attempted handoff and snatched it away a split-second before the other players crashed together.

Estil disappeared under a pile of tacklers while Arizona scored the game-winning touchdown. The opposing players rolled off leaving Estil on the ground twitching and flopping like a fish out of water. He writhed in pain clutching his passing arm.

~ 28 ~

An ambulance took Estil directly to the UCLA Medical Center. A team of specialists labored over him late into the night. One look told them he'd never play again. Their goal was to simply save the arm. After several weeks of recovery, Estil returned to Kentucky. He had been in rehabilitation for several months when Mary Jane made a visit to the Locust Grove Cemetery.

"Hi, Guys. It's me." She took her accustomed place on the base of her mother's marker. Mary Jane leaned over and patted her father's stone. "I'm going to talk to Momma, but you can listen in."

She turned to face her mother's marker. "Lately I've been feeling like I'd reached a dead-end in my life, not knowing which way to turn."

She smiled. "The Miss Kentucky Pageant worked out just the way I wanted. Winning Miss Cumberland Valley required me to compete in the Miss Kentucky competition. I didn't try very hard because the winner went to Atlantic City for Miss America and that's the last thing I wanted. I've had my fill of beauty pageants."

She took a deep breath. "So, I'm second runner-up. I got more scholarship money, and I'm off the hook." She laughed. "I bet I'm the first finalist in history who hoped she didn't win."

"As I left the auditorium, a man came up to me and handed me his business card. He said he wanted to hire me as a model. I stuck the card in my purse and forgot all about it. The whole idea seemed, um, a little weird."

Mary Jane fussed with the flowers she'd placed on her parent's graves.

"The more I thought about it, the more I decided maybe I should consider modeling. I mean, what do I have to lose? I remembered the card, dug it out of the bottom of my purse and called Mr. Bateman. He has a job waiting for me."

Mary Jane's excitement made it hard to sit still.

"This is my chance to finally spread my wings and fly. New York City, can you imagine? Me? I'm so excited I'm about to bust. I've already learned all the words to the song *New York, New York* by heart."

She lowered her head and let what she'd just said sink in. She had a tendency to over-analyze and knew if she allowed herself to think about it too long, she'd realize what a crazy long shot it was and lose her nerve.

Years ago her mother had advised her to trust and that's what she would do. This wasn't about logic; it was about faith, pure faith. An inner voice had told her, *Do this, or you'll spend the rest of your life wishing you had.* She'd trust that voice and the invisible hands she knew guided her life.

She sighed. "So, I guess you could say I came to say goodbye."

The words sent fear roiling across her stomach. She hugged herself and swayed back and forth until the feeling passed.

She leaned in her father's direction. "Don't worry, Daddy, everything's taken care of. The boys and I worked it out together. We sold the house and split the money three ways. Brian has enough for college. He'll be able to continue on and become a lawyer. Brent put his in a savings account. He's going to stay with Weezie and Cash until he graduates and then study accounting in college."

She glanced down at her mother's name etched in granite.

"I can hear you Momma. 'That takes care of Brian and Brent, what about you?' I'll be alright. I've got Mr. Bateman's job and my savings account until I get a paycheck. Marmalade and I are leaving tomorrow on the morning bus."

The tears she'd been holding back trickled down her cheeks. She blotted her eyes, sniffed several times and said, "I don't know when I'll get back, but I'll be thinking about you both every day."

She stood up, patted a kiss on both markers and whispered, "I love you."

BOOK TWO
NEW YORK, NEW YORK

~ 29 ~

New York, 1987

Mary Jane felt tingles of excitement as she muscled her luggage through the busy Port Authority Terminal. Here she was standing on the threshold of her dream, in line to claim her piece of the pie.

She hadn't bothered to look in a mirror, but knew she must look awful. Leaving the crackling static of an overhead speaker announcing arrivals and departures behind, she drug her luggage through the door and planted her feet on New York sidewalks for the first time. She drew a deep breath and looked up at the Empire State Building with a dizzying sense of exhilaration.

She had an appointment on the outskirts of the garment district the next day. On the bus she decided to go straight over and meet the people she'd be working with. But wanting to sightsee first, she headed east.

A quick block later she entered Times Square. Her pace slowed. Wide-eyed and frightened, she inched along the edge of the sidewalk cautiously eyeing the sleazy bars, sex shops and adult theatres.

Glancing through an open door, she saw a naked woman gyrating under pink lights. Mary Jane stopped and stared open-mouthed. She didn't become aware of the men loitering nearby until she heard their laughter. One of them wolf whistled. Another made an obscene suggestion. Clutching her suitcases tight against her, she spun on her heel and hurried back to the bus station to get a cab.

After double-checking the address, Mary Jane tapped on the dark oak door then tried the knob. A man in his mid-thirties sat at a desk sorting photos. He had a square face, stocky build and short, reddish-blond hair.

He looked up. "Hullo, Luv." His green eyes moved over her. He seemed not so much checking her out, as taking her in.

She stood there just as she'd arrived in New York. Hair tied up in a ponytail and pulled out the back of her Bly Marauders baseball cap, checkered shirt, wrinkled jeans and tennies.

The longer he looked, the more bewildered his expression became. "What can I do for ya, Darlin'?"

Her eyes flicked down to the paper in her hand and then back to him. "Would you be Mr. Rudolph Carson?"

"It's Rudy, just plain Rudy."

"Glad to meet you, just plain Rudy." She extended her hand. "I'm Mary Jane Combs. I have an appointment with you and a photographer in this building tomorrow."

"Chance?"

She glanced down at her paper. "Yes, Chance Crosley. You know him?"

"Mm-hmm."

"And you do makeup and hair styling."

Rudy nodded. "Shampoo your hair in the morning, but don't style it. Wear as little makeup as possible. Anything you put on, I'll have to scrub off." A light of understanding lit his eyes "You're the girl from Kentucky, one of Bateman's babes, right?"

Her cheeks warmed. "I wouldn't put it quite like that. Mr. Bateman recruited me for his agency. He said you'd do the makeup for my portfolio photos and bill him."

Rudy gave her a bored shrug of acknowledgement. "Drink tea?" He rocked a pot of thick, dark liquid and gave her a crooked smile. "I also have coffee."

"You don't look like the typical girl who comes through my door," Rudy said as he handed her a mug. "Is that some kind of cowgirl chic you're trying to achieve there?"

The mug quivered in her hands. "Do you insult everyone who comes in, or am I getting special treatment? How fresh would you look after spending twenty-some hours on a Greyhound bus, then fighting your way across New York City?"

"Sorry. This business has made me cynical."

"I'm going to need a place to stay. I came by early hoping you could give me some suggestions. But now," she lowered her eyes, "I'm not so sure it was a good idea."

"We got off to a bad start. Let's start over." Rudy leaned forward. "What you're looking for is an SRO."

"Standing Room Only? That doesn't sound very inviting."

He gave her a crooked grin. "*Single Room Occupancy*. It's a cross between a hotel and a boarding house. Think college dorm. You have a private room, but the bathroom's down the hall. They rent by the week or month. Women only and they serve a meal each day...or is it two? I can't remember. Anyway, they're run by Catholic nuns or the Salvation Army, so there's no monkey business."

"Sounds perfect." She gave him a triumphant smile. For the first time since she'd arrived, she dropped her guard letting the true Mary Jane shine through. She knocked her knuckles on the table. "See, it was a good idea to come here first."

The sudden glow and sparkle in her eyes lit the room. Rudy stared, basking in the warmth she radiated. He grabbed the phone book, jotted down several possibilities and handed her the list.

"You'll be rooming with lots of dancers, actresses and students. They're a pretty good group actually. I need to run down the hall." He slid the phone across the desk. "Feel free."

"I found one." She waved the list at Rudy. "The Markle."

"Super. I was telling Chance about you. He's looking forward to meeting you."

She grinned.

Putting his left elbow on the table, Rudy leaned into the palm of his hand and worked his fingers around his square chin. "Uh, Mary, there's something I need to ask you. It has to do with the modeling business."

"Okay."

"You know, one of the things you have to decide in this business is where you draw your lines."

A flutter of fear danced in her stomach. She put down the mug and crossed her arms. "I'm not certain I understand."

"I won't beat around the bush. How much are you willing to take off?"

"Clothes, you mean?"

"Yes. Will you get naked? I mean, if the shot requires it."

Mary Jane's cheeks turned fiery red. She jumped out the chair and began organizing her luggage. "Listen Buster, if you think I'm going to give you a strip show just for helping me find a place to stay, you've got another think coming. It'll be a cold day in Hell before I do that for you, or anyone else!"

She grabbed her suitcases and heaved them into her arms. "I'll keep my appointment tomorrow morning and if you try anything out of line, believe me, you'll wish you hadn't." She gave him an indignant harrumph worthy of Aunt Weezie's best and turned to leave.

Rudy ran around the table and blocked the door.

"Get out of my way, Mr. Carson."

"We need to talk, Sweetheart."

"We have nothing to talk about and I'm not your sweetheart."

"That's quite a temper you've got there. Come sit down, pretty please." He inched back toward the table, encouraging her with his hands. "It's okay, honest." He took two more steps. "I'm on your side."

Having only gotten snatches of sleep on the bus ride, she was too tired to argue. She left her suitcases by the door and cradled the pet carrier with both arms.

Rudy motioned her closer. "Let's talk about Bateman and this agency of his."

Her alarms went off. "What about Mr. Bateman?" She marched back and sat down, keeping the pet carrier in her lap ready for a hasty retreat.

"What's the kitty's name?"

"Marmalade." Her tone dared him to comment. The cat gave a little "Meowup" at the sound of his name. She slipped a finger in and rubbed him while she waited to hear what Rudy had to say.

"You were in a beauty contest, right?"

"The Miss America Pageant, Miss Kentucky competition."

"But you didn't win."

The flutters in her stomach came back double. Her mind raced imagining where this might lead. "I was second runner-up. How did you know?"

"That's where Bateman finds most of his girls."

"You make it sound like he's doing something illicit. On the phone he told me he had modeling jobs. He even works with movie producers."

"He does, but his jobs are in the skin trade and his movie producers make porn flicks."

"Why would you say such an awful thing?"

"Because it's true."

She furrowed her brow. "What's in it for you?"

"I'm not the only cynical one here, am I?"

"Just answer my question."

"Actually, nothing. If you're willing to do that kind of work, have at it. It's your life."

Rudy waited, giving her time to think.

In her mind, Mary Jane returned to Times Square. She recalled the lurid movie posters, the dirty little shops, the creepy men lounging against the buildings. She heard a wailing saxophone and wondered, is that what Bateman had in mind for me, dancing under pink spotlights?

"He's really a sleazeball, honest Injun?"

"Last year one of his clients won an award from the AFA,

the Adult Film Association. Poor thing brought it by to show me. The way she acted, you'd have thought it was an Oscar." He scratched his head. "It always seemed to me starring in a porn flick was analogous to being a pin cushion."

"You're telling the truth, aren't you?"

"Uh-huh."

Mary Jane buried her face in her hands. "What was I thinking? I can't believe I've done this to myself. How could I have been so stupid?"

Rudy came around the desk and stood beside her. He raised his hand and then paused, letting it flutter above her shoulder. "If I pat you on the shoulder, you won't sic your cat on me will you?"

"No," she said, chuckling through her tears.

He squeezed her shoulder. "All's not lost,"

She covered his hand with hers. "I'm sorry I was so bitchy. You don't understand. I've burned all my bridges. I sold our house. I quit my job. I bragged to everyone about my modeling contract. I'd be a laughingstock if I went back home. Besides, there's nothing to go back to."

"Why go back? You came to New York to be a model, didn't you?"

"You're not making sense, just plain Rudy." She wiped her face on her shirtsleeve and held out her hand. "Thanks for your help. You've saved me from a big mistake."

"And that's how it ends?"

"I don't have enough money to stay here indefinitely. What am I supposed to do?"

"Okay, here's the plan. First, call Bateman and tell him you changed your mind. Next, keep your appointment tomorrow. Once your portfolio's ready, I can steer you to some legitimate modeling jobs."

"I can't pay you for the portfolio."

"Not to worry. Your credit's good. We have a special, no-down-payment plan for Bateman babes."

“I wish you’d quit calling me that, it’s disrespectful.”

“I’m going to give you some more free advice. If you want to succeed in this business you’re going to have to develop a thicker hide. People are going to say things way more disrespectful than babe. I’d tell you a few, but I don’t want to spoil your fun.”

“Why are you doing this?”

“I don’t like Bateman’s tactics. Yeah, yeah, I know. Then why am I doing makeup for his recruits? Because it gives me a chance to head them off at the pass. I give each one of them the same little test I gave you.”

He pointed a finger at her. “You passed with flying colors, by the way. But more than that, I saw a little bit of it when you smiled. You’re special. Trust me, play your cards right and you’ll go places.”

Her mother’s words echoed in her memory. She wanted to believe there was significance to his choice of words while her logical side insisted it was only coincidence.

“I’m not so sure after what I’ve been through today.”

“I won’t steer you wrong.” He patted her hand. “Just trust.”

“I’m sorry I snapped at you. I’m edgy from the bus ride. And my watchword for today is *Circumspect*: to be heedful of circumstances or consequences.”

“Watchword?”

She shook her head. “It’s just something my Aunt started, a word for every day thing.”

Rudy walked Mary Jane to the door, handed her the last suitcase and gave her a peck on the cheek.

She hugged him tightly. “Thanks, just plain Rudy. I promise you’ll never regret this. Someday I’ll pay you back with interest.”

~ 30 ~

Mary Jane found The Markle in Greenwich Village right where Rudy said it would be. She unpacked and hung family photographs on nails already in the wall. While she worked, Marmalade inspected their new quarters.

After storing her empty suitcases in the closet, she opened the blinds. Marmalade jumped onto the windowsill beside to her. Together they watched lights flicker on as the evening sky darkened. She reached down and petted him. He rubbed against her, purring.

"This is it, Marmuls. I guess we're home."

Rudy grinned when he handed her the finished portfolio. "I knew it. The camera loves ya, Darlin'."

A few days later, Mary Jane answered a knock at her door and found a dark-haired young woman in a leotard.

"Hi. I'm Joann. A group of us from the Joeffrey Ballet meet downstairs every morning to exercise. I heard you're a model and thought maybe you'd like to join us. It'll help your flexibility and movement."

Mary Jane did, and made friends quickly. The young women supported each other's ambitions, splurging on dinner out when someone in the group landed a big job, and living frugally when they didn't.

One morning, Jill, another new friend looked up from a stretch and asked, "Ever done any acting?"

She admitted she hadn't.

"There's a walk-on in a show I'm in. Not much different from modeling. It's an easy way to earn a few bucks."

"Why not?" Mary Jane decided.

She got the part, which required her to join SAG, the Screen Actors Guild. Having a union card allowed her to pursue other small parts and short speaking roles. She had no long-term aspirations, but welcomed the income. It provided good experience and line items for her resume.

Modeling jobs came slowly at first, but she persisted.

"The easiest way to become an overnight success is to put in years of hard work," Rudy counseled one evening over pizza.

She eventually obtained catalog work modeling women's clothing. It was a good place for her to start since runways conjured up memories of pink lights and saxophones. Unlike the haute couture models with grandiose notions of their own importance, the people she came into contact with were down-to-earth.

In October, she answered a department store's casting call and spent her first Christmas season in New York impersonating a store mannequin. The job required her to stand stock still modeling one of the store's dresses. She quickly mastered the technique and enjoyed the startled look people gave her when she moved.

Beth looked up from the switchboard and waved a note at Mary Jane as she came through the Markle's lobby. "Man, you look tired. Everything okay at home?"

"Yeah, I had a great time, but a rough flight back." Mary Jane sat her suitcases down and took the *While You Were Out* slip Beth offered.

Beth watched her scan the message. "I bet it's a job offer."

"Think so?"

"Why else would they be calling? Somebody noticed you."

The department store wanted her for print ads. Mary Jane became as regular a part of the weekend edition as the entertainment section. Working one or two days a week for the department store and seasonally for the mail order folks assured her of a regular income. She began searching for her first apartment.

Her friends at the Markle took her out for a farewell dinner before she left. With candles flickering on the table, they sat in the darkened restaurant discussing Mary Jane's future.

Jill gave her a thoughtful look. "You need a name."

"I already have one."

"Yeah," Beth said. "A plain Jane name. Hotshot models need a name with flair like Rochelle, or Dominique."

"A weekly spot in the New York Times hardly makes me a hotshot model."

"How 'bout Aphrodite?" Joann suggested.

Mary Jane laughed until her sides ached. Wiping away tears with her napkin, she pointed across the table. "No more wine for that lady. I don't care if she begs."

The group eventually reached a consensus and, shortly after completing her first year of modeling, Claudia Monet, as Mary Jane now called herself, got her first magazine spread.

~ 31 ~

New York, 1991

"Your call surprised me," Rudy said, once the maitre d' seated them. "I've hardly seen you the last few months. When did you get back?"

"I flew in from Washington this morning. Brian had contracts for me to sign."

"And your nephews?"

"Didn't see them. It was strictly business."

Rudy swirled his wineglass, watching red waves rise and fall. "So are you going to tell me why you're here, or keep me guessing?

"I came to see you."

He gave her a lopsided grin. "Here I am, Darlin'."

She looked at him over the edge of her wineglass with a devilish smile. "I came to make you an offer you can't refuse." She touched the wine to her lips then licked it off seductively.

"And if I don't go along, you'll have a coupla thugs bust my kneecaps?"

"Nah. We'll slit yur throat 'n' dump ya in the East River."

She reached into her briefcase and extracted a pad and pen. She wrote a figure and slid the pad across the table. "This is approximately what you made last year, correct?" She offered a pen. "If you want to adjust the number, feel free."

Rudy tapped the pen on the tabletop as he studied what she'd written. "Care to tell me how you arrived at this?"

"Research, guesstimates, extrapolation. Am I close?"

"Doesn't look all that impressive when it's down there in black and white, does it?" He took a sip of wine and rolled it around on his tongue, pursing his lips as he swallowed. "Yeah, give or take a couple thou, that's about it."

"Let's give rather than take." Claudia wrote 5,000 below the original number drew a line and totaled them. She spun the pad around for his approval. Her expression asked, Good enough?

Rudy nodded.

"Yesterday I signed an exclusive contract. I want to hire you as my full-time stylist. It's eight months a year and requires travel, both domestic and abroad. Supplies, food, lodging and transportation are, of course, paid. The remainder of the year, you'll assist me on other assignments."

Claudia wrote another number on the pad and gave it a nudge in his direction. It sailed across the table's slick surface coming to rest in front of Rudy.

"This would be your starting salary. Interested?"

Rudy's eyes widened. She'd taken the previous total and doubled it.

"I like the way you negotiate. Sure, I'm in. Who are you working for?"

"A French firm called LEH Chemical Group."

"Never heard of 'em. What do they make toilet bowl sudser?"

She laughed and reached across the table to pat his hand. "I wish you could see your face. You look so disappointed. Who were you expecting?"

He took a deep breath. "Well, I thought... hoped we might be talking about the Souvanée deal."

"You've heard of it?"

"Rumors in the trade say they're under the gun to find a replacement for Bianca." He shook his head. "Jeez, that was a terrible accident, wasn't it? And they were almost ready to roll."

When Claudia didn't comment, Rudy cleared his throat and shrugged. "There've been no names, of course, but everyone knows they're looking."

Claudia raised her glass. "Surprise! LEH owns the Souvanée trademark."

Rudy raised his glass, toasting her. "Oh Baby, tell me more."

Although she never said so, this was her victory celebration. She'd whooped it up with Brian and Brent the night before, but they'd been in since the beginning. Rudy was technically the first outsider she'd told, though in a way he too had been in from the beginning. She couldn't imagine traveling and working so closely with anyone else. Rudy had been like a brother to her, and she knew his expectations would never go beyond friendship.

At times, she spoke in machine gun-like bursts, unable to control the words tumbling out of her mouth as her mood rose to exuberant heights.

"Brian's been working on this contract since a few days after the accident. I'd been kicking around the possibility of doing something like this for quite a while. After Bianca's accident, I knew LEH would be under the gun to find a replacement. Brent and I brainstormed, he cranked out the numbers and Brian put together a proposal. I've been to Paris four times for interviews, met all of the company execs and its Board of Directors. I've done test layouts for their ad agencies, even a couple of screen tests."

"They really put you under the microscope."

"It was a courtship, me getting to know them and them getting to know me. It's been grueling, and frankly," she gave a satisfied sigh, "I'm glad it's over."

"Why were they so picky?"

"You know the cosmetics industry, long on style and short on substance."

"But they're a tiny company. Souvanée's hardly sells enough to bother advertising."

Lowering her voice, she leaned closer. "That's the beauty of it. Their cosmetics division may be tiny, but LEH is huge. They've got the deep pockets. They've revamped their entire product line and want to make a serious run at building market share."

"Where do you fit in?"

"Everywhere." She blushed. "Excuse my modesty, but if things go according to plan, I'm poised to become a household name."

"You've always kept a low profile. Are you ready for that kind of exposure?"

"Probably not. We've been friends for a long time, Rudy. You know I've never sought notoriety or fame, but a couple of years ago I realized exclusivity offered me the greatest income potential. Since then I've been positioning myself, watching and waiting."

"So you'll do all their print ads."

"Their strategy is to build the brand around me. They're going to roll out a ton of print ads. There'll also be point-of-purchase materials, TV spots and personal appearances."

"Personal appearances?"

"It was the core of my proposal. I'm going to actively market their products. As you know, high-end cosmetics are sold in department stores. I'll be traveling to do in-store promotions, sales meetings and training sessions with the company's representatives. We'll start with the big markets and work down to the second tier cities, then third tier."

"I hope you're being well paid."

"We'll get to that in a minute. I'm not the only one who's going to be busy. You'll be traveling with me, applying my makeup at training sessions, answering questions and teaching technique."

"I don't recall teaching being part of our negotiations."

Claudia chuckled behind her napkin. "You didn't ask."

"Double my income, huh? I think you got off pretty cheap. Maybe we should re-open negotiations."

"I'm not finished yet. LEH is going to support us with a lot of advertising, but we've got to shoehorn our way into the department stores by making things happen at the grassroots level."

"With the sales clerks," he said.

"Yes. The competition isn't going to roll over and play dead. Our market share will come out of their hide."

"You talk like it's your business."

"In a way it is. Brian negotiated a three-pronged contract." She ticked them off on her fingers. "First, there's my remuneration, then there's an expense allowance and, finally, a share of the sales growth."

"I should have let Brian negotiate my contract."

"The expense allowance is generous. I'm buying my own jet. Well, actually Brian's buying it for me. I'll own it through a private corporation and lease it to myself."

"You've really worked this out."

"As I said, we've been crunching numbers for a long time. Now let's talk profit-sharing." She reached into her briefcase, pulled out a thick stack of trade magazines out and laid them aside.

Rudy gave a low whistle. "You actually read this stuff?"

"I sure do. I'm tired of being a showpiece. I'm a businesswoman, and I won't spend the rest of my life doing pretty."

This was a side of her she seldom showed outsiders. Claudia drummed her fingers on the table while they waited for the waiter to clear their dishes. She passed on dessert, encouraging Rudy to order whatever he liked.

"The color products will roll out first: lipsticks, rouge, blush, eye shadow, and so on. They're nothing but a pinch of product wrapped in a pound of promise. The margins are astronomical. That's why LEH can spend so much. They'll get it back in spades if they're, we're, successful."

"From where I sit, it looks like a long uphill climb," Rudy said.

"By starting off with a miniscule share of the market we have nowhere to go but up."

She leaned forward and whispered, "This is confidential, so keep it under your hat. The way Brian structured things I get a bonus linked to Souvanée's growth. Each 1% increase in their market share nets me an additional $1 million."

"Forever?"

"For as long as I represent them."

"What if their targets aren't met?"

"I still have my base salary. It's no secret. You'll see it in the trade papers, $8 million per on a five-year renewable contract. There's a multi-level buy-out clause LEH can exercise anytime after the first year. It depends upon growth and a lot of other stuff, but I don't intend to ever have to go there." She scribbled numbers on her pad as fast as she talked. "As you can see, anything above a 2% compounded increase doubles the take."

"So this is it then?"

"What do you mean?"

"This is the Big Time."

She seemed taken aback. Quickly regrouping, she smiled. "Yeah, I suppose it is."

"Nearly five years ago you walked into my studio, hair in a ponytail, kitty in a carrier. I said then and there you had it, didn't I?" He grinned. "Congratulations."

For a moment she seemed flustered. "Yeah, I guess you did. Even a blind squirrel finds an acorn once in a while, huh?"

"I'd have to have been blind not to see it, Darlin'."

Claudia cleared her throat. "Okay, for starters, I'm going to allocate 25% of the income derived from market growth to a profit-sharing account and divvy it up among my employees. There'll only be four or five. If we get the job done, the number I scratched on the pad will look like chicken feed."

"I'm feeling better already."

She reached across the table to squeeze his hand. "Let not your heart be troubled. I take care of my friends."

~ 32 ~

The first break in her schedule came between Christmas and New Year's. Claudia took possession of a business jet the first week of December and used it to shuttle between New York, Paris and Washington. This time, rather than pull her new crew away from their families so she could visit hers, she flew commercial.

Getting out of New York was as cleansing as a spring tonic. Her tension dropped away the moment the plane lifted off the tarmac. Leaning back in her seat, she sighed with contentment savoring the last crumbs of her anonymity.

True, she'd turned heads in the airport and, at the gate, felt a number of men's eyes inspecting her as she waited to board. That was something she'd grown accustomed to.

Even without Souvanée's notoriety, she was not invisible. While she waited at her gate, she noticed a woman several rows away staring. They made eye contact. The woman raised her magazine and pointed to Claudia's picture on the cover. Claudia smiled and nodded, acknowledging yes it was her.

She stowed her suitcases in the trunk of a rental car along with the shopping bag of presents she'd brought and headed south from Lexington. It was dark and snowing by the time she turned off of I-75 and headed east toward Bly.

Her anticipation grew with every mile she wound around the twisting, two-lane highway. She tuned the radio to WBLY, her hometown station, and sang along with the Christmas carols as she drove. Being back in the Cumberland Valley made New York and Souvanée seem like a dream. She planned to immerse herself in this place, this culture, these people, and drive her cares away.

The town's streets were snow-covered when she checked in at the Hereford House Inn. She had a top floor suite giving her a birds-eye view of downtown Bly. Blanketed in white, it had the crisp, fresh look of newly laundered bed sheets.

The exterior wall of her room had a sloped ceiling with a

wide dormer, reminiscent of her childhood bedroom. Claudia sat at the antique writing desk that filled the dormer and slid the lace curtain aside. Resting her chin in her hands, she gazed out the window watching snowflakes drift by. Christmas decorations hung from every telephone pole and colored lights twinkled in the store windows.

In the distance, she heard the muffled throb of a diesel locomotive and the rhythmic thump of rail cars banging against each other. She checked her watch, Chessie was right on time.

* * *

The following morning she walked over to see Weezie and Cash. She passed the Western Auto Store along the way. Seeing Del at the register, she rapped on the plate glass window. He looked up, smiled and waved. Continuing on to Stephanie's beauty shop, she opened the door and stepped into the buzz of a dozen conversations and the acrid smell of hair dye and permanent wave lotion.

Stephanie had her back to the door. When the bell on the door jingled, she said, "Sorry. We're booked. No walk-ins today."

"In that case, I'll go somewhere else."

Recognizing her voice, Stephanie spun around. Even with her smock on, Claudia noticed the swelling in her belly. They ran toward each other and embraced.

"Why didn't you tell me you were pregnant?" Claudia held her at arm's length for a second look.

"When you said you were coming for Christmas, I decided to surprise you."

"When is it due?"

"Early May. It's a girl this time. We're going to name her Trisha."

Weezie saw her coming. She was out on the porch, waving and calling, "Yoo Hoo" before Claudia reached their walk. In the living room, they hugged and she whispered, "Our watchword for today will be *Convivial*: sociable, relating to festive times and good company."

Her aunt took a step back. "Now let me have a look at you." She shook her head. "You're under too much stress. You're going to run yourself into the ground."

"I told you on the phone the first twelve-to-eighteen months were going to be hectic. Things don't look much different right now, but in a few months you'll understand."

They were still talking when Cash returned carrying several grocery sacks. "Here's everything you wanted, Weez."

Claudia noticed her uncle's flushed face and panting breath. Checking to be sure Weezie wouldn't overhear, she whispered, "Are you feeling alright?"

"It's the cold air. Don't worry, I'm healthy as a horse and stubborn as a mule."

She went into the kitchen to help her aunt. A few minutes later they heard a commotion in the living room. They ran in and found Cash lying between the coffee table and the sofa, thrashing and struggling to get up. He looked at them with a frightened expression and moved his lips, making noises instead of words.

"Oh Lord, he's having a heart attack," Weezie cried.

Claudia jerked the table aside. Together the two women lifted him onto the couch. Weezie patted his hand, asking where it hurt between short prayers.

Claudia dropped to one knee and studied Cash's face. "Can you talk?"

His mouth and tongue had a mind of their own.

"Smile for me."

Cash's face contorted into a lopsided leer. She glanced up at Weezie and mouthed the word stroke and pushed send on her 911 call.

"He's an usher at the Christmas Eve service. Whatever will we do?"

She assured her aunt everything would be taken care of,

and disappeared into the kitchen to make additional calls. When the ambulance arrived, Claudia leaned out the kitchen doorway and told the EMT, “Call the hospital for instructions. He’s headed for Lexington.”

Claudia sent Weezie with the ambulance, promising to rejoin her at the hospital.

* * *

“They haven’t told me anything yet,” Weezie said when Claudia walked into the waiting room. “The nurses spoke of a call from Lexington.”

“It’s the Neurology Department at Chandler Medical Center. After you left I called Brent.”

Weezie blotted her eyes with a flowered handkerchief. “I don’t have any idea what you’re talking about, child.”

“Brent’s firm does the accounting for several large medical groups. He made a few calls and talked to the top man.” Claudia pointed to the double doors. “They’ve been in touch with the doctors in there.”

She could tell by her aunt’s expression Weezie comprehended only half of what she said. She took her hand, hoping she’d remember the important parts. “The first hours after a stroke are critical. A life flight helicopter’s on its way. As soon as Cash is ready, they’ll transport the two of you to Lexington. Brent or Linda will be there to meet you. I’ll close up your house and join you.”

It’d been a long drive on a highway crowded with holiday traffic. Fatigue showed in Claudia’s face when she arrived at the hospital.

“How’s he doing?”

“They say he’s resting comfortably,” Weezie said. “He’s getting medicine to dissolve the clot. We won’t know how well it worked for several days.”

Claudia sat beside her on the waiting room couch.

"You just missed Brent and Linda. Brent wants me to stay with them since Cash will be in the hospital for several weeks." She dug a handkerchief out of her purse. "I can't put them out like that."

"Brent lived with you for a year. You can surely live with him for a few weeks."

"They'll have to take me places, fix my meals and do my laundry. They don't need a silly old woman fluttering around and getting in their way."

"You've got to let go, Weez." Claudia touched her aunt's arm. She'd never seen her look so frail and frightened. "You were strong when we needed you. Now it's someone else's turn."

Wheezie rolled her eyes. "And the cost of ambulances, helicopters, special medicines and intensive care is unbelievable. They say he'll need physical therapy. It all costs. Cash and I have a little saved, but we can't afford those sorts of things. We're humble people."

"Let go of those worries." Claudia slipped her arm around her aunt's shoulder. "I'll make sure you have whatever you need. I want you to move into the new assisted living complex, they have nurses and physical therapists there."

Weezie pounded her fist on her knee. "You haven't been listening. I just told you we can't afford it."

Claudia kissed her cheek. "You're the one who's not listening. I'm paying for it."

"You shouldn't be doing this."

Taking Weezie's hands in hers, she looked into her eyes. "I should do this and I will. What purpose is there to my crazy lifestyle if I can't help those I love?"

~ 33 ~

If, as Claudia suggested, the ramp-up to the Souvanée launch was like jumping onto a moving train, then the actual launch was the equivalent of having the same train plow into you at ninety miles an hour.

"Is this cool, or what?" Rudy tilted his head back and sheltered his eyes with a hand.

They stood side-by-side in Times Square watching a slide show of Claudia's images flash across an electronic billboard. This was Souvanée's opening salvo in the cosmetic wars. By morning her image would be on the sides and backs of buses and taxicabs, on billboards and in every department store in the Greater New York area. As she'd told Rudy six months earlier, she was about to become a household word.

Rudy kept his left arm resting protectively around her shoulder, gesturing with his right hand. "Remember the windy day when we shot at the beach?" The display changed. "Look! Look," Rudy shouted. "It's the red dress and upswept hairdo. Man I loved you in that red dress."

Claudia nervously eyed the crowd milling around them. "Will you keep your voice down? You're as excited as a kid at a fireworks show. People are staring."

They'd waited until dark to make the trip and she wore jeans and a car coat, pulling her collar up and tying a scarf over her head. Despite these precautions, she worried someone would recognize her.

It was one thing to sit around a table and hear someone say, "We've contracted to get the Reuters sign in Times Square for our kick-off." It's quite another to look up and see yourself projected 22 stories high to 1.5 million people a day. She scanned the whooping, hollering crowd and thanked God she peddled cosmetics, not lingerie.

By the end of the following week, sides of buildings in Los Angeles and Chicago would also carry her likeness, and within a month, she'd be on display coast-to-coast. Nationwide, warehouses disgorged their booty. Truckloads of counters, racks and shelving rolled out for installation. Pallets of cosmetics were in transit and training classes underway. For someone who'd consciously avoided the limelight, she found it unnerving.

They finished in New York, stopped in Chicago then continued west spending time in L.A., San Diego and San Francisco. Their next trip took them to Boston, Philadelphia and Washington, DC. While in Washington, she took a few days off and retreated to the serenity of Brian's Virginia farm. The full extent of her celebrity became clear when Brian's oldest boy, John, approached her for an autograph.

She looked up from the dinner table in surprise. "You're kidding, right?"

He shook his head and laid down a department store mailer with her photo on the cover. He rooted in his pocket. "I have a pen right here."

She reached out and mussed his hair. "What's the joke, Johnny? I'm Aunt Janie. I used to change your diapers. Why do you want my autograph?"

He hemmed and hawed before admitting, "It's for school. I told my friends you were my aunt and they didn't believe me."

"So you want proof?"

He nodded.

Claudia took the pen, smiled and wrote, *To my nephew, Johnny. Best wishes and lots of love, from your Aunt Mary Jane.*

When she finished, she returned the mailer and pen. He headed for his bedroom with a satisfied grin. He stopped at the foot of the stairway, looked down at what she'd written and hollered, "Hey, wait a minute. That's not what you were supposed to say."

Suppressing a smile, she asked, "Is something wrong?"

“Look at what she did.” He slammed the booklet down in front his father.

Brian burst out laughing. “She got you on that one. Always define the details of any contract.” Brian winked across the table at his sister. “There’s an evil heart lurking underneath your beautiful exterior, MJ.”

Claudia sent John into the den to retrieve her briefcase. She removed three different 8 x 10 publicity photos she carried specifically for autographs and spread them out on the table. She kissed him on the forehead and told him to take his pick, promising to sign it, “Anyway you want me to.”

~ 34 ~

London, 1994

Amanda Rivers paced the lobby impatiently. Stopping, she straightened the investment magazines spread across the coffee table. Were they to be read, she wondered, or simply part of the décor like the marble flooring, walnut paneling and oriental carpets? Who cared? She didn't own Kensington Partners, Alistair Whitestone did.

Kensington Partners, a member of the London Stock Exchange, occupied the upper floor of an office tower in Warwick Court at Paternoster Square. The building was at the heart of London. Sir Christopher Wren's masterpiece, St. Paul's Cathedral, stood nearby. The London Stock Exchange was equally close. The Bank of England was around the corner on Cheapside Street.

Amanda glanced at Whitestone's portrait beside the lift and shook her head. The young, virile Alistair Whitestone in the painting had panache. He'd built empires and slew dragons. Empire building he still did occasionally, but he hadn't slain a dragon for ages. She chuckled to herself. The only things he dreamt of slaying now were some of his clients.

The lift's bell chimed. Amanda checked her hair, smoothed her skirt and started toward its burnished bronze doors. At the first sliver of light, she buttoned her jacket.

Michael Cole exited the car. A longtime Kensington client, Cole had great ambitions and, at 38, time to accomplish them. He carried himself well, moving with the potent confidence of a man accustomed to being in control. His black hair, graying at the temples, was stylishly cut. He wore a three-piece blue wool suit and carried a leather attaché.

Cole's warm greeting surprised Amanda. He appeared ready to hug her.

She maintained her distance, politely offering her hand. "We have a conference room reserved. I'll have someone let

Alistair know you're here."

High-backed leather chairs surrounded the boat-shaped table with teak inlays. A kettle steamed on a burner in the adjacent kitchenette. Cole tossed his attaché onto the table and unbuttoned his jacket as Amanda adjusted the lighting.

"I saw you ogling the receptionist, Michael."

"Women appreciate a little attention now and again."

"She's hardly more than a girl. I think you frightened her."

He stared at her, his dark eyes feigning shock. "Really?" he asked, innocent as an altar boy. "Do I frighten you?"

Amanda bit her lip.

"A handshake, really Amanda, don't I deserve more?"

"Indeed you do. And someday you'll get what's coming to you. Would you like a cup of tea?"

"Have you forgotten everything?"

"I've certainly tried. Lord knows, I've tried."

She handed him the china cup and saucer. He sat it aside, slipped an arm around her waist and pulled her close. Feeling her body against his excited and frightened her. Every instinct told her to push him away. But she couldn't; he was an important client.

Cole traced the side of her cheek with the back of his hand and stared deep into her eyes. "I'm planning a trip to the Riviera. Why don't you accompany me? I'm sure Alistair can get along without you for a week or two."

Amanda waited a moment then laughed. It sounded contrived and forced. "You've always been such a kidder. I never know when to take you seriously."

Swept into a whirlpool of emotions, Amanda fought to maintain her composure. Cole's raw animal magnetism stirred up old feelings. Feelings she found hard to resist. Amanda sat on the edge of the table, demurely crossing her legs at the ankles.

Cole dropped into a chair beside her. “Come with me. It will be like old times.”

“It will never be like old times.”

“You’re right. It’ll be better. Have I ever told you how lovely you are? I’ve missed you, Amanda.”

“What about my husband?”

“I won’t take him to the Riviera, if that’s what you mean.”

“I can’t go running off with you; he needs me.”

“Does he? He didn’t appear to need you last year.” Cole clicked his tongue. “You’re a beautiful woman. You have needs. Don’t ignore your natural urges, it’s unhealthy.”

The tabletop gleamed from generous applications of carnuba wax and janitor’s elbow grease. A ruler stood on end would reflect a shine twelve inches deep. Slowly, almost imperceptibly, Amanda felt herself sliding toward Cole. Terrified, she hopped off and smoothed her skirt.

“You know full well Eric has a medical condition.”

“I’m concerned about you, not him.”

“I should never have shared my private life.”

“Nonsense, confession is good for the soul.”

Their eyes met and Cole’s wicked grin took Amanda’s breath away. He seemed to see into the core of her being. Know her darkest secrets. Sense her deepest desires.

“What unrequited fantasies do you keep hidden away? Whatever they are I can satisfy them.”

“Listen to yourself. This is a business office, not a pickup club.”

Cole dropped his eyes and sipped tea. “So it would appear.”

“I don’t need to repeat old mistakes.”

“Mistakes? There were no mistakes.”

Amanda felt only shame recalling their time together. But he knew her too well. Despite her best efforts, he could still awaken her darkest needs.

"Shall I speak to Alistair?"

"You're an evil force, Michael, a black hole destroying anything and anyone crossing its path. Have you no limits?"

Amanda moved to the opposite side of the table. It felt safer having a physical barrier between them. Straightening, she said, "We've made good progress this week, Mr. Cole. Your team and I ironed-out most of the details. I'm sure you'll be pleased."

"My offer still stands. The Riviera is lovely this time of year."

"I have work here."

"I have things for you to do there."

"I can just imagine."

"What if I insisted Alistair send you along?"

"I'd quit first."

"And lose your share of the commissions on my stock offering?"

Amanda leaned forward and looked him square in the eye. "Don't push your luck. You need the proceeds from this stock sale more than I'll ever need that commission. Go to the Riviera and hire yourself a prostitute."

Cole's people asked for half an hour up front to review the results of the week's negotiations. He pulled his chair close to the table and slipped on reading glasses to examine the charts and graphs spread before him.

His legal counsel, Ted Ballinger, waved at the papers on the table. "Most of this is standard boilerplate. We got everything you wanted. The interest rate's a few basis points higher than our goal, but manageable."

Cole smiled his approval. "Estimated timeline?"

"Approvals can be slow and then there's the escrow. But, unless there's an unforeseen problem, you'll net 700 million pounds before year's end."

Cole's eyes moved across the small group resting briefly on each man. "There will be no unforeseen problems. Understood?"

Cole held Ballinger's eyes until he couldn't stand it.

He looked away and began arranging papers. "Yes Sir, I understand."

"I'm glad you do."

Ballinger had no allusions. He'd seen the financing behind Paradise Getaway's recent acquisitions. He was also privy to the company's actual cash flows, not the doctored numbers they fed banks and stockholders. During the negotiations Cole maintained his usual breezy confidence, but Ballinger knew Cole was out on a limb. Way out. He lacked sufficient long-term financing to keep his far-flung enterprise afloat.

He's put all his chips on one spin of the wheel, Ballinger thought, tucking papers back into his briefcase. This was a make or break deal. Cole either became a player to be reckoned with, or he slipped into obscurity like so many other wannabe's.

Their eyes met. Neither man said a word. He knew. And Cole knew that he knew.

~ 35 ~

Alistair Whitestone leaned back in his chair and patted his stomach. “Great meal, wasn’t it? Good food keeps the wheels of financial progress turning.”

Cole nodded. “It’s a pleasure doing business with you, Alistair. I can’t imagine anyone else handling this deal.”

A waiter arrived carrying a humidor on a silver tray.

“How’s life on the South Side?” Whitestone asked as he removed a cigar.

“Wonderful. I have more space, a great view and parks nearby.”

“That’s quite a place you’ve gotten for yourself down at Putney Wharf. It listed for 3.75 million pounds, didn’t it?”

“Spending your afternoons reading the real estate listings?”

“People talk.”

“It’s about keeping up appearances. Besides, I crave privacy.”

Whitestone winked. “What you crave are women.”

“And you don’t?”

“I’m an armchair Romeo who follows your exploits from afar. At my stage of life I don’t know if I could handle the young women you entertain.”

“At the very least, you should stoke the home fire. Make a few subtle suggestions or leave a periodical or two lying about for your wife to find. She might surprise you.”

Whitestone took a long draw on his cigar. “At our age there are few surprises left. If I were to go about the house scattering randy photos, Anne would have a few rude suggestions for me.”

Cole blew several smoke rings. “My philosophy is, determine what you want, find it and take it.” His face relaxed when he smiled. “That applies to women, as well. If it’s a younger woman you want, then by all means have her.”

“What about Mrs. Whitestone?”

“Leave it up to her. The more the merrier.”

Whitestone’s ruddy cheeks flushed. “That isn’t quite what I meant.”

“That’s your problem, Alistair, you think small. Small thinking is the difference between want and have.”

Sensing his opening, Whitestone leaned forward in his chair. “Speaking of wanting and having, there’s a problem with this offering.”

“A problem?”

“I don’t think we can float this new stock.”

“Why not?”

Whitestone’s words came in a torrent. “You’re over-extended. You’ve been growing too quickly. Your debt-to-equity ratios aren’t strong. These additional shares will dilute earnings.”

Cole casually lifted the cigar and took a puff. He appeared relaxed and unconcerned. Meanwhile his left hand, hidden by the chair arm, flexed in and out of a tight fist. He’d learned long ago that you had to play along when someone else was in control.

“The postman brought you a letter today,” his Aunt Jessica said.

He recognized his mother’s script, *Master Michael Cole.* Then he noticed Aunt Jessica had already opened it.

Saving him the trouble of reading it, she said. “Your Mum’s coming home soon.”

The boy breathed a silent sigh of relief. Auntie Jess would finally go away. “Soon as she’s back, I’m going to tell her the nasty things you’ve been doing.”

“Are you now?”

The young boy’s face hardened. “You bloody well know I will. And I fancy she’ll have a thing or two to say about it.”

“Do you recall why they locked her away?”

"You said she had a nervous condition, she was disturbed."

Auntie Jess nodded. "Disturbed, those are my words, all right." She stroked her chin. "Those are serious charges you're making, Michael. What do you suppose I'll tell them when they come investigating."

He didn't know.

"I'll say poor Michael's been quite disturbed since they took his Mum away. Why he's so upset he's taken to wandering around the house without any clothes on. He walks about bare naked, and asks me to give him baths and rock him like a baby."

She put her arm around the boy's thin shoulder and kissed his cheek. "Now who do you suppose they'll believe, the disturbed little boy or the grown-up who's been caring for him nigh on two years?"

His head drooped.

She lifted his chin and spun his face to hers. "It's nothing to cry about, Sweetie." She wiped his damp cheeks with her sleeve. "You forgot who's in control, that's all." Auntie Jess sighed. "What do you suppose they do with disturbed boys...lock them away, perhaps?"

She leaned into the corner of the sofa and motioned to him. "Now be a good boy and crawl up here beside me."

Michael did what she wanted. He had to, she was in control.

Whitestone droned on. "Slow down. Give investors time to get to know you. Do it sometime in the future."

Cole straightened in his chair. "Without this money, I don't have a future. I'm paying you to make things happen. You've always gotten a fair share of the pie. What's happened?"

"If you want the God's honest truth, the phrase I heard most often was that you were over-reaching. Yes, you've had some successes, but you're still an unknown commodity to a lot of people."

Michael leaped to his feet. "All these years and the best you can say is I'm an unknown?"

"I'm your financial advisor and I advise shelving this plan. The average investor doesn't know Michael Cole or Paradise Getaways. Sit on your hands for a time. Meanwhile, hire a good publicist."

Cole fumed.

"You could learn a trick or two from that Trump chap. Increase your name recognition. Polish your corporate image. The worst thing we could do is try to force-feed the market."

"How do I survive in the interim? Since you're so full of advice, maybe you should run the enterprise."

"What about a short-term loan?"

"If the stock analysts pick up on it, they'll dilute my ratios even further."

Whitestone gave an exasperated sigh.

"What else?" Cole asked.

"Have you considered hiring a high-profile manager to give the firm some luster? I hear Admiral Schoonover is available. Someone with Reggie's reputation would boost your corporate image."

Cole ground out his cigar. "I'll think about it. In the meantime, let's not take the pot off the boil. I want to be able to pull the trigger on a moment's notice."

"We can't submit any paperwork for approval until we're ready to make the offering."

"Fine, allow two weeks for approval."

Whitestone shook his head. "A fortnight? Impossible. We've never gotten one through so quickly."

"Suppose you didn't have to wait for governmental approvals?"

"But they're required," Whitestone stammered.

Cole smiled. "Let me take control."

Cole followed Whitestone's suggestions.

He contracted the services of a public relations firm and hired Reginald Schoonover, a retired British Admiral. He also decided to become an author and hired a ghostwriter to produce a book on business. With the easy parts taken care of, his attention shifted to the harder aspects. Most importantly, to Anatoly Tereschenko who held the key to his survival.

An idea occurred to him on the way back from his meeting in St. Petersburg. Cole stopped at a Heathrow newsstand. Going directly to the women's section, he grabbed one of the fashion magazines and leafed through it, pausing occasionally to peruse the photos. The magazine was on its way back to the rack when, on a whim, he flipped it over.

After staring at the full-page advertisement on the back, he returned the periodical to the rack. Cole grabbed another and encountered the same woman. Returning to the first magazine, he faced the back cover out as a reference. Checking the next row down, he found her again on several more. His hand flashed across the rows of magazines, checking and flipping.

When he finished, Cole stepped back and crossed his arms. He stroked his chin as he studied the grouping he'd created. The last piece of the puzzle snapped into place. He smiled and pulled a black notepad from inside his jacket. He scribbled a reminder and left the shop.

A harried clerk passed the rack and muttered a curse. Someone had reversed several rows of magazines creating a montage of back covers...all with Souvanée ads.

~ 36 ~

Innsbruck

Claudia checked her messages when she returned to her room. Noticing a familiar area code, she grabbed the phone and punched in the number. It rang and rang before she heard Stephanie's sleepy voice on the line.

"Hi, Steph. I just got your message. What's up?"

"Try who's up? It's three o'clock in the morning. Where the heck are you?"

"I'm in the Austrian Alps. Sorry. I didn't even think about the time difference. That was a real blond moment, wasn't it? I saw your number and thought it might be an emergency."

Stephanie chuckled. "Austria, huh? I bet Rudy looks adorable in lederhosen."

"Rudy's not here. He's at an LEH research facility in Lyon, France. They're updating his line of salon products."

"It was nice of you to do that for him."

"All I did was point out to the VP of marketing how much exposure he gets. It's a no-brainer. Rudy had the name recognition and LEH didn't have a professional line of hair products."

"Well, I appreciate getting cases of freebies."

"Thank him, not me. After the barbecue you threw for us, Rudy insisted. Technically you're field testing."

"So what are you doing in the Alps? Skiing, yodeling and eating schnitzel?"

"Believe it or not, I'm working. LEH owns a corporate retreat here. Souvanée Worldwide is having their annual planning powwow."

"That sounds really tough."

"It's a dirty job, but somebody's gotta do it." Claudia chuckled. "I'm here with the North American Team. I spend a lot of time in meetings since I'm on the President's Advisory

Committee."

"Did you get my invitation?"

"I haven't seen anything. Where did you send it?"

"To New York."

"I'm heading back at the end of the week. I'll look for it. What am I invited to?"

"Our high school reunion is next spring and I know how far ahead you schedule. I'm on the committee. My mission is to make certain you're there."

Claudia hedged, trying to buy enough time to invent a polite refusal. "Gee. I don't know, Steph."

"Seriously, everyone's looking forward to it."

Claudia pushed the drape aside and watched a cable car climb toward the summit. Spotlights mounted at the top of the supports reflected onto the deep snow, illuminating skiers as they zipped past.

Letting the curtain fell back, Claudia dropped onto the bed. She disliked having her arm twisted. If it'd been anyone but Stephanie, she would've turned them down flat. She hadn't interacted with folks in Bly for several years and worried about the reception she'd get.

"It sounds like fun, but I'm just not sure."

"Aw, don't be a party-pooper." Stephanie dangled her bait. "It would give you a chance to see Aunt Weezie. She and Cash aren't getting any younger."

"I think I'd better pass, it just doesn't fit my schedule. I'll plan a trip back real soon to see you and Weezie."

"Come on, we're trying to get a hundred percent participation. Besides, your being there would make it special."

"I'm sorry, maybe next time."

"Look, you're not fooling me. We've known each other too long for this subterfuge. Tell me what's eating you."

"I'd love to come. I really would. I just don't want everybody making a big fuss."

"Well, La de da, aren't we special?" Stephanie laughed. "Okay, Miss High and Mightiness go ahead and drive up in a stretch limo with five uniformed bodyguards. See if we care? Everyone knows what a stuck-up snob you are. Wear a full-length mink coat and a diamond tiara if you want to."

"You know I'm not like that."

"Of course I do. What are you worried about? People remember you as the prettiest girl in the senior class. That hasn't changed. So you don't have an expanding waistline and fallen arches like the rest of us. We'll hate you for it. That never bothered you before."

She'd been away too long. "God, I miss you. Count me in. One way or another, I'll be there."

London

Cole waited in the back of the nondescript photo shop while John Applebee snapped a youngster's portrait. After his trip to St. Petersburg, everything had fallen into place nicely, bringing him closer to the planned stock offering.

Applebee's hand puppet bobbed and weaved through the air, swooping close to the child's face. At the last minute, the puppet's arms pinched the air in front of her. The brilliant flash caused her head to snap back. He'd captured the wide-eyed look of surprise Granny would treasure.

He glanced over at her mother. "That's the last one." He slipped the puppet off his hand and tossed it back into the small tray attached to the camera's rolling tripod. "The proofs will be ready a week from today. I'll print a couple with the Teddies, some on her tummy and a few with the beach background and sand bucket."

Applebee filled out the forms in his pad while Mrs. Wycliffe gathered her things and lifted her daughter off the table. When he finished, he tore off a copy and held it out. Mummy grabbed the slip as she passed and stuffed it into her purse. She hefted the child higher in her arms and spoke over her shoulder as he walked her to the door.

"Thank you so much, Mr. Applebee. Everyone says you're good with the wee ones. Now I see why. I'm sure her Father will love the pictures you've taken of our little Princess. We can't wait to see them, can we Penny?" She took the girl's arm and waved her hand. "Bye, Bye, Mr. Applebee. See you next Tuesday."

"I'll be here, Mrs. Wycliffe. Goodbye, Penny."

He swung the door shut and locked it. Flipping over a closed sign, Applebee pulled down the door's green blind and turned off the lights. He walked through the small waiting room to a drape-covered doorway and entered the back room.

Cole put aside the photography magazine he'd been browsing.

Even in the dim light, John felt the power of his dark gaze. "Sorry for the delay. The kiddies help pay the rent, you know." Applebee wiped his hand on the leg of his trousers and extended it to his guest. "Good to see you again, Mr. Cole. It's nice to have old friends pop in."

Applebee began fussing with his computer. "I worked late to get these done. I'm sure you'll be pleased with the results."

Young mothers in this working class neighborhood on London's East Side relied on Applebee's expertise. He had a knack for catching those special looks and, although his shop was small and dowdy, most customers returned year after year.

These loyal customers had no inkling children's portraiture merely supplemented Applebee's income. The real money, the under-the-table, strictly-cash, off-the-books-so-there's-no-taxman-to-deal-with money, came from another source altogether. And it would've shocked those young mothers.

As a trusted member of London's sexual underground, Applebee had seen it all. No matter what you did, if you took pictures he'd develop them.

"As usual, I scanned the entire set to a CD. It's late and I know you're busy. We needn't waste time looking through them. I chose the best ones," Applebee said. "I'll print them for you now."

The printer whirred and clicked as it pulled a sheet of photo paper out of its tray.

Cole detected movement in his peripheral vision. He glared at a spider skittering across the floor. He'd learned a bitter lesson as a boy; eradicate them promptly or you'll have problems.

One here, one there...he thought if he ignored them they'd go away. But they didn't. One day he returned from school and found his mother in hysterics. She'd seen those ugly black spiders again. She wouldn't let him hang up his coat. A particularly nasty one might be lurking in the closet. She saw spiders creeping along the baseboards cursing and muttering threats.

He was eight years old when they took his Mum away. Her youngest sister, nineteen-year-old Jessica moved in until his mother returned from the sanitarium. Two years of intermittent electroshock treatments made her a different woman. And two years of Auntie Jess made Michael a different boy.

Cole raised his foot and slammed it down hard, smashing the spider.

Applebee gave him a startled look.

Cole snatched up a rag to clean the smear off the sole of his shoe. "A spider, the bloody creatures are everywhere."

Applebee nodded and checked the prints. "I could fancy a romp with her," he mused as he slipped them into the envelope. "Do you know what would happen if anyone found out about these?" Applebee asked as he pocketed the wad of notes Cole handed him.

"You've never had a problem in the past."

"You never brought me anything like them before. I don't like developing photos of people I recognize from the evening news."

"You're on a one-way street, John. It's long past time for misgivings."

~ 37 ~

Paris

Six weeks before her high school reunion Claudia attended a party at the home of an LEH executive. Though she spoke French, she found cocktail conversation tiring. Small talk had never been her long suit and following an exchange of repartee, innuendo, insider observations and double entendres became more work than it was worth.

Excusing herself, she slipped away to the library. Double doors opened onto a balcony. Finding them unlocked, she made her escape. Grateful for the respite, she rested her elbows on the stone railing and gazed at the Eiffel Tower. The city of Paris, a mass of lights, lay at her feet.

As she often did at times like this, Claudia thought of her mother. Her mother had lived and died without ever leaving Kentucky. She would have loved to have taken her with her when she traveled. In a way she did. Momma went along on every trip in her heart.

Lost in her own musings, she didn't notice footsteps behind her. She was startled when a man's deep voice said, "Bonsoir, Mademoiselle."

She turned. A nice looking man in a dinner jacket approached her. Tall and dark, he carried a champagne glass in each hand. Her escape had become a trap.

Tensing, she replied, "Bonsoir."

A flicker of recognition flashed in his eyes when she turned. He smiled.

She returned a cautious smile.

He placed a glass beside her on the railing and put a finger to his lips. After a moment, in a British accent, he said, "You're the American model."

"Yes. Claudia Monet."

"Michael Cole." He took the hand she extended. "I watched

you leave and immediately knew we were kindred spirits. I said to myself, 'Michael, you're not the only one who wants out.'"

A sudden, stiff breeze snapped the edge of the canvas awning. Cole touched her arm. "You're chilled."

Without a word, he stripped off his jacket and draped it around her shoulders. The residual body warmth felt comforting against her cool skin.

He lifted his glass. "Join me?"

She touched glasses with him and put it to her lips, taking the tiniest of sips. "I'm afraid I don't enjoy champagne any more than I enjoy after dinner conversation," she said, realizing he'd noticed.

"Forgive me for pushing alcohol on you. I was only trying to be courteous. Allow me." Taking her glass, he sat them aside on a bench. "You mustn't let me forget them there. We can't have tipsy pigeons staggering about the gallery."

He stood beside her, grabbed the railing with both hands and took a deep breath. "Splendid evening, isn't it?"

She'd worried when he approached her. But Michael Cole behaved differently than most men she met. So many of them fawned over her and made fools of themselves by showering her with compliments. He seemed unaffected by her celebrity.

Finding his manner unpretentious and reassuring, she relaxed. They remained on the porch together, talking and exchanging histories. Forty-five minutes later, as they prepared to return to the party, Cole asked if he could call her. Although she expected nothing to come of it, she gave him her number.

Los Angeles

Claudia planned her April itinerary around the high school reunion. They finished filming on the West Coast and she sent her troupe home aboard commercial flights. She and Greg Harris, her chief pilot, continued on to Bly alone. Since they were flying against the clock, they left California early. On the way, they landed in Wichita to add three passengers.

Joey Spinoza spotted her as soon as she walked through the door and shouted, “Hey, Claudia!”

She dropped to one knee and opened her arms to the eight-year-old racing toward her. She held him at arm’s length. “I can’t believe how great you look. On the phone your Mom said you’d gone into remission. How are you feeling?”

The maturity in Joey’s voice belied his age as he spoke to her about his illness.

Claudia listened attentively. When he finished, she brushed her hand across his head. “What’s this fuzzy stuff all over your head? You’re not a baldy anymore.”

Joey beamed.

They’d met eighteen months before when she ferried him to Memphis for his initial treatment. Joey suffered from a neuro-blastoma, a brain cancer, and was one sick little boy. Each of the children Claudia transported became one of her special friends. She took them back and forth whenever she could and kept in touch by sending notes and little packages.

“I have a surprise for you,” Claudia said.

Joey grinned. “Puzzle books?”

“Oh, I didn’t forget your puzzle books, but this is bigger than that. I’ve got a brand new plane.” Rising, she put a hand on his shoulder. “C’ome out and take a look. Greg will show you how it flies.”

She’d chosen desert sand with chocolate accent stripes for the plane’s exterior. Joey studied the sleek jet end to end then ran up the stairs to meet Greg.

Claudia now traveled in a custom Cessna Citation X, a top-of-the-line business jet. Capable of near Mach speed, it cruised at 51,000-feet. She could go coast-to-coast in about four hours and do New York to Paris in around six.

Greg and Joey discussed the power of its twin Rolls-Royce engines and the plane’s instrumentation while she gave his parents a quick tour of the passenger section. Opening the freezer door, Claudia showed them a carton of rocky road ice cream.

Joey's favorite.

She popped her head into the cockpit. "Break it up there guys. We've got to get this show on the road."

She shooed Joey out of the cockpit and into a seat. Taking the empty co-pilot's position, she put on a headset and prepared for take-off. She'd earned her pilot's license four years before. Instrument-certified, she was fully qualified to handle the twin-engine jet and frequently did.

She and Greg said good-bye to their passengers in Memphis and headed for Bly. In the past, they would've flown into either Lexington or Knoxville, but, thanks to upgrades, the Blackstone County airport could now handle aircraft as large as hers.

She flew diagonally northeast. Tennessee spread out below them lush and green in the bright sun. Just before they crossed the Kentucky line Claudia checked in with the Control Center. Cleared for landing, she began her descent.

Greg pointed to their left. "Beautiful isn't it?

The Laurel River glistened like a ribbon of quicksilver as it snaked its way into Cumberland Lake. Across the horizon the Cumberland Mountains stood blue in the distance.

She smiled. "I can't wait to get back home."

Claudia circled the airport once. Then, with sun gleaming off the fuselage, she swung the plane around in a wide, slow arc and made a textbook landing. A crowd had gathered by the time she taxied to the hangars.

She throttled back the engines and parked the plane. "Would you look at all those people? We should have gone into Knoxville," she said as they ran through shutdown protocols. "What was I thinking?"

She removed her headset and ran a hand over her hair, smoothing it. Greg glanced out the window as he rose. Stepping aside, he offered his arm. "I think it's mostly other pilots, mechanics and folks who work close to the airport. I'll hang around and give them a walk-through if it's okay with you."

She jotted a phone number on a pad and handed it to him. "Here's Stephanie's cell. Conduct tours until you run out of customers or they tire you out. The Hereford House Inn is easy to find. Let's reconnect over breakfast."

Greg smiled. "Don't worry about me. Relax and enjoy your visit."

He lowered the stairs while she grabbed her traveling bag. The group applauded when she emerged from the plane. She paused on the top step.

Her job demanded she always look her best. The tailored wool slacks she wore accented her long legs. Her emerald blouse, tucked in at the waist, highlighted her blond hair. She'd left it open at the collar and pulled a tan cashmere jacket over it.

Recognizing several familiar faces, she made eye contact, waved and mouthed, "Hello."

She could have done without the attention. At times like this she wished she could put Claudia aside and simply be Mary Jane. But they hadn't come to see Mary Jane; they'd come to see Claudia. And that's who she'd be.

"It's nice to be home again." She took a deep breath and smiled appreciatively. "I wasn't expecting such a welcome. It's good to see you all." She glanced into the plane for a split-second. "I'd like to introduce my pilot, Greg Harris."

She stepped aside and Greg exited the plane to share the small platform with her. He'd put on a tie and slipped a charcoal blazer over his white shirt. With his dark hair and neat mustache, he was precisely what the pilot of a private jet ought to look like.

"Greg will be available if anyone wants to tour the plane. As for me, I guess I'll see y'all around town."

Claudia grinned, grabbed her bag and descended the stairs. She made her way through the crowd, moving quickly, but politely, always smiling and pausing to shake hands.

~ 38 ~

Claudia spent the day of the reunion decompressing. With Del at the store and the kids playing in the backyard, she and Stephanie had time for girl talk.

"So how's your love life?"

Claudia made an unpleasant face. "Do I ask you yours?"

Stephanie laughed. "No, but if you did, I'd tell ya."

"It's nothing to write home about. Truth is, they all blend together into Mister Generic. Nice looking with good prospects, personable, well-dressed, shallow and easily forgotten." She stirred her coffee, whipping it into froth. "They drift away as soon as they discover I'm not a dumb blond or an easy lay."

Stephanie gave her an understanding look. "What about Stephen Rutherford? Ever hear from him?"

"Now there's someone I haven't thought about in a while."

"I was certain he'd be the one. He was successful, good looking and wealthy."

"I remember you using a similar phrase to describe Estil."

"We were kids then. Besides, the Rutherfords are old money. The two of you looked great together. Didn't the family approve?"

"I had no problems with his family. Matter of fact, I still exchange Christmas cards with his mother. He's a confirmed bachelor."

Stephanie gave a knowing nod. "Why are the good-looking ones always gay?"

Claudia winked. "Steve may be a lot of things, but gay isn't one of them."

"Then what happened?"

"I just told you. We had great fun going to Broadway openings and concerts, sailed, spent weekends at his house in the Hamptons. I loved being with him, but I wanted marriage and children. "

"And he didn't?"

"Bingo. Once I realized he'd never change, I ended it." She noted Stephanie's disappointed frown. "I told you not to ask."

"But you're still looking for Mr. Right, aren't you?"

"Waiting would be a better description."

"Well, he'll come along, you'll see."

Stephanie smiled and hummed her way through the rest of the afternoon. When Claudia questioned her about it, she said, "Just feeling happy, I suppose."

She'd known Stephanie too long not to know something was up.

The reunion committee chose the school gymnasium for the dinner dance. Sufficiently large, the gym had a stage at one end and a sound system if they needed it.

The school's colors were crimson and gold. Caterers covered each table with a red tablecloth and added a centerpiece of dried flowers sprayed gold with matching candles. Steam tables for the buffet lined the back in front of folded-up bleachers.

Stephanie fluttered around the room like a mother hen counting her chicks. Del and Claudia watched her flit from table to table refolding napkins, smoothing tablecloths and aligning silverware. Satisfied, she pulled a stack of place cards out of her purse and began distributing them.

"The row of small round tables across the front is reserved for committee members," Del said. "You're sitting with us."

"I asked Stephanie to put me in the back. I don't want to be on display."

"What if we took the one on the far end?"

Claudia supposed it would do. The table was set for four. After giving Claudia her choice of seats, Del tilted the chair beside her against the table.

"Who's that for?"

"Steph just said hold it."

Claudia watched people arrive, smiling and waving to old friends and classmates. She wondered if Jeremy would attend. She hoped so. They hadn't seen each other since that horrible day when he'd dropped in unannounced. She shuddered, remembering the messy house and how awful she'd looked.

She knew he'd become a doctor and medical researcher. She also knew he'd married, had a son and that his wife died. She'd cried for him the day Stephanie gave her the news. She sent flowers, received a polite card back and nothing since.

Being committee chair gave Stephanie the right to worry and she'd started out her usual bossy self, barking orders and double-checking everything. Once things got underway, Claudia expected her to settle down. Instead, she grew more agitated. Claudia saw Stephanie glance at the door for the umpteenth time and wondered.

Stephanie's pensive look suddenly changed to a wide grin. Following her eyes, Claudia saw the reason. Even in the shadows, she recognized Jeremy's easy gait. An unexpected surge of delight rippled through her.

"Sorry I'm late," he said. "Trevor couldn't settle down."

Stephanie removed a place card from her purse. "So now I have to call you Doctor?"

"Call me Germy, like you always did."

"How have you been, Jeremy?" Claudia offered her hand. "It's been a long time."

He clasped her hand between his. Their eyes met and he smiled. "You look lovely tonight, MJ."

Over the next hour the two of them inched their chairs closer until they nearly touched. Candles flickered on the tables and soft music played in the background. Ignoring everything and everyone, they conversed in hushed tones punctuated by her occasional soft laughter.

When Jeremy rested his arm on the table, Claudia walked her fingers over and traced patterns on the back of his hand. "I've thought of you often," she said.

Stephanie noticed and nudged Del under the table. The band came on stage and Jeremy asked Claudia to dance. Stephanie watched him lead her to the floor with an arm around her shoulder and grinned with satisfaction.

Table talk rose to a boisterous roar when the band took a break. People milled about, stopping to visit. No one paid attention to the empty bandstand, or the dark figure moving across the stage with a high-powered flashlight in his left hand.

He wobbled, stumbled then caught himself. Staggering up to the microphone stand, he gave it a hard jerk. "Is this thing on? Hi kids. Is everybody having fun?"

Stephanie's mouth dropped. Del left to summon security.

Claudia watched the flashlight's beam move around the room knowing she was the object of Estil's search. Jeremy's arm went around her shoulder just as the light fell on them. They automatically raised a hand, shielding their eyes.

"I knew she was here somewhere." Estil moved the light to Jeremy. "Well for cryin' out loud, Germy's there with her. How's the old pill-pusher?"

Estil lost his balance and reeled backwards. His light swayed wildly when he bumped into the drum stand, sending cymbals crashing. Cursing, he staggered back to the microphone.

"Germy's got himself one hot date." He moved the flashlight in circles around Claudia. "There she is folks, the precious virgin Mary."

Jeremy shoved his chair back. "It's time to go."

Estil's light followed them. "Ol' Germy thinks he's gonna get laid."

Light from the hallway flooded into the dark room when Jeremy pressed the bar on the exit door.

"Don't bet on it. She's gelded better men than you," Estil hollered after them.

~ 39 ~

Jeremy's arm remained around Claudia's shoulder until they reached the parking lot. "Do you have a car?"

She shook her head and blotted her eyes with a tissue. "I have one rented, but I left it at Stephanie's."

"Should I take you to Stephanie's house?"

She nodded and slipped into the seat when he opened the door. Jeremy came around and eased his lanky frame behind the wheel. Resting his elbow on the back of the seat, he glanced over at her.

"You know, that dance will go on for several hours. And, since Stephanie's on the organizing committee, she and Del probably have to stay until the bitter end. We've got time on our hands."

The basement door where she used to wait after football games swung open. Two policemen emerged dragging Estil. Hands cuffed behind his back, he stumbled along muttering curses.

"What if we went somewhere and talked?" Jeremy asked. "I hate to leave you feeling so low."

"What did you have in mind?"

"I suppose 'Your place or mine?' is out of the question since neither of us has a place."

In the dim light of the school parking lot, grinning the way he was, Jeremy looked exactly as she remembered him. For an instant, she was sitting across from her Chemistry lab partner. The fondness she'd felt for Jeremy in high school and college came rushing back.

"After that scene, I'd prefer it be someplace private."

Jeremy turned the key. "Hennick's Hill, it is."

She reached across and patted his knee. "If I thought you were the least bit serious, I'd get out now."

They drove through town, neither saying much. When Jeremy left the city limits and continued into the country, she began to wonder. Ahead in the dark the lighted sign of a country market glowed like a beacon. Jeremy pulled in.

"Why are we stopping?"

"Only take a minute," he said. "I'll get us a Coke."

Jeremy disappeared into the store. She passed the time studying the rusting chewing tobacco and feed signs nailed to the building.

They'd been driving again for several minutes when she asked, "Are you lost?"

"I sometimes become temporarily disoriented for varying periods of time, but I've never been lost."

"Then where in the world are you headed?"

"Ever seen a moonbow?"

"You want to go to Cumberland Falls?"

"We can talk on the way. It'll be fun provided things come together the way they're supposed to."

"I'm wearing a dress and heels."

"Don't worry. The path is graded and paved."

Claudia got out of the car and looked around. "They've got a crowd tonight."

"They usually do. This is one of the few places in the world where you can see a moonbow, and only when the conditions are right." He squinted into the sky. "And I'm pre-t-ty sure this is going to be a special evening."

Taking her by the arm, Jeremy led the way to the observation area below the falls. As they walked he explained that as a young man he came every chance he got with the elusive goal of photographing a moonbow.

"It's sort of a magical process," he explained. "The sky has to be clear and there can't be any ground fog. You need a good flow of water over the falls so the mist coming off the river is just right. And, most important of all, it only happens one or two days either side of a full moon."

Jeremy called it right. The night was perfect, clear and cloudless. Trees along the eastern ridge stood silhouetted in front of the bright, rising moon. A murmur of excitement rippled through the crowd as the moon crested the trees and cast shafts of brightness toward them.

"Any minute now," Jeremy whispered to her from behind. He stepped closer, resting his hands on her shoulders. She did what felt natural and leaned back against him. When he slipped his arms around her waist, she clasped his hands in hers.

Moments later, a graceful arc of color sparkled from the base of the falls to the adjoining cliff. Claudia smiled, knowing her mother experienced a similar sight on her honeymoon.

They spent the return trip catching up on each other's life. In a short time they'd re-established the camaraderie they enjoyed in college. The sudden closeness she felt for Jeremy made her think of something else, something she was reluctant to broach.

They turned onto Stephanie's street. When he parked in front of the house, she took a deep, cleansing breath. "I had a wonderful time tonight in spite of the way it started. I'll always remember seeing the moonbow with you. It meant more than you can imagine."

"I'm glad you enjoyed it. It's been great seeing you. We should have stayed in touch."

She saw his hand move to open the door and stopped him. "Jeremy, there's something I want to suggest. I know we haven't seen each other in a long time. If you say no, I'll understand."

"Fair enough."

"I'm hesitating because, well, this may seem premature. You see, it's kind of personal." She'd begun wringing her hands.

"It could be embarrassing if word got around."

He waited.

She nibbled at the edge of her lower lip. "I, uh, have this foundation. It's my way of doing what needs to be done around here without leaving my footprints all over it."

His smile encouraged her to continue.

"I wondered if you would serve on my Board of Directors."

She plunged ahead, not giving Jeremy time to answer. "It's no big deal. It's a small board, my brothers, my banker and an investment advisor. We meet twice a year, alternating between Washington and Lexington. I reserve a meeting room at a hotel and the others come in the night before. All your expenses would be covered and each member is paid an honorarium for attending."

"I'd be happy to help any way I can."

She gave a sigh of relief. "How long are you going to be in Bly?"

"We're here for a week. I wanted to give Trevor time with my folks."

"I'm driving to Lexington tomorrow to see Brent. Could you tag along? He can give you a heads-up on foundation business." She frowned. "We'd have to stay over. Brent and Linda have room, but if you're not comfortable with that, I'll pay for a hotel."

"Can Trevor come too?"

"Sure, why not?" She leaned across the seat and kissed him on the cheek.

~ 40 ~

Claudia, Jeremy and Trevor wound through and around the Cumberland Mountains heading for Lexington. When they reached I-75, she headed north, set the cruise control and glanced into the rearview mirror. Trevor was slumped in his car seat, dozing. He looked like a miniature Jeremy except for his expressive brown eyes, which Jeremy said came from his mother.

Jeremy stared out the window, daydreaming.

"A penny for your thoughts."

He looked like a little boy caught with his hand in the cookie jar. "I was recalling the last time you and I drove this route together and how much has changed."

"It was our freshmen year at UK."

"Strange how life tosses you around. We both had things mapped out, but fate had other ideas."

She changed lanes, making room for a semi coming up the ramp. They lapsed into silence as they each explored memories and possibilities.

"Jeremy."

He turned.

"You've said very little about your wife. If you don't mind, I'd like to know more."

"What do you want to know?"

"Whatever you feel like sharing."

"Teresa was the most upbeat person I've ever known." He twisted in the seat to check on Trevor. "To her every day was a gift waiting to be opened."

Claudia smiled.

Jeremy's eyes sparkled when he spoke of his dead wife. "People were sometimes taken aback when they met her. They thought her enthusiasm and optimism were an act. But what you saw was what you got."

"How did you meet?

"She was in residency at Johns Hopkins when I was completing my degree."

"So you were both physicians."

"She was an OB/GYN. There was never any doubt in her mind what she wanted to do. The potential for problems in the delivery room has caused many physicians to shy away from delivering babies. As our society becomes increasingly litigious, it makes good economic sense, but that never stopped Teresa."

Jeremy turned to stare out the window and Claudia concentrated on the road.

"There are clouds on the horizon," he said. "Wonder if it's going to rain?"

"Nothing in the forecast, but you never know." She could make small talk if that's what he needed.

Jeremy took a deep breath and re-checked the back seat. "She was returning from delivering a baby the night she died. Her service called. She went in and finished at the hospital a little before two. I told her 'If you're tired, stay over.' When I heard a knock at the door, I thought she'd locked her keys in the car. Instead it was the State Police. A drunk driver ran a stop sign and plowed into the driver's side of her car." His jaw tightened. "She never had a chance."

Claudia placed her hand over his.

"It'll be two years this July." He motioned toward the back seat. "Trevor wasn't even 18 months old. He never got a chance to know her."

Jeremy faced the window again.

Claudia glanced over at him.

He felt her gaze and turned.

"I sense there's more, something you're not telling me."

"I've never told anyone. Not my parents, not her parents, no one."

She kept her eyes fixed on the car ahead, steering with one

hand, holding his with the other.

"When Teresa died, she was pregnant with our second child. We'd just found out. Given what happened, I felt knowing would only cause everyone additional grief."

"And so you've carried around this wonderful, terrible news for nearly two years without sharing it?"

His chin dropped to his chest.

"I'm so sorry, Jeremy. Sorry for Teresa, sorry for you, sorry for Trevor. I can only imagine how difficult it's been."

Linda turned to Claudia and whispered, "I think I know a girl who's been bitten by the lovebug."

Claudia and her sister-in-law, Linda, fixed snacks while Jeremy and Brent discussed foundation business and the kids watched TV.

"What in the world made you say that? Jeremy and I have known each other for years. We're just renewing an old friendship."

"Wipe that guilty look off your face." Linda pointed through the doorway. "I was talking about what's going on in the family room."

Claudia peeked in and grinned. Her two-year-old niece, Kathy, had snuggled into a chair beside Jeremy's son, Trevor. While he watched cartoons she spent most of her time staring at Trevor with stars in her eyes.

"Bu-u-ut, as long as the cat's out of the bag, Jeremy does seem really nice." The tone of Linda's voice brought back images of high school girls sitting in the bleachers discussing boyfriends. "Brent said you two went to the prom together."

"Did he also mention we were married for a short while?" Claudia withheld the clarifying explanation for several moments savoring the startled expression on her sister-in-law's face. "It was in our senior year Living Skills class," she said, laughing. "Jeremy and I were partners in the lesson section dealing with marital issues."

"Well, Jeremy's got everything going for him. Not only is he nice looking, but he's a doctor t' boot. He'll make a great catch for somebody." Linda smacked the countertop. "Why not you? It's high time you settled down."

"Is this where I get the, *You're not getting any younger*, speech? Or do you lean more towards the, *Haven't you always said you wanted children*, side of things?"

"Sheesh! Forget I said anything. I didn't mean to interfere." Linda jerked the plastic wrap off a vegetable tray. "I was only making conversation."

"I'm sorry, Lindy. I didn't mean to come off like Super Bitch. You're right on all counts." Claudia sighed, rocking on her feet. "The timing's just not right. He's a widower and I worry he's not ready to move on."

"Then let me set your mind at ease." Linda rested on her elbows and looked at her across the island bar. "I've seen the way he looks at you. The way your fingers find each other's when you think no one's watching. I was looking out the window this afternoon when you two came along the trail hand-in-hand. Somebody would have to be blind not to read your body language."

Claudia frowned.

Linda raised her hands defensively. "Okay, so I was spying. Get a gun and shoot me. All I'll say is you could do a lot worse."

~ 41 ~

The morning before she left, Claudia crossed the alley beside the hotel and noticed a pile of discarded clothing beside the Dumpster. She hurried on, muttering to herself about people dumping their trash anywhere and everywhere. It was easily forgotten; she'd seen worse in the alleyways of New York.

For some reason, she couldn't put it out of her mind. A nagging voice urged her to investigate. Investigate what, a pile of trash?

She debated with herself while she waited for a light. Why pick through someone's trash? The light changed. Instead of crossing, she retraced her steps to the alley.

Floating oil reflected a rainbow of colors in the puddles dotting the alleyway. With one arm extended and the fingers of the other tiptoeing along the building, she inched along a narrow sidewalk. Her fingers dislodged flakes of aging paint as she trailed them across a faded Dr. Pepper sign on the wall.

What she'd taken to be discarded clothing now appeared to be an olive-green bag. After double-checking the Dumpster, she charted a safe route around the puddles. As she lifted her leg to take a step the bag quivered. Heart pounding, she raised her purse prepared to bat away any vermin.

She saw hair. Not the gray coat of a rat, but brown hair, long and matted. A head emerged. Claudia gasped and rushed forward.

"Estil, how long have you been here?" She squatted in front of him, resting a hand on his shoulder.

At the sound of her voice, Estil turned and blinked. He smelled of alcohol and sour vomit. His cheekbone bore scabbed-over scrapes from a fall. He studied the neatly manicured fingers gripping his soiled jacket. Inch by inch, his eyes marched up the sleeve, reaching her shoulder and finally her face.

He squinted at her through swollen, blood-shot eyes. "Oh, for cryin' out loud."

"Let me help you up."

He jerked his shoulder away. "I can do it myself."

Estil grabbed the corner of the Dumpster and tried to pull himself up. He swayed and wobbled, sweat beading on his forehead.

He slumped back onto the ground and hung his head. "I can't do it myself."

"Okay, on three." She grabbed hold and counted.

Estil gripped the Dumpster and eyed her like a cornered animal. "What do you want?"

Despite his behavior at the reunion dinner, she found it hard to hate him. No matter what he'd done, he didn't deserve this.

"I want you to come with me."

"Where?"

"You'll see soon enough." She slipped an arm under his and pulled him along. Stumbling forward, he flailed his bad arm at her, trying to shoo her away. She stopped, grabbed the back of his jacket and spun him around. "You better cooperate or I'll slap you silly."

He gave in and lumbered along beside her chuckling to himself.

She led him out of the alley, around the corner and into the hotel. The desk clerk heard their shuffling footsteps and glanced up in time to watch them totter up to the elevator. The door opened and she led Estil inside, ignoring the stares of a gathering crowd.

He rolled against the wall breathing hard. He choked on his laughter. "You should be more discreet. Taking a man to your room in broad daylight might damage your sterling reputation."

"Most of the people in this town already have their minds made up about me."

Once inside her room, Claudia disappeared into the bathroom and turned on the shower.

She emerged with the hotel's plastic laundry sack and handed it to him. "Throw your clothes in here. There are clean towels and a robe in the bathroom." She dug into her purse and slapped a tin of aspirins and a roll of antacids on the counter. "These may help."

Steam billowed out the bathroom door. Claudia reached around the corner and flipped on the exhaust fan. "Take your time. There's an unlimited supply of hot water. I have an errand to run. When I get back, we'll order breakfast."

"Do you have any suitcases?"

The two clerks behind the counter at the town's small department store looked up in surprise. Recognizing her, the younger woman scurried around a corner and returned carrying a canvas bag with zipper and strap handles. "We have these. They come in two sizes; this is the large. We have them in—"

"I'll take it," Claudia said. "Leave it at the counter and follow me." She swiveled her head impatiently. "Where are your men's clothes?"

The clerk ran ahead, leading her to the back of the store.

She surveyed the jeans, estimating Estil's size. She grabbed three pairs, handed them to the clerk and crossed to the shirts. She piled a handful of shirts on top of the jeans then tossed in a couple of sweatshirts for good measure.

"Underwear?"

Arms overflowing, the clerk motioned with her head. "Over there." She ran back to the counter to dump her load while Claudia pulled packages from the display. Tossing them to the clerk, she reached for socks and a belt. She ended her impromptu shopping spree with a chestnut leather bomber jacket and matching shoes.

She packed the clothing into the bag as they scanned it. After signing the credit card slip, she smiled and left, leaving them to wonder.

~ 42 ~

Estil turned when he heard her enter the room. He'd showered, pulled on the robe and begun shaving. The muscular physique of Estil's youth was gone; his chest appeared hollow and sunken under the loosely tied robe. Feeling her gaze, he jerked the robe closed and returned to the mirror.

"You know, I fantasized about the two of us together in a hotel room." He slid the razor along the side his cheek as he spoke.

"Good to see you're feeling better."

He ran his hand over his chin. "I'm still a little ragged around the edges."

"Try this." She placed an extra-large cup of steaming coffee on the counter.

Estil took a long sip. "Where are my clothes?"

"In the incinerator." Seeing his alarmed look, she said, "I checked the pockets. Your wallet's out there on the desk." She dug into the canvas bag and tossed him a new outfit. "Try these on for size."

He came out looking like a new man. "You're good. Everything fits."

"There are shoes there by the chair."

She watched Estil rest the new shoe on his leg and undo the lace. Once he freed it, he knotted one end then re-threaded it starting at the bottom eyelet, criss-crossing as he went. He was repeating the process on the other shoe when he noticed her watching.

"Takes two hands to tie shoes," he explained. "This way there's only one string to deal with." He made a loop, lassoed the other shoelace and gave it a hard tug to tighten the knot.

"I'm impressed."

Estil smiled at her compliment.

"We need to do something with your hair. What if I tied it

back until you can get to the barbershop?"

She clamped a rubber band between her teeth and ran her comb through his long hair, accumulating it in her left hand.

He watched in the mirror. "You're enjoying this, aren't you?"

"Say what?"

"You're enjoying having me depend on you."

"Oh yeah, almost as much as changing a baby's stinky diaper." She jerked his hair through the band with enough force to make him wince.

Estil dug into the room service breakfast, admitting it was the first decent meal he'd had in several days.

"Why aren't you in jail?"

"Stephanie decided not to press charges. She said it'd take more than jail time to straighten me out." He concentrated on the plate. "You didn't deserve the other night, I'm sorry.

"Apology noted and accepted."

"Jeremy's a good guy."

"Yes, Jeremy *is* a good guy."

"In spite of the things I did, I always cared for you, MJ. I still do."

She picked up a water glass, turning it in her hands. "Um... Estil, maybe we shouldn't be talking about this."

"It's all right. Really it is." He chased scrambled eggs around the plate with his fork as he spoke. "I'm not a complete fool. I don't expect you to rush into my arms." He angrily stabbed a piece of sausage. "Arm!"

"You've got to let this go, Estil. You made a mistake; it doesn't matter."

"You think I haven't tried? When something you love doing

is taken away, that's what you do, pretend it never mattered. Lost an arm? No big deal. I've got another one right here." He waved his left one. "Can't anyone see, it did matter!"

"Of course it did. I wasn't referring to your arm. I meant the mistake you made on the field."

"Estil the football hero," he said with a rueful look.

"Don't be so hard on yourself. Under stress you reverted to form. When push comes to shove we are who we are."

He ran his eyes over her expensive clothing and jewelry. "How is it living my life?"

"Nobody can live your life except you."

"So you're telling me you haven't gotten everything you wanted?"

She folded her arms across her chest. "When did this get to be about me?"

He shrugged. "I just asked."

"Okay, then I'll just answer. An opportunity presented itself. I grabbed it. If that makes me superficial, or egotistic, or selfish, so be it. I've worked hard and I'm successful, very successful. For reasons I've never understood, that seems to bother people. I won't let you, or anyone else, make me feel guilty. Is this the life I hoped for? No. All I ever aspired to be was a wife and mother. Money doesn't buy happiness."

"I only meant I'd always dreamed of fame and fortune."

"Stop feeling sorry for yourself. Life's not a candy store. It's not what you get; it's what you give."

"That's easy enough for you to say. I don't have two nickels to rub together."

"Who said it had to be money? Human beings are designed to be conduits. Give what you've got." She gestured toward his feet. "Go to a nursing home and teach a stroke victim how to tie his shoes one-handed."

She sighed and shook her head "But instead of giving, we all behave like a bunch of monkeys with our grubby little hands stuck in a trap. We hang on to that nut for dear life afraid we'll never get another. Truth is, we're like wells. More water can't flow in until some of what's already there is taken out and used by someone else."

Chastened, Estil returned to his plate.

"Why didn't you go to work for your father?"

"He didn't want anything to do with me after I became a national joke. Not that it matters now. Estep Mining is nothing but a bad memory."

"I'm sorry about your father."

Estil took a deep breath. "For a while Pop managed to sweep the violations under the rug, but the inspectors knew where there's smoke there's fire. Then those six men died. You must've heard."

"I did. It was on the news for days. After they quit covering it I'd hear bits and pieces from Stephanie or Weezie now and then, but I was out of the country a lot."

"It may have dropped out of the news, but it didn't go away. The Kentucky Office of Mine Safety shone a bright light into every nook and cranny. Eventually they stumbled onto Pop's dirty laundry and they didn't like what they found, not even a little bit."

"So Daddy's accident..."

"Yep, Pop arranged your father's accident."

She rose out of her seat. "You knew and never told me?"

"I only found out years later. By then I didn't think your knowing would make much difference."

Closure always seemed such an elusive thing and she'd found it lying in an alleyway. Knowing the truth didn't bring the satisfaction she always imagined it would. Oh, she'd tell Brian and Brent, of course. They deserved to know. But Estil was right; it really didn't make much difference all these years later.

"And then they closed Blossom Gulch No. 3?"

"The insurance people jumped into the fray with the Mine

Safety folks and OSHA. The trio sharpened their knives, and went after Pop like they were butcherin' a fat hog. What they didn't get was divvied-up by attorneys, settlements, ex-wives, and creditors."

"And so, facing a prison sentence, your father put a gun to his head."

Estil looked away. "Anyone contemplating suicide ought to give a little thought to the poor SOB who's finds 'em."

"How are you getting by?"

"I get a disability check because of the arm. Ironic, isn't it? The biggest screw-up of my life supports me."

"You know you need to go to the Rescue Mission and get help."

"They kicked me out. I'm persona non grata." He shot her an angry glance. "What do you know about the Mission, anyway?"

"They'll take you back," she said, sidestepping his question.

"No they won't."

"Yes they will."

The reason for her certitude was a well-guarded secret. Only the Rescue Mission's Executive Director knew her foundation provided most of their annual budget. She handled her dealings with them the same way she handled the renovation at the high school and her support for Hospice and the Food Pantry, quietly and anonymously. The last thing she wanted was her name plastered all over town.

~ 43 ~

Jeremy attended the next board meeting and offered his input. He and Claudia formed a committee of two and continued meeting to evaluate his suggestions. They kept in close touch over the next few months, getting together in Baltimore anytime she wasn't traveling.

Foundation work gradually receded into the background as they rekindled the close and caring relationship they'd had in college.

One evening after he'd tucked Trevor into bed, Jeremy caught himself fantasizing about her. It shocked him. There'd been no one in his life, or even his imagination, since Teresa. The pain of her death and the difficult recovery had left him feeling asexual.

Spending time with Claudia made him realize how lonely he'd been and opened the possibility of loving again.

London

"Why bother with a taxi, my penthouse is only a stone's throw away." Cole's hand slipped under the table and up the side of her thigh.

"Not in a restaurant." Claudia pushed his hand away and smoothed her skirt. "How many times must I tell you, I'm not ready to sleep with you?"

He seemed genuinely hurt by her refusal. "What must I do to prove my affection?"

"Your affection or obsession?"

"I beg your pardon?"

"All the presents, the jewelry and flowers aren't necessary."

"How can I show you I care?"

"I care for you as well, but why must you always pressure me for sex?"

"We're both adults, surely you've..."

Anger flashed in Claudia's eyes. "I'm not here to discuss my sexual history. Can't you see your preoccupation with sex is an impediment to our relationship? When I'm ready, you'll know it."

"Is there someone else?"

"That's it." She reached for her purse. "You've exceeded the bounds of good taste."

Cole quickly backtracked, apologizing profusely.

Paparazzi attacked them when they left the restaurant hand -in-hand. Photographers seemed to materialize whenever she and Cole were together. Since the car hadn't been brought around, he suggested they humor them. Left with no other option, she posed with him while they snapped away.

He accompanied her to her hotel room and didn't ask to come in as he usually did, which pleased her.

"I'm just a love-struck teenager around you," he whispered before they kissed goodnight.

The contrast between Jeremy and Michael couldn't be greater.

Jeremy was like wearing a pair of her favorite weekend loafers. Slip them on in the morning and they'd get you where you wanted to go in ease and comfort all day. She put down her hairbrush and smiled. Jeremy was an easy-keeper.

Michael, on the other hand, reminded her of a pair of new high heels. Nothing wrong with them, they matched your outfit and looked dressy, but by the end of the evening your feet would be killing you. Michael was high-maintenance.

Claudia pulled the covers up and grinned. Jeremy also came with a bonus, Trevor.

"Why don't you and Trevor come to New York?"

Jeremy lowered his newspaper and glanced over it at her. As usual, Trevor was with his grandparents for the weekend.

They'd eaten brunch at a dockside restaurant, walked the waterfront then gone back to his house to read the Sunday paper together.

"Where would we stay?"

Was he honestly perplexed, she wondered, or searching for an excuse not to go?

"There are lots of hotels in New York, but you can stay with me." Reading his expression, she added, "I'll give you and Trevor the other master bedroom."

"The other master bedroom?"

"I bought the condo next door a few years ago, knocked out some walls and combined it with mine. I have three bedrooms now, two of them with their own bath."

He rubbed his chin. "New York? It's a big step."

"What do you mean a big step?"

"Just that it's a big step. Why do you want us to come to New York?"

She dropped onto the ottoman in front of him and began rubbing his feet. "Look how often I've come to Baltimore. Isn't it time you reciprocated? Trevor will love the Central Park Zoo. Don't be such a stick in the mud."

"Who are you inviting, me or Trevor?"

She stretched up and kissed him. "Silly boy, I'm inviting you both. I thought if you wouldn't come for your own sake, maybe you would for Trevor's. I'll be in Washington Tuesday and Wednesday meeting with Brian." She propped herself up on one elbow. "I could stop and pick you guys up on the way back."

"Does she really got her own airplane with a pilot 'n' everything?" Trevor asked.

"For the hundredth time, yes, she really has her own plane."

He spun his fingers in circles. "With propellers that go so fast you can't see 'em?"

“No propellers. Her plane’s a jet. It has two engines in the back.”

“Why didn’t you tell me this stuff?”

“It didn’t seem important.”

Trevor’s eyes grew wide with excitement. “Do you think she’ll let me fly it?”

Jeremy shook his head. “It’s not like the ones they have at the fair. Only grown-ups fly real airplanes.”

“How come you always call her MJ?”

“That’s her name, Mary Jane.”

“Isn’t her name Claudia?”

“It is...sort of.” Seeing the confused look on his son’s face, Jeremy explained in a way he thought Trevor would understand. “You know Superman, right?”

Trevor did.

“Well, when he’s a regular guy his name is Clark Kent. She’s like that. When MJ’s on TV or in magazines, her name is Claudia Monet.”

“You mean she’s got X-ray eyes, too?”

The door opened letting in a rush of air and the whine of jet engines. Claudia smiled when they looked up. “Hi guys, ready to go?”

Trevor walked onto the tarmac and stared up at the sleek business jet waiting to take them to New York. His mouth dropped. “Whoa. You weren’t kidding. She’s really got her own airplane.”

Claudia waited at the bottom of the ramp. As they drew closer, she saluted and said, “Welcome aboard, gentlemen. I’ll be your hostess today.”

Trevor grabbed her hand and scampered up the steps, leaving Jeremy to carry the bags.

~ 44 ~

New York

The nearer they got to her apartment the more nervous Jeremy became. She thought at first it was the heavy traffic, but eventually decided it must be something else.

"Is anything wrong?"

"I'm concerned about us sharing a room," Jeremy whispered. His eyes turned in Trevor's direction.

She patted his knee. "We're not sharing a room. You're staying in my apartment as guests. You guys will have your bedroom and I'll have mine." She took his hand and squeezed it. "If you'd rather get a hotel room, you still can."

He shook his head. "Ignore me. I don't know why I'm so nervous."

"Is this respectable enough, Dr. Tilden?" Claudia asked, as they stepped into her expansive condo.

Trevor pushed past, a backpack full of books and toys in one arm and a Teddy Bear under the other. He dumped his load on the sofa and ran to the window. His voice came from behind the drapes. "We're real high up, Dad. Come look at all the bitty cars."

Jeremy reached in and extracted him. "Get your things and put them in the bedroom."

Claudia pointed to a door on their right "You and your Dad will be sleeping in there, Trevor."

Claudia circled the apartment, opening curtains and turning on lights. Jeremy stepped up to the wide French doors opening onto her balcony and stared out at Central Park.

"What a view. I suppose you've lived here so long you hardly notice."

She rested her arm on his shoulder. "Nonsense. In the

spring and summer I eat breakfast on the balcony and in the Fall, the colors take your breath away."

"Hey, Dad, look what I found."

Trevor tottered into the room carrying a large brown cat. He hugged the cat against his stomach with its front legs draped over his arms. Its back half dangled nearly to the floor. The cat's tail swished back and forth and his feet made walking motions in the air.

The cat's coppery eyes went to Claudia. He made a plaintive meow, begging to be rescued. She scooped him out of the boy's arms and led Trevor to the sofa.

"This is my kitty, Mousse." She placed the cat in her lap and smoothed his soft brown fur. Mousse eyed Trevor suspiciously.

Trevor giggled. "That's a funny name." He put his hands on either side of his head. "Kitties don't have horns."

"He's a chocolate Persian. I named him for chocolate mousse."

Trevor seemed confused.

"You don't know what chocolate mousse is, do you?"

"Are they like chocolate Easter bunnies?"

"We'll get you some before you leave." Leaning close, she whispered, "You're going to love it."

Jeremy took Trevor's hand. "C'mon, Partner. Let's wash up for supper."

Halfway through the doorway to their room, Jeremy paused to glance back. "You know, we never saw your bedroom. I bet it has a canopied bed, marbled bath with sunken tub and gold-plated faucets, a wood-burning fireplace, and God-only-knows what else."

Her heart swelled as she watched Jeremy's face crinkle into familiar laugh lines. For a second, time stood still. She felt the sense of expectation she got whenever theater lights dimmed.

For an instant, Jeremy was her husband, Trevor their son and this apartment their home. She felt a sudden schoolgirl rush that turned her knees rubbery. She felt as if she were seeing Jeremy for the first time.

She noticed things she'd overlooked. The relaxed way he leaned against the doorframe, how handsome he looked in twill slacks, turtleneck and sport coat, and the way he didn't mind his sandy-brown hair being slightly windblown.

It took all her self-control not to run across the room, throw her arms around Jeremy and kiss him. They were, after all sleeping together. Umm, well, sort of. I need to splash cold water on my face, she thought. It's too soon for these feelings. Jeremy wasn't ready for a relationship.

Or was he?

She backed through the doorway with a shaky smile. "I guess I'll go into my fabulous marbled sink, turn on the gold-plated tap and freshen-up."

She closed her door slowly, lingering to watch Jeremy turn away. She wished she could read his mind. Or did she? She wouldn't have wanted him to read hers a moment earlier.

They started Thursday morning by going into the studio on the pretext of seeing how Claudia worked. She designed this elaborate ruse to create a surprise for Trevor.

Eighteen months after she began working for Souvanée, Claudia formed her own production company. Producing her commercials gave her control of the process and made good business sense. It grew into a lucrative venture with facilities and production staff on both Coasts serving a long list of clients.

She went in first to make sure they were ready. Ten minutes later, she popped out of the studio and invited them back. Trevor wandered around while she explained things. After he completed his tour, she called him onto stage in front of a green screen to film various action shots. She'd arranged for her postproduction people to add a soundtrack, insert computer-generated graphics and burn the footage onto a DVD.

After leaving the studio, they grabbed lunch from a cart then caught the tram to Roosevelt Island. They finished their day at the Children's Museum.

The rest of the week passed in a blur. On Saturday they stopped for chocolate mousse, which, as promised, Trevor loved. After his bath that evening, he emerged from his bedroom with cowboys galloping around his pajamas and a small book tucked under his arm. He approached Claudia with a shy smile.

"Would you like to read me my bedtime story?"

"I'd love to. What are we reading tonight?"

He handed her *Goodnight Moon.*

Jeremy came out of the kitchen with a glass of water. Trevor took his hand and led him to a chair. "You wait here, Dad." He handed him the paper. "Read this."

After jumping onto the couch to give Jeremy a hug and kiss, he hopped off and slipped his hand into Claudia's.

Trevor folded back his covers, turned on a lamp beside the bed, and slid his pillow aside. "You sit here."

He sat beside her. After studying her in the muted light, he reached up and touched her cheek. "You're real pretty."

"Why, thank you. That's a sweet thing to say." She hugged him.

"My mommy was pretty, too. Dad says so."

"I've seen pictures of her. She was *very* pretty."

"He says you were friends a long time ago."

"We were, in high school."

"Did you know my mommy?"

"No. I didn't."

"A bad man ran into her car. It happened when I was a little kid."

"I'm sorry about your mommy." She slipped her arm around him. "Sometimes sad things happen to all of us."

Trevor stared up at her. "I asked Dad if we could look for a new mommy."

"And what does your Daddy say?"

"He says, 'Maybe someday.' That's always his answer."

Leaving her arm around him, Claudia began reading. Trevor inched closer with each page. By the time they'd passed the page about the bowl of mush, he'd nestled himself tightly against her bosom. She kissed him on top of the head and hugged him, gently rocking. After a few more pages, she closed the book and put it aside. The steady rhythm of his breathing told her he was sound asleep.

She clicked off the lamp, letting the bathroom nightlight throw shadows across the floor. She held him for the longest time, watching him sleep. Realizing Jeremy must wonder where she was, Claudia reluctantly tucked Trevor in and tiptoed away.

Jeremy heard her footsteps and lowered his paper. She came around the sofa squinting in the light.

"Did you have trouble getting him settled in?"

"He was asleep by the time we said good night to the red balloon."

"What took so long?"

She swallowed hard. "He's so precious. I wanted to hold him forever."

Jeremy noticed the sparkle of a tear in her eye and slid beside her. "Thank you." He leaned over and kissed her. "Thank you for tonight and for these last few days. You've been a huge breath of fresh air into our very dull life."

The feelings she had on their first night returned. Along with it came desires so intense and graphic that she would've been embarrassed to share them. An inner voice warned, *Stop now, before it's too late. You'll both be hurt.*

Claudia leaned against him, resting her head on his shoulder. Jeremy snapped off the light and lifted her chin. He kissed her harder and longer. He wasn't saying thank-you now; he was knocking on the door and asking if he could come in.

~ 45 ~

Over the years, Claudia decided relationships follow a natural progression. A series of stages, each built upon greater trust and each with its proper level of intimacy. At some point, lovemaking became an appropriate means of sharing the feelings between two people. She was a big girl. She knew sometimes it occurred within a marital relationship, and sometimes it didn't.

She'd led a relatively chaste life. She valued herself too much to fall prey to the rampant promiscuity permeating her industry. She heard innuendoes, suggestions and propositions nearly every day, and turned them down. She didn't want intimacy without love.

Then, out of nowhere, Jeremy re-appeared. She never imagined a situation like this. She'd built defenses to protect herself from exploitation and now she found herself afraid of exploiting him.

For both of their sakes, she needed to cool things down. And, for the first time in her life, she found herself questioning her motives. Could Estil have been right? Was she a prude, a cold fish? Did she hide behind an elaborate moral framework to avoid confronting her fears?

She took a deep breath and reached for Jeremy's hands. An unsettling sense of déjà vu swept over her. She'd held Estil's hands this same way the night he tried to rape her.

Claudia looked into Jeremy's eyes and found the reassurance she sought. She lifted his fingertips to her lips and kissed them. "Jeremy, we need to talk before we, well, before."

He nodded.

Don't mention Teresa, she warned herself. *Whatever you do, do not say that name.*

"I've always enjoyed your company. Even in high school we communicated easily. We were friends then and I think we've rekindled that friendship."

He pushed away. "Friends? So this is a brush-off. The part

where you politely let me down? It's been great fun, but it was just one of those things?"

"No, not at all. I'm feeling much more than just friendship for you now. Earlier this week, when we first got home, I felt something. A little tingle, a spark."

"Yeah, I felt it too. I don't think your light switches are properly grounded."

She poked him in the ribs. "You aren't making this any easier." She took his hands again. "These last few days have been wonderful, but I worry. I don't want to push too hard and get the cart before the horse. I don't want to put what we have at risk, take you places you're not ready to go."

"We're both adults. There's something here. You felt it. I felt it. It could be nothing but a short in the electrical system. Or maybe it's more, much more. I'm willing to find out if you are."

She took Jeremy by the hand and led him to her bedroom.

"I wish you didn't have to go." Her fingers trailed across Jeremy's shoulders and down his arm as he sat up on the edge of the bed. She clutched his hand in hers, not wanting to sever the connection between them.

He turned and leaned back to kiss her. "It would be heaven to fall asleep with you in my arms."

"Someday," she whispered, "someday."

Jeremy began gathering the clothes he'd strewn on the floor. "I could stay. He's young and wouldn't think anything of it."

"No. Trevor expects you in his bedroom when he wakes and that's where you'll be." She made shooing motions with her hands. "Go. I can't be this strong much longer."

Claudia fell asleep thinking of Jeremy. The memory of being in his arms enriched her dreams and she awoke wanting him. Only when she touched the cold sheets beside her, did she recall insisting he return to Trevor's room. Even though she knew it'd been the right thing to do, she regretted it. Every cell in her body ached for him.

She didn't want to end up old and alone, sleeping with her cat. She wanted to curl around the man she loved. Lie in bed at midnight, talking and touching. Make love in the morning as the sunlight crept in.

She wanted someone waiting on the other side of the door when she came home. And she wanted babies. Tiny cherubs with round little bottoms, tummies full of giggles and soft skin that smelled oh so nice. She wanted to hold them and cuddle them, diaper and dress them and rock them as they fed at her breast.

Claudia replayed events of the previous evening in her mind as she showered. She suddenly gasped and dropped her washcloth. The bar of soap squirted out of her hand and thumped against the tub.

They hadn't used any protection.

Teresa was pregnant when she died, Claudia remembered, so she and Jeremy weren't using birth control. And, since she was the first woman he'd been with since Teresa's death, it probably hadn't occurred to him.

I could be pregnant.

Joining the tips of her thumbs, she brought her index fingers together forming a heart and pressed it to her abdomen. Here was where her baby would be. She watched the warm water sheet across the patch of skin her fingers outlined. It would grow as the baby grew, swelling to contain and nurture the life inside. She smiled and leaned back, rinsing conditioner out of her hair.

Claudia was deep into imagining what color hair and eyes a child of theirs would have when her brow knotted. How would Jeremy react? She turned in the warm spray and shrugged. She'd go it alone if she had to. Although she'd never planned on being an unwed mother, she certainly had sufficient resources.

~ 46 ~

Claudia dressed quickly and hurried into the kitchen to start breakfast. She whistled to herself as she set the table. When Jeremy and Trevor came out of their bedroom, she glanced up and smiled. "Hi there, Big Guy, did you sleep well?"

Jeremy stretched and returned her smile. "I slept like a log."

Trevor grabbed his father's pant leg and gave it a tug. When their eyes met Trevor gave him a hard frown. "She was talking to me, Dad. Don't you know I'm the big guy around here?"

Claudia chuckled. "You can both be my big guys. Okay?"

Father and son sat at the round table with Claudia between them. Jeremy scooted his chair close, pressing his leg against hers. Trevor sat in his chair tapping his heels and munching sausage. As he ate, he periodically checked Claudia's hand to see if it still rested on his father's. A satisfied smile lit his face each time he did.

As she cleared the table, Claudia noticed Trevor arranging his souvenirs along the couch. She walked over and knelt on the floor beside him. "How was your visit to New York?"

He spun around and threw his arm around her neck. "It was great, just like you promised it would be."

"Well, I'm pleased you had a good time. Did you get to see everything you wanted to see?"

"Everything but the Umpire State Building. Can we go there right now and ride the elevator to the top?"

Claudia patted his hand. "I'm sorry, Sweetheart. We have to be to the airport by noon. I'm afraid there isn't time. We'll go on your next visit."

"Promise?"

She crossed her heart. "The next time you come to visit, the first thing on our list will be the Empire State Building. Okay?"

Trevor couldn't hide his disappointment. "I guess so."

"Stay right there. I have something for you." She disappeared into her bedroom and returned carrying a snow globe with a miniature New York skyline inside. The Empire State Building stood in the center of the group. She pulled Trevor into her lap and handed it to him.

He studied it then held it out to his father. "Look, Dad, it's the Umpire State Building."

"I bought this globe during my first week in New York. I want you to have it. It'll remind you of my promise to take you to the Empire State Building."

Claudia's last words to Jeremy as she hugged him good-bye in Baltimore were, "See you Friday in Washington."

The foundation had a Board Meeting scheduled at the end of the week and knowing she'd see him again in five days made his leaving almost bearable. She'd count the minutes until they were together again.

New York

Claudia considered calling Rudy from the airport, but didn't. The way she felt she wouldn't be fit company for man or beast. Instead, she went home, stopped in the lobby to grab her mail and got into the elevator long-faced and glum.

Her dark apartment matched her mood. She tossed the mail aside unread and snapped on a light. Artificial illumination might drive away the shadows, but it couldn't relieve the emptiness she felt. She sat her purse on the Hoosier cabinet in her entryway and hung up her jacket.

She glanced over at the oak cabinet full of doors and drawers and bins. It'd been in her parent's kitchen since before she was born. She entrusted it, along with her mother's treadle sewing machine, to Weezie's safe keeping when they sold the house. She moved them to New York after buying her condo. These pieces of her past had always been a comfort. Even they seemed to have lost their restorative magic.

Her eyes went to the framed picture of her parents on their wedding day. She quietly stared. They looked so young and hopeful.

Did I do the right thing, Momma?

Mousse looked up expectantly. She bent to pet him, but it wasn't pets he wanted. He turned away, walked into the guest bedroom and meowed several times. Then he made a thorough search of the living room, peeking behind the drapes and under the coffee table. He padded throughout the apartment meowing around doorways and checking closets.

He felt it, too.

Something was missing. *Someone* was missing. It wasn't the same inviting place it had been on Wednesday. In the years since she and Marmalade spent their first night in their little room at The Markle she had never felt so utterly, desperately alone as she did then.

She missed the echo of Trevor's laughter and found herself mimicking Mousse. She lazily wandered from room-to-room looking for...she didn't know what. In the guest bedroom she noticed a pair of eyes peeking out from behind the bed. She smiled and reached for Trevor's rumpled teddy bear, Mr. Teddy Bumpkins.

She carried the bear into her bedroom and dialed Jeremy's number. When she asked for Trevor, Jeremy said he was under the bed looking for his bear. When Trevor came on the line she told him about a teddy who tried to run away to New York, but got caught and promised to return him on Friday.

Baltimore

Jeremy went downstairs after Trevor settled in. He picked up a medical journal, leafed through the pages before tossing it aside unread. He wandered into the kitchen and opened the refrigerator. Nothing looked good. He returned to the living room carrying a glass of water, sat it on a table but never drank it.

Jeremy opened the blind and stared out at the dark sky. He hadn't felt this forlorn since the first weeks after Teresa's death. It's Sunday night, he reminded himself. Weekend's over. He looked forward to the hustle and bustle of work the next day.

Things felt simple in New York. How did everything suddenly get so complicated? You knew the risks when you agreed to go, he told himself. Or did he? He wasn't prepared for the rush he'd felt when they kissed. Looking back, he remembered wanting her more than anything in the world.

Now what?

His pain drew Jeremy to the bookcase. He rummaged in his pocket for his keys, unlocked an upper cabinet and contemplated the row of VCR tapes. He'd watched them so often he knew every movement, every gesture, smile and giggle. He ran his finger along the row of worn boxes, realizing he hadn't watched any of them in nearly a year.

He slid a tape into the VCR and settled back on the couch. The dark room flickered with the familiar brightness of Teresa's smile. He stared at the screen with tears in his eyes. She looked so alive, so vibrant.

He 'd loved her so much. How could he have betrayed her so easily?

~ 47 ~

Washington

Claudia arrived at the board meeting with a briefcase in one hand and a chubby teddy bear under the other arm. She positioned an extra chair at the end of the table and propped Teddy Bumpkins in it. Crossing the room, she looked back at him, shook her head and returned to the bear, re-adjusting and checking again. After several attempts, she managed to position him with one of his paws resting against the side of his head as if in deep thought.

When Brian and Brent came in, she threw an arm around their shoulders and gave them each a peck on the cheek

Brent chuckled and began distributing financial packets.

Brian looked from her happy grin to the bear in the chair and back again. "Funny," I remembered Germy being taller. He wore more clothes, too."

"We've got two new members." Extending her arm, she made an elaborate bow. "May I present the esteemed and well-traveled raconteur, Mr. Teddy Bumpkins."

"Be sure to have him fill-out a W-9 so Brent can keep the books straight." Brian tossed his briefcase into a chair and headed for the coffee service.

She glanced over at Brent. "What did you do him? He's wearing one of Daddy's frowny faces."

Brent shrugged and resumed work on an easel display.

Claudia joined Brian at the coffee. "Boy! Somebody sure got up on the wrong side of the bed. If everyone's as grumpy as you are, it's going to be a long day." She pointed to the bear. "I'm returning Trevor's teddy bear via Jeremy. He left it in my apartment when they visited last weekend."

"Weekend visits now, hmm?"

"Yeah, got a problem with that?" She waited a moment savoring Brian's shocked expression then laughed. "See. You're not the only one who can be grumpy." Lifting her head, she tossed her blond hair aside. "But I don't want to be grumpy, so I'm going to be happy instead."

She sashayed over to her place at the head of the table, looked back over her shoulder and winked.

Jeremy arrived on time and conservatively dressed. He remained studious and businesslike throughout the day's meeting. He'd prepared a presentation and distributed notes as he spoke.

During breaks, Jeremy avoided small talk and responded with polite smiles. He treated Brian and Brent with the same remote professionalism. Claudia assumed his behavior reflected his relative newness to the board.

She anticipated having private time with Jeremy on Friday evening, but after dinner she looked around and he was nowhere to be seen..

The next morning the Board followed their agenda and ended the Saturday planning session on time. The members visited with each other briefly, then drifted away. For the first time, Claudia and Jeremy were alone.

"I didn't think they'd ever leave." Moving behind him, she leaned over his shoulder and kissed his cheek. "I can't stop thinking about last weekend." She massaged his shoulders. "You're all in knots, Sweetheart, relax."

"Last weekend's been on my mind, too." He kept his eyes on the report folder in front of him, poking it and tapping his pen.

"Stand up so I can get a good look at you."

He did as she commanded.

Claudia stepped close, wrapped her arms around him and rubbed her body against his.

Jeremy remained rigid, arms dangling at his side.

"What's the matter, worried someone might come in? Give me a little hug. It's all right, honest. If we hear the doorknob turn,

I'll jump back and pretend I don't know you."

"It's not that."

She hopped onto the table letting her skirt ride up and not caring that it did.

Jeremy's eyes instinctively went to the slice of creamy thigh above the top of her hose. He stared for a moment then forced his eyes away.

"What is it? You're on a late flight; we've got time." She laughed. "We'll get a room and I'll make sure you go back to Baltimore tired, but happy."

He stepped back from the table. "You're not making this any easier."

"The only way I could make it any easier is if I lay down on the table." She dropped back onto one elbow and pointed at the room's entry. "Make you a deal. If the door locks, my underwear comes off."

Jeremy took a deep breath and waved at a chair. "Sit down, MJ. We have things to discuss."

Blushing, she jumped off the table and straightened her skirt. She sat on the edge of the chair, back straight, knees together and hands folded in her lap. Panic danced in her stomach as she waited for him to speak.

"As I said earlier, I've been giving a lot of thought to what happened between us last weekend."

His tone said everything. She barely heard his long-winded explanations, rationalizations and apologies. Instead, she spent the time thinking about what a fool she'd made of herself. She should've seen it coming the moment he walked in the door and shook her hand. She'd written it off as mere formality on his part, concern they not appear too friendly in front of Brian and Brent. The signs were all there and she chose not to see them.

"I told you in New York we didn't have to move so fast. Things were going along fine before that. Let's take a step back, return to where we were, and pretend it never happened."

"We both know that won't work." Jeremy shook his head as he paced. "We can't undo what's been done." He pointed at the tabletop. "You more than proved it a few minutes ago by offering to do a striptease."

She snapped her fingers. "And so, just like that you throw it all away? What's going on here, Jeremy? Do you think just because I'm pretty I don't hurt? Well, I've got news for you. If you cut me, I bleed."

"It was a mistake for you to seduce me in New York." Jeremy turned his back. "I don't think we should see each other. You're more than I can handle right now."

She leaped out of the chair. "Just one doggoned minute, Buster." Grabbing his shoulder, she spun him around. "Don't lay the blame at my doorstep. In case you've forgotten, you're the one who wanted to test the wiring."

"It was a figure of speech."

"You want to end it, we'll end it. But don't go wimping-out and try to paint me as the seductress. I didn't invite you to New York to get you into my bed."

Claudia snatched her briefcase off the table. Noticing a package sticking out, she removed the thin, gift-wrapped box and offered it to Jeremy.

"I brought this for Trevor. Will you see that he gets it?"

Jeremy took it from her and she stormed away without another word.

Baltimore

"What is it?"

"A gift from MJ. Go ahead, open it."

After stripping off the wrapping and cellophane tape, he folded back the flaps and removed a card.

"Care Bears!" He waved the card in the air for his father to see. "How did she know I love Care Bears? She knows just about everything, doesn't she, Dad?"

A smile swept across Trevor's face when he opened the card. "Look," he pointed to the line of X's and O's beneath her name, "hugs and kisses, too." He ran his finger over them and sighed. "She loves me."

He pulled out a thin plastic case containing a DVD and passed it to his father. "What's the name of this movie?"

"*Now You See It, Now You Don't.*"

"Can we watch it?"

Trevor fidgeted on the edge of the couch while Jeremy loaded the DVD. He pushed play and returned to the couch as the TV screen exploded in a flash of light and sparks. They faded away leaving a cloud of smoke. The music rose, playing the intro to *Coming to America*. As drums pounded, the smoke thinned to a silvery mist and Claudia appeared, smiling as she walked toward them.

Jeremy recognized her outfit. This was film she shot with Trevor on their first morning in New York.

Fanciful lights and shadowy images danced on the curtains behind her. A white fog swirled around her feet. The camera pulled in tight until her face filled the screen. Jeremy felt as if she was looking right through the screen at him.

Trevor felt it too. When she gave them her million-dollar smile, he grinned back and waved hello.

Jeremy swallowed hard. Her eyes were such deep sapphire blue, as blue as a bottomless lake. A man could get lost in those eyes. Drown in them. And the way she moved, so graceful, so free...she appeared to float.

Trevor, too excited to sit still, wiggled beside him rocking and bouncing against his leg in time with the music. The camera pulled back. Claudia extended her arms and rotated her hands. She tugged at her sleeves making the magician's classic nothing up my sleeve gesture.

She brought her palms together, held them there for a second, and slowly eased them apart. As she did, Trevor materialized between her hands, head first, then the rest of him. She removed the top hand, appearing to balance him in her palm. After Trevor bent forward in a formal bow, she put her hand back on his head and collapsed him into her left hand. When her hands met, she opened them to the camera proving they were empty.

"How'd she do that?" Trevor asked. "She must be really, really strong to hold me up with only one hand."

Jeremy tried to explain trick photography and animation techniques as the image faded to black, but never succeeded in making Trevor understand.

To create the next sequence they'd filmed Trevor on his tiptoes reaching into her cupped hand. In the studio, she'd instructed him to pretend to remove something from her hand and dance in circles, waving his arm as he turned. In the enhanced version they stood on clouds and as he spun he twirled rainbows off his fingertips. Trevor leaped off the sofa and circled their living room, dipping and weaving, mimicking the action on the screen.

Giggling and applauding, Trevor watched as one fantasy after another unfolded. Where he'd swooped across the stage with his arms extended, now he soared above New York City like Superman. Flocks of white doves swirled above him when he danced. He swam with dolphins and rode an elephant.

"She's magic," Trevor said, as the DVD ended. After clapping and clapping, he glanced at his father. "Can we watch it again?"

Jeremy pushed the play button. He was in the kitchen by the time the music started. He sat on a stool at the island bar staring into his hands. Glancing up, he noticed a photo of Teresa on the bulletin board. He stared at the woman he'd loved trying to explain to her what he couldn't understand himself.

He bowed his head again. The genie was out of the bottle; what could he do now?

~ 48 ~

Ten days after the board meeting Claudia started her period. Given everything that happened, it seemed appropriate. She'd been so full of hopes and dreams and love, yet when all was said and done, she ended up with nothing.

Jeremy's behavior at the Board Meeting left her feeling adrift and betrayed. She'd gone from two men in her life to just one. With no competition, and sensing her vulnerability, Michael Cole courted her aggressively.

A month later the two of them left on a week's vacation to the French Riviera. On their second night there, a man in a white coat and starched chef's hat approached their dining table carrying a silver tray.

He bowed slightly. "The chocolates you requested, Mr. Cole."

The polished tray sparkled in the candlelight. The round chocolate truffles on it were bite-sized and gaily decorated with piped leaves, flowers and swirls of icing.

"The chef makes these chocolates especially for me. You simply must have some, they're exquisite." He lifted a light tan one and said, "I believe you prefer milk chocolate," as he placed it on her tongue.

She closed her eyes as it melted, savoring its rich texture. When she bit into it a burst of flavors filled her mouth, fresh raspberry and mocha mingled with the creamiest chocolate she'd ever tasted. There was a hidden hint of something else she couldn't quite put her finger on.

"You're right, those are wonderful. How does he do it?"

Cole popped a dark one into his mouth. "I've tried to make him tell, even threatened violence, yet he still refuses. I eat them anyway, they're too good to forego."

He paused, picked up another light one and held it out to her. "Have another. You can't stop at one."

She bit into it and smiled. "It's orange, my favorite." She

wrinkled her brow as she chewed. "There's something in them I can't identify. What is it?"

He ate another dark one. "It's his secret. Perhaps cognac or a fruited brandy, I often imagine I taste Drambuie, but it's gone so quickly I'm never sure."

He studied the tray and selected two with identical decorations. "The decoration indicates the flavor. We'll both eat the same one and solve the mystery." He offered her the lighter of the two.

She raised her hand. "No more. I don't want to spoil my dinner."

"Why don't we have chocolates for dinner?" His dark eyes crinkled at the corners when he laughed. "Surely you dreamt of doing it when you were a child. I know I did." He put the truffle back on the tray and rested his elbow on the table. "Have you ever eaten a chocolate bar?"

"Who hasn't?"

He swept his hand over the tray. "Look at these. They're tiny. The whole tray wouldn't make two respectable bars."

A wave of nausea swept over her as he spoke. She grabbed her napkin and covered her mouth, coughing and swallowing hard. It passed and she took small sips of water to settle her stomach.

"I'm not used to eating sweets on an empty stomach. I don't think I should."

Michael appeared hurt. "How can we solve the mystery if we don't have one more?"

She took the chocolate from him and reluctantly put it into her mouth. Its cherry flavor reminded her of *Pepto Bismol.* She struggled to identify the fleeting taste that eluded her, but couldn't. She frowned and shook her head.

"I couldn't either." He scrutinized her for a moment. Sliding around the booth, he moved beside her. "You're not feeling well, are you?"

Giving him a half-hearted nod, she tried to make apologies before burying her face in the napkin again.

"Let me help you." He eased her head onto his shoulder. "Close your eyes for a few moments and rest. If this doesn't pass, I'll take you back to the room and call for the hotel physician."

It felt good to relinquish control and close out the spinning room. She nestled into his shoulder and drifted, blaming the sugar. Feeling his arm tighten around her, she kissed his cheek. At that instant, she felt more loved and protected than she'd ever felt in her life.

"Feeling better?"

"Much, much better." Claudia raised her head.

Cole covered her eyes with his hand. "Careful. You've had your eyes closed; the room lights may seem bright at first."

He slowly lifted his fingers. She blinked at the bandstand. The spotlights seemed to pulse with the beat of the music. She closed her eyes and rubbed her temples. Putting her arm around Michael, she leaned over and kissed him.

"That was scary. I don't know what I'd have done without you."

"Rest for a few more minutes and then, if you like, we can dance."

"I'd like that." She took a drink of water then shook her head to get rid of the cobwebs. "The sugar's made me thirsty." She drained the glass. Michael caught the waiter's attention. He refilled her glass and she drank again.

"I'm ready for that dance now."

They made a handsome couple. He in a dinner jacket and she in a blue sleeveless dress with flared skirt and matching jacket. Michael was a skilled dancer and she enjoyed feeling him hold her close. Heads turned as they swept across the floor.

As they danced, she realized how much she missed being touched. Having his arms hold her felt right. The physical exertion of dancing made her feel better. Burning the sugar, perhaps, she thought. The earlier nausea became nothing but a bad memory.

"What is it that you most want in life?"

"I'd like to marry and have children," Claudia confided without hesitation. She was usually more reserved, but tonight, with him, things felt different. She could speak her heart without fear of reproach. It was refreshing to be herself instead of playing a part.

"Don't children imply giving up your career?"

"I'll cross that bridge when I come to it. What are your unfulfilled dreams?"

"Strangely enough, they're quite similar to yours. I find myself approaching the midyears of my life alone, and to be frank, frequently lonely. Success, I've found, comes at a cost."

His reply struck a chord deep within her. For the first time, she'd met someone who understood her struggle.

"Do you have any children?"

"No. Oh, I married once, but we were both young and busy building careers. Starting a family seemed easy to postpone. Since the divorce, I have to confess I haven't met anyone. I keep telling myself there's still time, eventually the right person will come along, but it's never happened." He looked into her eyes. "That is until now."

They kissed and she rested her head on his shoulder.

"How are you feeling? We could go out on the balcony and get some fresh air if you'd like."

"I feel wonderful, but the view's magnificent. Let's go out for a few minutes."

On the balcony the wind off the water ruffled her hair. Giggling like a child, she grabbed the balcony rail with both hands and leaned back. "If I let go, will you catch me?"

Michael moved behind her and rested his hands on her shoulders. "Perhaps I should take you back to the room. We could order room service."

"No, I'm fine, actually I'm finer than fine."

He took her in his arms and she relinquished herself to him. They kissed and hugged for several minutes, pressing against each other with growing passion. When at last he relaxed his grip, she begged him not to let her go.

They returned to the dining room and had a light dinner, waving away the dessert cart before it came close. Throughout the meal, they continued talking about their dreams and life expectations, their discontent with their current situations and their mutual desire to find a place in the country, settle down and raise a family.

They flirted and brushed legs under the table as they talked. When the waiter came to clear their dishes, Michael absentmindedly stroked her thigh as the man worked. Beneath the tablecloth, Claudia grabbed his hand and stuffed it between her legs.

Four truffles remained on the tray. Michael grabbed two of the dark ones and popped them into his mouth. "Dessert," he said and slid the tray toward her before excusing himself to go to the men's room. Two candies remained one milk chocolate and one dark. Rather than eat them, Claudia slipped them both into her pocket.

As soon as the elevator door closed, they rushed into each other's arms. After they'd kissed, Cole held her at arm's length and smiled. "I'm in the mood to do something deliciously outrageous. What about you?"

Her eyes widened. "I'm not going to get naked and do it in an elevator, if that's what you mean."

He straightened to his full height. "I certainly did not. What sort of man do you take me for?"

"I'm sorry. I said the first thing that came into my mind. I know you'd never suggest such a thing."

Cole dropped to one knee and took her hands. "Let's get married."

"Sure, when?"

"Right now...tonight."

Fear fluttered in her stomach. Her fascination with walking on the wild side had reached its limit.

"People don't just go out and get married on a whim. It takes forethought, planning." Feeling the elevator slow, she tugged at him. "We're stopping, Michael. Get up before someone sees you."

"I don't care if they do. You're beautiful and I want to marry you."

A bell chimed and the doors opened. Two couples started through the door, but halted when they saw him kneeling on the floor.

Claudia blushed and shot them an apologetic look.

Cole glanced up at them over his shoulder. "You folks seem to have intruded upon my proposal. Since you're here, why not stay? You can attest that I'm in full possession of my faculties, sober as a judge and madly in love with this beautiful woman." He stared into her eyes. "Claudia, make me the happiest man in the world. Marry me and have my children."

The people outside the elevator grinned and clapped when Claudia tearfully nodded.

In what seemed like seconds, Michael rounded-up a magistrate and collared two hotel employees to act as witnesses. A bridal bouquet suddenly appeared. The next thing she knew, they were side-by-side, ready to make their vows.

Panic flooded over her. She stepped away, releasing his hand.

"I can't do this, Michael."

His eyes flashed angrily for a split-second then he smiled. "What is it, Darling? All brides are nervous. We love each other. What else matters?"

"I'm so confused." She buried her face in her hands. "This isn't the way it's supposed to be. I don't have the necklace!"

"What necklace, Dearest." His voice remained calm, controlled.

"The one my mother left me. The one I'm supposed to wear when I get married." She rubbed her forehead wishing she could make him understand.

Cole put his arm around her and led her back to where they'd been standing. Taking her face in his hands, he spoke softly. "We're throwing off the rules and giving ourselves over to the moment, to the impulse of love. Neither of us began this day planning to get married. That's the beauty of it, its wonderfully crazy spontaneity. Imagine telling our grandchildren about this night. I'm certain your Mum would understand and approve."

They said their vows and people threw rice. There were balloons, and flashbulbs, and movie cameras, and photographers, lots and lots of photographers. Claudia glanced around in shock. Where had they all come from?

It was almost as if they knew ahead of time.

~ 49 ~

In the news business, the person with the earliest lead frames the debate and, more often than not, determines the course of the story.

By the time he'd shepherded his new bride to their room, Cole's publicists were already hard at work. Tired and confused, Claudia fell into bed and lapsed into semi-consciousness.

He'd planned things with care. The six-hour time difference between Southern France and America's East Coast allowed time to imbed the story in the evening news and create segments for the tabloid TV programs. By morning, newspapers on both continents would carry the wedding photos.

Leesburg, VA

Brian went into the family room to call the boys to supper. He started to click off the TV when his sister's picture flashed across the screen. He shooed them away and dropped onto the couch. Jennifer and the boys ate without him.

He tried to reach Claudia, failed, and left a voicemail. He called Brent to coordinate. Working together, they implemented what they called their Doomsday Plan. Several years earlier, with her approval, they'd developed a plan to erect a defensive wall around her holdings in the event of a catastrophe. For Brian and Brent, her marriage to Cole qualified.

Over the years her brothers had channeled Claudia's earnings into a diverse and far-flung portfolio of investments. She had a group of corporations that revolved around her modeling — shell companies that owned assets leased by her other entities, production companies, the clothing business and, of course, the Souvanée cosmetic contracts. She also held stock portfolios, passive ownership in several hotels and partnerships in others. She had her condo in New York, another on the West Coast and a chateau outside Paris, plus financial instruments, notes and other negotiable instruments.

Utilizing an existing Power of Attorney, Brian assumed control of her assets. He executed quit claim deeds and shuffled ownership to Swiss banks. Meanwhile Brent froze her checking accounts, shut down her credit cards and began auditing recent activity for spurious transactions. By the end of the evening they'd completed their work. Technically, Claudia was penniless.

Cannes

Slipping out of bed so as not to wake his sleeping wife, Cole tiptoed onto the balcony and dialed Whitestone. "Mission accomplished. Pull the trigger."

"What mission? Why in the dickens are you calling me? I hear you've married that model friend of yours. If anyone could take your mind off business, I'd think she would."

"I warned you to be ready to pull the trigger on the stock offering at a moment's notice."

"Shouldn't I recheck with the members of my syndicate first?"

"Time is of the essence. I've done everything you suggested. I contracted with a public relations firm. Pick up any newspaper or magazine and you'll see my picture. I even wrote a book on business management." Cole chuckled. "Or at least my ghostwriter did.

"I also hired Schoonover just as you recommended. I even courted and married an international supermodel. I've done my part. Now the ball's in your court. Get with it, man. I'll be in your office first thing tomorrow."

"You're on your honeymoon, Michael. Kick back and relax." Whitestone gave a manly chuckle. "Surely you have more important things to do."

"Stow the sentimentality. I'm in control now. I've already gotten everything I need from Claudia."

Whitestone sucked in his breath. What socially acceptable comment did one make to such a remark? "I, I don't know what to say. You've left me speechless."

“Forget it. Just put your people to work on those forms. Forward them directly to Bernard Chesley when they’re ready.”

“What you’re suggesting is out of court.”

“Who appointed you referee? I’m in control here and we’ll do it my way. Direct it to Chesley. I’ll see you in the morning.”

Claudia Monet was an incredibly beautiful woman. She could have anyone she wanted. Why, Whitestone wondered as he cradled the phone, of all the men in the world had she chosen Michael Cole?

Returning to the bedroom, Cole sat on the edge of the bed.

The movement made Claudia’s head pound. Despite the pain and the light, her eyes sprang open. “Michael.” She sighed, closing her eyes again. “What in the world are you doing?”

“I’m celebrating our first morning as man and wife.”

Man and wife? What in the world was he talking about?

Opening her eyes again, she saw the light glint off the gold band on her left hand. Things came together... bits of random memories and a jumble of mental images. What felt like fragments of a long-forgotten dream gradually coalesced. The restaurant, chocolate truffles, the elevator and, and doing something *deliciously outrageous*.

He glanced down at her. “What is it, Lovey?”

“Tell me we did the right thing last night.”

“I’ll always love you.” He wrapped her in his arms and kissed the top of her head. “There now, everything all better?”

She nodded, wishing it were.

Cole sprang up and reached for a tie. “Almost forgot. An urgent issue’s come up. I’ll be taking the early flight back to London.”

“If I’m to be your wife, we need to communicate on things.”

“You needn’t come along. There’s an evening flight, or if you prefer, you can even fly in tomorrow. I’ll be up and out early. Meetings, you know.” He glanced at her in the mirror as he knotted his tie. “Do you have any pressing commitments?”

“I have to be in New York on Monday. I’m sorry. I never dreamed I’d be getting married.”

“I’m booked too, so much for spontaneity, hmm?” Cole pulled on his jacket, adjusted the shoulders and shot the cuffs. He latched his valise, gave her a peck on the cheek and left without a backward glance.

Claudia showered after Cole left, dressed and then turned on her cell phone. Her voice mailbox was full. Repeated messages, all marked urgent, from Brian, Brent, Rudy, Natalie, Patsy and Stephanie competed for space. There was even one from Weezie asking, “Is everything all right, Dear?”

Greenbrier State Park, Maryland

Jeremy was the last to get the news. He and Trevor were away on a camping trip when Claudia married Cole. After several days of hiking, canoeing, cooking over an open fire and sleeping in a tent, he went into town for supplies. He put his groceries on the counter and noticed her picture on the cover of a tabloid magazine. While he waited to be checked-out, he picked it up and scanned the article. Halfway through, frustration overtook him and he ripped the paper to shreds.

“Hey fella, what do ya think you’re doin’?” the proprietor hollered.

Jeremy looked at the scraps of newsprint littering the floor and mumbled an apology. He paid for the copy he’d destroyed and bought another. After reading and rereading it several times, he used it to start the evening’s fire.

He relived their time together in New York as he stared into the embers. She’d been so giving. And like a man finding an oasis after a long trek in the desert, he’d drunk deeply, taking, and taking until he was sated.

At the Board Meeting it had seemed so clear cut. Simply end it and everything would be like it was before.

How wrong he’d been.

~ 50 ~

London

Cole arrived late in the day. He went directly to the penthouse knowing he'd have the place to himself until the next afternoon. He poured a tumbler of Scotch and opened Applebee's envelope. The photos tumbled out. Looking at them reminded him that with Claudia in the house he'd need to be more careful.

Cole's smile twisted into a sly grin. She traveled. With the cat away, he'd have plenty of time to play. Like always, he'd call the tune and the girls would dance. They had to; he was in control.

Resting his feet on the coffee table, he dealt the photos out beside him in a semi-circle like a winning hand of cards. He glanced down at them lying there and chuckled. How many to send? He'd need a secure courier. He reached for another picture. This little bomb would make quite an explosion when delivered to Chesley's office.

The invitation seemed decidedly spur-of-the-moment to Bernard Chesley. His day had gone bad enough without Michael Cole insisting they meet for drinks at the Exchange Club. A modest, but exclusive establishment, the Club catered to associates of the London Stock Exchange.

Cole glanced up from the bar when Chesley arrived. "Good to see you, Bernard." He studied his face as they shook hands. "You look pale, feeling well?"

Assured that he was, Cole asked what he'd like. After the bartender took the order, Cole requested a refill and directed they be sent to an out-of-the-way table. He draped his arm across Chesley's shoulder. "Come, let's talk."

After several minutes of standard give and take, their conversation reached a natural lull. Chesley used it to move the meeting along. "What did you want to see me about, Mr. Cole?"

"You're familiar with Alistair Whitestone's firm, Kensington Partners?"

"Absolutely."

"Then you may also know they're handling Paradise Getaway's upcoming stock offering."

"No, I didn't."

"I completed the arrangements today. Whitestone will forward the paperwork to you for approval tomorrow."

Chesley took a sip of his drink, shaking his head as he swallowed. "Not the way it's done." Career bureaucrat that he was, Chesley outlined the labyrinth each offering traversed on its way to completion.

The menacing look in Cole's eyes caused Chesley to gasp.

"I'm in control of this offering and I recommend you dispense with the usual formalities."

"I'm sorry, rules are rules you know."

Cole smacked his glass down on the table. Only its thick bottom kept it from shattering. "Forget about your bloody hoops and wickets. You listen to me. When you get those papers tomorrow you will find a way to approve them. Have I made myself clear?"

"Now see here, you can't—"

Cole cut him off. "Otherwise, the whole world will find out what you do when you stay over in the City. How will your wife react when she sees you bumping bellies with a little tart young enough to be your daughter?"

Waves of terror swirled through Chesley. Ever since the courier delivered the photos he'd wondered who held the trump cards. Now he knew.

Unbuttoning his collar, Chesley loosened his tie. He glanced into Cole's dark eyes then lowered his head. "What is it you want from me?"

"I knew we could handle this sensibly once you understood who was in control."

~ 51 ~

London

The dark limousine signaled a turn and pulled under the canopy of the fashionable high-rise overlooking London's Thames River. As soon as the vehicle rolled to a stop, the driver jumped out and grabbed the rear door handle.

"G'day, Mr. Cole," he said as he swung the door back.

Cole wore a Saville Row three-piece suit with monogrammed shirt and striped silk tie. Ignoring the driver, he stepped aside to allow his wife to enter the vehicle first.

"Fine morning isn't it, Miss Monet?"

Like most people, the driver automatically addressed Mrs. Cole as Claudia Monet. Although she legally ceased being Mary Jane Combs when they married, her professional name was her franchise and she continued using it.

"Yes, it is a lovely day," she smiled, "and you're looking well this morning."

The driver beamed.

"Metropole Hotel, front entrance." Cole barked and slammed the privacy window shut as the car inched into traffic. He handed Claudia a small velvet box. "Here, for you."

"Diamond earrings, what's the occasion?"

"I'm glad you came back. I know it was short notice."

"I came back to London because I'm your wife, Michael. You don't have to pay me."

"I never imagined I did. You made a special effort to be by my side today and I wanted to show my appreciation."

True, she'd juggled and postponed in order to return, but she'd been happy to do it at the time. Now she wished she'd told him to take a flying leap out the nearest window. Just weeks into her marriage she was already sleeping in the guestroom . Not that it seemed to bother Cole. He hardly acknowledged her presence.

"Why couldn't you show your appreciation by keeping your

pants zipped while I was away?" Claudia snapped the jewelers' box shut and threw it back at him. "Save these for your girlfriend. Apparently, she's for sale. I'm not."

Anger flashed in Cole's dark eyes. "Why now? You knew I wasn't a monk when you married me."

"I didn't expect to marry a monk, but I didn't plan on marrying Don Juan either."

"I haven't spoken to Amanda in over a year."

"Whatever her name is, I found her underwear in the bathroom," she said in answer to his unspoken question.

"You must have left them there. Something you intended to pack."

"Give me a little credit. I know my own underwear."

"You're being ridiculous."

"How did they get there?"

"The only person in the apartment while you were away was the cleaning lady."

She rolled her eyes. "Mrs. Garrity is old, arthritic and seriously overweight. It's hard to imagine her frolicking around the apartment in lace undies."

Claudia noticed the taut muscles in his neck. He was clearly under a lot of strain. She'd taken a prospectus with her on the plane and read it carefully, even the fine print. The lion's share of the proceeds went into Michael's pocket.

That didn't strike her as particularly noteworthy. Business was business. She'd watched Brian manipulate her contracts, and personal corporations for years. Her intuition told her, despite his protestations this wasn't as routine as he pretended. Something ominous lay hidden under the legalese and boilerplate.

Cole took a deep breath, forced a smile and took her hand. "Let's not fight. Neither of us is at our best. I've been under pressure and you've been traveling."

"That doesn't explain what I found in the bathroom."

"I recall asking Mrs. Garrity to clean out the drawers. You know how forgetful she can be. She probably sat the underwear aside for the dustbin and forgot it. Your finding it was a hurtful reminder of my past. I'm truly sorry it happened."

Claudia watched him closely, trying to read his face.

He returned the earrings. "Take them, please. I want you to have them."

She knew no marriage could survive unless both parties were willing to forgive and forget. This would be her turn, but she'd watch him closer in the future.

Their car stopped at the entrance and Cole got out before the driver reached the door. He gallantly offered his hand to his wife. Cameras clicked and flashed as she emerged. The photographers continued shooting until one of Whitestone's assistants appeared.

Henry Wexford extended his hand. "Mr. and Mrs. Cole, welcome. We're in the King's Suite. Your people have done a masterful decorating job."

Inside the hotel, Wexford lengthened his stride and led the way.

Cole slowed, putting distance between them. "This is an important day," he whispered. "I've got a lot riding on this."

Claudia cast him a sidelong glance. The smile he'd painted on his face looked tenuous at best. Tight lines formed around his eyes and his jaw muscles were set and rigid. She wondered again what made this so important.

"Take time to mingle. Get around the room and press the flesh. Most of these clowns don't get out of the office much. With a pretty girl hanging on their every word and an open bar, they'll be putty in my hands."

A pretty girl?

She'd canceled her plans and flown across seven time zones to be a pretty girl? Claudia had no illusions. All most people saw in her was an attractive face and a good figure. She could live with that, but she didn't want her husband treating her like a commodity too.

"I'll introduce you to Clayton Hemphill. The little weasel works in Regulatory Affairs. There've been rumors about him digging into our books. Hemphill must be neutralized. Spend time with him, flatter him, and butter him up." He caught her eye and winked. "Give him something to fantasize about when he slips into bed tonight."

"Is that all I am, your shill?"

She'd been tempted to use a more vulgar term. Even though she hadn't said it, that's how he made her feel.

His hand tightened around hers.

"What if I don't feel like being the entertainment de jour for your little gala?"

They climbed the stairs in silence.

"You're hurting my hand. Let go."

"This is more important than you realize." He relaxed his grip. "I asked you to come back early because I need your help."

This was as close to begging as he came. Reading the fear in his eyes, her heart softened. Even if he couldn't bring himself to ask, she'd help him for the good of their marriage.

"Let's not fight. I know the part; I'll be the dutiful wife. Now why don't you learn your part, the faithful spouse?"

The room quieted when they entered the King's Suite. Claudia wore a frosty chocolate, full-length dress with a sweeping flared hem. She had a matching three-quarter length, long-sleeved jacket over it. Cole led her to the center of the room and eased the jacket off her shoulders. A murmur rippled through the crowd as she stepped forward. Her beaded, V-necked dress was a Paris original. Gathered and crisscrossed from bodice to waist, the silk fabric shimmered in the bright lights.

Cole passed her jacket to an aide and began working the crowd. As he circled the room, Claudia trailed a half-step behind, content to let this be his show.

He led her to a man in a plain grey suit. “Darling, I’d like you to meet Clayton Hemphill.”

Hemphill extended his hand shyly.

Claudia took his hand between hers, looked him in the eye and smiled. “How are you, Clayton? Michael speaks very highly of you.” With Hemphill’s hand still in hers, she glanced at Michael. “You won’t be jealous if I spend time alone with Clayton, will you?”

Michael nodded his approval and drifted away.

Claudia was still with Hemphill when Admiral Schoonover strode into the room. He caught the eye of one of the company’s boatswains. At Schoonover’s signal, the man reached into his vest pocket and extracted a short, silver pipe. The boatswain put it to his lips and piped attention. The shrill notes stilled conversation.

The room lights dimmed as Schoonover, presenting a regal appearance in full dress uniform, stepped onto the podium and opened the meeting. When he finished his opening remarks, Schoonover turned the meeting over to Cole.

A palpable sense of expectation filled the room. Cole delayed, taking a sip of water and adjusting his notes to build tension. Surveying the room, he made eye contact here and there. Satisfied, he slipped on his reading glasses and began speaking from a prepared text.

Schoonover approached the boatswain, clapped him on the back and continued across the room. He paused at her table when she touched his hand. Claudia patted Hemphill’s knee, thanked him for keeping her company and rose to accompany Schoonover to a quiet space near the back of the room. She had questions that needed answers.

~ 52 ~

Everything went according to plan in the weeks following Cole's announcement. He had nearly achieved his objective when the course of events took a nasty turn. And, like the deepest of blizzards, the first few flakes seemed insignificant.

He picked up the phone when it buzzed to find Schoonover on the line. "Sorry to bother you at home, Michael, but I've just received troubling news."

"What is it?"

"Hemphill's regulators have begun investigating Paradise Getaways' accounting practices. They've made no official announcement, but it's already found its way onto the news. Could be nothing of consequence, of course, but it's been my experience these things seldom turn out that way."

"Why did you allow this to happen?"

"I'm not in control of the world's events. I didn't allow it to happen, any more than I allow it to rain. I'm simply apprising you of our circumstances."

"What about my stock offering? Isn't there some way to keep this quiet?"

"I don't believe there is."

"What if we refute the charges?"

"I'll schedule a press conference tomorrow," Schoonover said. "The best way to deal with unpleasantness is forthrightly, especially if there's nothing to hide."

"Stow your forthrightness, I want damage control."

"Should I or should I not plan a press conference?"

"Do so, but handle this with care. I don't want anything said or done that impinges on the stock offering."

Cole paced the dark room, weighing his options. Glancing out the window, he noticed a clock tower poking through the murky fog. He stared at its round face, watching the minute hand pause, lurch ahead then pause again. Tereschenko won't accept another postponement, he thought.

Monte Carlo

Claudia saw the red and white lights of the approaching helicopter before she heard the steady thump of its blades whipping the night sky. A thousand yards out the pilot flipped on two powerful landing beams. Welcoming the diversion, she concentrated on them.

She pulled her coat around her and watched small waves appear and disappear as the lights strafed the water. Seconds later the chopper's strobes marched up the shoreline and swept across the deserted beach, illuminating abandoned beach chairs and shuttered refreshment stands.

An orange-jacketed hotel employee in headphones and mike with a lighted baton in each hand directed the Heli-Air Monaco shuttle onto the hotel's landing pad.

Claudia pulled a scarf around her head and turned her back to the noise, wondering about Michael. She'd tried to contact him several times, but hadn't succeeded. He must know by now. It was on every channel.

Claudia was in Monte Carlo taping promos for an upcoming awards show. After a long day followed by staff meetings over dinner, she returned to her room. She'd showered, and was brushing out her hair when Natalie knocked.

"There's something on the news you have to see."

The grim expression on her face made Claudia's heart race. A thousand grisly possibilities ran through her mind. Whatever it was, she knew it wouldn't be good.

Natalie aimed the remote at the screen. "See for yourself."

Claudia saw the familiar Paradise Getaways logo overlaid by an announcer speaking French. Tendrils of fear twisted her insides. "Why is the company's logo on television? See if you can find the BBC, or CNN International."

"Your husband's been accused of cooking the books."

Claudia felt goose bumps rising on her arms. She tugged her robe tighter and crossed her arms. "Has Michael made any response?"

Natalie shook her head.

Claudia jumped up and walked to the dressing room. "I have to get back to London. Michael will need me. Put everything on hiatus. I'll be back as soon as I can."

Remembering Monaco had no commercial airport, she paused in the doorway firing instructions at Natalie. "Greg's in Nice with the plane. Page him. Tell him to have it ready and waiting. It's only 600 miles to London, I'll ride shotgun. Call Air Monaco and order a helicopter. Pay whatever it takes to get one here. I'll be on the rooftop in half an hour."

Michael had urged her to fly commercial since it cost less. Claudia was well aware of what it cost to maintain her private jet. It was a convenience she allowed herself. She was thankful she'd ignored his advice.

As soon as the pilot throttled back the engines, Claudia jogged to the helicopter. She was several feet away when a side door opened. The copilot jumped out to assist her. Taking her bag, he extended his arm to help her in. Claudia snapped her seat belt and they lifted off, preparing to head back in the direction from which they'd come.

As they swung around, Claudia took one last look. The towering Le Meridien Beach Plaza Hotel where she'd been staying sparkled in the night. She had the impression of a glittering jewel imbedded in this rocky palisade overlooking the Mediterranean.

A passing glance with no time for regrets or second thoughts was all she got. In seconds they were streaming over the dark water heading toward Nice.

~ 53 ~

London

Cole frowned. “What recourse do I have other than hoping for a sudden assassination attempt or a terrorist attack?”

“That’d be one way to get off the front page.” Claudia watched him move restlessly in the limo’s seat. “Like it or not, Paradise Getaways is the biggest draw in town.”

He instructed the driver to avoid the firm’s main entrance, directing him to a receiving dock instead. They’d take a freight elevator to the fourth floor, then switch.

All she’d taken on the helicopter was a small carry-on with a few personal items and a cosmetic bag. Natalie would pack her things or the clothes could wait in Monaco until they resumed shooting.

That morning she pulled a dark pantsuit out of the closet, matched it with a soft pink blouse, contrasting scarf, pearl necklace and earrings. It was tasteful and businesslike without appearing ostentatious.

“I hate the press. Always have, and always will,” Cole grumbled.

“Reporters are drawn to bad news like vultures to a rotting corpse. You have to outlast them. Once they pick the carcass clean, they’ll move on.”

The media’s feeding frenzy had begun. Television vans lined both sides of the street. Morning traffic backed-up throughout the district as vehicles tried to worm their way through the mayhem surrounding Paradise’s offices.

Schoonover was waiting when they walked in.

“Give me a minute to get on top of these then we’ll talk.” Cole snatched a stack of phone messages from the corner of his secretary’s desk and headed into his office riffling through the slips.

When Cole headed for his office Claudia joined Schoonover

on the couch.

Cole threw most of the messages away and placed all but one of the survivors under a paperweight. He waved a message slip at his secretary when she put down his tea tray. “Ring Whitestone.”

While he waited for the call to go through, he took off his suit jacket and draped it over the back of his chair. His phone buzzed. Cup in one hand, phone in the other, he leaned back and swiveled to face the window.

“What’s on your mind, Alistair?”

“I was hoping you could update me on these charges. Brokers want to know what impact this will have on the stock offering.”

Cole was deliberately matter-of-fact in his reply. “I’d love to give you all sorts of inside information, but the truth is we don’t know any more than what’s being reported in the news.”

He listened for several minutes.

“I understand your concern. I’ll meet with your investors, if you think it would help. The important thing is not to let this adversely impact our offering price. I’m counting on you to carry us through.”

Cole patiently listened as Whitestone poured out his anxieties. As expected, the London Stock Exchange had suspended trading in Paradise Getaways Limited before the opening. It was a standard precaution to avoid a run on the stock. In planning the offering, they’d established a target price for the new shares above the current market.

Whitestone reminded him each time the offering price declined it removed millions of pounds from the proceeds. If it declined too much all those crisp stock certificates would become worthless scraps of paper. Whitestone again suggested they postpone the offering.

“I’m in control and I say we press on.”

Whitestone continued to pour out his concerns.

"You needn't remind me of what is at stake here. I know better than you."

Cole sounded as confident and persuasive as ever. The last thing he needed was Whitestone getting cold feet. He'd find a way through this like always. He continued assuring Whitestone he'd keep him informed.

"Schoonover's waiting to see me," Cole said. "He's holding a press conference later this morning. Try to catch it."

The way Whitestone carried on you'd think his dear old Mum had died, Cole thought, cradling the phone. He headed for his private conference room. Schoonover waited along with Sheldon Weems, Director of Advertising and PR, and Ted Ballinger, the company's legal counsel.

"What's our status? Give me the short list."

"I have a press conference scheduled for ten. Weems is narrowing the participating news agencies to a manageable number," Schoonover said. "I've installed a toll-free hotline for recorded updates to stockholders. Other than that, we're rolling with the punches."

Cole faced Weems. "Just the A List at the press conference, we don't need anyone building their resume at our expense. Restrict the number of questions and set a time limit. Otherwise they'll keep repeating the same questions until the cows come home."

"I have my staff writing the Admiral's speech," Weems said. "It'll be short and sweet. Paradise didn't do anything. Paradise doesn't know anything. Thank you and goodbye."

Cole liked that, especially with Admiral Hornblower there. Dressed up in a sailor suit with his white hair and regal bearing the press would believe him if he announced little green Martians abducted the Royal Family.

"What about the travel agencies?" Cole asked, scanning the group.

"I've got three people on it. Major accounts have already gotten a call. The Sales Department will boost short-term incentives to maintain volume."

"What haven't we covered?" It was his way of ending a meeting. The others began shuffling papers, preparing to leave. Schoonover rose to speak.

"Two things need to be touched on here, Michael. First, I've scheduled an employee's meeting following the press conference. Your wife has graciously agreed to attend. Right now, she's conducting ad hoc departmental meetings."

"She doesn't know anything about the company."

"It doesn't matter what she does or doesn't know. Most times it's not what you say, but how you say it. She's a bright and articulate woman. She'd be a tremendous asset if you'd let her."

"Keep your marriage counseling to yourself. What else?"

"We need to make a public commitment to full disclosure." Schoonover ignored the irritated scowl on Cole's face and continued. "We must assure the investing public we intend to get to the bottom of this. Assure them that everything will be satisfactorily accounted for. That –"

Cole waved his hand, bringing him to a stop.

Schoonover looked shocked.

Cole chose his words carefully. "I'm sorry to cut you off, Admiral, but I know you'll need time to prepare for the press conference. I think I speak for everyone in the room when I say I agree with your sentiments. I won't rest until there is a full and complete explanation. You have my unqualified support in this matter."

Schoonover glanced at his watch. "Thank you. I should begin preparing."

Cole leaned back in his chair. What a brilliant solution. Of course the company would never rest in its search for the truth. Committees could study the problem from now until doomsday... or at least until the proceeds of the stock offering were safely in his pocket.

~ 54 ~

Willoughby Bay, Antiqua

Claudia slid the door back and stared out at the iridescent turquoise sea. A warm trade wind swept through the screen and into her room. She'd stayed over an additional day in London after the press conference. Then, faced with a full schedule, raced back to Monte Carlo, finished there and flew to the Caribbean.

She'd had enough of London's dreary weather and crowded streets. The Caribbean's relaxed, easy-going atmosphere was more her style. Smiling, Claudia closed her eyes and inhaled deeply. The fresh sea air was just what she needed.

She'd be in the Caribbean for two weeks, island-hopping to film a series of cable infomercials for a consortium of resorts. Management housed the crew in freestanding bungalows near the beach. For security reasons, they placed Claudia on the top floor of the main hotel.

She glanced into the mirror and frowned at the bruises on her upper right arm. Four purple-brown stripes like ugly bars, or fingers on a hand that'd twisted until she yelled, "Stop!"

They'd want to shoot from the right. It was her best side. Maybe Rudy could cover them, she thought, as she slipped on a skirt. A knock interrupted her thoughts.

"Up yet, Darlin'?" Rudy asked, through the door.

She threw on a blouse. "Up and at 'em."

"But are you decent?"

She laughed and swung the door back.

Rudy wore an outrageously bright tropical shirt, white cotton pants tied at the waist and sandals. With a floppy straw hat over his auburn hair and sunglasses dangling at the end of a bright yellow strap, it was clear he was already in the island spirit.

She winced when she lifted her arm to straighten the collar on her blouse. Rudy noticed the bruise and pushed her sleeve aside.

"Can you cover it? I slipped on a stairway at home."

"I do makeup, Darlin', not miracles. They can airbrush them out of stills, but we'll need to tack your sleeve down for filming." He placed his fingers over the four stripes on her arm. "By the way, the next time I'm in London, I'd love to see that stairway of yours."

London

There may be something about a man in uniform when it comes to a woman's heart, but Schoonover's frequent press conferences and televised interviews couldn't halt the stock's decline. Regulators, meanwhile, were maddeningly slow in releasing specific details regarding the charges against the company.

Whitestone leaned forward and tapped Cole's desk. His face flushed with anger as he spoke. "See here, Michael, you've got to find a way to stanch this continual loss of capitalization. You're bleeding to death, man."

"It's only temporary."

"So were the Great Depression and the Second World War."

"What are you implying?"

Whitestone shook his head like a doctor giving a fatal diagnosis. "Look at the numbers. Examine the charts. Paradise Getaways is sinking like a rock."

Clanking his cup into its saucer, Cole glared across the desk. "The press hates me."

"They surely loved you when you were wining and dining Claudia."

"I was paying them to love me. Investors aren't as easily manipulated as the tabloid-reading public."

"Your problems don't seem to have diminished her popularity at all."

Cole leaned across the desk. “If you’re suggesting she become a company spokesperson, forget it. She and I are barely speaking.”

Whitestone’s face had the look of a man who’d opened the water closet door and found his mother-in-law on the throne. He developed a sudden, keen interest in the nautical prints behind Cole’s desk.

“If you do your job, we’ll ride this out.”

“My traders have been stepping in to support your stock most every day. I can’t do all the heavy lifting.”

Cole’s eyes narrowed. “Know this, Alistair. So long as I’m in control, I will not kowtow to anyone. Not to you, not to Claudia, and especially not to the press.”

“Your stubbornness will be your undoing,” Whitestone said as he rose to leave.

Baltimore

As much as Jeremy tried to forget those days in New York, he couldn’t. Trevor wouldn’t allow him to. Every night when he put his son to bed, there sat Claudia’s New York City snow globe on the bookshelf.

Trevor stood on his bed and took it down. “Look, Dad, it’s snowing on the Umpire State Building.”

Jeremy believed he could end his relationship with Claudia without repercussions. He hadn’t counted on her stealing his son’s heart. Trevor had become an aficionado of everything New York. When he needed a new baseball cap, he happily tossed aside his Orioles hat in favor of one with the Yankee Y on it.

If a store advertised New York-style anything, Trevor pestered his father to buy it. During the preceding months, they’d dined on New York-style hot dogs, New York-style bagels, New York-style cheesecake...pretzels...pizza...New York-style anything and everything.

In a restaurant, Trevor asked if he could order a New York

steak. When asked if he knew what it was, Trevor answered, “Sure. It’s the kind Claudia eats.”

Jeremy came home from work one day and found the young boy engrossed in the evening news. When questioned about his sudden interest in network broadcasts, Trevor explained, “It’s live from New York.”

Jeremy picked up the globe.

Trevor reached to protect it. “Be careful, Dad. It could break if you drop it.”

Jeremy raised his arm, keeping it beyond his son’s grasp. “What’s so special about this snow globe?”

“Claudia gave it to me.”

He made a spur-of-the-moment decision to explore Trevor’s feelings. “Why do you think she gave it to you?”

“She loves me.”

“How can you be sure she loves you?”

“I could tell by the way she says my name.”

What had she done to him? It’d been eight months since their trip to New York, yet Trevor talked about her as if it were only yesterday. She’d taken possession of him. What happened in the bedroom while she was tucking Trevor in?

Forget Trevor, Jeremy thought. What happened to me in her bedroom? What has she done to us?

“Hey Dad, remember when we were playing Frisbees in the park and she threw it too high?”

“Uh-huh. I remember.”

“You lifted me up so I could reach it. We really caught it, didn’t we, Dad?”

“Yeah,” Jeremy sighed. “We caught it all right.”

~ 55 ~

Willoughby Bay, Antiqua

The Caribbean project followed a tight schedule giving Claudia the final two days free. She'd brought the latest production samples from her clothing line and used the time doing still shots around the island. Claudia and Natalie were zipping garment bags when a bellboy knocked.

Natalie overheard enough from the other room to know he'd delivered flowers. Curious, she walked into the living room. A box of long-stemmed roses lay open on the couch. Natalie noticed a long, velvet-covered box and opened it.

"Oh, wow! Look what you missed." She removed a gold tennis bracelet with diamonds and draped it across her wrist.

Claudia glanced at it, shrugged, and continued arranging roses.

"I should be so lucky."

Claudia angrily jammed the last rose into the vase. "I wouldn't wish my kind of luck on my worst enemy."

Natalie appeared confused.

Claudia sat on the couch and patted the cushion beside her.

"Every girl dreams of the man who will surprise her with flowers and gifts when it's not her birthday or their anniversary. I've been married to Michael long enough to know expensive gifts for no reason mean he's feeling guilty. Flowers? He strayed while he was out of town. Flowers and earrings? He got a gal drunk and she spent the night when I was away. Flowers and a diamond bracelet? "I've been away three weeks, plenty of time for whatever."

It had hurt terribly the first time Michael strayed. He begged forgiveness, swore it would never happen again and showered her with gifts. But it did happen again, and again, and again. Every time they were apart. In spite of it, she'd flown back from Monaco to stand by his side like a good, supportive wife. Rather than appreciating the effort, he resented her presence.

"Why would he treat you that way?" Natalie asked.

"I've asked myself the same question. I think Michael has deep-seated problems, sexual issues and a need to control." She laughed. "Listen to me I'm a pop psychologist now. Next thing, I'll have my own call-in show."

Natalie didn't laugh. "You must have reasons for thinking that."

Claudia hesitated. "The love went out of our lovemaking as soon as we married. He's become coarse and self-centered when it comes to sex. I've wondered if he wasn't disciplined harshly, restrained, or abused as a child."

"Does he ever talk about his childhood?"

"Not much. An aunt cared for him while his mother was in a sanitarium. He refuses to talk about it.

Natalie put the bracelet back in its box and tossed it onto the coffee table. It'd lost its sparkle.

The producers arranged a wrap party on the neighboring island of Barbuda. The group arrived at sundown prepared to feast on catered island fare. Smoke billowed from commercial grills and a steel band played. The buffet featured various shellfish, conch fritters, swordfish and snapper, and jerked chicken by grilled vegetables, mango-papaya salsa, and fried plantains. Bartenders dispensed drinks as the crew celebrated.

Claudia and Rudy retreated to a private spot away from the crowd. Relaxing in canvas chairs, they ate from plates balanced on their knees.

Rudy adjusted his floppy straw hat. "Man, I can't get enough of this island life. Where are you headed from here?"

"I'm heading back to London to be the hostess at a party Michael's throwing."

"If you can't pull 'em in with free food and liquor draw 'em with eye candy hmm?"

"It's not like I'm going to do a striptease. I'd rather not even be there, but it's important to him."

“You’re always the dutiful helpmate.”

“Don’t look at me like that. I promised.”

“Just like Michael promised to forsake all others.”

She spent the next several minutes explaining the problems Michael had encountered with his stock offering.

Rudy sat quietly, munching the spicy chicken and offering a sympathetic ear.

It was a bittersweet time. Her brief marriage to Michael Cole had failed. Even if she pretended otherwise, it was obvious to everyone around her.

Rudy read her thoughts. “You know, you’re going to have to leave him.”

“We’ve only been married a few months. Leaving him now would be so...so Hollywood. The tabloids would have a field day.”

“Why did you wait so long to explain? It matters more what the tabloids think, than that you’re married to a creep who cheats on you.”

She took a deep breath. “The truth is I’m afraid of what Michael might do if I left.”

She spoke so softly that Rudy could barely discern her words over the sound of the steel drums. Why did you marry him in the first place?”

“Would you laugh if I said I don’t know? It was a spur-of-the-moment thing. In retrospect, I suppose I just wanted to be married.”

“Sounds like every girl’s dream.”

“Yeah, but my dream turned into a nightmare. After Michael’s party, I’m going to Washington. Brian can help me untangle this mess.”

“Why not leave the bastard and never look back.”

“I need to be careful. Since we’ve been living together, I’ve found out things. Things I’m not supposed to know. Michael might try to harm me if I left.”

~ 56 ~

London

Claudia returned from the Caribbean early, landing late on a Friday evening. Rather than bother Michael she took a taxi from the airport.

As they drove, Claudia clicked on the reading light and checked her makeup. She'd had a wonderful time in the Caribbean and it showed in her happy glow. Michael's party was Monday evening. She'd try to make the mood last until then, she decided, pouting into the small hand mirror as she refreshed her lipstick.

They'd had words before she left. Perhaps he sent the flowers and bracelet as a peace offering. He had a lot on his mind right now. She promised herself she'd keep an open mind.

The doorman saw her and swung the door back. "Good evening, Miss Monet. Running a bit late tonight, are we?"

Warren spoke to all the tenants as they came and went. Most barely acknowledged him, but Claudia always smiled and occasionally lingered for short conversations. She knew his wife's name and regularly inquired about his children.

"Here are some chocolates for the children from the Caribbean." She handed Warren the colorful tins she'd brought.

"Why thank you, Ma'am." He reached for the phone. "I'll buzz Mr. Cole and let him know you're on your way."

"Don't bother. I'll just go on up."

Warren dropped the candy onto his desk and chased after her. "Uh, Miss Monet..."

She turned.

"I really should buzz, Ma'am. It's my job to announce visitors."

"But I'm not a visitor."

"Still, it may not be the best thing...to not buzz, I mean."

"Why do you say that?"

Warren paused, struggling to form an answer. "Uh, well, it's rather late. Mr. Cole could be, uh, sleeping. We wouldn't want to startle him." His face brightened. "I'll buzz just to be on the safe side."

The lift chimed. When the doors parted, Claudia stepped in. Warren reached out and grabbed the door before it closed.

"I insist, Ma'am. It'll only take a second."

"How can I make you understand? It isn't necessary." She smiled. "If I surprise him, I surprise him."

He gave a rueful nod. "Yes Ma'am, as you wish."

Claudia wondered what Michael might be doing. He'd most likely be reading business reports. That's all he ever seemed to do. He'd be sitting in his black leather chair with it spun around facing the terrace.

On the table beside him would be a tumbler of Scotch, neat. And he'd have the floor lamp bent forward so the light fell over his shoulder. Despite everything she'd confessed to Rudy, there was comfort in coming home and knowing what she'd find.

Claudia eased the door open and stepped into the dark foyer. The living room drapes were open and light from distant buildings created a hodge-podge of shadows. Michael's leather chair sat in its usual position, untouched and empty.

Her skin tingled. The darkened room seemed out of character. Her instincts told her to leave.

Instead, she stayed.

Stepping into the living room, she tossed her coat over the back of the sofa and slipped off her shoes. The thick carpet felt good under her stocking feet. She crossed the room and glanced through the open door into Michael's dark office.

At the end of the hall, a thin bar of light glowed under their bedroom door. As she drew closer, Claudia heard rock music thumping on the other side. A shiver tiptoed up her spine.

Michael didn't listen to heavy metal bands. He barely knew Marilyn Manson from Marilyn Monroe. Ignoring an overwhelming urge to turn and run, she eased the bedroom door open a crack. The loud music masked her entrance.

Claudia squinted as her eyes adjusted to the sudden brightness. Hazy smoke wafted over the room. One breath told her it wasn't Michael's Cuban cigars. It had a distinct herblike smell she hadn't encountered since college. A sickening wave of revulsion and disappointment swept over her.

She'd mistakenly believed she was beyond shock. Her modeling career obliterated whatever naiveté she once possessed. She knew how the world worked and experienced firsthand its ability to be rude, crude, or both. There wasn't a come-on, innuendo or indecent suggestion she hadn't heard. She'd been felt-up and patted-down more times than she cared to remember and knew all about the drugs and sex.

In spite of this, she'd maintained a cockeyed belief in the underlying fairness of life., until now. This went beyond the pale. It was her moment of truth. The instant when the fabric of her ill-fated marriage ripped apart like the threadbare knee of an old pair of jeans.

Michael had two naked prostitutes in their bed.

Stepping away, Claudia eased the door shut. Her knees felt wobbly and her cheeks burned like they were on fire. Tears welled in her eyes. She willed them away, forcing them into the dark place where unrequited tears remain. Turning, she quickly retraced her steps down the hall and out of the apartment.

She began sobbing uncontrollably once she stepped into the lift. Her makeup streaked and her nose ran. She had only one goal now, to get out of the building without confronting Warren.

He looked up when he heard the doors of the lift open.

Claudia yanked up the collar of her coat and took long strides toward the door.

He sprinted across the lobby after her. "Miss Monet, wait. Please. Let me help you."

She turned to face him.

He held out a box of tissues to her. "You've been weeping."

She grabbed them by the handfuls, cramming them into her pockets.

"I'm so sorry, Ma'am. I should have done more, stopped you, buzzed the apartment...something, anything."

A look of understanding passed between them. He'd seen Michael come in with those tramps. When she told him not to buzz, he knew she'd walk in on them.

"It wasn't your fault," she whispered, "you tried to warn me." She sniffed and headed for the door. "I hope the children enjoy the chocolates."

"Oh no, Ma'am, don't leave. It's late. Let me call a taxi. I'll have one here in a jiffy."

She nodded. "I'll wait outside."

The cool night air felt good against her hot cheeks. Life was funny, she thought. On the flight to London, she'd worked hard to brighten her mood because she expected Michael to be in a funk. In spite of the pain, she was grateful she's come home early. If she hadn't, she might never have known about those women. How many others had there been?

Michael would pay for this, she promised herself. He would pay.

~ 57 ~

She'd stopped sobbing by the time they reached her hotel. Always the pragmatist, her mind turned to dealing with the situation at hand. Her best defense would be a strong offense. It was time to circle her wagons.

Ignoring the time difference, she dialed Brian's home number. To her great relief, he'd anticipated a sudden breakup and developed counter measures. Understanding now that the marriage had been nothing but a sham, Brian constructed a legal barricade to protect her from Cole. Before they hung up an hour later, he assured her all the necessary instructions would be in the hands of his London correspondents when they arrived for work the following Monday.

Cole was scheduled to leave town on Wednesday. Until then, she holed-up in her hotel room biding her time. After he left, she returned to their penthouse to gather and box her belongings. With them stowed on her plane she left London vowing never to return.

New York

Claudia swallowed her disappointment and forged ahead. The first weeks back passed in a blur of activity. In addition to an already full schedule, she had to squeeze in numerous trips to Washington for conferences with Brian.

Though Cole's team remained surprisingly quiet, the press raised a riotous clamor. Magazines and tabloids feasted on her troubles, publishing story after story rife with speculation and innuendo. Their ridiculous conclusions bordered on the humorous, but with so much at stake, neither she nor Brian found much to laugh about.

Whenever she had a free evening Claudia unpacked one of the boxes from London. She found it onerous and depressing and hated doing it nearly as much as she disliked seeing the unopened boxes piled in a corner.

Even with Cole gone, she'd packed in a rush. Each box contained a hodge-podge of whatever happened to be close at hand. Rather than confront the entire stack, she carried them into a spare bedroom one at a time. She dealt with the lingerie, mementos and other personal items as she encountered them. The clothing, she sorted by type, temporarily piling them on the bed to send to the cleaners.

One particular evening, with nothing else to do, she grabbed a box and headed for the bedroom. She'd spent the afternoon in Washington and smoldered all the way back. Rehashing their brief courtship and equally short marriage always upset her.

She'd been trusting, naïve...downright foolish. How could Cole's manipulation have drawn her in so easily? She shook her head in dismay and dropped onto the corner of the bed.

She recalled the night they'd married, how lighthearted she'd been. An indefinable power flowed through her. She felt invincible and utterly, blatantly sexual. Meanwhile, Michael seemed suave and sophisticated and unbelievably handsome.

In retrospect, nothing made sense. She'd thrown caution to the wind and acted on impulse. It seemed so romantic when he dropped to one knee in the elevator and proposed. From her current vantage point, she saw it as the silly theatrics it was.

Sighing deeply, she went to work.

Her wedding outfit came out the box first. She loved the blue dress when she bought it and wore it for the first time the night they married. Holding it at arm's length, she knew she'd never wear it again. The dress and matching jacket were on their way to the donation pile when her hand froze in midair.

She poked a finger into the pocket, knitting her brow in concentration as she moved it around. Then, dropping the jacket onto the bed, she dashed into the kitchen. She returned a moment later with two plastic zipper bags. She dug two chocolate truffles out of the pocket, popping one into each bag.

Baltimore

"I'm glad you're home, Dr. Tilden." Mrs. Carruthers had her coat over her arm, ready to leave. Trevor's nanny typically departed as soon as Jeremy came home. Today, for some reason, she lingered.

He loosened his tie and glanced at her expectantly. "Is anything wrong?"

"Trevor's keeping a magazine in his room."

"A magazine?"

"Yes. He was sitting on his bed studying it when I came around the corner with the clean laundry. When he noticed me, he crammed it under his pillow and pretended to be playing with his Teddy Bear."

"Which magazine was it?"

"I don't know. I asked to see it and he denied having it. Of course, I could have reached under the pillow and gotten it, but it didn't seem like the proper approach. I decided it'd be better for you to deal with it. In case it was," she made an uncomfortable face, "something he shouldn't see."

Jeremy sat on the edge of his son's bed and motioned him to sit beside him.

"How was your day?"

"Okay."

"What are you up to?"

"I'm playing with my farm set. One of the horses is missing. He must've run away."

"I bet he's here somewhere." Jeremy made an inspection of his son's room, pretending to search for the horse. He bent over checking behind the dresser. "I think I see something, but I can't reach it. Do you happen to have any magazines I could use to sweep it out?"

"Why does everyone think I keep magazines up here?"

Jeremy gave him a sidelong glance. “Do you?”

Trevor hemmed and hawed for a moment, then crossed his arms. “No.”

The tremor in his voice gave him away. At four he hadn’t perfected the art of lying to his father. With practice, he’d get better. By the time he became a teenager he’d be adept at it.

Jeremy walked back to the bed and picked up Trevor’s Teddy Bear.

“You know Teddies never lie.” He stared the bear in the eye and, in his best prosecutorial tone, asked, “Teddy Bumpkins, does Trevor have a magazine?”

Jeremy held the bear next to his ear, pretending to listen. He sat the bear back on the pillow and lifted an eyebrow. “He said you had a magazine.”

The boy’s face dissolved into panic. His best friend had just turned state’s witness. Trevor turned his big brown eyes up at his father and gave a guilty nod. “I was only looking at the pictures. You know I can’t read many big words.”

“Can I see it?”

Hoping for an easy escape, Trevor shook his head.

“Where did you get the magazine?”

“I found it. Honest.”

“Where did you find it?”

“It was in your wastebasket. You were done with it, so I didn’t think you’d mind if I looked.”

“It’s not a good thing to be going through wastebaskets.” Jeremy took a deep breath and lifted his son onto his lap. “Let me see it.”

Trevor slipped off of Jeremy’s knee and walked to his closet with the enthusiasm of a condemned man approaching the gallows. He dug into his toy chest and returned with the crumpled magazine. He handed his father a *People* magazine with Claudia’s picture on the cover and lowered his head awaiting his punishment.

He lifted his son's chin. "Can we talk about this?"

Trevor grinned and hopped up on the bed beside him. He pointed to a picture.

"Who's this guy with his arm around Claudia?"

"His name is Michael Cole." Jeremy cleared his throat. "He's her...uh, husband."

A look of fright spread across the little boy's face. "Does she have kids, too?"

"No. This article says they're getting a divorce."

Trevor's face brightened. "Then she won't be married anymore. She could marry somebody who had a kid 'n' be their mommy."

"Grown-ups don't usually get a divorce and marry someone else right away." He slipped his arm around him. "It just doesn't work that way."

Trevor's voice was firm with conviction. "I can wait."

Jeremy bent over and kissed his son on the top of his head. Trevor said these types of things over and over. Claudia had become an obsession. He regretted ever letting Stephanie talk him into attending the reunion dance.

He also regretted letting Trevor accompany him on the trip to New York. It was his fault, not Trevor's. He'd known how desperately Trevor longed for a mother. Claudia overwhelmed him with attention, causing the boy to invent fantasies about her coming back for him.

Perhaps a child psychologist could help Trevor work through this, he thought.

Happy again, Trevor rocked on the bed. "After she takes me to the top of the Umpire State Building, she's going to take me home to her apartment and read me *Good Night Moon* at bedtime." He smoothed the wrinkled page and lovingly touched her photo. "Look how pretty she is, Dad,"

"Yes," Jeremy whispered, "she is very, very pretty."

~ 58 ~

Leesburg, VA

"What are you saying? That can't be."

When Brian invited her to spend the weekend at his Virginia farm overlooking the Potomac River, Claudia assumed it would be a family visit. She'd spent the day walking the fields with her two nephews and their big Golden Retriever. After they returned to the house late in the afternoon, she helped her sister-in-law, Jennifer, prepare dinner.

Only when they retired to his study did Claudia realize his invitation had been a ruse. He'd known of the problems with Souvanée all along and hadn't mentioned them.

"How can Souvanée not be certain they'll extend my contract?"

"It's Michael."

"What about him?"

Brian put on the confident smile he used whenever he delivered bad news to a client. "The tabloids haven't been kind to you. He manipulated facts to make it appear he's the aggrieved party in the divorce. There are suggestions of infidelity on your part."

She leaped out of her chair. "Infidelities? After what he did how can anyone accuse me of anything?"

"I'm sure Michael's feeding it to them."

"And they're lapping it up like barn cats around a bowl of warm milk. Can you stop it?"

"I can paper their walls with injunctions, for all the good it'll do. It only gives them something else to report."

"Okay, let's table it for now." She sank back into the sofa. "What about Souvanée?"

"As I told you, this quickie marriage and sudden divorce has undermined your public image." He waggled his fingers in the air. "The divorce makes you appear, unstable, flighty. The folks in

Paris are wondering if you're the right person to represent them."

"I worked like a dog for Souvanée and nearly had a nervous breakdown getting their program off the ground. I've grown that brand from zero market share to a household name. Thanks to me, they have 14% of the worldwide cosmetics market. They earn hundreds of millions of dollars from cosmetics every year and now that I've delivered the goods those disingenuous jerks stab me in the back. You'd think they'd show a little gratitude."

She slumped into the sofa to sulk.

"You know better. Their reply would be, 'Yes, and you've been generously compensated for the work you did."

She shot him an angry look. "Whose side are you on?"

"Yours, I'm just pointing out their side of the story. The situation at Souvanée has changed since you signed-on with them. When their other model suddenly died, they were in a bind. You showed them a way out."

"Why now? We're only a few months into a new contract year."

"I always begin negotiating next year's renewal as soon as the current contract goes into effect. It gives me time to deal with whatever crops up, and, believe me, something always does. I don't usually involve you until the very end. This year things are, well, different."

He led her over to his latest addition to the room, the fireplace. All summer he and the boys collected flat stones on his farm. In August, he hired a stonemason to assemble them into a fireplace and hearth. To give it a rustic look, Brian refinished a post from the farm's 150-year-old barn for the mantel.

He settled her into one of two wingback chairs angled in front of the fire. They sat quietly, watching the flames.

"Fire's nice, isn't it?"

Claudia mumbled a reply, feigning interest for Brian's sake.

He warmed his palms. "Notice how shallow the firebox is and the wide angles of the side walls? It's based on a design by

Count Rumford."

"Counts design fireplaces nowadays? What next, space shuttles by Dukes and Viceroys?" He'd drawn her into a discussion of fireplaces. Fireplaces! She couldn't believe it.

"Count Rumford was born in the late 1700's in Massachusetts."

"They had American Counts back then?"

"His name was Benjamin Thompson. He became a Count later." Brian pointed into the firebox. "Notice the herringbone pattern in the firebrick on the back and sides? Really gives it an authentic touch, doesn't it?"

Here's a man who desperately needs to get himself a hobby, Claudia thought. "What got Rumford interested in fireplaces?"

"Fireplaces were high science in those days; everyone heated with them." He rotated to face her. "Think of it this way. Suppose someone could modify an ordinary car engine so it got 150 miles to the gallon? That's essentially what Rumford did."

"I see. But the big oil companies are suppressing his technology so everyone doesn't start running their cars on sticks and twigs, right?"

"Boy, aren't we in a mood tonight?"

She wasn't of a mind to discuss the aesthetics of fireplaces, or the BTU output of various hardwoods any longer. "Let's get back to Souvanée. From what you said, this won't come to pass for nearly a year."

"Right, I simply wanted you to be apprised of the situation."

"It's hard to imagine they could consider doing this."

Brian rested an elbow on the chair arm and leaned closer. "The people in charge today weren't even there six years ago. They inherited a thriving business with a robust market share. They're happy to take credit for your efforts."

"So that's that? 'It's been great doing business with you; don't let the door smack you on the butt on the way out?'"

"You're making too much out of this. For all we know, it's

nothing more than a negotiating ploy. We always knew this could happen. That's why I negotiated residual payments on existing market share if your contract isn't renewed.

"You're not exactly being thrown onto the breadlines. I asked Brent for projections. If Souvanée's market share holds, you'll earn about $30 million in residuals. Your perfume line is a branded product. Without you they can't sell it. Then there's your clothing business, real properties and other investments."

"It's not about money. Call it pride if you want, but I don't like going out this way. Truthfully, I'm not even angry with Souvanée; it's Michael I'm upset with. To build his business, he trashed mine."

Most of her staff supported the cosmetics portion of her work. Their jobs depended upon Souvanée as much as hers did. Those people weren't just hired help, they were practically family. A number of them had been with her from the beginning. Michael may have gone after her, but he'd affected the whole organization. She fidgeted in the chair, seething over what Cole had done.

Brian made soothing motions with his hands. "You're starting to frighten me, MJ. I've seen that look before."

The fire threw flickering shadows across her face as Claudia developed her strategy. Clearly a divorce wouldn't solve her problems with Cole. She needed to settle his hash once and for all.

"There's that expression again. What are you thinking?"

"You take care of Souvanée and I'll take care of Michael Cole."

"You can't go slamming people into walls. You're not a kid anymore."

She patted Brian's arm. "You're right. It's taken me a while, but I've learned how to get the job done without the drama."

"What are you going to do?"

A sly grin curled her lips. "I'm going to rip Michael's heart out."

~ 59 ~

Washington, DC

Brian Combs glanced up at his sister. Even dressed casually, she looked lovely. The denim jeans and large silver belt buckle she wore accented her long legs and trim figure. Her white cotton blouse had feminine ruffles along the placket and she'd laid its pointed collar over the lapels of her plum-colored jacket.

"When you called, I expected to discuss your divorce. Are you sure you about this?"

"That's why I'm here."

"Speculating in stock is risky business. As your attorney, I'm against it."

"Trust me. I've given it a lot of thought."

He thumped the thick stack of research papers she'd faxed him. "Clearly you have."

"You'd be right if said, 'Hey Brian, I got this great idea while I brushed my teeth this morning. Lets plop down half a million on XYZ Computers and see where the market takes us?' That's not what I'm doing. This is PGL."

"And the principal stockholder of Paradise Getaways, Limited is your soon-to-be ex-husband, Michael Cole. I don't know if the timing's right."

"This is the perfect time."

"How so?"

"Both the British Government and British press are on my side."

Brian appeared confused.

Reaching into her briefcase, she removed a *London Times* and laid it on his desk. She'd highlighted a column in the financial section. "Living in the States, you probably haven't heard about this. They're investigating Michael's accounting practices. This article tears him to shreds. What kind of impact will this have on the stock price?"

"It'll drive it down."

"But those are only paper losses unless we divest Michael of the company."

She flipped through the papers in her briefcase. Whipping out several pages of stock graphs, she dropped them on top of the newspaper. She bent forward to trace the descending line with a neatly manicured fingernail. "He's already up to his eyeballs in alligators, what better time to attack?"

"What if he's exonerated?"

She glared at him. "This is Michael Cole, not Mother Teresa. Do you honestly believe there's a chance he's not guilty?"

"I wish I shared your confidence."

"Do you remember how, when we were running low on groceries, Momma would crumble up the bacon and scramble eggs over it? And you and Brent always complained you didn't get any bacon because you couldn't see it on the plate?"

Brian smiled. "She'd always say, 'Trust me, it's in there."

"The same goes for Michael."

"I feel you're too close to the situation to be objective. I sense this has more to do with revenge than investing."

"You betcha it's about revenge. I've told you what he did... the women, the abuse. And there's the problem he's created for me with Souvanée."

Brian's chair squeaked when he leaned back. He swiveled to one side and crossed his long legs.

"Can I ask you something, MJ?"

"Sure."

"Why did you choose to marry him in the first place?"

"I didn't choose to marry him."

"You could've fooled me."

Claudia lowered her eyes and took a deep breath. "You know how hard it's been for me to file this divorce. A sudden marriage followed by a quickie divorce goes against everything I believe in."

"I never knew what you saw in him."

"Oh, he was quite charming in the beginning. Unfortunately you came in during the second reel."

"But that doesn't require you to take over his company."

"You don't understand, there's more to it than that."

Brian slowly rocked the chair. Interlacing his fingers across his stomach, he said, "Tell me about the *more to it than that*, MJ. Then I'll understand, too."

"Okay. First, there's Souvanée. Claudia Monet is more than just a name. Claudia Monet is a brand, the foundation on which I've built my career. You know more about the trouble Michael's created for me there than I do."

Brian nodded.

"What would McDonald's do if you besmirched their fries? Would Campbell's twiddle their thumbs while you bad-mouthed tomato soup? I have every right to fight back."

She gave him a resolute look, grabbed the lapels of her jacket and gave them a tug, closing the matter to further discussion.

"And number two." She leaned over and extracted several sheets of paper from her open briefcase. "Which type of chocolate do I prefer?"

Brian answered without hesitation. "Milk chocolate, you never liked the dark stuff."

"The evening he proposed, a waiter brought a tray of Michael's special chocolate truffles to our table. As luck would have it, I tucked several into my pocket. When I got back to New York, I had them analyzed. Here's the lab report on the dark chocolate ones."

She tossed a sheet of paper at him.

Brian read aloud. "Expected ingredients found in dark chocolate sample: sucrose, cocoa, cocoa butter, soy lecithin, salt, vanilla, butter, cream, orange extract, orange peel. Unexpected ingredients: None." He shrugged.

"Michael ate the dark ones. Here are the expected ingredients found in the milk chocolate ones."

Another sheet of paper zipped across his desk. He looked it over. The two sheets were practically identical except for the milk.

She rattled a third sheet. "We're not done yet. Milk chocolate sample Page Two. First unexpected ingredient: 3,4 – Methylenedioxymethamphetamine, a physco-active drug known on the street as Ecstasy, the Love Drug, and X. It increases brain activity and triggers a massive release of dopamine and serotonin. Effects: a sense of euphoria, followed by a feeling of calmness. Users feel more sociable, often in a sensual, uninhibited way. Side effects: nausea, dry mouth, elevated blood pressure and dehydration. MDMA is banned in the US as a dangerous narcotic."

Brian's mouth dropped. "So he—"

Her raised hand stopped him. "Second unexpected ingredient: Gamma hydroxybutyric acid, a physco-active drug known as GHB, Fantasy, and Easy Lay. Effects: intoxication, happiness, desire to socialize, affectionate and playful feelings, sensuality. Side effects: nausea, dizziness, amnesia, loss of consciousness and paralysis, followed by death. GHB is manufactured from its precursor, GBL, a solvent found in floor cleaners, nail polish and super glue removers."

She tossed the page at him. "Just for the record, I almost tossed my cookies right there in the restaurant. All evening I was so thirsty I couldn't get enough water. And I barely remember anything."

"Jeez, MJ, I don't know what to say."

Claudia leaped out of her chair and planted her palms on Brian's desk.

"Say you'll help me nail Michael's worthless hide to the barn door! Listen, I may have gotten Momma's good looks, but my strong-willed determination came straight from Daddy. I am going to do this. It's time to either fish or cut bait. Are you with me, or do I start shopping for another lawyer?"

Claudia didn't wait for his answer. She spun around, stormed across the room and stared out the window.

Brian watched her blot the corners of her eyes with a tissue. If Cole had been willing to put her life at risk to achieve his goals, what else might he do? Brian feared she still underestimated her former husband.

He crossed the room and touched her shoulders. "M.J.?" His voice conveyed the love he felt for her. She turned to look up at him. He pulled her into his arms and hugged her.

"Years ago I promised I'd always be on your side, and I will be."

~ 60 ~

"Don't let her beautiful exterior fool you. She can be tough as nails," Brian whispered.

The men's conversation ceased when Claudia entered. She'd come to do business and dressed accordingly. She wore a tailored, champagne-colored pantsuit with a discrete pinstripe, a tropical wool blend, Italian made. Her jacket was a classic two-button style with notched lapels. She'd matched it with a Wedgewood blue silk blouse and gold jewelry.

The pantsuit and blouse were among the fall offerings in her signature line of clothing. Unlike many celebrities, Claudia frequently wore her trademarked outfits. She could do this because she insisted upon quality, a quality product and a quality presentation. She wouldn't put her name on cheap or shoddy merchandise, and she didn't want her clothing dangling from a pipe rack between the beach balls and a pyramid of motor oil in some discount store. Her line was available only at the best department stores in a dedicated kiosk.

The men at the table stared.

She stood tall and gave them a knee-weakening smile. Shoulders back, face forward and eyes straight ahead, she crossed the room with a briefcase under her arm. She took her time, giving them a good long look.

When she reached the conference table, she plopped her briefcase down on the corner and glanced around the table. Her eyes circled the group, briefly pausing to memorize each face. "Good morning, gentlemen."

Brian rose and took his sister's arm. "These are your partners, MJ. I'll introduce you," He led her around the table and, one-by-one, introduced her to each of the venture capitalists, brokers and investment bankers he'd invited to the meeting.

A stack of color-coded pasteboard folders sat beside Brian's place near the head of the table. He looked at his notes and slid the first stack of papers over to her.

"These are the various incorporation documents. The corporation we're forming today will be known as The PGL Acquisition Group and based in the Caribbean." Brian pointed to one of the men at the table. "Walter is your corporate representative. All funds will be deposited in, and cleared through, his bank."

He directed her eyes to the other side of the table. "Alfred, Gerald, and Timothy represent venture capital firms. They'll extend financing to your new company."

The men smiled at the mention of their names.

"Martin's firm will be the company's broker. His London trading office will execute the orders through correspondents. His Merger and Acquisition team, specialists in hostile takeovers, developed our strategic plan."

Brian handed her a pen. "Before you sign the papers, let's review. Part of the financing comes in the form of loans and part in the form of equity. The strategic plan calls for us to take PGL private, deal with the regulatory problems and eventually do an IPO for the new company."

Claudia glanced around the table, smiling at her partners-to -be.

"You'll be signing two notes today. One, as CEO of the new corporation, pledging the PGL stock you acquire as collateral for the margin loans. The second is a personal guarantee secured by your future earnings. Clear?"

She took a deep breath and nodded. "That's the way you laid it out yesterday."

For first time since she'd started down this path, the full impact of the undertaking became clear. If she ended up on the losing end of this fight, she could consign herself to a lifetime of indentured servitude.

"I also have papers here temporarily pledging some of your stocks and other investments as collateral on a $75 million loan from Walter's bank. He'll disburse those funds into PGL

Acquisition Group's account immediately, giving the firm working capital."

Claudia adjusted the first document and brought the pen down. Pausing, she glanced up and smiled. "I hope one of you is planning to buy lunch today, because after I sign these I won't be able to afford it."

London

PGL stock continued to plummet. Looking away from the ticker when his phone buzzed, Whitestone hoped for the best and steeled himself for the worst. "Michael, how are you?"

"What bad news do you bring today?"

"I wanted to see if your efforts to find support for PGL stock had yielded fruit."

"As market maker, it's your job to support PGL stock."

"We've been down this road before. You can't float a leaking vessel. Besides, we both know, as market maker, Kensington Partners is the buyer of last resort."

"Are you buying?"

"Yes, we're buying. But I can't accumulate shares at this pace indefinitely."

"We need to stop Hemphill," Cole said. "He'll ruin me."

"Hemphill is merely a bureaucrat."

"You sound like Chesley. Every time I bring it up with him, he whines and cries and wrings his hands. I'm going to have to show them who's in control."

Cole wasn't the only one without a friend, Whitestone thought. He'd invested too much of his firm's capitol in a futile effort to stabilize PGL stock. The bank hounded him daily for additional margin deposits. If PGL sank, it might suck Kensington Partners down with it.

Cole's tone unexpectedly brightened. "Maybe I could have Hemphill shot. I'll line the bastards up and shoot them all."

"I don't believe that would be wise."

"Either they get shot, or I do."

"I want you to listen very carefully, Michael. Kensington Partners cannot support PGL stock much longer."

"What about my new offering?"

"It stumbled coming out of the gate. I'm sorry."

"What am I going to do?"

"You need to begin exploring the possibility of restructuring the company. Most likely, you'll have to declare insolvency."

As soon as Whitestone hung up, he rang his trading desk and instructed them to reduce their purchases of PGL stock until they rolled-over their current holdings.

Though neither Cole nor Whitestone knew it, PGL's fate was already sealed. A new, well-funded, professionally savvy, and ruthlessly aggressive force entered the market on the overnight trading session. Stepping into the vacuum created by Whitestone's retreat, PGL Acquisition Group scooped-up all available shares and quickly accumulated a commanding position.

~ 61 ~

Washington, DC

The restaurant, on the second floor of a renovated warehouse, sat in a trendy section off Washington's Beltway. Its newly refinished wooden floor proudly displayed the stains, nicks and dents of its former life. Interior designers left the ceiling open, exposing duct pipes, conduits and reinforcing rods as further proof of the building's history. Together with the high, multi-paned windows and old freight elevator, it created an industrial chic justifying the expensive menu.

Claudia sat near a huge concrete pillar surrounded by *Ficus bejamina* trees in planters. She'd almost given up on Brian when he rushed across the room.

He dropped his briefcase beside the table. "Sorry. I was in court."

"Arguing ground-breaking precedents before the Supreme Court I imagine."

"I was fighting an eviction notice for a Legal Aid client."

"Good for you."

A busboy filled their water glasses then disappeared. In the bar a pianist tapped out the opening bars of Cole Porter's *Night and Day*.

"I assume you called because you have news," Claudia said, after they ordered.

"I do indeed. Thanks to continued press coverage, and Michael's stubborn refusal to withdraw the stock offering, you're well on your way to accumulating the shares you need, and at considerably less than we budgeted."

Claudia smiled.

"I've got to hand it to you. It looks like you're going to pull this off. You're going to be rich, well, at least richer."

"This was never about getting rich. It's about refusing to be taken advantage of."

"Should we order a bottle of champagne to celebrate?"

"Not yet. The time to dance on the grave is after the corpse is safely buried."

Brian grinned. "Really Sis, grave, corpse, buried? Your analogies are, well, downright shocking."

Claudia put down her fork. "We're not home free yet. There isn't a bottomless pit of PGL shares. Michael controls maybe 30% of the outstanding shares. We already have," she rocked her hand, "what, 45%?"

Brian nodded and twirled his fettuccine. He could see where she was going. If Cole controlled 30% and they owned 45%, that left a swing vote of around 25%. Whoever controlled those shares determined the company's destiny.

He frowned. "It's going to be tight."

"We need every share we can lay our hands on. What about institutional holdings – banks, investment funds and the like?"

"They're low-hanging fruit. Martin picked them off early-on."

"Is there anyone else buying shares?"

"In the beginning a few day-traders tried to get into the game, but they got caught in our downdraft. I don't think anyone has the nerve to run against us now."

"Well then where are those shares?" Claudia reached into her briefcase, removed several graphs and opened them between their plates. "This tracks our purchases against the total daily volume of PGL shares traded. Notice the shaded area? That's the spread between what we've purchased and the outstanding shares Michael doesn't control." She rapped the page with the end of her pen. "We need those shares."

"Kensington Partners supported the stock in the early stages. Martin says word on the street is Whitestone took a big hit when the market went south. They say he's losing his taste for the game."

Claudia sipped her coffee, swirling it on her tongue as she thought. After a moment, she retraced the lines on the graph. "Of course, it's Kensington. The spread is narrowing. We're buying increasingly greater percentages of the market each day. Martin's right. Whitestone's pulling back."

"Do you know him?"

"We're not bosom buddies, but he'll take my calls. Can Martin give us an idea how many shares he holds?"

"I'm sure his traders could. Martin also suspects Michael negotiated a hold harmless agreement with Whitestone."

"So he'll reimburse Kensington for any losses incurred on his behalf."

"Given that, how do we bring Whitestone over to our side?"

"Whitestone's agreement is with Michael and, if Michael goes the agreement goes with him."

They were nearly alone in the restaurant now. The pianist sat at the bar smoking a cigarette and joking with a waitress. A busboy moved around the room spreading clean tablecloths for the dinner trade.

"Having Whitestone's shares gives you control," Brian said, "but it doesn't get rid of Michael. He'll never sell, and we can't take the company private without his agreement."

Michael had to go, and Claudia thought she knew how to do it. "Let's wrap this up. I've got a couple of other things I want to discuss."

"I'll talk to Martin and get an estimate on Kensington's shares."

"Super. I'm flying to Europe tomorrow. I want to meet Whitestone face-to-face." She gave him a confident smile. "I'll get those shares."

Brian slid his long legs out from under the table and crossed them to the side. Placing one hand on his knee, in a syrupy-sweet falsetto he said, "Why Alistair dear, it's so nice to see you." He ran his hand up his leg. "My goodness, would you look at my skirt.

It's hiked-up clear to Montana. I just can't seem to keep that little thing down where it's supposed to be. What's a girl to do?" he asked, tugging at the hem of his suit coat.

"That is *not* what I had in mind."

Chuckling, Brian flipped over a fresh sheet on his legal pad and scribbled reminders. "What else?"

"What's the divorce status?"

"Michael's solicitor was relieved to hear we'd settle on what the nuptial agreement called for."

"I don't have to rely on any agreement. I'll beat him at his own game, fair and square." She sighed deeply. "Money is all Michael cares about. I intend to take it all, right down to his last penny."

"What if Whitestone double-crosses you?"

"The man's not a fool. He'll see which side his bread is buttered on."

Brian scribbled more notes then raised his eyes expectantly.

"Also, there are some things I want to retrieve while I'm in London. Can I legally go in and out of the penthouse?"

"What is it you want to get?"

"It's personal."

"Isn't this all."

"Can I get in, or not?"

"Is your name on the deed?"

"Michael insisted."

"Since you're still his legal wife and your name is on the deed, you can come and go at will. I'd recommend you take someone with you and choose a time when he's away."

"But I can get in?"

"Just don't do anything crazy like trash the place." Brian leaned forward. "Whatever it is, why not let it go."

"I can't let it go."

"I'd feel better if you did."

"You know I never take unnecessary risks, but I won't turn tail and run either. That runs counter to every promise I made to Momma."

"Legal right or no legal right, If Michael finds you inside the apartment, you'll be in more trouble than you bargained for.

London

"How large of a position have they accumulated?" Cole asked.

Whitestone lied. "I'm not sure. It takes time for transfers to be settled, booked and recorded."

"Who are they?"

Whitestone lied again. "Typically, the street knows, but this time everyone's tight-lipped."

Cole's fears finally broke through. "What are you implying?"

"The handwriting's on the wall, someone clearly intends to take your company away."

"You're my broker, Alistair, my market maker...my friend. Together, we have a controlling interest. You still have those shares, don't you?"

"Yes, I have them."

"I knew I could count on you. Remember, I take care of my friends. Be smart. Go with the winning side."

Cole was right. He should go with a winner. Whitestone rested his cigar in the ashtray and dialed the phone.

"Martin, Whitestone here. I promised Claudia I'd respond before day's end. I'll option my PGL shares on the terms she and I discussed."

Whitestone walked to the window and folded his hands behind him. Sunlight sparkled off the dome of St. Paul's Cathedral. Despite its shaky start this might be a good day after all. He wouldn't miss Michael Cole.

~ 62 ~

London

"I know it's a lot to ask without more of an explanation, but there's no one else I can turn to." Though she tried not to sound frightened, the telephone receiver felt slippery in her damp palm.

"This afternoon would work for you then?" Schoonover asked.

"Yes, it would be perfect. Can you do it?" She drummed her nails on the hotel's bedside table, awaiting his reply.

"I'll do my best, but you know how unpredictable he can be."

"I only need a half-hour, although longer would be better." She glanced around the rented suite nervously. Michael couldn't know I'm in London, she told herself.

"I'll provide you with as much time as possible. You'll need confirmation. How can I reach you?"

A call through the hotel's switchboard would reveal her location. She gave him her cell number.

"You'll hear from me one way or the other."

"You can't imagine how much I appreciate this."

"I'm happy to be of assistance." Then, in a paternal tone, Schoonover added, "You know, this is a very foolhardy undertaking."

"I understand the risks."

"For your sake, I hope you do. One last thing, Miss Monet."

"Yes?"

"Godspeed."

Schoonover excised himself from the meeting when he saw Cole pass in the hallway. He leaned out the door. "Michael! May I speak with you?"

Cole stopped. By the time he turned around, Schoonover stood beside him.

“What is it?”

“There is something I must discuss with you.”

“Can’t it wait?”

“I only need a half-hour or so. I have some intelligence on the takeover attempt.”

“Come by at teatime.”

Whitestone watched Cole walk away and smiled. He’d taken the bait.

Claudia dressed all in black with dark sunglasses and a scarf over her hair. Instead of carrying a purse, she had a fanny pack tucked under her leather jacket. She hurried across the marble lobby, hoping to reach the elevator without being recognized.

Warren, the doorman, dashed her hopes. “Excuse me, Ma’am. Do you have business in this building?”

Claudia turned into a small alcove.

Warren followed her around the corner.

She raised the glasses.

“Miss Monet. The news said the two of you are divorcing.”

Claudia nodded.

“I can’t say as I blame you.”

She took his hand in hers and squeezed. “You didn’t see me here, Warren. Do you understand? Michael can’t know I’m in London.”

“Are you going up to the penthouse?”

“Yes, there are things there I must retrieve.”

Concern clouded Warren’s face.

“I’ve checked with my attorney; he says it’s all right.”

Warren motioned her back behind a coat rack. “Stay here until you see my signal.” He glanced around the corner. “I’ll summon your lift."

When Cole didn't show for their meeting, Schoonover walked down the hall to his office. "Michael and I had a meeting planned. Has he been delayed?"

Cole's secretary checked. "He didn't note it. Sorry, Admiral, he's left the building."

Schoonover exhaled sharply. "When did he leave?"

"About fifteen minutes ago. He took a call from a woman, then left. He won't be back until tomorrow."

He had no way of warning Claudia.

Too anxious to leave and too worried to work, Schoonover remained in his office, pacing and staring out at the dark skyline as he waited for news.

Claudia set her watch alarm for 15 minutes and entered the penthouse. Ignoring the light switch, she relied instead on the tiny beam of her penlight. It helped knowing the way in the dark. She dashed into Michael's home office, clicked on the computer and rocked from one foot to the other while she waited for it to boot.

The screen lit up and she went to work. Plugging a Flash Drive into a USB port, she selected the folders on his desktop and copied them en masse. Like a burglar, she had to grab what she could and get out. She'd review the files later and discard what she didn't need. As soon as the transfer finished, she popped it out and inserted another.

There was more around there somewhere. She aimed the light into one drawer at a time, and sifted through their contents. She found a case of CD's labeled *PGL Files* in the top drawer. Good stuff. She transferred them one-by-one, swapped out the Flash Drive and resumed her search. She copied everything she found in the second drawer and moved down.

In the back corner of the bottom drawer Claudia discovered another cache of CD's. She put the one into the computer. It held nothing but JPG's. Hitting Select All, she moved them over without opening them. She pulled the last Flash Drive and began shutting down.

Out in the hall the intercom buzzed long and hard.

"Mr. Cole in the lift with female companion," Warren said twice.

Her blood ran cold. Claudia ran her eyes around the room. She stared at the only hiding place available, the kneehole of the desk.

She couldn't fit in there.

But Cole's key was in the lock and, with seconds to spare, fit she did. Once she'd squeezed in, Claudia stretched out her arm and snagged the base of the desk chair. She rolled it over, covering the opening. Her watch beeped just as the door opened. "Fat lot of good you do me now," she muttered and clicked

~ 63 ~

Baltimore

"Whoa, Partner. Break time."

Jeremy rounded a curve and headed for a bench. Slumping forward, he rested his hands on his knees and hung his head, breathing hard. He and Trevor ran several times a week. Actually, Jeremy did the running. Trevor rode alongside on his bike.

He snatched the water bottle off of the frame of Trevor's bike as he rolled to a stop and dropped onto the bench. Jeremy was gulping water when Trevor drew his attention to a woman jogging on the path below them.

Young and attractive, she had her blond hair tied back. Moving with a steady, relaxed rhythm, she rounded the curve legs churning. She pulled even then passed by them in an instant. The two of them watched her ponytail swish across her back as she disappeared down the path.

"Did you see her, Dad? She looked like Claudia."

"You say that every time you see a woman with blond hair."

"No I don't."

Jeremy shook his head. "MJ's taller and her hair has pretty undertones. Her nose isn't as big and her cheekbones are higher. She also moves a lot smoother. That lady looked like she might trip over her own feet." He took another sip of water. "She didn't look much like MJ at all."

Trevor sat down beside him, waiting his turn. "Whaddaya think she's doin' right now, Dad?"

"I don't know." He handed him the bottle with a faraway look. "I don't even know where she is."

Trevor held the bottle with both hands. "I bet she's doin' something exciting."

"How would you know?"

Trevor swept a sleeve across his lips. "Cause she's always doin' exciting stuff." He seemed surprised his father didn't know this.

Jeremy sighed. “What did Dr. Baldwin tell you?”

Trevor stared at the ground.“I’m sorry, Dad.”

“Dr. Baldwin wants to help you, but you’ve got to do your part.”

“I’m trying, Dad. Honest. But when I tell Dr. Baldwin Claudia’s coming back, she doesn’t believe me.” He bit his lip, forcing back tears. “I bet she thinks I’ll never get to the top of the Umpire State Building.”

“Sure you will. You and I could go to New York by ourselves.”

Trevor jumped up off the bench, juggling the water bottle and nearly dropping it. “No, Dad, we can’t do that. She has to be there.”

“You’ve been told not to talk like this.”

Dr. Baldwin, Trevor’s psychologist, had made minimal progress in dealing with his obsession over Claudia. After their last session, she’d recommended anti-depressants. As a physician, Jeremy knew the side effects this class of drugs had on youngsters and rejected the idea.

A few weeks earlier, Trevor spent his afternoon scratching out a letter to Claudia. It broke Jeremy’s heart to see his son so committed to a hopeless cause. But, Trevor’s faith remained unshaken. She was coming back. Period. End of discussion.

“We were right there in her living room when I asked her. She gave me a snow globe as proof.” He stood at attention and put his hand over his heart. “She said, ‘Trevor, I swear I’ll take you to the top of the Umpire State Building no matter what.”

“I don’t think she swore any such thing. Grownups sometimes say things, even promise things, which they later find out they can’t do. It’s not because they’re mean or telling fibs, it’s because circumstances change. You’ve got to accept that.”

Trevor lowered his chin to his chest and covered his ears. “Sorry, Dad, something’s wrong. I can’t hear what you’re saying.”

Jeremy stood up and stretched. “It’s time to head back.”

After adjusting his helmet, Trevor straddled his bike and spun it around. A wide smile crossed his face as he rolled forward. He peddled hard in the direction his father had jogged, caught up and zipped past.

“What’s the big hurry?”

Trevor leaned into the handlebars. Feet flying, he never looked back. “Maybe she’ll be waiting for us when we get home.”

London

Crouched beneath the desk, Claudia listened to distant laughter and the muted clink of ice in glasses. She heard footsteps then a woman’s form appeared, silhouetted in the doorway.

“So this is your office?”

“Would you like to see it?” Cole reached around her, feeling for the light switch.

She stopped him. “Don’t turn the light on. It’s sexier in the shadows.” She scanned the dim room noting the trophies on bookcase shelves, hunting scenes on the wall and the brass statue on the credenza. “Very masculine, I can almost feel testosterone oozing out of the wallpaper.”

He nuzzled the nape of her neck. “I know more direct ways of experiencing testosterone.”

She wiggled away and entered the room. She danced her fingers around the desktop, toying with various items. “Nice desk.” She rapped it with her knuckles. “Good and solid.”

The thumping reverberated around Claudia like a bass drum.

She swept her hand in an arc. “Wood’s lovely, too. I don’t recognize it.”

With the hall light at Cole’s back, his shadow slithered ahead of him as he approached.

Claudia watched it advance and covered her mouth to suppress a scream. It crept into the kneehole, surrounding her in darkness.

He snapped on the desk lamp. “It looks best in the light. It’s custom made from a single slab of Ancient Kauri.”

“I’ve never heard of Kauri?”

“It comes from New Zealand. The tree grew to be the size of a giant redwood, died and toppled into a peat bog. The acidic environment preserved the wood for over 50,000 years.” He made scooping motions with his fingers. “They harvest the trees with bulldozers.”

“You lugged a slice of 50,000-year-old tree all the way from New Zealand to have it made into a desk?”

“I saw it, I wanted it, and now I have it.” He slipped his arm around her waist. “I always get what I want.”

Claudia cringed inches below, listening to them joke and flirt with white-knuckled interest.

“You’d be more comfortable without this.”

A woman’s coat thudded into the desk chair.

Scarcely breathing, Claudia stared out. The position of their feet told her he’d moved behind her. Piece by piece, the woman’s clothing gradually joined her coat.

“I can take it from here.” She gave a little wiggle and a pair of lace knickers draped themselves around her ankles. Pulling one foot out, she gave them a soft kick.

Claudia shrank back as they floated toward her. How had she ended up scrunched underneath a desk listening to her ex-husband seduce another woman? If Brian asked, she’d tell him, “It seemed like a good idea at the time.” It seemed much less so now.

“Funny isn’t it?”

“What’s that, Amanda?”

Claudia felt the icy tingle of recognition, Whitestone’s Amanda?

"How things work out."

Cole whisked the chair out of the kneehole. "Ever done it on a desk?"

"I'd rather be in the bedroom the way nature intended."

"I'm in control here. If I want you on the desk, you'll bloody well get up there.

Claudia sensed Amanda's shock at Cole's sudden mood swing. She couldn't warn her that this was the way his rages began.

"You sound angry. Calm down."

"You'll do exactly as I tell you, Claudia. Get on the desk."

Amanda spun away from him. "Claudia? It's not that dark in here. I'm Amanda, you crazy fool."

"I am not crazy!' Cole shouted. "I have never been crazy. I will not allow it. I am in control. Do you hear? In control."

Amanda gathered her clothes. "Forget it, I'm out of here."

Cole grabbed her, twisting her around.

She screamed as the clothes tumbled from her arms.

Claudia laid her fingers where a similar yank had left bruises on her arm.

"You're going nowhere except onto the desk. When someone else is in control, you do what you're told." Cole placed a hand on Amanda's back, bending her forward.

"There's a computer monitor in the middle of the desk. I couldn't get up there if I wanted to."

Cole grabbed the keyboard and monitor and flung them away. They smashed against the wall and crashed to the floor, exploding in a flash of electrical sparks and flurry of shattered glass. Claudia covered her face as shards of glass ricocheted off the panel behind her.

Cole's fingers formed fists.

Amanda inched away.

Claudia squirmed and kneaded her calves and thighs to

relieve the cramps.

"Get on the desk."

"No."

Under the desk, Claudia heard the thud of a fist against flesh. Amanda tottered backward and collapsed into the desk chair. She no sooner hit the seat than she jumped up. Twirling the chair around, she held it by the arms, ready to use it as a battering ram. She swept hair out of her face and retreated, pleading with him.

Claudia's eyes followed them as they moved around the end of the desk. This was her chance. She had a clear path to the doorway.

Claudia rocked forward, hesitated momentarily, and then settled back onto her haunches. She couldn't abandon Amanda to Cole's madness. Her mind raced trying to find a solution. A moment later, she smiled and slipped her hand into her jacket.

~ 64 ~

Bly, KY

"Same as always?"

""Uh-huh. Have you heard from MJ recently?" Weezie asked.

"Now that you mention it, I haven't." Stephanie lifted Weezie's fine gray hair with a comb, layering the back. She checked the mirror as she worked. The tension in the older woman's eyes worried her. "What about you?"

"I haven't gotten a call, a letter, not even an email for two weeks."

"She's probably up against some deadlines. You know how hectic her schedule gets." Stephanie tried to reassure herself as much as Weezie.

"Neither of her brothers knows where she is either."

Stephanie forced herself to concentrate. She didn't want to make a mess of Weezie's hair. "Maybe you're making too much of this."

Motioning Stephanie into an empty chair, the older woman took her hands. "This morning, during my quiet time with the Lord, thoughts of Mary Jane kept returning to me. I can't shake the feeling that she's in danger."

London

Ignoring her twitching legs and aching back, Claudia took out her cell phone. She said a silent prayer and hit the power button. Cupping one hand around the phone to shield its glow, she held her breath and pushed the speed dial. Down the hall a phone rang in the bedroom. She'd neglected to delete the number from her directory and was grateful for the oversight.

Cole jerked around. Only a handful of people had that number. Leaving Amanda, he headed for the bedroom.

"Cole here."

"Michael?" she whispered from under the desk. "Is it really you?"

"What do you want?"

"I'm lonely. Talk to me."

"I have nothing to say to you."

For a moment she worried he'd hang up. Her whispers became pleas. "Just listen then, just for a little while. I need to talk."

"Why are you whispering?"

"I'm afraid." She sniffed, pretending she'd been crying. "I'm lonely. I miss you, Darling. I wish you were here with me in bed."

The sound of a voice roused Amanda from her stupor. She eyed the room. There was no one there, yet she heard a woman's voice. She cocked her head trying to pinpoint its source.

"What do you want?" Cole asked.

"I need you. I always loved the way you took control. No one else can do what you do." The words made Claudia's skin crawl.

Amanda tiptoed toward the desk.

"We had some good times, didn't we? Let's start over. I'm yours, Michael. Take control."

"You're in London?"

She'd hooked her fish. Claudia inched forward, confident enough to come out of her hidey-hole.

Amanda's face suddenly appeared in the open square in front of her. Eyes wide, they peered at each other.

For a moment Claudia feared Amanda might speak. Shaking her head, she pointed to the phone and put a finger to her lips.

Amanda nodded.

"Yes, I'm in London. I can be there with you in half an hour."

Claudia whispered endearments to Cole while communicating with Amanda in sign language. She pointed to herself, to Amanda, to the clothes on the floor and then to the door, making walking motions with her fingers.

Amanda quickly dressed.

Claudia tried to stand, but the muscles in her legs refused to co-operate. She staggered, careening out of control.

Amanda rushed to her side and slipped an arm around her. Together they limped down the hall, out the door and to the lift while Claudia completed arrangements to return to Cole.

"Hold on; there's someone's at the door of my room."She muted the phone so Cole wouldn't hear the lift chime. As soon as they were safely inside she whispered, "I'm sorry, Darling. It was a drunk at the door. Will you wait while I come to you?"

He assured her he would.

"Give me time to call a taxi. I'll make your every fantasy come true."

Claudia ended the call with Cole swearing he'd wait.

When the door opened she dashed across the lobby to Warren.

He smiled when he saw her. "You got my message?"

"You're a life-saver, Warren." She kissed him on the cheek. "We need a taxi and a place to hide until it arrives."

~ 65 ~

Claudia examined the material she'd copied as soon as she got to her hotel. The stuff in the upper drawer related to ventures the firm eventually rejected. Dropping the Flash Drive back into her purse, she moved on. The files from the second drawer were interesting and diverse.

One set itemized the kickbacks paid to various travel agencies for bookings with Paradise Getaways. Another contained the firm's raw financial data before it was re-calculated and smoothed-over for public consumption. The investigators were right. Michael was running a Ponzi scheme.

The final one contained access codes and account numbers. He'd stashed cash under myriad names in multiple locations. It also had copies of communications and payments to a man named Tereschenko. That deserved additional research.

Lastly, she studied the JPGs she'd found in the bottom drawer. She opened one and gasped. Each set featured multiple shots of couples during sexual intercourse. As she opened others, she noticed the men varied, but the woman didn't.

These were not amateurish attempts at pornography. She recognized some of the men...Bernard Chesley, Chancellor of the Exchequer and Second Lord of the Treasury among them. Blackmail appeared to be another of Michael's business strategies.

Before she closed them, she took a long look at the young woman with Chesley. The girl triggered something in Claudia's memory banks. She'd seen her somewhere before.

In Michael's office?

No, that wasn't it.

Whitestone's?

No again.

She'd seen her recently...maybe a waitress in the hotel restaurant, a desk clerk, the *concierge*?

No, no, and no.

Claudia decided to take a break. Yawning, she grabbed a soda from the hotel refrigerator. She dropped onto the couch and slid some newspapers aside to rest her feet on the coffee table. The front page skittered away, fluttering to the floor. She bent to retrieve it and recoiled in horror.

The young woman who'd seemed so familiar stared up at her from the floor. Claudia slowly lifted the paper. The girl on Michael's JPGs was on the front page. Or at least an artist's likeness of her was. She'd been found floating in the Thames and Scotland Yard sought help in identifying the dead woman.

Claudia converted all she'd gathered to CD's. She made two sets, one for the authorities and one for Brian to hold for safekeeping. Although she wouldn't allow herself to dwell on it, she knew Cole would surely kill her if he found out what she'd done.

Brian's set could go by overnight courier; they had a drop box in the lobby. She enclosed a note instructing him to hold them for her in his firm's safe.

The second set needed to go to the authorities. But it had to be done discretely. She wanted to bring Michael Cole down, not the entire British government. She pondered for several moments then dialed Schoonover's home number.

As she waited for the call to go through, Claudia inventoried the room. It'd only take a few minutes to cram everything into a suitcase and flee, get out of London as fast as she could.

The reasonable thing to do would have been to head west. Fly home and hide out in New York, or Virginia with Brian, at Brent's in Lexington, or with Weezie in Bly.

Instead, Claudia left London flying north and east. She crossed the North Sea, Denmark, Sweden and then the Baltic Sea. She touched down in northwest Russia, at St. Petersburg. The old Northern Capitol and city of the *Beliye Nochi*, the White Nights had been home to the great Romanov Tsars. Now it was home to Russian Mafia kingpin, Anatoly Tereschenko.

~ 66 ~

London

Cole replayed the events of the previous weekend in his mind as the lift rose. He seethed each time he recalled how Claudia played him for a fool. Most probably she'd made the call from hone and then laughed about it. If he ever got hold of her, there'd be no doubt about who was in control.

He entered the penthouse, loosened his tie and tossed his suit coat over a chair. He was groping for the light switch when a table lamp clicked on.

"Good evening, Mikhail," Anatoly Tereschenko said.

The old man's voice was throaty and heavily-accented. "You seem surprised."

"Why didn't you tell me you were coming?"

"When the mountain does not come to Mohammed, Mohammed is left no option but to go to the mountain."

Through sheer force of will, Cole propelled himself forward. He extended his hand in greeting.

The heavyset man studied the outstretched hand with disdain. "What is this? Are we barbarians? No, we're cultured individuals, gentlemen who understand protocol and revere tradition."

Cole's arm dropped to his side.

"Who am I that come at me with your hand out...a stranger, an underling? This cannot be how your mother raised you. You and I, Mikhail, we have a history."

"Yes sir," Cole replied, humble as a schoolboy in front of his principal.

"Your father was a good man, a man who lost his life serving my organization. Afterward, I gave your mother money and promised to always help. She took you home to London and changed your name, but still I sent checks. I owed your father, don't you see? And a man must always pay his debts."

His voice rose as he tapped a finger on his chest. "This is Tereschenko, your benefactor. The uncle you never had. Or have you forgotten?"

"No sir, I would never forget you."

"Nor will I forget you, Mikhail."

Cole shifted nervously.

"Do you care nothing for your heritage? When she was alive you surely greeted your Ma-Ma with a hug and a kiss on both cheeks. When the Metropolitan of St. Petersburg gives us his blessing, do we not kiss his right hand? Do we not bow and murmur a prayer before the holy icons?"

Tereschenko rose to his feet and opened his arms wide. "Come kiss your Uncle Tolya on the cheeks, as you should. It's only right."

Cole stepped forward, put his arms around him and planted a light peck on each of his ruddy cheeks.

The old man gripped him tightly, returning the kisses with gusto. He left one arm draped around Cole's shoulder for support and swept the other in a wide arc. "So this is how you live."

Tereschenko's noticed a painting on the wall. "A Matisse?" He craned forward, taking a closer look. "It's original."

His knowledge of art surprised Cole. "Yes, I found it in an auction gallery."

"Hmm, so you favor *French* Impressionists." The old man raised his bushy eyebrows. "And overlook Nikolai Timkov. Or would the work of a *Russian* Impressionist not dazzle your high-class friends?"

"I...uh, saw it and liked it, so I bought it."

Tereschenko continued inspecting Cole's penthouse. He poked his toe into the carpet, testing its nap. Piece by piece, he inventoried the tables and lamps, chairs and couches like a buyer appraising an estate. Once he'd seen all there was to see he stared out at the London skyline.

"Nice view."

Cole nodded.

"Do you have vodka?"

Cole did.

Tereschenko poked him in the ribs. "Then why have not you offered your dear Uncle a drink?"

Cole returned with the vodka and handed him the glass.

He sampled it, nodded his satisfaction, and waved him onto the couch.

Cole's anger simmered as he watched the old man dither. They both knew why he was here. He wanted his money. If it weren't for the regulatory problems, the stock sale would have been completed by now. There would have been money enough for everyone. The brokers, the creditors, even dear Uncle Tolya would have gotten his due.

The old man settled into the couch's soft cushions. "You live well, penthouse apartment, expensive artwork, and a trophy wife. Very well indeed, too well perhaps, but then, you are an important man."

Cole gave an apprehensive quiver. "You're flattering me. I'm just a hard-working businessman. I'm not important at all."

"Not important?" Tereschenko stroked his ample chin, shoving fleshy folds of skin around. "How far is it from St. Petersburg to London?"

Cole struggled to calculate a reasonable estimate of the distance between the two cities. Who cared? He didn't. He couldn't imagine the old man did either. He hated all this subterfuge, formality, and ritual.

Cole shrugged. "I suppose about 1,200 kilometers."

Tereschenko brought his fingertips together while he digested Cole's reply. From force of habit, he formed his fingers into what school children called cathedral arches. He absentmindedly flexed his fingers, expanding the arches then collapsing them.

Cole's eyes followed the movement, noting the generous

sprinkling of brown age spots scattered across the back of Tereschenko's hands. As his arthritic fingers flexed, thick ribbons of blue-green veins bulged beneath parchment skin. Up and down they went, the massive gold ring on his finger rose and fell, the diamonds surrounding its large ruby sparkling when the light caught them.

How well Cole remembered that ring.

"Hurry along," his mother scolded. "We haven't much time and we dare not be late."

She held his hand, jerking him along the sidewalk, prodding him to keep pace with her longer legs. Nearly stumbling, young Mikhail leaped a puddle to keep his new shoes dry.

They entered a room bigger than any he'd ever seen. His mother sat in a mahogany colored leather chair and spoke in hushed tones to a big man at a desk. The winter sun streaming in the window, made it difficult for the boy to discern the man's features. What he recalled were the man's massive hands, and his ring.

His mother's weeping made the boy uncomfortable. He stood beside her chair fidgeting and poking a finger into the neck of his starched shirt. While he waited, his eyes followed that gold ring up and down as the man's fingers flexed.

New memories flooded in.

He recalled their cheap flat in London and a youngster on the way home from school passing a man opening a cigar. The young schoolboy politely asked, "Please, sir. Might I have the paper ring?"

He hurried home and tucked it into his nightstand. In the evenings, his mother sick and he lonely and afraid, Michael slipped on the paper ring, made arches with his fingers and pretended he was a powerful man behind a big desk.

"What would you want with this silly old thing?" Auntie Jess asked when she found the ring on his nightstand. She turned it in her hand and laughed. "It's nothing but a wee bit of paper." Crumpling it into a ball, she threw his ring, along with his dreams, into the dustbin.

"It's 2,094 kilometers," Tereschenko said. "Over four hours, even on my Learjet." He tapped the chair arm for emphasis. "A tired old man with arthritic joints sat in an airplane all that time just to see you. You must be an important man."

Cole swallowed hard.

"Have you eaten?"

"No, I haven't had dinner."

"Good, we will share a meal." The old man smacked his hands on his legs in anticipation. Grasping his cane, he leaned forward, looked Cole in the eye and whispered, "It will give us time to talk, hmm?"

Tereschenko concentrated on his plate. "Your wife, Claudia, is a beautiful woman."

"My ex-wife," Cole corrected. "But yes, some people consider her nice-looking."

Tereschenko put his knife and fork down. "She's considered nice-looking? That's the best you can say? Do you think an older man loses his appreciation for a woman's attributes? The mind still functions," he touched the side of his head then glanced at his lap, "even as other parts grow sluggish."

The two men resumed eating in uncomfortable silence.

Tereschenko wiped his fingers on the napkin and pushed his plate aside. "You're ex-wife, hmm?" He shook his head. "Divorcing Claudia was a foolish, foolish thing to do, Mikhail. A wise man never flaunts his mistresses before his wife."

How could he have known?

"You turned a valuable asset into a dangerous liability."

Cole lowered his head. "I'm sorry you're disappointed in

me. I've done the best I could."

"I recall a young man coming to his Uncle Tolya after his mother's funeral, a poor boy with his mother's surname instead of his father's. He had no prospects, but great ambitions, very great ambitions. What was he to do, start at the bottom and work his way up? Not this young man. He wanted to be in control. What became of that eager young man, Mikhail?"

"Those loans earned you handsome returns over the years."

"True enough, but now we have a problem. Does a banker reach into his own wallet when he lends? No, he lends his depositor's money. And those depositors, sooner or later they expect their money back. You see, I am like the banker and my... uh, depositors, are concerned they may not be repaid."

"I need additional time."

"I am an old man, Mikhail. I have little time left. And neither do you. If it was my money, if it were only between the two of us, perhaps accommodations could be made. But..." He raised his palms in a hopeless gesture.

Cole gulped the last of his Scotch.

"Someone has been shorting your stock."

"We've known for weeks for all the good it's done. They operate through multiple holding companies and secret bank accounts. Their orders come in from everywhere in the world and they're impossible to trace. They've been very adroit at driving down the market."

"My guess would be this is an enemy paying you out for some wrong done to them. Have you considered this?"

Cole pretended to be surprised. "I have no enemies."

"Do not assume your Uncle to be a fool. We both know this is not the action of a friend. I came today because they contacted me."

Terror rocked Cole's stomach. No one knew of Tereschenko. Not Schoonover. Not Whitestone. Not Ballinger. Not Chesley. No one.

And yet, someone did.

Cole leaned forward in his chair. "Who is it?"

Tereschenko shook his head. "I did not come to betray confidences."

Cole's face reddened. "Don't just sit there old man. I demand you tell me."

The old man's eyes narrowed. "Mikhail demands?"

Cole slumped into his chair mumbling apologies.

"Your actions have told me all I need to know." Tereschenko folded his napkin and slapped it down on the table. "You waste time threatening friends while your enemies destroy you. The value of the stock you pledged sinks daily. I cannot recover my investment and my depositors want their money. What would you do in these circumstances? Think on this, Mikhail. Think and then act quickly. Your time is running out."

~ 67 ~

Geoffrey Landsdown glanced around the conference room and leaned toward Schoonover. "Some meeting, it looks like everyone is here. What's up, Admiral?"

Schoonover appeared unperturbed. "I believe we all received the same memo."

"This is the big one, isn't it, Mate?"

"The big one?"

"Don't play foxy with me. We're all about to be terminated, aren't we? This is the royal kiss-off, the final handshake. Goodbye and good luck and all that rot."

"One never knows."

"Why else would that broker fellow, Whitestone, and the company solicitor be here? One thing is for certain. We're not getting our annual bonuses, are we? This accounting scandal has sunk the whole bloody company."

Schoonover's expression remained placid, inscrutable. "You'll know any minute now, my friend."

Conversation ceased when Cole entered the room. "What's our per share price this morning?"

"The Exchange has suspended trading," Whitestone said.

He appeared shocked. "That's it, trading suspended. It's over then?"

"No. I don't believe so."

Cole locked eyes with Schoonover.

"What do you have to say for yourself, Admiral Hornblower? This happened on your watch."

"Yes sir, it did."

"That's all you have to say? 'Yes sir, it did.'"

"To the extent my actions negatively impacted either this company or your stock offering I accept responsibility. To the best of my knowledge, that has not been the case."

Cole snapped his fingers. “So you’re absolved of all guilt. There you sit, pure as driven snow.

He glanced around the table. “This company may be on its last legs, but if Michael Cole goes under he will not go down alone. I’ll see that you’re all ruined, professionally, financially and personally. You will pay.”

The door opened, interrupting Cole’s tirade.

Claudia stepped into the room and smiled. Dressed in a gray wool suit with blue pinstripes, she wore a long-sleeved white blouse with ruffled cuffs under her single-breasted jacket and a cornflower blue scarf folded loosely around her neck. It contrasted nicely with her sapphire and diamond earrings. Her hair and makeup were perfect, her tailored suit and silk blouse tastefully stylish.

“Good morning, gentlemen. Sorry you had to start without me.” She glanced over at Cole. “You know, last night I did something I swore I’d never do.”

Cole chuckled.

“Don’t let your imagination run away with you. I returned to London even though I swore I wouldn’t.”

“What are you doing here?”

“Dear, dear Michael, you missed your cue. You were supposed to ask why I returned. So instead, why don’t you tell me what you’re doing here?”

“What’s the matter with you, woman, have you lost your mind? I own the place.”

Claudia sat on the corner of the table, crossing her legs at the ankles. She shoved Cole’s folders off and sat her purse where they’d been. Papers scattered like a flock of startled geese.

She swiveled on the corner of the table, catching his eyes and holding them. “You own this place? Michael Cole, the ultimate man’s man, companion to beautiful women and consummate businessman owns this place? Cruise ships, airlines, hotels, office furniture, computers...everything?”

He grunted in acknowledgement.

"I'm here to tell you, you don't."

"You don't understand the stock market."

Claudia stared at the ceiling like a schoolgirl searching for letters in a spelling bee. A moment later she ticked off all the pertinent metrics regarding Paradise Getaway stock.

"But there's more to this story than a bunch of dry old statistics, daily trading volumes and P/E ratios. The market's dropped through the floor. Your stock offering is dead in the water and someone keeps selling you short while they accumulate additional shares."

Cole silently stared.

"Want to know why the Exchange suspended trading?"

The room grew deathly still.

"How would you know?" Cole asked

"I asked them to. As PGL's new owner I wanted to facilitate an orderly transfer of ownership."

Claudia savored the startled expression on Cole's face.

"Oh, you'd be surprised the things I've found out. I know someone's been making illegal kickbacks, falsifying financial reports and, can you believe it, blackmailing people with dirty pictures."

"You have no idea what you're talking about."

"Don't I? You've managed to get an awful lot of people, shall we say, a wee bit peeved?"

For the first time since she'd entered the room, Cole's face brightened. "Even if what you say is true, you'll never get rid of me. I still have my shares. I'll always be a thorn in your side."

"Funny thing, your friend, Mr. Tereschenko, didn't see things that way. He optioned those shares to me. I made him an offer he couldn't refuse. The downside is, it barely made a dent in what you owe him."

The color drained from Cole's face.

She reached into her purse, extracted a legal form and tossed it at him. “This is our nuptial agreement. It pretty much wipes out your personal assets. I don’t know how the British define it, but where I come from people would say you pretty much don’t have a pot to piss in.”

“All along it’s been you. You set out to destroy me.”

“Yep, and I did a pretty good job of it, didn’t I?”

Cole leaped out his chair and took a wild swing at her.

She hopped off the desk easily avoiding the blow.

Several men at the table rose, forming a protective circle around her.

Claudia gave them a grateful smile. “A few minutes ago, you asked why I was here. I own the place. Now, do me a favor and get your worthless carcass out of my chair.”

Cole had the glassy-eyed look of a fighter on his way to the mat after a knockout punch. He buried his face in his hands.

She punched the intercom. “You can send those gentlemen in now.”

Two large men in dark suits entered.

She tapped Cole on the shoulder. “Some people from Mr. Terschenko’s office would like a word with you.”

Cole’s face went slack at the sight of the men.

One of the men whispered to him. Cole shook his head. They exchanged more whispered words. Cole continued gripping the arms of the chair and shaking his head. The men finally pried him out the chair and drug him to the door, thrashing and stumbling.

When the door closed behind them, Claudia ran her eyes over the men assembled around the table. “Welcome to a new era, gentlemen.”

~ 68 ~

Washington, DC

Brian looked up when Claudia opened the meeting room door. "I could swear I talked to you in London late yesterday afternoon."

She gave him a hug. "I've spent enough time in London. I handed everything over to Schoonover."

"You look pretty chipper for someone who just flew across the ocean. Want some coffee?"

"Yeah, thanks."

"How are you doing?"

"You mean in regards to Michael?"

He rocked his hand. "Yeah, Michael of course, but how are things in general?"

"I'm hanging in. Someday, years from now when we're both old and gray, we'll sit on the porch in our rockers and I'll tell you all the sordid details. For now, let's just say having him out of my life is like a breath of air when you've been underwater too long."

"You seem distracted. Is anything wrong?"

She stirred the coffee, watching it swirl. "I've got a lot on my mind."

Since this was a business meeting, she wore one of the new outfits in her signature clothing line. The line targeted the value-minded female executive whose work required she dress well. Claudia looked smart, tailored and businesslike in the cashmere-wool blend suit and contrasting blouse.

"Nice outfit. Is it in the stores yet?"

"Our Fall line debuts in a few weeks. I have catalogs in my briefcase for you and Brent. As usual, once Jen decides what she wants, she calls Patsy with the catalog number, color and size. The manufacturer will ship direct."

He chuckled. "I'd go broke if I had to pay for all the clothes you give her."

"They're promotional expense. Jen's a walking billboard for my line. Brent's wife, Lindy, does the same in Lexington. I have Patsy in New York and friends in Boston, Chicago and L.A. along with Millicent, our new Account Exec at the ad agency."

"How's Millicent working out?"

"She means well."

"Meaning she's not performing well?"

"She spent too much time studying and too little time living. She wears that MBA like a small town sheriff with a new badge."

"Always thinking of business, aren't you?"

"Guilty as charged. It's not like I have a life."

She'd exposed more of her feelings than intended and she could tell Brian picked up on it. Her success hinged on meeting people's expectations. Personal appearances required her to be upbeat and enthusiastic. She was. At photo shoots they asked her to smile. She did. She could look sexy on cue, or happy, excited, winsome, seductive, wholesome, and pensive. Take your pick. She was a jukebox; push a button and out came your tune.

Brian crossed his arms and his forehead wrinkled into a frown.

"You look just like Daddy when you do that. I bet you intimidate the beejeebers out of your kids."

"I can't. Their Aunt Janie's too busy spoiling them. They keep threatening to run away from home and go live with you."

"Now there's an idea I like. I'll round up all the kids and we'll run away to my hideout way back up the holler. We'll pop popcorn and make fudge and stay up past our bedtime every night."

"You're joking again, that's a good sign."

"What's the status of the stock transfers?"

"Right back to business, hmm?"

She shrugged.

"Well, on my side of things, we're seeing light at the end of the tunnel. I've reached an agreement in principle with the English authorities. It clears the way for you to take the company private. Your international reputation went a long way to smoothing things over. It would've been stickier without you."

"You've done a good job." She rested her hand on his for a moment. "How are things on Brent's side?"

"He's got things pretty well unraveled. The loans are paid off, so there's no more interest accruing and you're off the hook. The corporation will carry a lot of debt, but that's common for a leveraged buy-out."

She nodded and smiled as she listened.

"Brent's staying over with us tonight. Why don't you tag along? The three of us could kick things around in front of the fireplace after the kids are in bed."

A pen, pad and personalized maroon meeting packet awaited each member on the table. To pass time, she'd begun straightening the packets and aligning the pen and pad as they talked. She worked her way around the table, reading the names.

Brian glanced at her across the table. "What about staying over?"

"Can I let you know later?" She rounded the end of the table and stopped. "Jeremy's not here." She fought back tears. "Where's Jeremy's packet?"

"I thought you knew."

Her voice quaked. "Knew what?"

"He resigned from the board, submitted his letter of resignation weeks ago."

"Why wasn't I informed?"

"I assumed you'd talked to him about it." He paused. "Obviously you didn't."

"Would it have killed you to send me an email?"

"I didn't think it was necessary. You two are friends."

"We were friends."

Brian's cup clanked when he dropped it onto the saucer. He rushed around the table and took her by the shoulders. "You're crying. What's the matter?"

"I'll be all right. Maybe it's the lack of sleep, or jetlag," she blinked several times, "or, I don't know what. I've decided to name the pre-natal and early childhood clinic we're building in Bly *The Teresa Tilden Children's Health Center*. I looked forward to giving him the news personally."

Her hand went to her face. "I...I just nee–...had–...wanted to talk to him." She brought her fist down on the tabletop. "I flew all night and now you're telling me he isn't even going to be here."

"I'm sorry. I didn't know it would upset you so much."

She pushed past him, heading for the door. "I told you I'll be okay."

"You need to calm down."

"Give me a minute to freshen up." Halfway out the door, she stopped and glanced back. "Brian?"

She tried to appear calm. Watching his eyes, she knew he saw right through her. Years of performing under stress and every ounce of will power she could muster were going into this performance and she wasn't pulling it off.

"What can I do?" Brian asked.

"Let's cut this morning's meeting short. We'll do a quick run through on the financials, approve next year's budget and table the rest for a special session in a month or two."

"But everyone's come from out of town."

"And I flew all the way from Europe. Besides, I'm the one paying their travel." She took a deep breath. "Tell them if it's too much trouble they can quit, too. I'm not in the mood for a long, drawn-out meeting. Understand?"

"I'm sorry. Of course we'll reschedule."

"I'm going to take a rain check on your offer to stay over tonight. I have something to take care of after the meeting."

~ 69 ~

Baltimore

Claudia headed to Baltimore as soon as the Board meeting ended. A thousand questions, doubts and scenarios ran through her mind as she walked the hall to Jeremy's office.

She thought of Trevor, remembering the night she'd held him while he slept. Was he still intent on finding a new mom? She'd take the job in a heartbeat, if Jeremy would only let her.

Had Jeremy met someone new? If not, could they start over? Would he be ready to make the first, tentative steps to a relationship now? He clearly hadn't been the last time they'd spoken.

The doorway opened onto the smaller portion of Jeremy's Lshaped office. It held filing cabinets, two chairs, a coffee table and a couch. A small boy knelt in front of the couch driving a toy car over its cushions.

Trevor turned at the sound of the door. He burst into a wide grin and tossed the car aside. "She's back! Look, Dad, she's back! I told you she'd come."

He was on his feet in a flash, racing toward her. She dropped to one knee. He leaped into her open arms and wrapped himself around her, hugging her with all his might and covering her face with kisses. After hugging and kissing him, she sat him on her knee.

"This is a nice surprise. I didn't expect to find you here."

Trevor hadn't changed. He had the same cherubic face and his brown eyes still sparkled with the threat of mischief. His sandy brown hair reminded her of Jeremy's more than ever.

"Mrs. Carruthers had to go shopping," Trevor said, "so I'm helping Dad do his work."

"Mrs. Carruthers is his nanny," Jeremy explained as he rounded the corner.

Claudia let Trevor slip off her leg and stood up, extending her hand.

"How have you been, Jeremy? You're looking well."

"Fine. Busy with my work, but fine. And you?"

She forced a smile. "Busy too, but otherwise fine."

Claudia couldn't tell if her presence upset Jeremy or not. She was still mulling it over when Mrs. Carruthers returned. Jeremy seemed relieved to see her and instructed Trevor to gather his toys so she could take him home.

Claudia sat in one of the chairs, trying to stay out of the way. Trevor crossed the room dragging the backpack in one hand and his coat in the other. He stared at the floor, looking distressed and ready to cry.

"Do I gotta go?" He looked up at his father with pleading eyes and pointed to Claudia. "She just got here."

"The grownups need some time, Trev. I'll see you at home tonight."

Mrs. Carruthers took his hand. He jerked away from her and ran to Claudia's lap. "I don't wanna go." He forced himself under her arm. "I'll be real quiet and keep my snoopy little fingers outta stuff. You won't know I'm here. Tell me I can stay, please...please...ple-e-e-ez."

Claudia glanced up at Jeremy.

He shook his head.

"Can Trevor and I have a minute alone?"

He and Mrs. Carruthers stepped outside.

Trevor waited until the door swung shut, then turned his imploring eyes up at Claudia. Smiling down at him, she brushed his hair aside and kissed his forehead. She took out a tissue, blotted his tears, and then covered his nose and instructed him to "Blow."

She took his hands in hers. "I know you don't want to go, Sweetheart. And I know you'd be really good if you stayed, but I think its best you go home with Mrs. Carruthers."

"I won't say a word. I promise. I won't even listen."

"I love you, Trevor."

"I love you, too." He picked at one of his fingernails and sobbed. "I don't wanna go with Mrs. Carruthers."

She pulled more tissues out of her purse and assured him everything would be okay.

"Do you still read *Goodnight Moon* at bedtime?"

He shook his head.

"Gotten too big for it?"

"No. I'm saving it for you to read to me. Can't I please stay?"

"I wish you could, but you just can't. Not this time."

"Can I still go to New York with you and see the Umpire State Building?"

"Yes, I promise. You'll come and stay with me...sometime." Claudia took his little hand in hers and unfolded his fingers. "I've got something special for you."

She brought his hand to her lips, kissed his palm and carefully refolded his fingers.

"There's a kiss for you to keep forever and ever. Anytime you feel sad, or worried, or lonely, think of me. Remember I love you, and having one of my kisses to help make you feel better."

She held out her hand. "Can I have one of yours?"

Trevor leaned forward and gently kissed her hand. He watched in fascination as, one-by-one, her neatly manicured fingers closed over it. Smiling down at him, she pressed her fist to her heart.

He put his fist to his chest, mimicking her.

They quietly looked into each other's eyes for a long moment before she lifted his coat. "Ready?"

Trevor hopped down from her lap and shoved his arms into the sleeves. She zipped him up and took his hand to walk him to door. As they walked, he squeezed her hand three times and looked up expectantly. It was their secret code: *I Love You.*

She gave him three squeezes in return.

~ 70 ~

"I didn't realize Trevor would be here."

"There's no way you could have known."

Jeremy invited her to join him on the couch. They sat at opposite ends as they talked.

"He looks more like you every time I see him."

"That's what my mother says, too." Jeremy shifted on the cushion, examining the crease in his slacks. "But he got those big brown eyes from Teresa."

Claudia felt a guilty twinge of jealousy. How could she ever compete with a dead woman? She questioned the wisdom of rushing to Baltimore. Shouldn't she have at least called first instead of just showing up at his door unannounced like some shirttail relative on vacation with no place to stay?

"What brings you to Baltimore?"

"I was in Washington for the board meeting. I learned you'd resigned and decided to come see you."

Jeremy sighed. "I assumed Brian would tell you."

"He did, this morning."

"I felt it was for the best."

"The best for who, best for you...best for me...best for the foundation...for continued peace in the Free World?"

"If you must know, best for Trevor."

A look of fright came over her. "Something's wrong with Trevor? Why didn't you tell me? How can I help?"

Jeremy hadn't anticipated that mentioning Trevor would elicit such an emotional reaction. "It's nothing like that. Trevor's seeing a child psychologist. She's diagnosed him as having obsessive-compulsive tendencies."

"He's seemed perfectly normal a few minutes ago."

"He would, you're the focus of his obsession. He's made a little progress. Your showing up probably set him back to square one."

"Perhaps I could talk with him."

"You've done quite enough already, thank you very much."

Chastened, she folded her hands in her lap and stared into them. She glanced over at Jeremy.

He turned away.

She didn't believe him for a minute. Not about Trevor, anyway. Sure, he might be seeing a child psychologist, but that wasn't the reason behind Jeremy's resignation.

Her soft voice broke the silence between them. "Why did you resign from the board?"

He shifted on the couch. "For God's sake, you got married."

She'd known it all along, but needed to hear it from his lips.

"Brian said you resigned six weeks ago. The marriage was over by then. Michael and I were married just a few months and I was away most of that time."

"I read the papers. Married, divorced, it really doesn't matter."

"What does matter, Jeremy? What about New York?"

"I've already told you we made a mistake."

She shook her head. "No, don't say that. It was wonderful, pleasurable, and fulfilling. Two people sharing what was in their hearts and souls. It may have been many, many things, but never a mistake. I won't allow you to denigrate such a beautiful moment."

A pained expression crossed Jeremy's face. "That night, I believed I could handle it...you. I honestly did. I tried so hard. But...but, I made a commitment to Teresa."

"Yes you did. She was kind and caring and a sweet person, I'm sure. You loved her deeply and she loved you back. You can be proud of that. You had her for almost six years together. There are people who, in their entire life, never know a single moment of what you two had."

Claudia pounded the cushion beside her. "It's 'Til death do us part.' Teresa is dead, Jeremy. I know it hurts to hear me say it. You weren't ready. Trevor wasn't ready. She wasn't ready. Yet it happened. You've mourned. You've honored her memory. You're raising a fine son. What else can you do? She'd want you to move on."

"How dare you claim to speak for her?"

She looked at Jeremy and saw Trevor. He appeared so frightened, so fragile. She wanted to take him in her arms and rock away his pain.

"I'm someone who cares for you very much, someone who could help you if you'd let me. Time is a river. It flows in only one direction and can't be stopped. It carries us along whether we like it or not. Refusing to acknowledge the present won't change the past."

Jeremy rose and paced the room.

She reached out for him. "We've known each other for a long time."

He spun to face her. "Have we? I'm not sure I know you at all. I don't think you know yourself. One minute you're Mary Jane, the next minute you're Claudia." He moved his hands in front of himself pretending to toss a ball back and forth. "Claudia has one life; Mary Jane another. Mary Jane slept with me in New York, or was it Claudia? One, or the other, married Michael Cole on a whim."

"Hold it right there, Mister. You have no idea what you're talking about and, even if you did, it doesn't give you the right to judge me."

"So enlighten me."

"I didn't come here to discuss Michael Cole. I came to talk about us. Check your calendar. You were in New York before I got married. I never asked you for a commitment. I just asked you to give us a chance."

Jeremy jerked his head toward the door. "I think it's time you left."

"Not until I say what I came to say."

She began to sob. Taking his hands, she pressed them to her cheeks, wetting them with her tears.

"Don't let it end this way, Jeremy. If I pushed you too fast, led you into things you weren't prepared for, I'm sorry. If things I did hurt you, I'm sorry for that too."

When Jeremy tried to pull his hands away she gripped them tighter, covering them with kisses and tears.

"I love you, Jeremy. I knew it in New York; I know it now. Most people don't get a second chance like this. We have to take it. Run with it and never look back. If you want me to beg, I will. Just please, please don't shut me out."

His face remained as rigid and inscrutable as a statue chiseled out of stone. Jeremy jerked his hands away. Hand on his hip he circled the room running his fingers through his hair.

She looked deep into his eyes. "As far as Michael goes, can you accept that everyone does at least one really, really stupid thing in life? And no matter how much they regret it, it can't be undone. But that single event, that one mistake, doesn't define who they are."

"I wish I could say the past doesn't matter. I wish I could say I'm ready to move on. I wish I could tell you all the things you want to hear. But I can't. I'm sorry."

Jeremy turned on his heel and left her there alone.

~ 71 ~

She'd been wrong.

Jeremy and Trevor wouldn't be a part of her life after all. Losing him...them, a second time hurt terribly. For an instant she wished she could undo it all, make it never have happened. But she couldn't and, if she were honest with herself, she wouldn't have even if she could.

She'd left for Baltimore full of confidence. It would be easy to attribute it to false pride, a supermodel's ego. It wasn't. Rather, it was what she felt when they made love. Jeremy felt it, too. No matter how much he tried to deny it, she knew he had. She didn't expect everything to come together immediately, but never in her wildest imaginings did she think Jeremy would flat-out reject her.

On her way back to New York, Claudia realized she couldn't stay in her apartment with only Mousse for company. If she did, she'd go stark-raving mad. Become a recluse, one of those people you read about who haven't left their apartment in 32 years and have junk piled up everywhere.

She had work waiting for her, lots of work. But first, she needed to heal. When they landed in New York, she ran home, packed a bag and poked Mousse into his carrier. Then she headed back to Washington, rented a car and drove to Brian's.

At 1:30 the following morning, she tiptoed up Brian's flagstone steps and rang the bell. When he opened the door, she ran a hand through her tangled hair and blinked into the light., "I decided to take you up on your invitation after all."

Jennifer, who'd come downstairs with Brian, took one look and ran across the room with open arms. "Come here, you need a hug."

She dispatched Brent to light a fire in the den and sent Brian into the kitchen to make coffee. Then Jennifer settled Claudia on the sofa and gathered pillows, blankets and a box of tissues. After shooing the men off to bed, Jennifer returned with a tray of coffee and cookies. Mousse curled up beside them and slept while the two women talked through the night.

Baltimore

"Dr. Tilden, I was worried. I called your office and they told me you'd left. I tried your service, but they couldn't reach you. I didn't know how to find you."

"What's happened, Mrs. Carruthers?"

"It's Trevor."

She read the expression on Jeremy's face. "He's fine. Well, not fine, but he isn't bleeding or unconscious."

Jeremy dropped onto the bench, apologizing.

"He hasn't been himself since we left your office this afternoon. He didn't have three words to say all the way home. The last time I checked on him, he was sitting on his bed with his snow globe, sobbing."

He patted her arm and apologized again for not phoning.

Jeremy tapped on Trevor's bedroom door and eased it open. "I'm home."

He stepped into the dark room and looked around. Trevor lay on the bed with his back to him.

"Can I turn on a lamp?"

Trevor grunted.

Jeremy sat on the bed and touched his son's shoulder. "Is everything okay?"

"Did she come home with you?"

"No, she didn't come home with me."

Trevor's shoulders quaked as he began to cry. Jeremy ran to the other side of the bed. Light from the small lamp spread across the bed, glistening off of Trevor's tear-stained face. Jeremy knelt on the floor beside him. "We won't be seeing each other again. I'm sorry."

Trevor stared down into the palm of his hand. Between gasping sobs he whispered, “She came back, Dad. Just like I always told you she would. She came back.”

Jeremy noticed the odd way Trevor held his hand. “Is there something wrong with your hand? Does it hurt?”

“No!” Trevor shouted. He clamped his fingers over the spot she’d kissed, “My hand’s fine.” He pressed it to his heart and covered it with the other.

Jeremy sat on the bed next to him, Slipping his arm around the boy’s shoulder, he hugged him tightly.

Trevor coughed and hiccupped as he fought to control his tears. “Why wouldn’t she come home with you?”

Jeremy’s jaw tightened. “It wasn’t her, Trevor. It was me. I told her, umh...well, I said...” He buried his forehead in his open palm, kneading his temples.

“I wish there was a way to make you understand. I had to tell her we weren’t ready to have her in our life. That it would be best if she didn’t come around anymore.”

He grabbed his son by the shoulders and stared into his eyes. “Don’t you see, I had no choice.” His tone begged the boy to understand. “I had to tell her not to come around anymore.”

“But she came back, Dad. She wants to come around some more. She wants to take me to the top of the Umpire State Building.”

“Can’t you forget about the Empire State Building, just for five minutes?”

Jeremy’s eyes went to the snow globe on the shelf. To hell with Dr. Baldwin and her pills, he thought. I’ll toss it in the trash where it belongs and deal with Trevor’s obsession once and for all.

Reading his father’s intention, Trevor leaped up on the bed and snatched it off the shelf. Tucking his under his arm like a football, he ran across the room. He cowered in a chair and curled around the precious globe to protect it. “It’s mine. She gave it to me.”

As Father and son stared at each other in the shadowy silence. Jeremy realized how misguided he'd been to think breaking a simple trinket would correct everything wrong in his life.

Trevor remained on guard, ready to defend the globe with his life.

"I won't do anything to your snow globe. I know how much it means to you."

The boy relaxed a little.

Jeremy rested his elbows on his knees, gathering his thoughts. "Honey, life isn't always easy. One of the things you'll learn is sometimes stuff happens you didn't plan on. We think we know how everything's going to be, and then it doesn't turn out that way. I couldn't bring her home. She doesn't belong here."

"Why not? She loves us."

"Oh, how I wish it were that simple. This isn't about what she wants, or what you want, or even what I want. It's about your mother."

Trevor silently mouthed the word, '*Mommy*'?

"I can't do it, Trevor. Your mother and I promised there'd never be another. I know you're too young to understand, but I broke my promise." Jeremy shook his head and rubbed his eyes. "I can't bring someone else home. It would be unfair to your mother."

Trevor's eyes widened. He gasped then let out a terrified wail. The snow globe slipped from his fingers, rolled off the edge of the chair and spun circles on the carpet.

Jeremy was beside him in an instant, wrapping him up in his arms. "What's the matter? Where does it hurt?"

"I'm sorry, Dad. I'm sorry, I'm sorry," he repeated, over and over. " I didn't mean to. No one ever told me."

"Slow down. Take it easy. You didn't mean to what?"

Once Trevor calmed Jeremy ran a sleeve across his son's face, drying his damp cheeks. Trevor picked the snow globe off the floor and handed it to his father. "Throw it away. I don't want it anymore."

"But it's your Empire State Globe."

"Throw away all my magazines and the movie disc, too. I don't want Mommy to hate me anymore." In an unbelievably mature voice, he said, "I'm sorry, Dad. I didn't know I wasn't supposed to want a new mommy."

Jeremy stared into his son's brown eyes. How could he have so blind to Trevor's pain? "None of this is your fault. You didn't do anything wrong. I don't how things got so mixed up, but we'll fix it. I promise we will."

Trevor patted his father's hand. "It doesn't matter, Dad. Like you said, she's not coming back."

After tucking Trevor in, Jeremy went downstairs. He roamed the house restlessly, clutching the boy's treasures. In the living room he put the magazines and globe aside, opened the drawer under the TV and removed Trevor's DVD.

He felt a presence in the room and slowly turned. Jeremy's eyes went to the cabinet with the videotapes of Teresa and then down to the DVD in his hand. He wavered for several minutes then finally sat Trevor's DVD on the table with the other items.

Digging in his pocket for his keys, he walked to the cabinet. Jeremy removed a tape and lovingly turned the worn box in his hands. He eased it out, read Teresa's handwriting on the label, sighed, and slid it back into its box. Then he reached for the second tape and each one after it until he had them all. Wishing wouldn't bring her back. Jeremy carried the tapes into the garage and packed them away, carefully fitting tissue around each box. Someday, when the time was right, he and Trevor would watch them together. Until then, they belonged in a storage box.

~ 72 ~

Bly, KY

Only a second look convinced Stephanie it was actually Jeremy Tilden in line at the coffee shop. She hardly recognized him in jeans, flannel shirt and tan field coat. He looked her way and she threw her eyes back onto her newspaper.

Stephanie stared at his back, wondering what he was doing there.

Pocketing his change, Jeremy stepped away from the counter.

Stephanie raised her paper, pretending to read. His approaching footsteps sounded like an infantry column marching toward her.

Jeremy rested his hand on the back of the chair opposite her. "May I?"

"Sorry, that chair's reserved for a decent human being."

He stepped to the left side of the small, square table and tentatively touched the chair.

"Nope, it's for someone with at least an ounce of consideration."

He moved to the right, his hand hovering inches above the chair back. Stephanie slapped her paper down on the table and pointed to the farthest corner of the shop. "I see one for you over there."

Cup in hand, Jeremy crossed the room. He stopped beside the table she'd pointed to, slid a chair out a few inches and looked back for her approval.

She nodded.

He grabbed the chair, jerked it away from the table and hauled it back across the room. Shoving one of Stephanie's chairs aside with his leg, he sat down and pried the lid off of his coffee.

They drank in uncomfortable silence for several minutes before Stephanie asked, "What the heck are you doing here?"

"I need help."

"Maybe you can find a nice 12-Step Program for people who do really, really dumb stuff. Trust me, they'll let you in.

"Can't we at least talk?"

"What I'd rather do is beat you over the head with the ten-foot pole MJ wouldn't touch you with. We have nothing to talk about. Vamoose!"

"Give me a break."

"I'll give you as much of a break as you gave her."

"Please."

"I got a news flash, Jeremy. I'm not the one you should be talking to. Apparently you boarded the wrong plane. Look around you. Surprise! This isn't New York City; it's Bly, Kentucky."

"I've been trying to get in touch with her for weeks. They keep saying she's out of town."

"She travels."

Resting his elbows on the table, Jeremy interlaced his fingers and looked over at her. "You're her best friend."

"And you're the world's biggest jerk."

"Will she ever talk to me?"

"For her sake, I hope not."

"Maybe you could, you know, call her, and...uh..."

"Oh, oh I get it. This is like junior high. You're afraid to ask somebody for a date, so you have their best friend scope things out ahead of time. Sorry, no can do, Doctor."

"Then tell me what I should do."

"Take a long walk on a short pier."

"You're not being fair."

"Fair?" Stephanie rose out of her seat waving her arms. "I'm not being fair?"

She stopped and glanced around the room. The small coffee shop had come to a standstill and everyone's eyes were on her.

She gave them a feeble smile. “Show’s over, folks. Everything’s fine. Go back to whatever you were doing.”

She settled back into her seat and smoothed her smock. Folding her arms on the table, she leaned forward and spoke in a low snarl. “Listen here, you lousy bastard, you’re in no position to lecture anyone about fairness. The prettiest, sweetest, kindest girl in the whole world wanted to love you and you broke her heart.” She smacked the tabletop. “Not once, but twice!”

“She played a part in it, too.”

“Right, she was the victim. Unlike some folks I know, she cares about other people’s feelings. You can’t imagine how much she agonized about hurting you.” She rolled her eyes. “Hurting you, what a concept. She knew you might not be ready for a relationship, that maybe it was too soon after Teresa’s death. You encouraged her. You let her mother your little boy. You let her take you to her bed.”

“I wasn’t ready. I wanted to be, but I wasn’t.” He dropped his chin to his chest. “I panicked.”

“You better believe you did. She’d have given you all the time you needed to work through your grief. No commitments. She was willing to take her chances, wait and see. She’d have gone a country mile if you’d moved one lousy inch.”

“I didn’t think it’d be fair to her.”

“Don’t start that fairness crap again unless you want coffee in your face.”

She shook her head. “This supermodel stuff doesn’t count for diddly. All she’s ever wanted was to be a wife and mother. You dangled the bait in front of her and then yanked it away when she leaped to take it.”

Jeremy’s face hardened. “Well, she didn’t waste any time finding a replacement.”

“You’re overlooking a couple of things, Mister. One, you had already tossed her aside. And secondly,” she folded another finger, “men fall at her feet everyday of the week. She doesn’t have to go hunting for replacements; they line up outside her door."

"She could have at least made a better choice."

"When did this get to be about Michael Cole?" She nodded with understanding. "Ah yes, someone worthy to fill your shoes, a suitable replacement, someone with talent, breeding, noble bloodlines perhaps."

Jeremy's hand closed into a tight fist. "There's something about Cole that no one will talk to me about it."

"Cole screwed her over. She got pissed. She took over his company and booted his worthless butt out. There you have it. Cut and dried. Happy?"

Jeremy shook his head. "You know there's more to it than that. It has something to do with the whole marriage thing. She implied as much the day she visited me in Baltimore."

"*The day she visited me in Baltimore*," Stephanie echoed, sarcastically. "You have a way with words. You really do. Why not admit the truth and say, 'The day I broke her heart?'"

"I asked Brent. He cursed and hung up. Brian won't return my calls. I tried his home. I won't go into what his wife told me, but what she suggested is a physical impossibility. You're the only one left."

"You mean you're not going to terrorize poor Aunt Weezie? I almost wish you would. She'd thrash the daylights out of you with her cane. You're barking up the wrong tree if you think I'd ever betray her confidence."

Jeremy gulped the last of his coffee and crumpled the cup.

"Let me ask you something. Do you honestly think she loved Cole?"

"I don't know what to think anymore."

"Then let Aunt Stephanie tell you. She married Cole on the rebound. Isn't that obvious? He was good looking, successful and clever enough to tell her the things she wanted to hear. I'm sure she had one heck of a 'My God, what have I done now?' moment the morning she woke up wearing a wedding band."

“That isn’t the way it appeared in the papers and on TV.”

“Making a hobby out of checking the tabloids?”

“They’re in all the supermarkets. Sometimes you can’t help noticing things.”

“I suppose so. Look, here’s my take on things. MJ has been through more than her share of tough times and over the years she’s developed a strong self-protective streak. If her experience with Cole says nothing else, it says she’s had it up to here with people abusing her.” She rapped her knuckles the table “And that, brings us right back to Dr. Jeremy Tilden. She dropped her guard and let you land a haymaker not once, but twice. I can’t imagine her ever being so vulnerable again.”

Jeremy’s face mirrored his disappointment. “Thanks anyway,” he said sadly. “You’re probably right. It’s a waste of time to imagine she’d even talk to me.”

~ 73 ~

Natalie interrupted just as Rudy finished freshening Claudia's make-up. "The guard says someone's out front asking to see you."

"Did the guard give you a name?"

"No. The guy says he has to see you."

"Probably an over-zealous fan," Rudy said. "Tell the guard to give him a signed photo and send him away. This is how trouble starts."

Something told Claudia perhaps it wasn't an over-zealous fan.

Natalie's hand moved toward the phone.

Claudia caught the hem of her sleeve. "Do me a favor. Take a peek through the viewing window and see if you recognize him."

Natalie returned shaking her head. "Never saw him before."

"See, what did I tell you?" Rudy whisked away the protective cape he draped over her clothing. "I'll call out and tell the guard to give him the brush-off."

Claudia fluttered her hand to shush him.

"What does he look like?"

"He's tall, sandy-brown hair, and nicely-dressed. Not a movie star hunk, but wholesome, if you know what I mean. Nobody you'd be ashamed to take home to the folks."

Claudia's forehead wrinkled in disbelief. "Is he alone?"

"Yes, and he's pacing the lobby like they're coming to take him to the gallows any second."

Claudia scowled.

"You know this guy?" Rudy asked.

"Yes. No. I'll go find out."

Claudia peered through the small, one-way security window. The guard had his chair leaned back with a magazine opened across his stomach. He munched a Danish while Jeremy paced in front of his desk.

Claudia walked back onto the set and clapped her hands. After a pause to give people time to stop what they were doing, she said, “Why don’t you guys break now and take a long lunch?”

The crew began turning off lights and shutting down equipment. Claudia was on her way to her dressing room when she heard Millicent hollering, “No. Stop. Wait.”

She ran across the set chasing Claudia. When she caught up, Millicent gave a prim little cough. “Claudia, I think we need to talk.”

“What now, Millicent?”

“Do you know what you’ve just done?”

“Yes. I gave everyone a little extra time off.” Reading Millicent’s expression, she said, “Oh, dear. Is that a big No-No?”

Millicent crossed her arms and nodded. In her best MBA voice she said, “You see, we’ve pre-booked the studio time and those are all union people.” She lowered her voice as if coaching a slow student. “They’re paid by the session. They remain on the clock whether they’re working, or not. Spur of the moment decisions like this waste valuable advertising dollars.”

“Spur of the moment decisions waste ad dollars, hmm? So this could put us over budget.”

“It certainly could.”

Claudia sat on the corner of a desk. “I suppose we’ll have to find somewhere to cut. Of course, the clothing line is nothing more than a shell corporation. Our product costs and freight are fixed. Most of the advertising is already contracted.” She threw her hands up. “The only variable we have is wages. Natalie and Rudy are paid under Souvanée cosmetics and I don’t take a salary.”

Glancing over at Millicent, Claudia traced the edge of her lapel with a finger. “That jacket looks nice on you. It’s one of ours, isn’t it?”

Millicent smiled. “Mm-hmm, it’s brand new.”

“Doesn’t the cost of the clothing we give you come out of the advertising budget?”

Millicent gulped. “I...I suppose it does.”

“Come to think of it, my clothing line is the only account you manage. The agency bills your entire salary straight through. How much do you make a year, Millicent?”

The color drained from the young woman’s face; her eyes twitched and fluttered.

Claudia let Millicent stew for a long moment, then smiled. “Maybe we shouldn’t worry about this budget stuff too much. Things have a way of working themselves out. What do you think?”

“Oh, yes,” Millicent stammered. “Yes, I agree.”

“Great. Now be a good girl and tell everyone to break early for lunch.”

“No more than half-a-dozen people knew I was working at Axialis Studios. How did you find me?”

“Luck of the draw. I guessed.”

“I know better. My own studio was booked, so we came over here at the last minute.” She lifted her chin and tossed her hair over her shoulder. “You never heard of this place until you walked through the front door.”

“So I made some phone calls.”

“The heck you did. Anyone who knew where I was wouldn’t speak to you. Quit beating around the bush, Jeremy, you’re not a good liar.”

“Okay, I hired a private detective to find you.”

She stared at him, dumbfounded. “You had me followed? Have you never heard of anti-stalking laws? I should have you arrested.”

“He wasn’t stalking you; he was just...well, sort of...seeing where you went."

"I fail to notice the difference."

She walked over to a desk and picked up the phone.

"What was I supposed to do? You won't take my calls. Nobody in your family will speak to me. Stephanie wanted to wring my neck."

She let the receiver dangle in her hand. "You went to see Stephanie?"

"Yeah, I asked her to give you a message." He sighed. "But she wouldn't get involved."

"Smart girl." Returning the phone to its cradle, she crossed her arms. "Why are you here?"

"I want to talk."

"You said it all in Baltimore. I have deadlines." She motioned toward the lights and props and backdrops cluttering the stage behind her. "Can't you see we're busy? Now leave before I call the cops."

She reached for the phone again. He put his hand over hers, preventing her from lifting it.

"Can't you trust me for just one minute?"

She glared at him with fire in her eyes. "You're a fine one to talk about trust. You've been paying someone to follow me around and snoop into my private life. To rummage through my trash, for all I know."

He raised his right hand. "I can assure you he absolutely did not rummage through your trash."

"Well now, doesn't that give me a warm, fuzzy feeling?"

He dropped down onto one knee. "Two minutes. Just give me two minutes."

"Cut the theatrics. Say what you came to say then get out of my life. I'm busy."

Jeremy reached up and grabbed for her hands.

She tried to pull away, but wasn't quick enough.

He caught them and held on tightly.

Her instincts told her to turn away. The expression on his face begged her not to. She relaxed a little and stopped trying to extricate her fingers.

He cleared his throat. "I'm the dumbest guy in the world."

"At last, something we can agree on."

"I came here to tell you I love you, MJ. I knew it that night in your apartment. I knew in it Baltimore. I've known it every second of every day since I saw you at the reunion, but I was afraid to acknowledge it. You were right. We could have something special."

Had he looked up, Jeremy would have seen her frown softening into a smile. He paused to catch his breath, kissed her fingertips and said what he'd come to say.

"I know I've hurt you. If you want me to grovel, I'll grovel. If you want me to beg, I will. Just please, please give me one more chance."

She rocked from one foot to the other, not knowing what to do or say.

The dam broke and his words flooded out. "Living in the past is tearing me to pieces. It's destroying Trevor. It's time we moved on. Trevor helped me see that Teresa would want this for me, for him, for us."

He inched closer, ready to grab her if she tried to bolt. He swallowed hard. "You know, everyone does at least one really, really stupid thing—"

Recognizing the words she'd spoken to him, Claudia dropped to her knees, threw her arms around him and cut him off with a kiss.

When she pulled away, he picked up where he'd left off.

"...stupid thing in life. And no matter how much they regr—"

She kissed him again, longer this time.

"... re, regret it, it can't be undone. But that one event,—"

She put her hands on either side of his face, yanked him to her and smashed her lips against his. He struggled to speak, but she kept kissing.

Breaking away, he gasped for breath. "...bu, but that one mistake doesn't define—"

She pulled him back and, out of the corner of her mouth, said, "I won't stop kissing until you stop talking."

She hugged him with all her might, half-afraid it was a dream, a dream that couldn't slip away as long she held him.

A shiver passed between them. They laughed and cried and hugged. They kissed again and again, tasting the salty mingling of their tears.

Jeremy wrapped her in his arms, holding her close. She rested her head on his shoulder the way she had in her apartment. They remained in each other's arms for several minutes, kissing and touching.

She smiled. "Ah, blessed silence."

He leaned away from her. "I can't be stopped that easily." Lips pursed, she lunged at him. Before she reached him, Jeremy whispered, "MJ, will you marry me?"

She froze for a heartbeat then tumbled into his arms, murmuring, "Yes. Oh yes...yes...yes...yes."

Jeremy took Claudia's hand and helped her to her feet. She rocked for a moment and he grabbed her elbow, steadying her. Taking a box of tissues from the makeup table, she offered it to him.

"Here, you need these as much as I do."

After they'd wiped their faces and dried their eyes, she glanced into the mirror. "Look at me. I'm a fright. Rudy spent all morning getting my makeup just right. He's going to have a conniption fit when he comes back and sees what you've done."

She winked at Jeremy and giggled like a child doing something naughty. "Not that I care."

Claudia rummaged around behind a screen and returned

with a sheet of poster board and Natalie's bold marker. Laying the sheet across the dressing table, she wrote 'Change of plans – Take the afternoon off.' She cocked her head, studying what she wrote. After nibbling on her lip for a second, she added, 'Take tomorrow off, too.' She looked it over for a moment and scribbled another line, 'Take the whole week off. See you Monday.' In teensy, tiny letters, she added a postscript. 'Maybe.'

She capped the marker and propped the poster board on an easel where her crew would see it when they returned. She picked up her purse, tossed her jacket to Jeremy and glanced back at him as she slipped an arm into the sleeve.

"Where's Trevor?"

"He's at home with Mrs. Carruthers."

"Well, what are you waiting for? Let's get a move on." She grabbed his hand and dragged him along as she made long strides toward the door. She pulled out her cell phone as they walked and punched the speed dial. She tilted her head to Jeremy as the call went through. "I'll have them get the plane ready."

She checked her watch as they crossed the lobby. A quick nod to the guard and they were out on the street.

She snapped the phone shut "We'll fly down, pick him up and zip back to New York."

She stepped off the curb and waved for a cab. "You'll stay at my place," she shouted over the traffic. "The Umpire State Building stays open 'til midnight."

~ 74 ~

When Claudia finished her shower, she was pleased to find the breakfast tray Weezie ordered.

Souvanée remained on her mind as she ate. They'd been ominously quiet since she took control of Paradise Getaways. She shrugged. They'd either renew her contract or they wouldn't. She'd learned long ago not to let things she couldn't change upset her.

Turning her attention to the old glove box, Claudia lifted the lid. She removed her mother's letter and reread it. She silently stared at those final words for a long time. Momma truly had seen into her future, she thought, refolding the letter and putting on the necklace.

Rudy arrived and gave her the upswept hairdo they'd agreed upon, did her makeup and left. Stephanie and Weezie were helping her into her dress when they heard a light tapping at the outer door. Stephanie opened it and found Trevor dressed in a tuxedo.

"I'm here to see Mommy. Dad said 'cause it's their wedding day he's not allowed to see her with her clothes on. But it's okay if I look." He poked his head into the room, checking.

"You'll have to wait. She's still dressing."

Trevor pushed out his stomach and pointed to his vest pocket. "I've got Mommy's ring right here in this pocket. I can't take it out, 'cause I'd probably lose it."

The bedroom door opened. "I recognize that voice."

Trevor stared up at her open-mouthed. "You're the prettiest lady in whole world."

"That deserves a hug," she said. "But no kisses. We don't want to smear my makeup."

Claudia glanced over at Stephanie. "Call downstairs and tell the photographers I'm ready. Better they get their pictures now than have them jumping out from behind bushes all day." She winked at Trevor. "Want to tag along and watch those silly people take pictures of your Mom?"

When the photographers finished, Claudia and her party left for the church in a rented limo. She could have gotten married anywhere...New York, Baltimore, Washington, Lexington, even Europe, if she chose to. She surprised many people by selecting tiny Bly, Kentucky.

Gazing out the window, she watched memories sweep by as they drove. She recalled making this same trip to Church on a January day when ice sparkled on every tree limb and lamppost. As a youngster, Bly felt like a place where nothing changed. Instead of bothering her, now she found it reassuring.

She smiled. She'd made the right choice; nowhere else would've felt quite right.

They passed familiar landmarks along the way, Del's Western Auto store and further up the block, Stephanie's beauty shop. Instead of weekly specials, the Piggly Wiggly Market's sign read: Congratulations Mary Jane and Jeremy.

Farther down, they drove by a large construction site. Scaffolding and piles of sand, pallets of bricks and bags of concrete surrounded the partially completed structure. In front of this skeleton of a building a sign identified it as the future home of The Teresa Tilden Children's Health Center.

Turning a corner, they passed the Rescue Mission. She saw a familiar figure in a blue suit and asked the driver to slow down. As they rolled up beside him, Claudia lowered her window.

"Give ya a ride, sailor?"

Estil grinned. "Sure, if you've got room."

He climbed into the limo, taking a seat beside Trevor. Estil had filled out since she last saw him and his face had good color. There was a light in his eyes.

"Thanks, MJ," he said, as they rolled away. "It was kind of you to stop."

Trevor scrutinized him. "Who are you? You called Mommy, MJ. Did you know her in the olden days?"

Estil contemplated Trevor's words. "In the olden days... yeah, that's what they were all right. As for who I am, I'm the guy who thinks your Pop's the luckiest guy on God's green earth."

Claudia asked both Brian and Brent to walk her down the aisle. Her brothers were waiting at the back of the church when she arrived. Brian pulled her aside and pointed out two well-dressed men sitting on undersized chairs in the Sunday School Room. "Thought you ought to know, we caught a couple of gate-crashers

Her expression changed. "What are they doing here?"

"They tried to tell me they came for the service." He chuckled. "Thing is, they're actually here to eat humble pie, not wedding cake. Since your takeover of Paradise Getaways, you've been on practically every magazine cover. I think they realized they're about to lose the most valuable asset they have."

"I'm getting married."

He shrugged. "They wouldn't take no for an answer."

Lifting the hem of her dress, Claudia marched over to the men. "Messieurs."

The men rose in acknowledgement.

As Claudia conferred with the men, Stephanie stepped beside Brian. "Know those clowns?"

"The tall, gray-haired man is Henri La Martinière, Chairman of LEH. The other one is Jean-Paul Boulanger, President of Souvanée USA."

"What do they want?"

"They want MJ. They're saying, 'Please, don't leave us. We'll give you anything you want.'"

"Anything?"

"They're offering less travel, shorter hours, twice the base, increased profit sharing and a seat on the Board."

"I can't believe this. They're negotiating a business deal in the back of the church on her wedding day?"

"That's about the size of it."

Stephanie stormed across the room and forced herself in-between Claudia and the men. She started to protest, but Stephanie shushed her.

"What do you two monkeys want?"

"And who would you be, Madame?"

Stephanie jerked a thumb in Claudia's direction. "I'm someone who'll tell you what she's too polite to say. You're holding up the show. Move it, or I'll have you both tossed out on your keister."

"But Miss Monet—"

"Forget Miss Monet. Mrs. Crandall says, if you want to stay, an usher will find you seats."

She grabbed Claudia's arm. "You're here to get married, not gab with these geeks."

Tall and proud, her brothers escorted her down the aisle. As she walked arm-in-arm between them, she recalled a young girl sitting with her brothers around their kitchen table. They promised to remain true to each other, and they had. They'd stuck together just like she promised Momma they would.

Jeremy took her hand.

She looked into his eyes and everything else faded away.

The wedding went just as they'd rehearsed it. Reverend Martin pronounced them husband and wife and Jeremy kissed his new bride. When they turned to face the congregation, everyone rose, clapping and cheering. Claudia stood on the altar steps, her heart swelling to the sound of their applause, her smile as radiant as the noonday sun.

She felt a small hand slip into hers and looked down in time to see Trevor take his father's hand. He'd linked them together; they were a family now.

Everything that matters is right here, she thought, staring across the sea of faces. In the front pews she saw Brian and

Jennifer, and Brent and Linda, with her nieces and nephews. Across the aisle were Jeremy's family and behind them, Teresa's parents. Stephanie and Del were on the steps beside them. Aunt Weezie stood in a side aisle next to Cash in his motorized chair, blotting away tears of joy.

Claudia's eyes found Rudy and Natalie and Greg, her pilot, and others who worked with her. She was surprised to see Admiral Schoonover and Alistair Whitestone and their wives. She hadn't expected them to make the trip. She smiled at Mr. Pence, her first boss, and at old friends and neighbors.

As Claudia, Jeremy and Trevor started down the aisle, people began reaching out, touching their hands, congratulating them as they passed. Her parents, she knew, were there, too. She was all the more certain when she heard her mother's voice echo in the depths of her memory reminding her of something Momma once promised.

It's true, she thought, as fingers brushed past hers. I may not have taken the path I expected, but I ended up right where I'm supposed to be.

The End

The action ranges from Delhi, India to San Francisco, from Annapolis, MD to London, England, and from the Oregon Coast to the Gulf of Alaska.

Claudia Monet's newest adventure —

LOST

By
E. G. Lewis

Book Two
of the
Mountain Memories Trilogy

When Three Good Ideas Converge in One Great Catastrophe

LOST is first and foremost a story about love, the kind of love which binds two hearts together transcending time and space. Told through parallel storylines, their point of convergence is the disappearance of the cruise ship, *Paradise Voyager*. And the common thread tying them together is the impact they have on the life of Oregon newspaperman, Thomas Jenkins, whose wife and granddaughter were aboard the ill-fated ship.

When officials declare the *Voyager* irretrievably lost and close the investigation, Tom strikes out on his own. Bringing together the unlikely team of two Vietnam Vets, an Indian Scientist, and an International Supermodel, he goes on the offensive, eventually unraveling the mystery behind the ship's disappearance.

However, the final piece of the puzzle lies not in the Gulf of Alaska as he thought, but in the Oregon woods. Undaunted, Tom sets off into the forest alone determined to either save his wife and granddaughter or die trying.

Sample Chapter

LOST

Pine Crest, Oregon

It was mailing day at the Pine Crest Courier.

Billy Nevins showed up at ten on the dot and began stuffing and collating his way through the stacks of newspapers. As soon as Billy completed a paper, Tom took it from him and ran it through the addressing machine. Tommy got it next. He sorted them by zip code and bundled them with crisscrossed strips of yellow plastic strapping. Then the bundles of newspapers went into mailing bags, the bags into the van, and the van to the Post Office.

Shortly after they'd finished the papers the man from Domino's Pizza tapped on the back door. Billy let him in and arranged the lunch table before popping his head around the partition and hollering, "Pizza Time!"

As the crew ate their pizza, the talk turned to the Mothers of Song. Everyone around the table speculated on where the cruise ship might be and what those aboard were doing at that very moment.

Tom started to speak, when a sharp knock at the door interrupted him. He wiped his lips on a paper napkin and dropped his pizza onto his plate. "I'll get it."

He looked through the front window as he walked to the door and saw a uniformed man. At first he thought it was a policeman, but quickly recognized it as a military uniform. The man, in his mid 30's and a shade over six feet tall, stood ramrod straight. He looked directly at Tom as the door swung back.

"Mr. Jenkins, Thomas Jenkins?"

"Yeah, I'm Tom Jenkins." His pulse began to race. Fear tightened his stomach.

The man removed his hat and slipped it under his left arm. "Sir, I'm Coast Guard Lieutenant Albert Darrow, from Coast

Guard Air Station North Bend. May I come in?"

Tom's imagination raced. In the split second needed for his response dozens of scenarios cascaded through his mind. He felt his worst fears were about to be confirmed.

"Okay...sure, I guess so." He opened the door wide and re-locked it behind the Lieutenant. "What's this about?"

"Sir, the United States Coast Guard received notification earlier today from the executive offices of Paradise Getaways. They've lost communication with one of their ships, the *Paradise Voyager*." His eyes went down to a scrap of paper in his hand. "I understand your wife, Martha, was aboard."

Tom felt like he'd been hit by a truck. He grabbed the counter for support. Seconds ticked by in slow motion as fearful apprehension welled up within him. The room grew cold, deathly cold. "What exactly does that mean?"

"They aren't sure. That's why they contacted the Coast Guard. You see—"

Tom's raised hand stopped him in mid-sentence.

"There are some other people who need to hear what you have to say." He pointed the way to the rear of the building. "Come on back."

Darrow followed him around the partition and over to the lunch table where everyone sat laughing. The air was heavy with the smell of spices and pepperoni. While Tom was away, Billy had opened a container of his mother's oatmeal cookies and put them in the middle of the table for dessert.

All talk ceased at the sight of the man in uniform.

The Lieutenant nodded to the group and remained standing.

"I'm sorry; let me get you a chair." Tom disappeared for a moment and returned rolling the chair from his desk. "Sit here."

After Tom introduced him, Darrow unbuttoned his jacket and sat down in the black office chair. He transferred his hat from under his arm to his lap. His hands, pale white against the dark blue of his uniform, rested on his thighs. A crisp crease dropped straight off of each knee to cuffs that angled out above highly polished shoes. He glanced around the room as Tom repeated what Darrow told him.

An eerie silence settled over the group. One by one, everyone at the table put down their partially eaten slices of pizza. The sudden quiet magnified even the slightest sounds; a faint car horn on the street outside, the hum of the refrigerator.

Darrow's sudden appearance had ruined Pizza Day.

Tommy was the first to speak. "You said they'd lost communication with Mom's ship. What exactly do they mean? Did someone on the ship forget to check in on time or something?"

"The home office in London maintains a nearly continuous line of communication with each of their ships. It's computerized, of course, but it's still unprecedented to have a ship just blink off like this."

"How do they know it wasn't a computer glitch?" Tom asked.

"It very well could be. You have to understand, however, we're not talking about just one computer talking to one other computer. There's a whole net of communication links. For instance, there's a constant interface to the bridge. There are multiple email conduits, perpetual inventories kept of supplies, food and fuel tracked on multiple platforms. In some cases, the ship transmits data directly to suppliers rather than through the corporate office. The redundancies built into a system like this pretty much preclude a total blackout."

"But still, in the event of a complete power failure isn't that exactly what would happen?"

Tom's mind raced in the short time it took Darrow to answer. What would cause a total power failure? Their engines must generate electrical power just like a car. So, if the engines shut down could that cause a power failure? What would shut the engines down? Running out of fuel...a collision...a fire...sinking.

None of those possibilities sounded like anything he wanted to explore in depth.

"Yes, that *would* happen in the event of a power failure, were it not for a couple of things," Darrow said. "First, the ship's computers have a UPS, an Uninterruptible Power Supply. The system automatically switches to battery back-up in the event of an electrical outage. This keeps the essential systems running for several hours, more than sufficient time to report an emergency. And, secondly, there were several satellite phones aboard. They pack their own power source and bounce signals off other satellites besides the home office relays."

"When did you hear about this?" asked Beth.

Reaching into his jacket, Darrow unbuttoned a pocket flap and pulled out a small notebook. He folded the black leatherette cover over and scrutinized his notes.

"Coast Guard offices in Washington, DC received the notification today, Thursday, at 1435 hours, Eastern Time."

"If that's when you were notified, when did whatever happened happen?" Tommy asked.

Darrow frowned for a moment then glanced up. "Now things get a little stickier. Keep in mind Thursday, 1435 Hours in Washington converts to 1935 in London. That's well beyond their normal business day. We don't know how heavily they staff their second shift. We can only guess at how much time elapsed between the actual event and when someone noticed the lines were down."

Great, really great. Everybody goes home to dinner leaving everyone to fend for themselves. How long did it take them to notice something was wrong? What were they doing in the meantime? The pencil in Tom's hand began to quiver.

"So you're saying ships just blink off the computer screen and nobody gives a damn!"

"No Sir, that *isn't* what I said. They monitor 24-7. As soon as they noticed, they back-tracked the logs to determine when the last report came in. The last communication from the ship was received at—" he paused to check the book again. "Here it is. It came in to London at 1753. Overlaying that on a 15 minute reporting cycle places the event somewhere between 1745 and 1800 hours."

"What did the Coast Guard do once you were notified? Did you send out those little orange helicopters we always see flying around?" Tommy asked.

"Washington immediately relayed the Ship Missing Status to all stations from North Bend north to Air Station Kodiak. They also alerted commercial shipping in the North Pacific to the existence of a possible emergency situation. Then they formed a Unified Response Team. As for the helicopters, no, we didn't send them out."

Seeing their wide-eyed reaction, Darrow raised his hand.

"The *little orange helicopters* you referred to are HH65A Dolphins. They can fly up to 150 miles off shore, hover for about 20 minutes and return. Reaching the *Paradise Voyager* is beyond their operational capability. Instead, they launched two fixed-wing aircraft, HC130's, to initiate the search and rescue. A cutter set out to provide support once the incident site is located."

"How did your planes know where to begin looking?"

"Paradise Getaways provided the ship's last reported position."

"When did they last report their position?" Beth asked.

"As I was about to say , their system does this automatically. The last position report, the coordinates where the Coast Guard initiated its search sequence, came in at 1745...London time, of course. The final contact with the ship occurred at 1753. It was a perpetual inventory restock request ordering more hand soap and toilet paper when they docked."

Tom's voice grew thick with sarcasm. "Wonderful! At least we know all the important things are taken care of"

"That tells us more than you may realize," Darrow said. "Inventory requests are normal, day-to-day procedure, certainly not something done during a perceived emergency. It's a strong indication that whatever overtook the *Paradise Voyager* was quick and unexpected."

Tommy asked the question on everyone's mind. "What did your planes find?"

Darrow's face fell. "So far, nothing."

"Nothing?"

"That's correct. There's no sign of the ship, nothing on radar, no oil slick , no flotsam." Darrow took a deep breath. "And no lifeboats. I'm sorry."

The little group fell silent.

Darrow rolled his chair back and rose. "Here's my card. I'm one of the Public Information Officers at the base. You can call me anytime; it'll roll over to voicemail if I'm not there. I'll let you know of any new developments. I'm sorry to rush away, but I have other families in town to contact."

Although he never said so, Darrow appeared to already have more than enough on his plate for one day.

www.ingramcontent.com/pod-product-compliance
Lightning Source LLC
LaVergne TN
LVHW020531100826
845148LV00010B/1422
9780982594919